CLOSE CALL IN COLORADO

CINDI MYERS

BISCAYNE BAY BREACH

CARIDAD PIÑEIRO

MILLS & BOON

First Published in Great Britain 2023
by Mills & Boon, an imprint of HarperCollins*Publishers* Ltd
1 London Bridge Street, London, SE1 9GF

www.harpercollins.co.uk

HarperCollins*Publishers*
Macken House, 39/40 Mayor Street Upper,
Dublin 1, D01 C9W8, Ireland

Close Call in Colorado © 2023 Cynthia Myers
Biscayne Bay Breach © 2023 Caridad Piñeiro Scordato

ISBN:978-0-263-30709-2

0123

MIX
Paper | Supporting
responsible forestry
FSC™ C007454

CLOSE CALL IN COLORADO

CINDI MYERS

Also by Cindi Myers

Eagle Mountain Cliffhanger
Canyon Kidnapping
Mountain Terror
Disappearance at Dakota Ridge
Conspiracy in the Rockies
Missing at Full Moon Mine
Grizzly Creek Standoff
Investigation in Black Canyon
Mountain of Evidence
Mountain Investigation

Also by Caridad Piñeiro

Lost in Little Havana
Brickell Avenue Ambush
Cold Case Reopened
Trapping a Terrorist
Decoy Training

Discover more at millsandboon.co.uk

Chapter One

On the list of activities Carrie Andrews would like to be doing on a frigid March Saturday, rappelling into an icy canyon didn't even make the top twenty. Yet here she was, standing on the edge of the canyon wall, in helmet, climbing harness and crampons, awaiting her turn to complete the descent as part of a required training exercise with Eagle Mountain Search and Rescue.

"I'll send you down as soon as Tony and Danny are safely at the bottom." Training officer Sheri Stevens came to stand beside Carrie. A tall blonde who regularly competed in—and won—ice climbing competitions, Sheri thrived on this kind of thing. Like several others on the search and rescue team, she made dangerous exercises like this one look easy.

Carrie clapped her gloved hands together, trying to force more warmth into her fingers. "I don't know why I always get so nervous about these climbs," she said. "I've done them dozens of times."

"Just remember your training and take your time," Sheri said. "Safety is way more important than speed, even in real-life situations where an injured person is awaiting rescue down there. You can't help someone if you don't get to them safely."

Carrie nodded. "I know." But after five years with

the team, she also had a mental catalogue full of terrible climbing accidents they had responded to—a graphically illustrated memory bank of everything that could go wrong.

She forced her attention back to the two men currently rappelling into the canyon. SAR captain Tony Meisner descended swiftly, comfortable enough to use both hands to navigate around icy outcroppings, relying on his harness and the Prusik loop that provided a backup to the belay loop to keep him safe, whereas Carrie was never able to let go of her death grip on the rope as she descended.

Positioned several yards over from Tony, Danny Irwin was a more tentative climber. Like Carrie, he had trained extensively and could be counted on in an emergency to do everything required, but he wasn't one to climb for enjoyment. Fun and easygoing on the ground, he was all business when it came to anything dangerous. A nurse in his day job, he had a reputation as a bit of a player, having dated every single woman on the team except Carrie, who had turned down his overtures when she first joined SAR five years previously. He hadn't pressed the issue, and they worked well together on the team, but they weren't close.

"Tony is really booking it today," Sheri said. She moved over to get a better look. "He's almost to that last tricky part where the canyon wall juts out."

"Why did he choose that route?" Carrie shifted closer to Sheri. "Why not move over where he doesn't have to negotiate around that spot?"

"He said he wanted a challenge." Sheri shrugged. "You know Tony. He does things his own way."

"I guess it's good practice for difficult situations we might get into," Carrie said. "But still, I—"

A shout went up from within the canyon. Carrie stared in horror as Tony's rope hurtled into the chasm below. "What's going on?" Sheri rushed to the edge of the canyon and dropped to her knees to look down.

"What is it?" Carrie asked, and hurried to Sheri's side.

"Tony's fallen." Rookie Austen Morrissey joined them, his face ashen. The thirty-something had signed up with the team several months before, after relocating to Eagle Mountain. His expression reflected all the horror Carrie felt. "Everything looked fine and then…the rope just came loose."

SHOUTING DISTRACTED DANNY from focusing on the descent. He steadied himself and turned his head to look across and down at Tony, who had been climbing ten yards away, skimming down the icy rock with his usual flair. Except Tony wasn't there. The ropes he had been using in his descent were no longer there, and Danny's heart rose into his throat. "Tony!" he shouted. "Tony!"

"What happened?" Sheri called down, using a battery-operated hailer. "Where is Tony?"

"I don't know!" Danny looked up his own ropes, momentarily frozen. He had made similar climbs dozens of times in training and in real-life rescues, but he was never entirely comfortable. As a registered nurse, his chief role in search and rescue was to deliver medical aid, but he strove to be as physically competent as he could be, too. He never wanted to be the weak link in any rescue operation. But he didn't have the natural talent people like Tony and Sheri seemed to have.

"Get down there and see if you can find him!" Sheri shouted.

The order got him moving. Danny focused on completing the descent as quickly as possible, his mind running through all the possibilities. The last time he had checked, Tony had been about fifteen feet deeper into the canyon than Danny was. Which meant he had fallen—what—twenty yards? Thirty? Had he had his crampons set in the ice at the time he fell? He forced himself to look over, half-expecting to see his friend hanging head down, leg bones snapped by the force of the fall. But he saw nothing except empty ice-and-snow-covered rock.

He tried to tell himself that was a good sign, but he only felt sick inside. There was a lot of rock and ice between the place where he had last seen Tony and the bottom of the canyon—lots of tree branches and rock outcroppings he could bash against or be snagged by. He divided his attention between his own descent and checking to his right for signs of Tony, but he saw nothing.

Nothing, that is, until he was almost to the canyon floor. Then he looked down and saw what at first appeared to be a pile of discarded clothing on the edge of a trickle of icy water from Grizzly Creek where it flowed through the canyon. He made himself move faster, though still methodically, until his crampon-shod boots crunched onto the canyon floor. He fumbled releasing himself from the ropes, then hurried toward his friend, shedding his pack as he went.

He dropped to his knees beside Tony, who lay with his legs bent under him, face bone white beneath his beard. The ropes he'd been using to descend—red-and-yellow climbing ropes—were still fastened to his harness and lay in a tangle over and around him. "Tony, it's Danny. Can you hear me?" He unpacked medical gear as he spoke, even as the radio mounted on his shoulder squawked.

"What's going on down there?" Sheri demanded. As training officer, she was leading today's exercise.

"I've found Tony," Danny said. "He's alive. Hurt, but

alive. Get a team with a litter started down right away and call for a helicopter." The canyon was too narrow to get a chopper down into. They'd have to bring Tony up in a litter, the very exercise they had been training for this morning.

He touched Tony's cheek. "Tony. It's Danny. Open your eyes for me."

Tony groaned, but opened his eyes. His pupils looked normal. His climbing helmet appeared undamaged, so maybe he hadn't hit his head on the way down. "What happened?" Danny asked. He found the pulse at Tony's wrist and started counting, eyes on his watch. The pulse was irregular but strong.

"Rope...came loose." Tony forced out the words, then groaned again as Danny began to gently examine his legs.

Danny stared. Was Tony disoriented by the fall? Basic climbing procedure was to tie a firm stopper knot at the ends of the ropes to keep them from slipping out of the anchor chain. He had heard of people forgetting this step, but Tony was always so careful. He had been a member of search and rescue for almost two decades, and had trained many other people on safe climbing techniques.

Had the rope broken? Ropes were meticulously checked before and after each use and retired after a specific number of hours, whether they appeared to be worn or not. And yet either the ropes themselves or the gear they were attached to had failed to do their job. He shook his head and focused on assessing his friend, treating him as he would any other accident victim, which meant ignoring his groans of pain as he sorted out Tony's various injuries.

By the time Hannah, Carrie, Eldon and Austen joined him in the canyon, Danny had started IV fluids and administered morphine. Hannah, a paramedic, and Carrie, second-in-command of the team, joined him, while Eldon and Austen began setting up a long line to transport the litter to the rim of the canyon. "How's he doing?" Carrie asked. She rested a hand on Tony's shoulder.

"We won't know everything without X-rays, but he's got fractures in both lower legs and probably one ankle. Probable rib fractures, and he may have a broken pelvis." Danny forced himself to deliver the news in a flat tone, without emotion. It was a terrible laundry list of damage and didn't begin to cover possible internal injuries.

"Let's get him immobilized and warmed against shock," Hannah said, already unpacking a thermos of hot water and several blankets.

"We need to get him untangled from these ropes," Danny said. "Give me a hand here, Eldon."

The two worked to carefully unwind the nest of ropes from around and beneath their friend. Danny worked his way to the end of the ropes, then froze, his brain not quite registering what his eyes were seeing.

"What are you staring at?" Carrie asked. She moved around to crouch next to Danny.

"Tony said the rope came loose," Danny said. "I didn't believe him. That just doesn't happen. But look." He held up the frayed and torn ends of the two ropes.

"We'll take a closer look at this later," Carrie said. "And we'll check all of them. Maybe there's some kind of defect we haven't noticed before."

Danny nodded. He hated to think of some flaw in their equipment that had escaped notice until now, but what else could it be? "Who's up top with Sheri?" he asked as he and Hannah prepared to ease Tony onto a backboard.

"Ryan and Ted are up there," Hannah said. She took out a cervical collar and began to fit it to Tony's neck. Like Sheri, Ryan was a competitive climber, though he was still recovering from injuries incurred earlier in the year. The oldest member of the force at sixty, Ted was also an experienced, capable climber, but a good person to have helping to bring the litter up to the canyon lip.

"Ted pitched a bit of a fit about staying up top," Carrie said as she positioned the backboard. "He wanted Austen to stay up there while he came down." Austen was a rookie, not as experienced with climbing. Sheri had probably wanted him to get the practice today in a real-life rescue.

"We don't need to be worrying about Ted along with Tony," Austen said. He joined them and looked down at the captain. "How's he doing?"

"He's holding on," Danny said. He didn't want to say more with Tony able to hear them. "Is the helicopter on its way?"

"Sheri was talking to the air crew when I started down," Hannah said. She was filling hot water bottles to tuck around Tony for the ride up to the top.

"What happened?" Austen asked.

"His ropes failed," Carrie said. "We don't know why yet."

"How did that happen?" Eldon leaned over Danny's shoulder to stare at Tony. "I saw him inspect all his equipment before he set up for the rappel. There was nothing wrong with the ropes then, or he wouldn't have used them."

"We'll inspect all the gear when we get back to headquarters," Carrie said. She stood. "Are we ready to take him up?"

Hannah tugged on the straps holding Tony into the litter, and double-checked the IV line running beneath the blankets. "He's good to go."

"Let's get him on the line," Carrie said.

How many times had Danny done this, in both training exercises and real-life scenarios, fastening the litter
to the line and threading the ropes through the pulleys to
haul the patient up to a waiting helicopter or ambulance?
Every other operation he had focused on procedure—the
mechanics of making sure the trip went safely. But Tony
was their captain, the leader who ran every mission. He
was also a close friend. Having him seriously injured in
such a freak accident rocked Danny more than he cared
to admit.

He wanted to go up with Tony, but Eldon was a stronger climber, so he made the trip, leaving the rest of them
to gather their gear and follow at a slower pace.

He and Carrie were the last to reach the canyon rim,
arriving just as the helicopter lifted off. "They're taking
him to St. Joseph's in Junction," Sheri said.

"Is here somebody we should notify?" Austen asked.
"A girlfriend or his parents?"

"Tony's parents live in Florida and he doesn't have a
girlfriend that I've ever heard him mention," Sheri said.

"I think we're his family," Carrie said. "I'll drive over
to St. Joseph's this afternoon and see if I can get in to
visit him."

"I'll go with you," Danny said.

She looked surprised. "You don't have to do that,"
she said.

"I want to." He clenched his hands into fists since he
couldn't lash out at the anxiety that coiled in his stomach. "I was right there with him when he fell. I need to
see him."

Her expression softened. "Of course." She cleared her
throat. "It would be good to have some company."

He had ridden to the training exercise in the Beast, the
team's aging search and rescue vehicle, but it had already

pulled away without him. "You can ride with me," Carrie said as they watched the modified Jeep drive away.

He didn't especially feel like talking, but Carrie apparently needed to deal with her emotions out loud. "I still can't believe that happened," she said as she headed down the mountain road toward the town of Eagle Mountain. "Did you see him fall?"

"No." He shifted in his seat. "I don't look around all that much when I'm climbing."

"Me either," she said. "It's the part of this job I dread most."

"I don't dread it," Danny said. "It's just not the most comfortable thing." He glanced at her. She was an attractive woman, with honey-blond hair and a strong, compact frame. She was friendly, but not overly so. Self-contained, he would have said. He knew she was divorced and had a couple of little kids and worked as an architect, but she wasn't one to socialize after hours, and the one time he had asked her out she had made it clear she wasn't interested in him that way. If she was dating someone, she definitely kept that person's identity to herself.

"I don't like heights," she said. "But I make myself do it because it's part of the job."

"We've had other people join and end up quitting because something scared them," Danny said. "There's no shame in that. Not everyone is cut out for this work."

"I do it because it scares me," Carrie said. "I think it's good for me to face my fears."

Do you have a lot of fears? he wondered, but he didn't ask. Some other time he would have, but not now, with the memory of looking over and seeing empty space where Tony should have been still an icy spot in the center of his chest.

Carrie pulled her SUV into the parking area next to

search and rescue headquarters and Danny followed her into the barn-like building where the others were already busy unloading gear and hanging it to dry. "Let me see Tony's ropes," he said to Carrie.

"We all want to see those ropes," Sheri said.

Carrie plopped her pack onto the table at the front of the room, and the others gathered around as she took out Tony's climbing ropes and uncoiled them.

"The ends don't look cut," Ted said. He reached out and pointed to the frayed fibers, uneven and fuzzed.

"They look more worn than anything else," Carrie said. "But the rest of the rope is in good shape."

Danny picked them up to examine the ends more closely. He ran a finger across the torn fibers, then looked along the length of the ropes. Both lines had severed near the end, just below where the stopper knot would have been. There was fuzzing in places on the rest of the rope—normal for something that was dragged across rock on a regular basis. "It looks a little discolored, on the end by where it broke," Eldon said.

"Nothing unusual about that," Sheri said. "The material fades with sun and sweat and water exposure."

"Where's the anchor chain?" Danny asked.

"I've got that." Austen stepped forward and laid the bundle of chain on the table. The stopper knot Tony had tied held firmly above the chain link, the frayed ends of the rope dangling below.

Danny brought the torn ends to his nose and sniffed. The sharp odor made his mouth pucker, as if he had tasted lemons. He turned to Eldon. "Let me see one of the other ropes," he said.

Eldon fetched a purple coil and brought it to the table. Danny laid it beside Tony's and studied the trio. The purple was a little discolored, though not as much as

Tony's, but the purple rope might be newer. They were constantly replacing gear as it became too worn to be safe or reached the end of its useful life. Danny sniffed the line. It smelled of rock dust and fabric. Not lemons.

"What is it?" Carrie asked. She wasn't looking at the ropes anymore—she was studying Danny's face.

"I'm not sure." He handed her the end of one of Tony's. "What does that smell like to you?"

She brought the rope to her nose and sniffed. Her eyes widened. "It smells like acid," she said.

"What?" Sherri grabbed the line and sniffed, too. She stared at Danny. "Do you think someone poured acid on Tony's ropes?"

"I don't know." But acid would eat at the fibers and weaken them. The damage might not be noticeable until too late.

"How did acid get on the ropes?" Eldon asked. "Did he spill something on it? Some kind of cleaner or something?"

"I don't think we use anything that strong to clean," Carrie said.

"If it wasn't an accident, it was deliberate," Ted said. His face looked craggier than usual, thick gray eyebrows drawn together in a scowl.

"You mean someone did this on purpose?" Eldon asked.

"I think someone meant for Tony—or someone else— to get hurt," Ted said. "Sabotage."

Chapter Two

Sabotage. The word sent a chill through Carrie. After a long moment, she became aware of everyone looking at her. With a start she realized that, now that Tony was out of commission, it was up to her to lead the team. It wasn't a role she had ever aspired to, but it was too late to worry about that now. "Let's look at the other ropes and harnesses," she said. "See if anything else has been tampered with."

Everyone pitched in to collect the climbing gear they had used that morning and laid it out on folding tables at the front of the room. "I'm not seeing anything amiss," Sheri said.

"Nothing over here," Ted added.

"Maybe it really was an accident," Eldon said. "Something spilled on those ropes and Tony just didn't notice it."

"Maybe," Carrie said. "But Tony is usually so careful."

"We should call the hospital and see how he's doing," Sheri said.

Carrie took out her phone and found the number for St. Joseph's. The others started putting away the gear, but she knew they were listening. "I'm calling to check on a patient who was transported by helicopter this morning," Carrie explained to the woman who answered the phone. "His name is Tony Meisner and he was injured in a climbing accident in Eagle Mountain."

"Are you a family member?" the woman asked.

"No, but I—"

"I can only provide information to immediate family."

Carrie stared at the phone.

"What did they say?" Danny asked.

"She said she could only give out information to family."

"There are privacy laws," Hannah said.

"Let's go to Junction and see what we can find out in person," Danny said.

"Go," Sheri said. "We'll finish cleaning up here."

Carrie called her mom, who was looking after Carrie's two children, and let her know it would be a couple more hours before she was home, then headed for her SUV, Danny on her heels. He settled into the passenger seat, his tall frame filling the space, making her more aware of him physically. It wasn't that she didn't like Danny. He was a great guy, and a good teammate. But being near him distracted her. He was too good-looking. Too masculine for her to be entirely comfortable. Most of the time she thought of him as the playboy type, but that glimpse of raw emotion when he had talked about being with Tony when he fell had unsettled her. It made her realize there was more to Danny Irwin than flirtatious remarks and a wicked sense of humor.

"I don't think that acid spill was an accident," he said as soon as they were on the road. "Tony isn't careless like that. And whatever is on that rope, it had to be strong stuff to weaken the fibers like that."

"I wonder if we can have it tested," she said.

"Where would we do that?"

"I don't know." She ran her hands down the steering wheel. "The police?"

He made a face. "And what do we tell them? We think somebody may have sabotaged Tony's gear, but we don't know who. Or why?"

"'Who' would almost have to be someone with search and rescue," she said. The thought made her physically ill, but she couldn't think of anyone else who would have access to their gear. "But none of us would do that."

"Someone from outside could have done it," he said. "They could have come in after we left on a call."

"The building is supposed to be locked." They stored a lot of valuable equipment there, not to mention narcotics, though those were kept in a separate secured cabinet and only Danny and Hannah, as medical personnel, had the key.

"I'm not sure we're always good about locking up," Danny said. "The drugs, yeah, but you know how it is when we scramble to go out on a call. Things can be chaotic. And what about former volunteers? One of them might have a key."

"But why would anyone want to hurt Tony?"

"We don't know that Tony was the target," Danny said. "We all use the ropes. Maybe whoever did this just wanted to hurt any one of us?"

She shivered. "Who would do something so terrible?"

"I don't know. Ex-spouse? Ex-lover? A former volunteer who washed out or was dismissed for some reason? Or maybe Tony really was the target—as captain, he might have felt responsible if someone was injured on his watch."

"He's only been captain a couple of years." The group elected its own officers by general consent. There was no definite schedule for changing office, but the members tended to rotate the various positions. Carrie had been second-in-command since last year, and she had accepted the role only after she had been reassured her primary function would be to assist Tony. The idea that she might have to step in to lead the group had seemed so remote it wasn't worth considering. "Maybe we should ask around and see what we can find out before we involve the police," she said.

Danny settled back into his seat. "When was the last time a SAR member had a bad accident like this?" he asked. "Do you remember?"

"Ryan and I were caught in that avalanche when we were training earlier this year." She still remembered the terror of a river of snow washing over her and pulling her under, though the others had found her and pulled her free within minutes. Ryan had escaped injury also, since the slide had been small. "And Ryan was badly hurt when Charlie Cutler pushed him off the side of Mount Baker." The convicted serial killer had been running from the police. She glanced at him. "Cutler tried to kill you, too, didn't he?"

Danny shrugged. "I got out of it with a few bruises and a sore knee. But, escaped serial killers aside, this kind of thing is really rare."

"It's kind of amazing, given the nature of the work we do," Carrie said. Personally, she tried not to think about the danger involved in rescuing people from remote wilderness, high mountains, deep canyons and rushing rivers. Better to focus on what a great service they were providing, and not personal risk.

"Barb and Cecil Kellogg slid off the road into the creek on a rescue call six years ago," Danny said. "Cecil broke his collarbone and Barb tore up her knee. They both left the team not long after that."

"This is different," she said. "Tony could have been killed if he had fallen from a great height."

"He might still not make it," Danny said. "We don't know what kind of internal injuries he might have, and all those injuries—sometimes the body can't cope."

"Don't say that. He's going to make it." She had depended on Tony so often, her role model for getting past those things about the search and rescue that threatened to overwhelm her.

They fell silent, an aching tension filling the car as they both contemplated their friend's possible fate. "How long have you been with search and rescue?" she asked as she turned onto the highway toward Junction, desperate to shift the conversation somewhere less dark.

"Seven years? Something like that. They put out a call for volunteers with medical experience and I thought it sounded pretty interesting."

"So a little longer than me," she said.

"I remember your first day," he said. "If I was a betting man, I would have said you wouldn't stick around. I guess I owe you an apology for that."

She hazarded a look at him. He wore an amused expression. "Why do you say that?" she asked.

"For one thing, most of our volunteers are climbers or have previous SAR experience, or have a medical or military background. They have a lot of outdoor experience."

"You make it sound like I was some couch potato who'd never been on a hike." She couldn't keep the huffiness from her voice. "I was trained in CPR and first aid and I'd been a life guard. I like hiking and I wanted to help people."

"I'm pretty sure you're the only member we've had who's a single mom with two little kids."

"What's that supposed to mean?"

He blew out a breath. "Don't get upset. I just mean the training we do, not to mention the actual calls, require a lot of time away from home. Seems like that would be hard with kids."

Was he implying that she neglected her children? "My kids understand search and rescue is important work. And I'm lucky enough to have my mom to help look after them."

"I get it," he said. "You're a great role model for them. Most people just aren't willing to make that sacrifice."

"It's not a sacrifice for me." When she had moved to Eagle Mountain following her divorce, she had been lost, wondering what to do with her life. She had a good job as an architect, but it wasn't enough. She felt helpless and was desperate for something that would make her feel stronger and more confident. When she saw a poster calling for recruits for the local search and rescue team it struck a chord in her. "I like challenging myself," she said. "And I like working with our team."

"You're good at it. I mean that."

"Why did you join SAR?" she asked. "I get that you thought it was interesting, but you've stayed all this time, so you must get more out of it than that."

"Like you said, it's a good team. And unlike you, I have a lot of free time—I work three twelve-hour shifts a week in a surgery unit and have the rest of the week to do what I want. In the winter I volunteer with backcountry ski patrol, but that's not very demanding. I have plenty of time for search and rescue. It's kind of addictive, you know?"

She nodded. She wasn't as much of an adrenaline junkie as some of her fellow volunteers, but she recognized the rush of taking big risks to save lives. When you succeeded, there was no other feeling like it.

"I didn't mean to insult you," he said again. "I admire you. I really do. And you've done a great job. I'm glad you stayed. And I'm not just saying that because you're in charge now." He grinned, a charming grin that sent a flutter through her stomach. That flutter surprised her so much she had to jerk her attention back to the road before she drifted onto the shoulder.

Danny was known for charming women, but he had certainly never charmed her. Her divorce had rendered her charm proof, she was sure.

OPEN MOUTH, INSERT FOOT, Danny thought as they neared Junction's city limits. He usually handled himself better with women. In his defense, he hadn't been trying to flirt with Carrie or anything. She was his fellow team member. Sure, she was an attractive woman, but she had made it clear from day one that she wasn't interested in anything but a professional relationship, and he tried to respect that. Just as well, since she probably thought he was an idiot now.

She parked her SUV in the hospital's garage and they made their way to the main entrance and approached the front desk. "We're trying to find out information about a patient here, Tony Meisner," Carrie said.

The woman behind the desk—gray hair, gray glasses, gray sweater—tapped out something on her keyboard and frowned at the computer screen. "Mr. Meisner is in ICU. Are you a relative?"

"We—" Danny began.

"I'm his sister," Carrie said.

The woman frowned. "Let me check his file."

She started typing again, and Danny took Carrie's arm and pulled her toward the elevator bank. "Why does she have to check his file?" Carrie asked.

"She's probably seeing who is listed as next of kin." He checked the directory for ICU and hustled her inside an open car, where he pressed the button for the right floor, then the button to close the elevator doors. "The thing about hospitals is if you look like you know where you're supposed to be, most of the time they won't stop you," he said. "If I'd been thinking clearer, I'd have worn my scrubs."

"Have you worked at this hospital before?" she asked.

"No. I'm at a surgical center in Delta. But I doubt things are much different here." He led the way to the ICU, marching past the nurses' station, though a sideways glance told him it was unoccupied at the moment. The Intensive Care Unit was set up with rooms in a half circle, the patient's name clearly marked next to each door. Tony was midway through the circle, the door half-open.

He slipped into the room and Carrie followed, both of them moving as silently as possible. They stood at the end of the bed and stared. Tony, a tall, thin man, looked less tall and much thinner in the hospital gown, festooned with tubes and lines for IV, catheter, pulse oximeter, blood pressure, oxygen cannula and heart monitor. Beside him a screen traced a continuous EKG and registered his oxygen saturation and blood pressure readings. He wore casts on one arm and one leg and probably had other bandages they couldn't see under the blankets draped over him. His eyes were closed, sunken and shadowed in a face that looked gaunt and pallid.

Carrie covered her mouth with her hand but said nothing for a long while, then she straightened, removed her hand and murmured softly, "Tony? Are you awake?"

The door opened behind them and a woman in blue scrubs, dark curly hair pulled back in a bun, approached.

"Hello?" she said, the question mark at the end of the single word leaving them to fill in the blank on the query.

"This is Tony's sister, Carrie." Danny stepped aside so the nurse could see her more clearly. "I'm her husband, Danny. I'm a nurse over at Delta."

Some—but not all—of the tension went out of the nurse's face. "Your brother has been out of surgery about thirty minutes," she said. "The doctor is keeping him heavily sedated."

"How is he doing?" Carrie asked. "I see the bandages, but what is the extent of his injuries?"

"We were with him when he fell," Danny said. It wouldn't hurt to let the woman know they were aware of the circumstances of the accident. "It was quite a shock."

"He was climbing?" the nurse asked.

"Rappelling into a canyon," Carrie said.

The nurse shook her head. "I don't know why these young men want to risk their lives like that."

Danny could have pointed out that Tony had been training to save lives, but he didn't bother. He couldn't be sure the woman at the front desk wouldn't decide to send security after them, so they shouldn't waste any time. "Can you tell us about his injuries?" he asked.

"Broken right leg—tibia and fibula. Several broken ribs. One of them punctured his lung on the way over here. Broken radius of the right arm. Various minor contusions and strains. He had surgery to pin some of the bones together and deal with the collapsed lung. He's stable, but still critical."

"Is there anything we can do?" Carrie asked. "Donate blood or something like that?"

"Nothing right now." The nurse checked Tony's IV. "Please limit your visit to five minutes. Even though he's sedated, he may be aware you're here. That's good, but we don't want to tax him."

Neither of them spoke after the nurse left. Danny tried to assess the situation as he would one of his patients at the hospital in Delta, but the knowledge that this was Tony—his friend—kept interfering. Besides, there was too much he didn't know, medically, to make any kind of accurate guess as to Tony's prognosis.

Carrie took a step back. "Let's get out of here," she said.

He followed her out of the room and back along the hallway to the elevator bank. When they were in the car alone, she turned to him. "Husband?" she asked.

"I wasn't sure they'd buy that I was a brother, but a sister's husband is close enough to be allowed into the ICU." He took out his phone. "I took a photo of the whiteboard in his room."

"Why?"

"It has the nurses' station's direct number." He showed her the image. "Now you can call and identify yourself as Tony's sister and get an update, bypassing the main switchboard. Give me your number and I'll forward it to you."

Her expression softened. Maybe she didn't think he was such an idiot after all. "Thanks."

"Can we grab dinner? And coffee?" Now that the rush of adrenaline following the accident had faded, he could use both.

"Just something fast." She checked her phone. "I really need to get home. My mom is great, but it's Saturday and I'd like to spend a little time with my kids."

"Sure."

They ate burgers and fries in the parking lot of a fast-food restaurant, with the SUV's heater running. Neither of them had been up to the brightly lit interior of the place, with half a dozen children racing about in the aftermath of a soccer game or something. "Tell me about your kids," he said.

She glanced at him. "Do you really want to know?"

"Yeah, I really want to know." He dunked a French fry in ketchup. "I like children."

"Dylan is nine and Amber is eight." Something like a smile softened her face. "They're great kids. I know every parents says that, but they are. Smart and kind and just...great."

"You must have had them pretty young." He had pegged her as being pretty close to his own age, which was thirty.

"I was nineteen when Dylan was born, and I had Amber thirteen months later." She met his questioning gaze. "I married my ex a month after we graduated high school."

"Wow. I didn't know people still did that."

"Yeah, wow."

"So, how long have you been divorced? Or is that too nosy?"

"Six and a half years. I found out he was cheating while I was pregnant with Amber."

"Ouch."

"People tried to warn us. Or they tried to warn me, at least. We were too young. He wasn't ready to settle down. But my mom was only eighteen when she had me. She was seventeen when she married my dad—he was twenty. And they were happy together for twenty years until he was killed by a drunk driver."

"I'm sorry for your loss."

"Thanks. I think with my ex and me, it wasn't really

immaturity that killed our marriage, it was the fact that he really didn't want to be married."

"Do you still see him?"

"Occasionally. He drops in and out of the kids' life, which drives me crazy, but they seem resilient, and at least I'm not relying on him for support. I'd be out of luck if I was."

He heard the bitterness behind her words, but who could blame her?

"What about you?" she asked. "Have you ever been married?"

"No way."

She laughed. "Well, tell me how you really feel."

He dug around in the paper bag, searching for more fries. "I don't think I'm marriage material."

"Well, if you think that, it's probably a good idea not to get married." She turned the key in the ignition. "You ready to head back?"

He was, and they did. They didn't say much on the way home, and he found himself watching her in the fading light. She really was pretty—honey-blond hair past her shoulder blades, strands coming loose from the braid she wore today. She was fit—that was a given for search and rescue. Doing the math, he knew she was only twenty-eight or twenty-nine, but she had an air of maturity about her. Maybe having kids did that. He knew she worked as an architect—her name was on the plaque at an office just off Main of a firm that designed high-end houses. The only woman on that list, he remembered. Did that feel odd to her, or did she even care?

He thought of himself as being good at reading people, but he had never been able to read Carrie. He didn't like to admit how much that bothered him, but there it was. She kept herself to herself, much like he did. People thought of him as outgoing, but that was just another way of keeping them from getting too close.

They saw the flashing lights as they climbed the hill toward search and rescue headquarters. Red-and-blue strobes bathed the snowbanks around the building in a kaleidoscope of light and shadow. Two fire trucks and two sheriff's department vehicles filled the lot, along with several cars he recognized as belonging to fellow SAR volunteers. "What is going on?" Carrie asked, fear tightening her voice.

Sheri trotted up to meet them, her husband, Colorado State Patrol detective Erik Lester, close behind. Carrie stopped the SUV and lowered her window. Icy air rushed in, along with the smell of smoke and hot metal. "What happened?" she asked.

"The Beast is gone," Sheri said. "Burned up." She glanced over her shoulder at what Danny could now see was the blackened hull of a vehicle. "I hated that old thing most of the time, but what are we going to do without it?"

The Beast had been the primary transportation for SAR volunteers and gear. Ancient and outdated, it was still the best thing they had for those purposes, and the organization—always strapped for cash—had never had the money to replace it.

Erik nudged Sheri aside so he could address Carrie. "I understand you're in charge, with Tony in the hospital."

"How is Tony?" Sheri asked before Carrie could reply to Erik.

"He was out of surgery and critical but stable," Carrie said. "He's in intensive care."

"He was sedated, so we didn't get to talk to him," Danny added.

Carrie turned to Erik. "Do you need me to sign papers or something?"

"I need to ask if you know of anyone who might have a grudge against search and rescue or someone in the group." Erik said.

"I don't understand," Carrie said. "What does that have to do with this fire?" She looked toward the charred remains of the Beast.

"We don't think this fire was an accident," Erik said. "We're pretty sure someone torched the Beast deliberately."

Chapter Three

Carrie tried to comprehend this statement, but the words floated on the surface, refusing to sink in or have meaning. "Are you talking arson?" Danny asked. "Someone deliberately torched the Beast?"

Erik nodded. "We'll know more after the investigator's final report, but everything points to that right now."

"I told him about Tony," Sheri said. "How his fall might not have been an accident."

"Sheri said you suspected chemical damage to Tony's climbing ropes," Erik said.

"Yes." Carrie finally found her voice.

Sheriff Travis Walker, his tall, broad-shouldered silhouette recognizable even in the darkness, strode toward them. He nodded to Carrie. "Where was the search and rescue vehicle parked when you last saw it?" he asked.

"Right next to the building." She looked toward SAR headquarters, dark and silent. And unharmed. "There's a designated parking spot for the Beast right by the door," she said. "How did the Jeep burn and the building isn't touched?"

Travis and Erik exchanged looks. "The Jeep was parked up by the road when it burned," Travis said. "Between a snowbank and the asphalt. Nothing else impacted."

"Who has the keys to the vehicle?" Erik asked.

"They're kept on a hook just inside the door of the headquarters," Sheri said. "Anyone could access them."

"Anyone with a key to the building," Carrie said.

"And who is that?" Travis asked.

"Any member of search and rescue," Danny said. "Probably some former members, too."

Travis's frown told Carrie what he thought of such lax security. "We have to be able to respond to an emergency at any time," she said. "Whoever reports here first starts loading up the gear we'll need." It was a process that had worked well for over thirty years.

"I want to take a look at the ropes Tony was using when he fell," Travis said.

"Do you really think there's a connection between the Beast being destroyed and what happened to Tony?" Even as Carrie asked the question, she realized how desperate she sounded. The SAR captain had almost been killed this morning, and the only vehicle the organization owned had been destroyed tonight. What else could they think but that someone was trying to harm Eagle Mountain Search and Rescue?

She unlocked the side door to the building and flipped on the lights, flooding the large concrete-floored expanse with a harsh white glow. "Does anything look out of place?" Erik asked.

She scanned the area. Gear hung on hooks and was stored in bins along the back wall, and long tables at the front of the room held a couple of coffee cups, some recruiting brochures and a box of nitrile gloves someone had forgotten to stow. A sagging sofa and an assortment of folding chairs occupied most of the rest of the space. The air smelled of coffee, disinfectant and the lingering odor of the pizza they had ordered in a couple of days before. "Everything looks fine," she said. The very ordinariness of it chilled her, considering what had happened.

"Where are the climbing ropes?" Travis asked.

"Over here." Danny led the way to the table where the broken climbing ropes were laid out. "You can see where the fibers disintegrated," he said, pointing to the place where the strands had separated. "And there's discoloration around the breaks. It's hard to see, but if you take a whiff, you can smell some kind of acid."

Travis bent close to the ropes and sniffed, then nodded. He looked up at Erik. "Can you have the state lab test this for us?"

"Sure thing. I'll get an evidence bag from my car." He left, and Travis moved away from the table.

"Who might have tampered with the ropes?" Travis asked.

"All the search and rescue team members know where the gear is stored and would have access to it." Her stomach knotted as the implication of that sank in. Of course they had talked about one of the other volunteers being responsible, but having law enforcement reach the same conclusion made it seem more real. She trusted her fellow volunteers with her life. They were a team. Who would betray them this way?

"Someone else could have come in and done it," Danny said. "People monitor the emergency channel. They would know when we were out on a call."

"We're supposed to lock up every time we leave, but maybe someone was careless," Sheri said.

"What about the Beast?" Carrie asked. "Why do you think that was arson and not just, I don't know, something wrong with the engine? We're always having problems with it."

"We'll have a full report in a couple of days, but the

fire crew that responded said they could smell diesel and it looked like someone soaked the area around the vehicle and tossed in a match," Travis said. "It went up like a bomb."

She wrapped her arms around herself, cold to the bone despite the murmur of the building's furnace.

Erik returned and collected the severed ropes. Sheri left with him, and the sheriff followed them out. Danny put a hand on Carrie's shoulder. "Are you okay?"

Just like that, she was hyperaware of him again, of his quiet strength and the warmth in both his hand and his voice seeping into her. It would be so easy to lean into him, to imagine some connection between them that entitled her to take comfort from him.

Instead, she uncrossed her arms and straightened. "I'm fine. It's just a shock, something like this."

"Yeah. You should go home," he said.

"I will. You too."

"Yeah."

They walked out together and she made a point of locking the door and trying the knob to make sure it was secure. Danny waved, then drove off in his car, and she followed him down the hill and into town. Foot traffic on the sidewalks had died down and only a couple of restaurants and Mo's Pub showed signs of life. She turned off Main Street and drove to the small house she shared with her mom.

"I heard fire engines go by an hour ago," her mother, Becky, said when she met Carrie at the door. Not yet fifty, Becky was petite like her daughter, with naturally frosted blond hair cut in a chin-length bob. "I was afraid you had to go out on another search and rescue call."

"I would have phoned you if I had." Carrie hung up

her coat and dropped her purse and keys on the end of the counter. "Are the kids in bed?"

"They went sledding with Ruthie and Evan Morris this afternoon and were tired out," Becky said.

Carrie tiptoed down the hallway and peeked into the first room on the left. Dylan lay on his back, one hand thrown across his chest, one leg out of the covers, blond hair fallen across his forehead. At peace. Smiling, she moved to the door across from his, where Amber lay curled on her side beneath her pink quilt, her princess night-light bathing the room in a muted pink glow.

Back in the kitchen, her mother switched on the electric kettle. "I thought I'd make some tea," Becky said. "Do you want some?"

"Yes." Carrie sank into a chair at the table, exhaustion pulling at her like lead weights.

"How is Tony?" Becky asked. "Were you able to see him?"

"He was out of surgery and I saw him, but he's sedated. His condition is listed as stable but critical."

"Did you have anything to eat? I could warm up some soup."

"We stopped for a burger on the way home. Thanks."

"Someone went with you. I'm glad to hear it." Becky dropped tea bags into cups and took out a jar of sugar. "Who was it?"

"Danny Irwin. He was climbing alongside Tony when Tony fell. I think it probably shook him up a lot." Danny hadn't shown any outward signs of distress, but there had been real concern beneath his calm, and his normally jovial manner had been more subdued.

"I hope Tony gets better." Becky poured water over the tea bags. "I don't know him as well as you do, but he's always struck me as a really nice man."

"He is," Carrie said.

"Do they have any idea how the fall happened?" Becky brought two mugs to the table and slid one toward Carrie. The scent of mint perfumed the air. Chamomile-and-mint tea, her mother's solution to every worry.

"We're not sure." That was all she had intended to say, but the rest came rushing out. "But it might have been deliberate. The sheriff took the ropes Tony was using to be tested. Danny thinks someone might have poured some kind of acid on them. The damage wasn't really evident, but the ropes failed and Tony fell."

"That's horrible! Who would do something like that?" Becky's voice rose and Carrie cast a worried glance toward the hallway and the children's rooms.

Becky leaned forward and lowered her voice. "Seriously, does anyone know who would do something like that to Tony?"

"No idea." Carrie sipped her tea. She really didn't want to say anything else, but Eagle Mountain was too small a town for her mother not to find out about the Beast as soon as she reported to the courthouse Monday morning for her job with the county clerk's office. "Those fire engines you heard earlier were responding to a fire at search and rescue headquarters," she said. "Someone set fire to the Beast."

Becky's eyes widened. "You're kidding. Why would someone target search and rescue? You help people."

"I wish I was kidding. I know the old thing was a pain in the butt sometimes, but now we'll have to replace it and we really don't have the money."

"You'll have to hold a fundraiser or two," Becky said. "People will want to contribute."

Carrie nodded and pushed aside her cup. "I'm beat. I'm going to take a shower and crawl into bed."

"Sleep well," Becky said.

But Carrie knew that wasn't going to happen. Not tonight, and maybe not for a long time to come.

DANNY WOKE TO find a wet spring snow beginning to fall but wasn't surprised when he received a text from Carrie calling a special meeting at search and rescue headquarters. Better to get everyone together to talk about this now, on Sunday when most people would have the day off and be able to attend. He usually spent his Sundays working ski patrol in one of the popular backcountry areas around town, but after yesterday's ordeal he had sent a text to the volunteer coordinator begging off. He had planned to spend the day sleeping and watching TV—a whole day to himself, when no one needed him.

But he wouldn't pass up the opportunity to hear the latest news and speculations about Tony's accident or the destruction of the Beast.

Shortly before he had to leave for the meeting, his phone rang. The familiar mixture of panic and dread filled him as he stared at the caller ID. He sucked in a breath and answered. "Hey, Joy. How are you?"

"Not so good." His sister sounded as if she hadn't slept in a while, his first clue she wasn't just calling to complain or ask for money. "Mom isn't doing so well," she said. "She's been talking about how she doesn't need to take her medicine anymore. The way she's been acting, I'm wondering if she's already stopped taking her prescription."

"You keep track of the pills, right?" Danny asked.

"Yes, but maybe she's throwing them away when I'm not looking. You know how devious she can be."

Their mother was smart, which sometimes worked against her.

"Something's not right," Joy said. "After all this time, I can tell."

"I'll talk to her," Danny said. Sometimes, he could reason with Mom and take some of the load off Joy.

"Call tonight. She left this morning. She said she was going out with friends, but she doesn't really have friends, so I don't know where she is. And she never answers her phone when she's gone like this."

"I'll call tonight," he said, the familiar fear twisting his stomach in a knot. "Have you talked to her doctor?"

"Of course. He says he can authorize inpatient treatment for a little while, if Mom will agree to go."

A big *if.* "I'll talk to her," he said again.

"Great. I'm going to lie down now." *Click.*

Danny signed. Joy was probably depressed. Caring for their ill—and uncooperative—mother was taking its toll. But what else were they going to do? His mother and sister lived in Iowa. Danny's life was here in Colorado. Their mother refused any other assistance. And much of the time she refused to help herself. They were all doing the best they could, but he had stopped pretending it was enough.

He set a reminder in his phone to call later and headed to the SAR meeting. He wasn't surprised to find the parking lot already full of cars when he arrived shortly before noon. It looked like everyone who had even a peripheral role with the team had shown up. Like Danny, they were probably hoping for an update about both Tony and the Beast.

"Thank you for coming on such short notice," Carrie said from the front of the room. Every chair and the sofa was filled with volunteers, and several people, including Danny, stood along the walls. "I know you're all worried about Tony. I spoke with the hospital a little while ago and he's awake and they've even had him up and moving about a little. He's still in critical condition and can't have visitors, and he's in a lot of pain, but we know he's tough."

"Tell him I said he's too mean to die," Ryan said, and received a few laughs.

"Where's Austen?" Eldon asked. "Why isn't he here?"

"I had a text saying he'd be here." Carrie frowned. "It's not like him to be late." As the newest member of the team, still in his training program, Austen had been more dedicated than most, showing up for every call and every training session.

"Ted isn't here, either," Sheri said. "But don't wait for them. Have the police discovered anything about the damage to Tony's harness or the fire that destroyed the Jeep?"

"I called the sheriff, but I haven't heard anything," Carrie said. "He indicated last night that it could take several days to get results from the state lab on the climbing ropes Tony was using, and from the arson investigator."

"Why destroy the Beast?" Eldon asked. "Does someone seriously not want us to be able to go out on rescue calls?"

"I've wanted to torch the old clunker plenty of times myself," Danny said. "But I would have waited until we had a replacement to do it."

"Even if they find the lowlife who set the fire, we've still lost our only response vehicle," Sheri said. "What are we going to do now?"

"We'll have to use our personal vehicles," Carrie said. "I filed a claim with our insurance carrier this morning, but we're only going to be able to collect a couple of thousand dollars at most. The Beast wasn't worth that much to anyone but us."

The door opened, letting in a blast of cold air, and Ted stamped inside. He brushed snow from the shoulders of his jacket. "Sorry I'm late," he said. "It's snowing hard out there." He hung up the jacket and joined the others. "What did I miss?"

"We were just talking about the Beast," Sheri said.

"We'll have to find a replacement," Ted said.

"The Beast was specially modified for search and rescue work," Danny said. "Getting something to replace it is going to run upwards of a hundred K."

"We'll need to raise money," Carrie said. "I want a couple of people to work on a contribution plea to send out to donors who have supported us in the past, and to come up with ideas for other fundraisers."

Silence met this announcement, as the volunteers avoided looking at each other. "I'll volunteer," Sheri said finally. "Eldon, you can work with me."

"Sure," Eldon said.

"Thank you." Carrie glanced down at the tablet on which she had apparently scribbled some notes. "The sheriff asked me to compile a list of everyone who has a key to the headquarters building. I'll need help figuring out who—besides those of us in this room—might have access." She looked across the room. "Ted, I'm hoping you'll help me with that. You've been a member longer than anyone else."

"I don't see the point," Ted said. "It wasn't a search and rescue volunteer who did this. The older members know how hard we worked to get the Beast in the first place. We held spaghetti suppers, car washes, silent auctions, sold T-shirts. We worked our tails off to pay for the thing. And the newer volunteers know how much we relied on the Beast to get us and our gear to accident sites in the mountains. I've known every volunteer with search and rescue for the past thirty years and none of them would do this."

"Maybe it wasn't a volunteer," Danny said. "Maybe it was a friend or family member of a volunteer who resented the organization taking up their time."

"Or just a nutcase who decided it would be fun to set something on fire," Eldon said.

"What happened to Tony wasn't a spur-of-the-moment decision," Sheri said. "Someone planned to ruin his ropes and put him in danger."

"Whoever did it ought to be charged with attempted murder," Eldon said.

Everyone started talking at once, voices rising with anger and outrage. Carrie let them talk but said nothing. Danny was silent, too, watching her. She looked so calm, only a tightness around her eyes and mouth betraying her concern. They were lucky to have her to assume command in Tony's absence. He had never thought of her as a leader before, but she was exactly the person they needed right now.

"Ted, I want a list of all the people who have worked with search and rescue so far," she said when the conversation had died to a murmur. "Danny, I want you to make a list of everyone in Tony's life—friends, relatives, people at his job. I want to know everyone who might have had a grudge against him or against SAR."

"Okay, but why me?" he asked.

"You know Tony as well as anyone. And since you're a nurse, you can get in to see him in ICU and ask him if he has any idea who did this."

"Maybe we should leave all this 'making lists' and questioning people to the cops," Eldon said. "I mean, that's their job."

"And I'm sure they're going to investigate," Carrie

said. "But I want to do whatever we can to help them. Tony is one of our own. I want him to know we're doing our part to stop whoever damaged those ropes and to keep them from hurting someone else."

"Did the same person damage the ropes and set fire to the Beast?" Sheri asked.

"We don't know," Carrie said. "But I'm curious to see if any names show up on our lists of people with a key to headquarters and people who interacted regularly with Tony."

"Every one of us will be on both lists," Eldon said.

Silence. They had probably all been thinking the same thing, but having it said out loud—that the saboteur was one of them—was too terrible.

"The cops are going to look at all of us first," Danny said. "We might as well be ready for that. And if we can find someone else we think they should look at instead, then we need to do it."

The door to the outside burst open and banged against the wall. They turned as Austen Morrissey staggered inside. Blood ran from a gash on his head and his clothes were wet, his pants legs smeared with mud. "Austen! What happened to you?" Sheri rushed forward and took his arm.

"I was on the way here and someone ran my car off the road." He sank into a chair and looked up at them, eyes wide. "They came straight at me. I ran into the ditch. I guess I hit my head." He touched the gash and winced. "I must have blacked out for a little bit. I managed to get out of the car and hike up the road, but I'm a mess. I mean, it's crazy, but I think somebody tried to kill me."

Chapter Four

Blood ran down Austen's face and stained his light gray jacket. "Sit down and let me take a look at you," Danny said. He took Austen by the elbow and guided him to a folding chair.

"Should I call an ambulance?" Carrie asked.

"No! I'll be fine." Austen tried to stand, but Danny gently pushed him back into the chair.

Danny checked Austen's pupils, which looked normal. He guessed Austen was in his early thirties, with a broad face, wide-set blue eyes and a dusting of freckles, which combined to make him look young and guileless. "Let's get some of this blood cleaned up and see what we're dealing with," Danny said. "You might need stitches."

Carrie brought him a bottle of saline and a packet of gauze pads, and Danny used these to clean the blood from what turned out to be a fairly shallow gash just above Austen's right eyebrow. "This doesn't look too bad," Danny said. "Head wounds always bleed a lot, and you've got a good-sized lump. How many fingers am I holding up?"

"Three," Austen said. "Honestly, I'm fine—just shook up."

"What happened?" Ted asked. He and the others had gathered around.

Austen gripped his knees, his knuckles white as Danny dabbed antiseptic on the wound, but he didn't flinch. "It was snowing pretty hard, so I didn't see much," he said. "I was headed up the big hill toward headquarters and I saw the headlights of a vehicle coming toward me. They were superbright, and I flashed my lights at the driver to remind him to dim them, but instead, they kept coming right toward me. By the time I realized he was in my lane and he wasn't slowing down, all I could do was steer toward the ditch. I banged my head when I went off the road."

"You say the driver was a man?" Carrie asked.

"I don't know." Austen touched the lump on his head and winced. "The car's headlights were blinding me. I can't even tell you what kind of vehicle it was."

"Where is your car?" Danny asked.

"I left it in the ditch and walked up here." He looked down at his boots, the leather dark with dampness. "I guess that was a dumb thing to do."

"We should call the sheriff," Carrie said. She pulled her phone from her pocket.

"They're not going to be able to do anything," Austen said. "I can't tell them much."

"Maybe they'll find something," Carrie said. "And if nothing else, I want this on record."

While Carrie moved away to speak to the 9-1-1 operator, Danny finished bandaging Austen. "Any other injuries?" he asked when he was done.

"Only to my pride," Austen said.

"A deputy is on his way." Carrie rejoined them. "How are you doing, Austen?"

"I'm okay." He continued to stare at his shoes.

Carrie put a hand on his shoulder. "I imagine this was

pretty upsetting, after the accident you were in a couple of years ago."

Austen's mouth tightened. "Yeah, it was a bit of déjà vu."

Danny sent Carrie a questioning look. What was she talking about?

She shook her head. *Later*, she mouthed.

"Austen, I've got my truck with me," Eldon said. "Maybe I can pull your car out of the ditch once the deputy has had a look."

Austen looked up and seemed to gather himself together. "Thanks," he said. "I'd really appreciate that." He looked around. "Do we have any coffee?"

"I'll get you a cup," Sheri said.

The others talked among themselves and to Austen as Danny packed up the first aid supplies. Carrie met him at the medical closet. "I don't think Austen should be driving," she said. "Would you mind taking him home? He can worry about the car tomorrow."

"Sure. What was that about him having been through something like this before?"

"Don't you remember?" She glanced over her shoulder toward Austen, who was surrounded by the others, deep in conversation. Carrie looked back at Danny. "Summer, two years ago? He and his girlfriend—she may have been his fiancée, I don't remember—were in a horrible accident on Briar Patch Road. The Jeep they were in slipped off the road and rolled in Poughkeepsie Canyon. Austen was thrown clear near the top and only suffered a broken shoulder, but his girlfriend was seriously injured. They had to airlift her out of the canyon. She was alive when we got to her, but she didn't make it."

"I heard something about that," Danny said. "But I was away for almost a month that summer, dealing with family stuff." His mother had been struggling through a particularly bad period back then. He glanced back at Austen. "Was he living here then?"

"No. They were on vacation from Texas or Arizona or someplace like that. He moved here later. He said he was so inspired by the work search and rescue did that he wanted to be a part of that."

"No wonder what happened today shook him up so much."

She nodded. "I'll feel better if I know someone is seeing him home safely—someone with medical experience, in case that knock on the head was worse than it seems."

The door from the outside opened again, bringing in a swirl of snow and Rayford County sheriff's deputy—and new SAR recruit—Jake Gwynn. He surveyed the room, then focused on Austen's bandaged head. "I understand there's been some trouble," he said.

"Someone ran my car off the road," Austen said. "But before you ask, I didn't see who it was."

Jake pulled up an empty folding chair and sat in front of Austen. "Start at the beginning and tell me everything that happened."

Austen told the same story he had shared with them and wasn't able to provide more details, despite Jake's questions. When he was done, Jake tucked his notebook back into his pocket. "I'll stop and take a look at your car on my way back into town," he said. "But it's snowing hard enough it's probably already obliterated any tread patterns from the other vehicle."

"I told Carrie she shouldn't even bother to call you," Austen said. "I'm sorry we got you out on such a nasty day."

"I called because I wanted this on record," Carrie

said. "Jake, you know about the other attacks on search and rescue?"

Jake nodded. "I know about the damage to Tony's climbing ropes and the burning of the SAR Jeep. Have there been others?"

"Not until this attack on Austen," she said.

"What makes you think this accident is related to those other incidents?" Jake asked.

"Austen told you this other vehicle headed straight toward him, with its bright lights on," Carrie said. "Who has their bright lights on in the middle of the day, even if it is snowing? It wasn't an accident, it was a deliberate attempt to harm one of our members."

"It could have been a drunk driver," Jake said. "Or even someone who didn't see Austen in the snowstorm until it was too late. How would this other driver have even known who Austen was and that he's a member of search and rescue?"

"There are no other homes and businesses up this road," Danny said. "Anyone driving up here was most likely with SAR."

"For all we know, whoever is doing this knows all about us," Sheri said. "From what kind of car we drive and where we live to whether or not we have a partner waiting at home."

"It's a pretty tenuous connection," Jake said. "I'll do what I can, but we don't have much to go on."

"What about the sabotaged climbing ropes and the burned-out Jeep?" Eldon asked. "Do you have any clues as to who is responsible for those?"

"No." Jake looked around at them. Their faces reflected anger, worry, annoyance or a combination of all three emotions. "Can you think of anyone who might have a grudge against search and rescue?" he asked.

"Someone you angered or maybe the relative of someone you weren't able to save."

"Most people are grateful that we try to save their loved ones," Ted said. "Even when our job is to retrieve a body from a remote location, the families are relieved to have that closure."

Jake nodded. "Keep thinking. And we'll keep looking for clues. In the meantime, everyone be careful."

He left and Austen stood. "Let's see about my car, okay Eldon?" he said.

"The car can wait until morning," Danny said. "The cops probably aren't finished with it yet anyway. I'll take you home."

Austen hesitated. "I don't know…"

"Let Danny take you home," Carrie said. "You probably shouldn't be driving right now anyway."

Austen nodded. "I guess you're right. Thanks, Danny."

Austen followed Danny to his car, a battered green Honda that had seen better days but served him well. He followed Austen's directions to a new set of condos on the outskirts of town, built as part of an affordable-housing initiative. "What do you do for work?" Danny asked. "I don't think I ever heard."

"I'm the manager for these condos," Austen said.

"What led you to join SAR?" Danny asked. Though Carrie had told him the story, he was curious to hear what Austen would say. "We recruit heavily in the climbing community and among medical personnel like me, but I'm always curious what brings others to the group."

"Eagle Mountain Search and Rescue saved my life," Austen said. "A couple of years ago I was in a bad accident in Poughkeepsie Canyon. I thought you knew."

"I was out of town a lot that year," Danny said. "Family stuff. I guess I wasn't here for that call. Looks like you made a full recovery." No mention of the girlfriend, but maybe that was too painful to talk about.

"Yeah, but I figured the SAR training would help me get in better shape, and it has." He unbuckled his seat belt. "You want to come in? I'm going to make more coffee."

"Thanks. Coffee would be good." He was curious to know more about this rookie he hadn't interacted with all that much.

Austen unlocked the front door and led the way into a small foyer that opened into a combination living/dining room, with a galley kitchen along the back wall. "Make yourself comfortable," he said. "I'll get the coffee."

While Austen fiddled with a coffee-pod machine, Danny studied the simply furnished room. Where his own place was cluttered and messy, Austen's condo had the look of a hotel suite or a real estate show home. The furniture had the same neutral colors and clean lines that blended into the white walls and light wood flooring. There were no books or art. The only ornament at all was a photograph in a silver frame on a table by the sofa.

Danny studied the image of a smiling woman with brown curly hair, a slight gap between her upper front teeth.

"That's Julie, my fiancée." Austen spoke from right behind him.

Danny flinched and turned around. "I didn't mean to be nosy."

"It's okay." Austen set two mugs on the coffee table. "She died before I moved here. That's one of the reasons I came to Eagle Mountain. I wanted to make a fresh start."

He sat on one end of the sofa and Danny took the other and sipped from his coffee, trying to think of a suitable reply. "That must have been hard," he said after a moment.

"It was," Austen had a tightness around the mouth again, as if he was reining in emotion.

"I'm off tomorrow," Danny said. "I could pick you up and take you out to your car."

"Thanks, but I think I'll just call O'Brien's for a wrecker." He forced a smile. "That's what insurance is for, right? I guess I was so shaken earlier, I didn't think of it. I should have called them right away, come home and cleaned myself up and not said anything."

"No, you did the right thing, coming to the meeting. We need to know about this stuff."

Austen grimaced. "You heard the deputy—he thinks it was just a careless driver. But I know that car was headed straight for me." He set his mug on the coffee table and leaned forward, his elbows on his knees. "I wish I could figure out who wants to hurt us—to hurt search and rescue."

"Maybe it's like Jake said—someone has a grudge. Maybe someone who didn't make the cut to join the group."

"Does that happen very often?" Austen asked. "You kick people out?"

"Not everyone can meet the rigors of training or keep up with the demands on their time," Danny said. The coffee was already lukewarm, so he set the half-full cup aside. "And occasionally we get people who are so set on being heroes that they can't work as a team. The one thing you have to accept to do this kind of work is that it really isn't about you—it's about the community, the team and the people we're trying to help."

"I still struggle sometimes when people get into trouble because they did something stupid and we have to go out and save them," Austen said.

"Yeah, that can be annoying, but you learn to put that

aside. You're doing a good job. I can see how you've improved in your training."

Austen straightened. "Thanks. That means a lot."

Danny stood. "I know you're probably worn out. I won't keep you. Thanks for the coffee."

"Thank you for the ride home." Austen walked with him to the door. "I guess SAR is kind of my family now," he said. "All these attacks feel personal."

"Yeah, it feels that way to me, too," Danny said.

"I want to find out who's doing this," Austen said. "And I want to stop them."

"We all want that," Danny said. "Maybe we'll think of something that can help the sheriff."

"If I figure out who this is, I'm not going to wait for the sheriff." His gaze met Danny's, the anger in them sharp and bright. "I'm going to make sure they never hurt anyone again."

"I worry about you taking on too much, stepping in as SAR captain in addition to everything else you have going on." Becky sat across the kitchen table from Carrie and regarded her daughter with a look of concern Carrie had seen so often it was the expression she most associated with her mom—a slight furrowing of the forehead, a narrowing of her eyes, lips pressed together in a way that deepened the lines on each side of her mouth. She had been startled, after her children were born, to recognize an identical expression on her own face at times.

"It's okay, Mom." Carrie pushed aside the stack of incident reports, training schedules and inventory sheets she had been studying. Though she had helped Tony with some of the paperwork a few times, the sheer volume of record keeping involved in running one rural, search and rescue operation had surprised her. "You know I like to keep busy," she said, and smiled in a way she hoped was reassuring.

"Sometimes, staying busy is a good way to avoid thinking about the rest of your life," Becky said.

Ouch. "What's that supposed to mean? My life is the kids and you, my job, and search and rescue. All things I love."

"What about your personal life?" Becky asked. "You're still a young woman. You should be dating."

"Says the woman who hasn't been on a date in how long is it now, ten years?"

"I'm not twenty-nine. You are." A flush stained Becky's cheeks, making her look even younger than her forty-eight years. "And my situation is different. No one could replace your father."

Carrie wanted to reassure her mother that she didn't have to replace Dad, but she didn't have to spend the rest of her life alone, either. But that would open the door for her mom to turn Carrie's words back on herself, and she didn't have the energy for that argument this evening.

But her mom wasn't going to drop the subject. "You live in a town where the men outnumber the women two to one, or something like that," she continued. "And they're all skiers and climbers and runners and outdoor guides. You could have your pick of sexy, fit men."

"Why would I want a guy who spends all his spare time climbing rocks or riding mountain bikes?" Carrie asked. "And why are you bringing this up now, Mom? What's happened to make you suddenly concerned about my single status?"

Becky's lips thinned and the lines on either side of her mouth deepened even more. "I overheard Amber talking with her friend, Kiley, today when we were all walking home from school. Kiley asked where Amber's daddy was and why didn't he live with them, and Amber said her dad didn't live with them because Mommy didn't want a daddy around, so she guessed that meant she'd never have one."

It wasn't the first time something one of her children said made Carrie feel like she'd swallowed rocks, but the sensation wasn't easier to take, no matter how much practice she had. "Don't you think having different men move in and out of my life while I tried to find 'the one' would be a lot harder on the children than leaving all that until they're older?" she asked.

"I think children are resilient and you can't be afraid to let someone into your heart because of what might happen." Becky caught and held Carrie's gaze. "I didn't raise a coward, Carrie Ann."

The words stung. "I am not a coward. Even when I hate something, like heights, I do exactly what you taught me—buck up and get on with it."

"You're the bravest person I know when it comes to saving other people's lives," Becky said. She reached across the table and squeezed Carrie's hand. "If it helps, think of relationships as another challenge to be overcome, like climbing a peak or rappelling into a canyon, only this time the person you're saving is yourself."

Carrie searched for some sharp reply to this remarkable statement but drew a blank. She was still struggling to find words when the doorbell rang.

Becky released Carrie's hand and checked the time on the microwave. "It's after seven. Were you expecting someone?"

"No." Carrie stood and hurried to the door as the bell rang again. She flipped the switch for the porch light and checked the security peep, and was surprised to see Ted staring back at her.

"Ted! Is something wrong? Did I miss a callout?" Dispatch was supposed to automatically send her a call and a text in case of emergency, but maybe something had gone wrong.

"Nothing like that." Ted shoved both hands in the pockets of his blue Eagle Mountain Search and Rescue parka. "Can I come in and talk to you about something?"

"Of course." She stepped back and let him pass into the living room. He was a tall man, a little hunched now, and he carried himself like someone who had probably taken up more space at one time. She wondered if he had played football when he was young. He had the frame for it, if not the weight.

He pulled off the green fleece hat he had been wearing and ran one hand through his still-thick white hair, which did nothing to neaten it. "I'm not interrupting your dinner or anything, am I?"

"No. Come on into the living room." She flipped on the light as she entered the small room with the sofa that turned into a bed, mostly used when her aunt Dorothy came to visit from Phoenix. "What did you want to talk about?" she asked.

He looked around the room, at everything in it but her. "Any news about Tony?" he asked.

"He was moved out of ICU into a regular room today," she said. "I'm going to see him tomorrow."

Ted nodded. "That's good. I remember when he joined search and rescue. He was just eighteen, the youngest member we'd had until then. This skinny kid who didn't know anything—had to learn everything from scratch. But he stuck with it. Terrible, that rope being damaged like that."

"Do you know something about what happened?" she asked. "Is that why you're here?"

He looked up, startled, as if he had only just remembered she was in the room. "No. I wanted to talk to you about the way I'm being sidelined with the group," he said. "I've got more experience than anyone on the squad, but because I'm older, I'm being skipped over for leadership roles and asked to take a secondary role on rescue missions. It isn't right."

The complaint didn't surprise her, but the force of the anger behind it did. "Let's sit down," she said, and motioned him to sit beside her on the sofa. He did so, perched on the edge of the cushion, as if prepared to spring up at any second. "We all respect your experience with search and rescue," she began. "You've been a mentor to so many of us."

"I'm not a mentor. I'm a fellow team member," he said. "An active member, not a consultant, but that's what Tony has been trying to make me, and I won't stand for it."

"I don't think Tony has been doing that," she said.

"I wanted to be the training officer this year," he said. "It's a job I've done before. I've done all the jobs before, but I'm especially good at that one. It's like you said, I'm good at teaching others—mentoring them. But Tony gave the position to Sheri instead. He said she's a stronger climber and that's something we all need to work on more. Just because I messed up tying a knot one time, he's never going to let me forget it."

Carrie remembered the incident he was referring to. Ted had started down a rappel before he secured the end of his rope with a stopper knot so it would slide through the anchor chain when it reached the end. It was the kind of careless mistake that could cost a climber his life. Tony had seen what was happening and stopped Ted before he met with disaster. How ironic that Tony had been injured when his ropes slipped through the anchor, though in his case it had been no accident.

There hadn't been any other missteps by Ted that Carrie was aware of, but even she had noticed that Ted was the slowest of the squad now, lagging behind on long hikes and tiring more quickly under duress. "Ted, you've been doing this kind of work a long time," she said.

"Almost thirty years," he said. "Longer than you've been alive."

She nodded. "Your body has taken a lot of beating in that time," she said. "Long hours, tough hikes, lots of nasty weather."

"It's part of the job. I don't complain."

"I guess what I'm trying to say is, it's normal that at some point you have to slow down. Your body is forcing you to, whether you want to or not."

"I'm not slowing down!" He jumped up and glared at her. "That's age discrimination. What is it going to take to stop this? Do I have to sue?"

"Don't let your pride endanger yourself or one of your teammates," she said. "Instead of trying to keep up with people thirty years younger, use that experience of yours to coordinate our rescue efforts, analyze situations and communicate with other agencies. We could really use someone like that, and you would be perfect for the job." She had no idea where the idea had come from, but she saw it was the perfect solution. Normally, people rotated through the role of incident commander, but Ted would be ideal for the position, as long as he didn't let a fantasy that he was still an athlete in his prime get in the way.

"Don't patronize me," he said.

"I'm not patronizing," she said. She would have to talk to Tony about this, and the others, too, but it could be a great innovation that would benefit everyone. "At least consider it," she said. "What would a role as full-time incident commander look like to you?"

He was shaking his head when both their phones went off. She pulled out hers and read the text: Missing hiker, Grizzly Ridge.

"Looks like we got a missing hiker," Ted said.

"I'm calling for details now." As she waited for dispatch to answer, she shoved her feet into boots and found her keys. "I'll meet you at headquarters, Ted," she said. "We'll talk about this later."

Her mother came into the living room, Carrie's SAR parka and pack in her hands. "I heard your phone," Becky said. She glanced at Ted. "Hello, Ted. Are you going to ride with Carrie?"

"I have my own car." He opened the door. "See you there."

"Thanks, Mom." Carrie took the jacket and pack as the dispatcher, Rayanne, said, "Hey Carrie. You've got a fifty-four-year-old male and a fifty-two-year-old female, married couple from Dallas, George and Angela Dempsey, who set out to hike Grizzly Ridge this afternoon. They were supposed to meet friends for dinner and never showed and their vehicle is still at the trailhead."

"Any medical conditions we should know about?" Carrie asked as she slipped on the parka.

"Kids say not. They're both healthy, though there's always the altitude to consider."

"Right. Thanks. We'll get right on it." She ended the call, her mind racing with a running list of procedures and equipment they might need. It would be dark soon and that meant the temperature was dropping fast. If one or both of the couple were injured, the team would have to bring them down a rugged trail along an exposed ridge in the dark. If they were lost, they might have to suspend the search until daylight in order to protect the searchers. Going off-piste in winter darkness without knowing exactly where they should head would be foolish.

And that, Carrie realized as she started her car, was what she should have told her mother. She wasn't being a coward about relationships. Instead, she was being prudent. She wasn't acting only for herself anymore. She had Amber and Dylan to protect as well. By limiting her risks, she was really looking out for them all.

Chapter Five

"We need a hasty team to head up the Grizzly Ridge Trail ahead of the main group," Carrie addressed the team at search and rescue headquarters as they gathered gear for the search for missing hikers George and Angela Dempsey. "Danny, I want you with me, and we need one other person."

"I'll go," Ted said.

"I want you to stay at the trailhead as incident commander," Carrie said.

"Sheri or Ryan can do that," Ted said. "I'll go with you."

Everyone else held their breath, Danny included. How was Carrie going to handle what bordered on insubordination? Tony would have shut Ted down or even sent him home. The struggle showed clearly on Carrie's face—give in to Ted and risk weakening her authority or get into an argument that could waste precious time?

"I'll be incident commander," Sheri said. "I don't mind."

"Fine," Carrie said. "Ted, you're with us. Get a move on, everyone."

Danny slid into the passenger seat in Carrie's SUV, while Ted climbed into the rear. He could have cut the tension with a scalpel, but he didn't know how to diffuse the situation. Ted had been out of line, but making a big deal out of it probably would have made things worse.

Ted acted as if nothing had happened. He sat forward as Carrie sped out of the parking area and said, "There's a place two-thirds of the way up Grizzly Ridge trail where there's a lot of beetle-kill pine. If one of those trees came down, it would block it and force a detour. It's a likely place for someone who isn't familiar with the trail to get offtrack."

"I'll keep that in mind," Carrie said. She signaled the turn onto the county road that led to the trailhead and switched on the wipers. A mix of rain and ice had begun to spit from the sky. "This moisture is liable to be snow farther up on that trail," she said.

"Hypothermia risk, for sure," Danny said, mentally running through his supply of instant hot packs and blankets in his medical kit.

"There's a ledge about two miles up that trail with a northern exposure," Ted said. "If we don't find these folks before then, we should check around there in case one of them slipped and fell."

"Thanks, Ted," Carrie said. "We'll do that."

"This is why you need me with you instead of back at the trailhead," he said. "No one else on the team has my knowledge of these trails."

"Knowledge you could have passed on as incident commander," Carrie said. Her hands tightened on the steering wheel, knuckles whitening.

"Showing is better than talking," he said. "You'll see."

They made the rest of the drive in silence. Carrie parked at the trailhead next to a white Toyota 4Runner with a camper shell—the Dempseys' vehicle. As the three of them climbed out of the car, a Rayford County sheriff's black-and-white SUV pulled in and Sgt. Gage Walker got out. "Anything you need from me?" he asked.

"Not yet, anyway," Carrie said as she shouldered a pack. She keyed her radio and hailed Sheri. "We're starting up now," Carrie said.

"Ten-four. I've got Ryan, Jake, and Eldon headed your way."

"Tell them to stage at the trailhead until we know what we'll need and where," Carrie said.

She hooked the radio to the shoulder strap of her pack and started up the trail. The precipitation was steadier now, thin pellets of ice that stung Danny's bare cheeks and danced hypnotically in the beam of his headlamp. The frozen mud was slick underfoot with a fresh crust of ice. They traveled at a slow jog, and it wasn't long before he heard Ted's labored breathing as the older man brought up the rear of their trio.

Carrie stopped abruptly and looked back. "Ted, are you all right?" she asked.

"I'm fine," he gasped. "I'll get my second wind in a minute. Keep going."

Carrie started out again, feet pounding the trail. Danny made a mental note not to challenge her to a race anytime soon. He did trail running to keep in shape, but he was having a hard time matching her pace.

After a hundred yards of switchbacks the trail leveled out, still climbing, but at a less punishing rate. Carrie stopped and unstrapped a hailer from her pack. "George!" she shouted. "Angela!"

They waited, but only silence—and Ted's still ragged breathing—greeted them.

Carrie repeated the calls twice more, waiting a full minute each time, but there was no answer. "We'll try again in a bit," she said, and set out jogging once more.

When she stopped again, Danny realized Ted was no longer behind him. "Where's Ted?" he asked. "Ted!" he shouted.

"I'm…coming." The reply came from some distance back. Danny glanced at Carrie, who stared down the trail, expression impassive.

It was a full two minutes before Ted staggered into view. He stopped and bent over, hands on his knees, gasping. Carrie checked her phone. "We've only come a mile," she said. "We have probably several more to go."

Ted looked up. His headlamp made seeing his expression impossible, but Danny heard the anger in his voice. "You're doing this on purpose," he said. "Trying to prove I'm no longer fit."

"I'm doing what a hasty team is supposed to do," Carrie said. "Our job is to get to the person in need of help as quickly as possible. It's why we do trail running as part of our training."

Ted said nothing.

Carrie took out the hailer again and called for George and Angela, again with no reply.

"We don't even know where these people are or what's wrong with them," Ted said. "There's no need to run."

"We don't know," Carrie said. "But we know the odds are they are either injured or lost, or both. It's how the majority of these calls play out, so we respond accordingly. Let's go."

She turned and headed out again, slowing a little as they reached a steeper section, through stands of dead trees, the black trunks glittering with ice in the glow of their headlamps.

"Is this where you thought they might have become lost?" Carrie asked.

But once more Ted had fallen behind and didn't answer. Neither did the Dempseys.

"There aren't any trees down on the trail," Carrie said. She took out a flashlight and played its beam along the route. "Do you see any boot prints that look fresh enough to have been made today? I wish I knew for sure they came this way."

Danny joined her in the search. They spotted a couple of clear prints rimmed with ice—one large enough to be a man's and a smaller one with shallower treads that probably belonged to a woman. "That could be them," Danny said. They stood very close, staring down at the prints. He smelled peppermint on her breath—gum or toothpaste or maybe lip balm? "Should I go back to look for Ted?" he asked.

"I guess so," she said. "I hope he hasn't had a heart attack."

But a wavering beam of light, accompanied by muttered swearing, announced Ted's arrival. He leaned against a tree trunk and drew out a water bottle but failed in an attempt to unscrew the cap and just stood there, eyes closed, body sagging.

Alarmed, Danny raced to him. "Sit down," he instructed, and helped his friend slide down the tree trunk until he was in a sitting position on the wet ground. He checked the older man's pulse—strong but irregular. Ted's skin was clammy. "Are you having any chest pain?" Danny asked.

"I'm not having a heart attack," Ted said.

Carrie ignored him. "Danny, will Ted be all right waiting here by himself for a bit?" she asked.

"Let me check him out." He examined Ted, despite the older man's weak attempts to push him away and grumbles that he was fine. When he was satisfied, Danny stepped back. "He's taxed, but he's not having a heart attack. But I don't think it's a good idea in these conditions to have anyone hiking by themselves."

Carrie nodded and turned back to Ted. "I need you to wait here," she said. "I'm going to radio for someone to come up and go back down with you. I don't think it's safe for you to go on, and I don't want you heading down on your own. Not in your condition."

Ted's protest consisted mostly of swearing. Carrie didn't even blink. "I don't have time to argue. I'm ordering you to stay here." She keyed her radio and made her request for someone to fetch Ted.

"I'll send Eldon," Sheri said.

"Thanks," Carrie said. She turned to Danny. "Are you ready to go on?"

He nodded. It was probably a testament to how beaten Ted was that he didn't say anything as they moved on without him.

Neither of them said anything until the top of the next set of switchbacks, where the trail finally leveled off to traverse the top of the ridge Ted had mentioned before. "You're sure Ted will be okay by himself?" she asked. "I'm furious with him right now, but I definitely don't want him to die."

"No guarantees," Danny said. "But I think he's in good condition for a man his age, with no history of heart trouble. And Eldon will get to him in less than an hour, probably."

"I should have insisted he stay at the trailhead," she said. "Tony would have."

"Ted might not have opposed Tony so openly," Danny said.

"You think he was trying me out because I'm a

woman?" she asked. "Or because this is my first time as captain?"

"Both, probably."

"He came by my house this evening," she said.

That surprised Danny. "What did he want?"

"He wanted to complain about being discriminated against because of his age. He said Tony was trying to push him out. He was upset that Sheri was chosen as training officer instead of him."

"What did you tell him?"

"I tried to emphasize how important his experience and knowledge of the area and of search and rescue history in Eagle Mountain are to the group. And I tried to persuade him that the best way to utilize that experience and knowledge was as incident commander."

"That makes a lot of sense," Danny said.

"He hated the idea. And you saw how he reacted when I suggested he take that role tonight. He put himself in danger and he's left us short one person."

"I'm glad I'm not you right now," he said. "But for what it's worth, I think you're doing a good job. With Ted and with everything else that has happened—the vandalism and stuff. You're exactly the person we need right now." It had been a revelation, seeing this aspect of her personality emerge. Before, she had been the attractive woman who had turned him down. Now he had a much more complex view of her.

"Thanks. That means a lot." She let out a deep breath. "And now we really need to find the Dempseys. It's miserable out here." She raised the hailer once more. "Angela Dempsey! George Dempsey!"

No answer. Carrie tried again. "Angela! Geor—"

"Help! Please help!" The woman's voice was high-pitched and tinged with panic.

"Angela! Is that you?" Carrie called.

"Yes! George fell and is hurt and I couldn't leave him."

"Where are you?" Carrie asked.

"On a ledge below the trail. He slipped on the ice. I climbed down, but I can't get back up."

"Keep talking to me. We're with Eagle Mountain Search and Rescue and we're coming to help." She lowered the inhaler and looked at Danny, smiling. "We found them," she said softly.

"Almost." He pulled a large Maglite with a spotlight beam from his pack and switched it on, then aimed it to their left, on the downhill side of the trail. He and Carrie walked slowly forward, staring at each area lit by the beam, until it came to rest on the white face of a woman thirty feet below. She stood and waved both hands at them. A darker shape lay on the ground beside her. "Thank God you're here," Angela Dempsey said.

"Stay right there," Carrie said. "We'll come to you. This is Danny. He's a nurse. He's going to ask you about your husband's injuries."

"I think his leg is broken," Angela said.

"Which leg?" Danny asked.

"Um…left."

"Can you see bone protruding from the skin?"

"No. He just…landed funny. And he said he heard something pop. And he's in a lot of pain."

"I'm in pain. I'm not dead." The man's voice—George's—was strong. "And I'm freezing my tuchus off out here."

Danny grinned. "We'll see if we can get you warmed up. Hang on a little bit."

Carrie was already on the radio with Sheri, relating the Dempseys' situation. They'd need climbing gear to get the couple off the ledge, materials to stabilize George's leg and a litter to transport him down the mountain. Hot food and coffee for all of them. An ambulance waiting to transport.

Danny and Carrie spent the next hour talking with the Dempseys, trying to keep their spirits up. They were able to lower blankets and hot packs to them and promised more help was on the way.

Jake was the first to arrive. He jogged up the trail, bringing an air cast for George's fractured leg and some of the gear they would need to safely move him back onto the trail.

"I came up with Eldon," he said as he slipped his pack from his back. "He's taking Ted back down. What happened? Ted looks terrible and he was cussing a blue streak."

"Never mind Ted," Carrie said. "We've got to set up to get Danny down to the Dempseys on that ledge."

"Are you going to go with him?" Jake asked.

The idea of climbing down there in the icy dark made her heart beat a little too fast. Of course she would do it if she had to, but in this case, she didn't have to. "No, I'm going to wait for the others."

"They're on their way." He began unloading the rest of the gear and laying out the ropes and other climbing gear. He worked quickly and competently, impressive for someone who had been training only a few weeks.

Approaching voices announced the arrival of Ryan, and Hannah. They set to work, everyone knowing their roles in getting this couple back to safety. Danny and Hannah climbed down to George and Angela, where they were able to stabilize George's fracture and give him some pain relief. Thermoses of hot coffee and soup warmed them, then they assisted Angela in the climb up to the trail and brought up George's litter. Then everyone fell into line for the trek back down the mountain. Carrie brought up the rear, doing a last check that they had left no equipment or debris behind.

IT WAS AFTER 2:00 a.m. by the time they saw George, accompanied by Angela, loaded into the waiting ambulance. "That went about as smoothly as a rescue could," Sheri said as they watched the taillights of the ambulance dissolve into the darkness.

"It did," Carrie agreed. The adrenaline of the rescue effort had faded, leaving her bone-tired and craving warmth and sleep.

"What happened with Ted?" Sheri asked. "He just glared at me when I asked, and insisted Eldon drive him back to headquarters right then."

"He couldn't keep up on the trail," Carrie said. "I should have made him stay down here in the first place, but I didn't want to waste time arguing with him. As it is, he could have been seriously hurt, and the rescue would have been delayed even further. I should have stood up to him and I didn't."

"Ted is stubborn enough he might have tried to follow us anyway." Danny joined them. He looked as weary as Carrie felt, shadows under his eyes, skin abnormally pale in the glare of the work lights set up at the trailhead. "At least having him with us allowed me to monitor him. He's in better shape than most men his age, but he wasn't up to running that trail."

"If he can't do the job, he shouldn't be on the team," Sheri said. "If he can't be depended on to pull his weight, he puts other people in danger."

"He has a lot of experience and knowledge," Carrie said. "I thought that could be put to good use as incident commander."

"But everyone has to be prepared to step in and take an active role," Sheri said. "If Ted can't do that, it's time to retire."

Carrie nodded. "I know. And Ted probably knows it, too. I'll talk to Tony about it when I see him tomorrow."

Sheri nodded and moved to help Ryan take down the lights. Carrie started to join them, but Danny put a hand on her shoulder. "You're doing a good job," he said. "Don't second-guess yourself."

She told herself it was only because she was so tired that tears stung her eyes at his words. "Thanks," she managed, and quickly turned away. She felt too vulnerable to face him right now. Too close to revealing how much she needed those words. How much she wanted someone to care. That that someone would be Danny—the serial dater, who went through women the way some people adopted and abandoned hobbies... It was too depressing to think about.

Chapter Six

When Danny had suggested he accompany Carrie to visit Tony in the hospital on Monday, he halfway expected her to tell him she was tired of him tagging along. It wasn't as if the two of them had been close before Tony's accident. They had been thrown together a lot since then and he was surprised how well they got along.

"What do you like to do for fun?" he asked as they set out for Junction Monday afternoon. He had a half day of comp time he needed to use up before the quarter ended and had decided today would be a good day to clock out early. Carrie was driving them again. She seemed to like being behind the wheel and he was happy to let her. Her SUV was more comfortable than his old Honda anyway.

"Fun?" She glanced at him, one eyebrow raised in question.

"Do you have hobbies?" he asked. "Things you like to do to relax?"

She laughed, though the sound wasn't exactly joyful. "You have obviously never been a parent. I don't have time for hobbies. Or relaxing."

"That doesn't sound very healthy," he said, then wanted to take back the words. "I mean, I don't see how you do it all."

"Yeah, well, I don't do it all. Not well." She smoothed

her palms down the steering wheel. "I guess search and rescue is my stress relief. Not that it isn't intense sometimes, but it gets me out of my own head. And it feels really good to help other people, you know?"

"I know," he said. "When I signed up I thought I would just do it for a while, to help out in a pinch, but I got hooked. And hey, it impresses women."

"Yeah, I'm so impressed."

He laughed, and she did, too, a real laugh this time. He found himself searching for a way to make her laugh again. "Yeah, they're always impressed when they find out I save lives in my spare time. And then I have to cancel a date because I get a callout and they aren't so amused. After the second or third time that happens, they're moving on."

"One more reason not to bother dating," she said.

Was she saying she never dated? That he wasn't the only man she had turned down? Because surely others had asked her out. "I like being single," he said. "But I'd rather not be alone all the time. So I guess the pluses and minuses even out."

"I'm not alone," she said. "I live with my mom and two children. There are days when I'd pay for a few hours to myself."

Did he detect a bit of false bravado behind her words? "I could give up dating," he said. "But I'd really miss sex."

A pink blush lit her cheeks. "Um, well, yeah, there is that."

He wondered how long it had been since a man had held her intimately. She had a combination of femininity and strength a lot of men would be drawn to. A sensuality beneath her no-nonsense veneer. Then he told himself he shouldn't be thinking about her this way.

He looked away, at the first spring wildflowers beginning to splash the roadside with pinks and purples, blooming despite patches of snow. Probably time to change the subject. "I don't guess you've heard anything else from the sheriff's department about the fire that destroyed the Beast."

"Nothing," she said. "And nothing on Austen's accident, though maybe Jake is right and it was just a driver being a little reckless on a snowy day."

"I don't think what happened with Tony was an accident," Danny said. "It's going to make me even more nervous about climbing."

"Me too. We'll just have to be extra cautious when it comes to inspecting our gear." She slowed as they reached the edge of Junction. "I wish I had something to tell Tony," she said. "When I talked to him on the phone yesterday, he said he doesn't remember the moments leading up to his fall, but he's sure he would have said something if he noticed anyone tampering with SAR gear."

"Maybe he'll remember something today," Danny said.

A short drive around the south side of town took them to the hospital. This time they bypassed the information desk and went straight to the elevator and rode the car up to the patient floor where Tony had been transferred.

They found him sitting in a wheelchair by his bed, still hampered by casts and looking pale and almost frail, in a green hospital gown, wire-rimmed glasses magnifying his blue eyes. His beard was neatly trimmed, damp hair curling around his ears. "It's great to see you out of bed," Carrie said, and leaned down to give him an awkward hug. "You look better already."

"I'm a mess, but it's better than being dead," Tony

said. He nodded to Danny. "Have they found out who did this to me yet?"

"We haven't heard anything," Carrie said.

"Can you think of anyone who was upset enough with you in particular or with SAR in general to have damaged those ropes?" Danny asked. He leaned against the end of the hospital bed, facing Tony.

"I've had plenty of time to think about it and I can't come up with even one person." Tony frowned at the cast on his right leg, propped in front of him, rigid and off-white and uncomfortable looking. "Maybe it was just someone random."

"Someone who had access to our equipment," Danny reminded him. None of them wanted to think that someone close to the organization would do something like this, but ignoring the possibility didn't make it any less so.

"Ted has been upset about how some issues are being handled with search and rescue," Carrie said.

"What makes you say that?" Tony asked.

"He came to see me at home yesterday evening," she said. "He complained about being passed over for the training officer position and said you were trying to push him out altogether."

Tony scowled. "I'm not trying to push him out. But it's clear he's not up to some of the physical challenges we face. I wanted to work with him to find a role that would focus on his skills without hampering the rest of us."

"Ted's always been a bit of a curmudgeon," Danny said. "But do you really think he would do something like this?"

Tony's face slackened with shock. "I can't believe Ted would hurt someone," he said. "He's devoted to Eagle Mountain SAR. He helped found the group." He studied Carrie's face. "Do you seriously think Ted put acid on my ropes and burned the Beast?"

She shifted from foot to foot. "I don't know. But he was pretty angry yesterday. He accused us of age discrimination and threatened to sue."

Tony's eyes widened. "He's a lot more upset than I thought. Were you able to calm him down?"

"Not really. I suggested that with his experience, he'd be really valuable as our incident commander, but that only made him angrier. We got a call last night to search for a couple of missing hikers and Ted insisted on being part of the hasty team."

"How did he do?" Tony asked.

"It was awful. Danny and I jogged up the Grizzly Ridge Trail and Ted couldn't keep up. I was afraid he was going to have a heart attack and ended up ordering him to wait for someone to come up and take him back down to the trailhead. That meant we were two people short. I never should have let him try to come with us. I know you wouldn't have."

"Maybe letting him realize the limits of his capabilities that way was a good thing," Tony said. "Have you talked to him today?"

"I tried to call him this morning to see how he was doing but he didn't answer," she said. "I left a message, but he hasn't responded. I wondered if he was upset enough to want to lash out at us all."

"He was late to the meeting Sunday morning," Danny said. "He showed up only a little while before Austen did." He turned to Tony. "Austen was delayed because another car ran his off the road."

"Ted said he was late because of the weather," Carrie said. "It was snowing pretty hard."

"He could have waited until he saw Austen's vehicle

approaching and raced down the hill to run him into the ditch, then turned around and drove to the meeting as if nothing happened," Danny said. The idea that Ted, someone he had always liked and even looked up to, would do something like that made him physically ill.

"We shouldn't jump to conclusions," Tony said. "Ted is a lot of things, but I've never known him to be violent. And he really is devoted to SAR. I can't see him wanting to destroy it."

"I'm sure you're right," she said. "Now I feel bad even bringing it up. I just wish we knew who was responsible. With your fall and losing the Beast to arson and the attack on Austen, I'm holding my breath, afraid of what will happen next."

"We're all on edge," Danny said. "But that will make it harder for whoever this is to do anything else."

"What are you doing about a new search and rescue vehicle?" Tony asked.

"The insurance company is sending us a check for $5,000," she said. "It's not nearly enough, but more than I expected, honestly. And Sheri is working with some others to come up with ideas for raising money."

"We should ask the county to chip in," Tony said. "They're always saying they don't have any money, but they should contribute to this. Everyone in the county, not to mention a lot of visitors, benefit from the work we do."

"Maybe when you're home again, you can speak to county officials," Carrie said.

"Why wait?" Tony said. "I don't have anything else to do between rehab sessions. I'll start making calls now."

Carrie brightened. "That would be terrific."

Tony looked up, over her shoulder. "Speaking of rehab." He raised his voice. "Here comes my favorite torturer now."

A petite redhead in blue scrubs glided into the room. "Time to get back to work, Mr. Meisner," she said.

"Mr. Meisner is my old man," Tony said.

"All right, Tony." She grinned. "Say goodbye to your friends and quit goofing off."

"No rest for the weary." Tony shook his head. "Thanks for stopping by, and keep me posted on developments."

"We will," Carrie said.

She and Danny left the room. He waited until they were in her car again before he spoke. "Do you really think Ted could be behind these attacks?" he asked.

She started the SUV and backed out of her parking slot. "All I know is that he was truly angry when he came to my house yesterday. And you saw him last night—he was furious."

Danny nodded. He had dismissed Ted's rage last night as typical of the older man, who had a reputation for salty language and a short fuse. But would he really go so far as to hurt Tony—his friend and someone he had known since Tony was a teenager? "I guess all we can do is keep an eye on him," he said. "Make note of anything suspicious." He glanced at her. Tendrils of hair had come loose from her braid and curled around her cheeks. His fingers itched to brush them back so he could see her expression more clearly. And to feel if her skin was as soft as it looked. "Just to be safe, maybe you shouldn't be alone with Ted for the time being," he said, his voice coming out rougher than he intended.

She glanced at him. "Oh, I don't think Ted would hurt me."

"If he hurt Tony because he was upset with Tony's assignments, why wouldn't he go after you after last night?" The idea chilled him. "You said yourself he was furious. And he blamed you for putting him on the spot."

She huffed out a breath. "You have a point but don't worry. Like I said before, it's rare that I'm ever alone. I work in an office full of people, my mom and kids are around when I'm home, and on a search and rescue call, I have the whole team around me. So I guess I'm safe."

"You're alone with me now."

Silence. She braked for a red light, then turned to look at him. "I am, aren't I?" Her lips curved in a slow smile. "But you don't scare me, Danny."

"That's good." He settled back into his seat. He'd never tell her, but when he was being honest, she scared him just a little, the way she unsettled him, and made him think about her the way he had never thought about another woman. As if the idea of her being hurt, by Ted or anyone else, caused a physical pain. He wasn't that kind of man, but it seemed with her, he was.

CARRIE WAS IN the middle of a meeting at work Tuesday morning when her silenced phone buzzed against her hip. She ignored it and tried to focus on what the senior partner, Greg Abernathy, was saying about changes the client wanted to a proposed condo development north of Eagle Mountain. "If we put the community room where he wants it, that will eat up half a dozen parking spaces, at least," Carrie said. "He'll be out of compliance with the county regulations for a new development."

"The client thinks he can get a variance," Greg said. "Our job is to draw up the plans the way he wants them so he can take them to the county."

Right, and the implied message was that Carrie, as the junior architect, was to keep her mouth shut and do as she was told. Which she would, because this was the only architectural firm in town and she had negotiated a flexible schedule that allowed her to take off early or work from home when her children needed her or she had a callout from search and rescue. Greg had told her when he hired her that he liked the idea of having a young woman on staff because it made the company looked progressive—as if she was a generic placeholder labeled Token Female instead of a talented architect in her own right.

But being close to home and available was more important than acknowledgment of her skill, she reminded herself as the meeting ended and she headed back to her office.

Another perk of the job was that she had an office to herself—what had probably once been a bedroom in the old Victorian home on Main Street. The room had good light, polished hardwood floors and plenty of room for a desk and a drafting table. And a door that shut so she could have privacy when needed.

She slipped her phone from her pocket and frowned at the number. Local but unfamiliar. She hit the button to call back and was startled when a brisk female voice answered. "Rayford County Sheriff's Department."

"Oh, um, hello. This is Carrie Andrews. I missed a call from this number."

"One moment."

Instrumental music of a song she didn't recognize replaced the woman's voice, then a man said. "Hello, Carrie. Thanks for calling me."

She recognized this voice—Deputy Jake Gwynn, "Has something else happened related to search and rescue?" she asked.

"We've received the reports back on the fire that destroyed the Jeep and the tests done on the climbing rope," Jake said. "When can you stop by and talk to us about it?"

She glanced at the clock. She was supposed to get off at four today to attend Dylan's youth lacrosse game. If she left at three thirty she should be able to talk to Jake and get to the game on time or close to it. "Can you meet me at three thirty?" she asked.

"That's fine. You're welcome to bring someone else from search and rescue with you, if you like."

They said goodbye and she stared at the phone in her hand. She thought about calling Danny and asking if he wanted to meet her at the sheriff's department, but she immediately rejected the idea. He was probably working, and besides, she didn't need Danny to hold her hand through all of this, though it felt like that was exactly what he had been doing so far. Maybe not holding her hand, but certainly supporting her, providing a sounding board for her concerns and offering encouragement when she needed it.

Not a role she would ever have pictured for Danny Irwin. Sure, he was a competent caregiver and member of the search and rescue team, but he was also a flirt who fit the mold of so many other men in this town—ski bums, rock hounds and bike jocks who lived to play and prided themselves on avoiding commitment but also stress. They were good-looking, charming and fit, and thus always had a woman for company when they needed one, but none of those relationships lasted long. Wives and kids would only cramp their style.

Come to think of it, Hannah had dated Danny for a while, before she met Jake. They had managed to break things off with little awkwardness, probably because Danny had never let things get serious.

A good example for Carrie to follow. Not that she would ever get serious about Danny. She wasn't that foolish. From one perspective, he might have been a perfect match for her. He was handsome, easygoing and about her age. They shared a common interest in search and rescue. And best of all, like her, he wasn't interested in a long-term commitment. It might be nice to have someone to go out with, someone with whom she could share dinner or movies. And sex. She grew warmer, remembering how he had brought up the subject yesterday. Women talked, and they especially talked about men, and she had heard that Danny was, well, talented in bed.

But she knew herself too well. She couldn't give the rest of herself without handing over her heart, too. She didn't think she was capable of the kind of no-strings-attached relationship men like Danny specialized in. Spending so much time with him lately had been nice, and she was developing a certain fondness for the man. She just had to remember not to let that go too far.

At the sheriff's department that afternoon, Carrie waited less than a minute before Jake came out to meet her. A slender man with short, dark brown hair and brown eyes that were almost black, he was training to work with search and rescue, but he hadn't yet participated in many calls, so Carrie didn't know him well. "Thanks for stopping by," he said. "Come right through here."

She followed him through the door and down the hall, trying not to stare at everything they passed. This was the first time she had ever been in a law enforcement office and she felt a little nervous.

Jake stopped at a door and knocked, and a familiar voice said, "Come in."

Sheriff Travis Walker stood from behind his desk. "Hello, Carrie," he said.

"Hello." Nerves made the word come out a little shaky. No reason for her to be nervous, she reminded herself, but why was the sheriff involved in what she had assumed would be a simple report?

"Sit down." Jake gestured to a chair in front of the

sheriff's desk and he moved a second chair over beside her while Travis resumed his seat.

The sheriff's desk was neater than her own, with only a laptop, a tiered In and Out box and a framed photo of Travis's wife, Lacy, a beautiful brunette standing in a mountain meadow.

Jake opened a folder on the desk in front of him. "The arson investigator concluded the search and rescue Jeep was deliberately set on fire," he said. "Unfortunately, the fire destroyed any forensic evidence the arsonist might have left, and we haven't found witnesses who saw anyone near the Jeep before the fire."

"SAR headquarters is pretty remote," Travis said. "The arsonist could be fairly confident no one would see him or her."

"Does SAR remember seeing anyone around that evening who shouldn't have been there?" Jake asked.

"No. Everyone had left headquarters hours before. I was in Junction, at the hospital with Tony Meisner. Another volunteer, Danny Irwin, was with me."

"So someone might have gone back to headquarters after everyone left and no one would have seen them?" Travis asked.

"I guess so." She had to force herself to admit this was true. "There aren't any other buildings around headquarters, and no one lives up that road, so it doesn't get much traffic."

Jake flipped to another page in the folder. "We also received the results for the lab analysis of the climbing rope Tony was using. The fibers were soaked in hydrochloric acid, also known as muriatic acid."

"I've heard of it," she said. "But I don't know much about it."

"I spoke with some experienced climbers, and with

the lab," Jake said. "For someone not to notice the damage upon your initial inspection, and for Tony to have gotten as far into the canyon as he did, we believe the acid must have been poured onto the ropes either immediately before or immediately after he inspected them. But probably immediately before."

"But we were all there," she said. "Somebody would have seen any tampering with the ropes."

"Not necessarily," Jake said. "We're talking maybe half a cup of acid. A person could carry that in a small vial or bottle in their pocket and tip it onto the rope without anyone noticing. Was there a particular team member helping Tony that day?"

She tried to remember. "We were all assisting each other," she said. "I was getting into my climbing gear, waiting my turn to descend. Danny and Tony were going to go down together, spaced along the canyon rim. Sheri, as training officer, was supervising all of us. Ryan and Austen and Eldon and Ted were helping everyone else. And Hannah was there, too." She shrugged. "You should talk to Tony. He told me he doesn't remember anything about that day, but maybe his memories will start to return."

"I will talk to him," Jake said. "Was there anyone else in the area that day—somebody not part of the SAR training exercise?"

"No."

"You're sure?" Travis asked.

"I'm sure. We always clear the area of other people before we start, but that morning there wasn't anyone else to clear. We had the canyon to ourselves." She swallowed hard as the meaning behind that admission sank in. "So whoever poured that acid on the ropes, it had to be one of us."

"Do you have reason to believe somebody wanted to harm Tony?" Jake asked. "Maybe a volunteer he had argued with?"

"No. Nothing like that." Even as she said it an image of Ted, accusing Tony of trying to push him out, popped into her head. But she couldn't believe Ted would do something like this. It was too...calculating. "Where would someone get muriatic acid?" she asked.

"You can buy it at most hardware stores," Travis said. "They use it to etch concrete."

She shuddered at the idea of something like that eating through rope fibers.

"We'll ask at the local stores," Jake said. "But it's the kind of item someone might already have at home."

This whole conversation felt surreal. She shook her head, as if that could somehow settle her thoughts into a semblance of order. "What about Austen's accident?" she asked. "Did you find anything there?"

"No," Jake said. "It was snowing too hard to draw conclusions. And we don't really have evidence to link that with the Jeep or the damaged ropes. It's a steep road and it was snowing hard when he ran into the ditch. It's possible someone made a wrong turn, and in heading back down the mountain, they were going too fast for the weather and panicked when Austen drove toward them. There was no damage to his vehicle. He simply slid into the ditch, bumped his head and dented a fender." He closed the folder. "That's all we have now. Let us know if you think of anything that might help us in our investigation."

"Of course." She stood, anxious to be out of here.

Jake escorted her back to the lobby, where she muttered goodbye and fled. As she drove toward the ball fields, his words replayed in her head. What kind of information, exactly, would be useful? The search and rescue team was like a family—siblings and cousins who mostly got along but sometimes disagreed, said things they shouldn't say or displayed fits of temper. That only proved they were human, not people who would destroy a valuable vehicle or try to kill their captain.

Except one of them was. Icy fear gripped her at the thought, and she held more tightly to the steering wheel to control the shaking that overtook her. Someone had tried to kill Tony. Would he—or she—try to finish the job, or target someone else? Were they all in danger from one of their own?

Chapter Seven

After seven years at the surgical center, Danny had the routines of his job burned into his body. Every procedure had a protocol to follow, and he had a knack for placating even the most difficult patients. He liked the work, but mostly he liked what else the job enabled him to do. Working three twelve-hour shifts a week allowed him plenty of time off and a salary large enough to support his interests. Over the years he had seen various coworkers come and go, many to take better positions at hospitals or other facilities. Danny didn't mind that there wasn't a lot of room for advancement where he was. He found his challenges in other areas of his life, not at his job.

Wednesday evening as he prepared to drive home after work, he checked the weather forecast on his phone, a habit he had developed since joining search and rescue. Rescue calls had seasonal patterns: summer saw more lost hikers, accidents on Jeep roads in the high country and swift-water rescues on local rivers. Deepest winter brought more ice-climbing accidents, missing backcountry skiers and traffic mishaps on icy roads.

Now, in late March, was an in-between time, with periods of heavy, wet snow broken by stretches of warmer, sunny days. This was avalanche season, and a time when hikers and mountain climbers, eager to hit the trails after a long winter, sometimes got caught by the ice and snow that still lay deep at higher elevations. A few more weeks and they could add in mudslides and rock slides and rivers flooded by snowmelt to the list of potential hazards.

Tonight's forecast called for temperatures just above freezing. Snowmelt that had run onto the roads would refreeze into black ice. SAR would be lucky to make it through the week without at least one callout.

An hour later, he was just pulling the plastic film from a microwave lasagna when his phone's message alert sounded. He set aside his dinner and read the brief summary—a car had slid off the highway near the top of Dixon Pass. Danny stuck the lasagna back into the refrigerator and went to round up his gear. A few minutes earlier, he had been thinking about how tired he was after being on his feet all day, but now the familiar adrenaline buzz kicked in, fizzing in his body as he anticipated what they might find at the accident scene. The message hadn't said where the car went off, but there were a couple of likely locations, spots known to be particularly hazardous, especially for ice. Whoever had been in the vehicle would need medical care, provided they survived the trip into the canyon.

Fifteen minutes later, he joined the rest of the team at SAR headquarters. Or rather, the portion of the team who were available. "We're shorthanded tonight," Carrie informed them as they gathered around her to get the details of this call. "Tony is still in the hospital, of course, but Hannah is also sick with the flu. Sheri and her husband are in Denver. I've asked Jake to join us to help make up numbers."

Jake Gwynn lifted a hand in greeting.

"Where's Ted?" Austen asked, looking around at the

group, which consisted of Carrie, Jake, Danny, Ryan, Eldon and Austen.

"Ted isn't responding to my calls," Carrie said. She picked up her pack. "Come on. We should be able to go in two vehicles, with only six of us."

The blue-and-white strobes of two sheriff's department SUVs and a state highway patrol cruiser lit up the red rock walls that edged the highway on the climb up through Grizzly Creek Canyon, like a garish light show. A sign indicated the highway was closed, but the deputy on duty waved the search and rescue team through. Danny climbed out of Eldon's pickup and the sudden grip of cold made him suck in his breath.

Sgt. Gage Walker joined them by their vehicles. "A passing motorist saw the fresh skid marks and called it in," he said, and pointed toward the tire tracks that cut through old snow on the side of the highway, ending at the edge of a sheer drop-off. "I shined a hand-held spotlight around and I can see what I think is the top of a vehicle," he continued. "I shouted, but nobody answered."

"We'll get a couple of people down there to take a look," Carrie said.

All of them except Jake had climbed in this area before. Eldon and Austen began hauling out the gear while Danny and Jake inspected everything. Danny made a point of sniffing the equipment for any hint of acid, but found nothing.

Carrie and Ryan unloaded a couple of litters, extra helmets, splints and other medical gear they might need. "An ambulance is on its way," Gage told them. "And we've got a medical helicopter on standby to land at the soccer fields if we need transport."

Right. The canyon was too narrow at this point to risk maneuvering a helicopter, especially at night. The ambulance could have a patient to the soccer fields in five minutes.

As the most qualified medical person on scene, Danny would go down first, along with Eldon. Carrie would remain up top as incident commander, while Ryan, Austen and Jake would handle the ropes and transport of any other gear.

Danny carried a medical pack with basic supplies, while Eldon hauled the chains and anchors they might need to stabilize the vehicle, if it had come to rest in a precarious position. They also had headlamps and handheld lights to illuminate the accident scene as much as possible.

"Take your time and be careful," Carrie said as Danny indicated he was ready to start down.

He nodded. He didn't like climbing in daylight, when we could see what he was doing. At night, with ice slicking the surface of the rock, it was a matter of doublechecking every move. He remembered watching Tony and being envious of the way he swung out over obstacles and skimmed down sheer rock walls. Danny moved at a crab's pace in contrast. A very slow crab, but one who would arrive at his destination alive and unharmed.

The car, a minivan, lay on its side on a rock ledge halfway to the river below, the passenger door wedged hard against a slanting pine tree that grew from the ledge. Eldon and Danny stopped above the ledge and swept their spotlights over the scene. "Hello!" Eldon shouted, and the sound came back at them, hollow and distorted. "Hello! Can anyone in the van hear me?" he called again.

"Help! Somebody please help!"

"We're coming down to help you!" Danny shouted. "Hang on tight." He tucked away the light and started climbing down again, toward the van. He landed on the ledge just behind Eldon, Together, they chocked the van's tires, and Eldon slid under the vehicle to wrap a chain around an axle, then secured this around a boulder up against the canyon wall. That didn't guarantee the van would stay where it was, but it upped the odds.

As soon as Eldon nodded in his direction, Danny hoisted himself onto the front tire and leaned across the hood to shine a light through the windshield.

A man sat slumped forward, forehead against the steering wheel, the white mass of the deflated airbag surrounding him. Blood, like a trickle of chocolate syrup in the harsh light, matted the back of his head.

A cry of pain made Danny shift the light to the passenger seat, to the white face of a woman, a fall of dark hair obscuring one eye and cheek, her lips twisted in a grimace of pain. She lay against the door, the seat belt taut around her, forcing her head over at an odd angle. "Hang on, ma'am, I'm coming," he said, and crawled back across the hood, toward the driver's side door.

Eldon joined him and the two of them tugged at the door, which wouldn't budge. It was probably locked, since most vehicles automatically locked once the car was in motion. Eldon pulled a metal bar from his pack, ordered the woman to close her eyes, then hit the driver's-side window, shattering the glass. Danny brushed away the pebbled fragments, reached inside with a gloved hand and opened the door.

He stopped to assess the man first, aware of the woman sobbing just across from him. The man was breathing, and his pulse was strong, but he had obviously hit his head and was unconscious. He would need transport to the hospital. "Ma'am, I'm going to get the driver out where he'll be more comfortable, then I'll help you," Danny said. "Can you tell me where you're hurt?"

"My baby," she wailed.

Danny looked around them. There was no sign of a car seat or anything having to do with a child in the car. "Where is the baby?" he asked, forcing his voice to remain calm even as panic climbed his throat. If the child had been thrown free, it could be anywhere. And if it was outside the vehicle and alive, it could be freezing to death.

"The baby!" the woman said again, and moaned and clutched at her stomach.

Danny directed the beam of his headlamp toward her, and his eyes widened as he took in the mound of her stomach. He swallowed and focused on remaining calm. "It's going to be okay," he said. "How far along are you in your pregnancy?"

"Thirty-seven weeks." She fixed her eyes on him—big brown eyes, shiny with tears. "It's not supposed to be here yet."

"Tell me what's going on." Danny looked at her over the man—her husband's?—inert body.

"I'm having this baby," she said, her voice sharp.

"You're having labor pains?" Danny asked.

"Yes!" She clutched herself again and moaned.

"Okay. Hang on. We're going to see to your husband, then take care of you and your baby. Just…hang on."

He and Eldon fixed a cervical collar and a backboard to the man, then got him out of the car and into a litter. They wrapped him in blankets and tucked in some chemical heat packs, then Danny radioed Carrie. "We've got a man, the driver, unconscious with a head wound. Send a couple people down with a litter to get him up and into the ambulance. The passenger is a woman. I'm getting ready to assess her, but she says she's thirty-seven weeks pregnant and in active labor."

"Well." A pause. "I assume you've delivered a baby before?"

"I work in a surgical center. Not labor and delivery."

"So you've never delivered a baby before?" Carrie asked.

"I have not." He had studied the subject in nursing school of course, and even seen a film detailing the process. But that was different from trying to bring a child into the world in the cold darkness in a frozen canyon. "Let me see how far her labor has progressed. With luck we have time to get her to the hospital, where she'll be more comfortable."

While Eldon attended to the man, Danny climbed back into the vehicle. His headlamp lit up the woman's terrified face. "Hi, I'm Danny," he said. "I'm a nurse with Eagle Mountain Search and Rescue. We're going to get you out of here, to somewhere safe." He studied her seat belt and decided the first order of business was to cut her out of it. "I'm going to cut this seat belt, then maybe we can get you free of the car."

He took out a tool designed for the purpose and sliced through the safety belt. The woman yelped as she fell back against the door, then the cry changed to a wail of pain.

Danny took her wrist and found her pulse. It was strong, but rapid. "What's your name?" he asked.

"Rosa," she said. "My husband! Is he—"

"He's going to be fine," Danny said. "He's got a bump on the head. Now, do you think you can climb out? I'll help you."

Rosa grabbed the dash and the side of her seat and made an effort to haul herself up. Danny took hold of her upper arms and pulled, and together they managed to get her to the edge of the door, where she fell into Danny's arms, the hard curve of her abdomen pressed against him. He tried to steady her and keep her on her feet, but she sank to the ground. "Ohhhh!" she moaned.

Danny crouched beside her. "How far apart are your pains?" he asked.

Her eyes met his, wide and frightened. "Not far. This baby is going to come soon."

"Is this your first?" he asked.

She shook her head. "Third. The others were fast, too." She tipped back and lay on the ground, knees up. "I think I'm going to have this baby now."

Eldon moved over. "Should we get some blankets under her or something?"

"Yeah." Danny's hopes of getting her into a litter and out of the canyon before the child came were fading. "Let's do that, then I'll examine her."

They made a makeshift pallet while Rosa alternately moaned and cursed. Danny examined her and discovered she was well dilated, her water had broken and the baby's arrival did indeed seem imminent.

By this time Austen and Ryan had arrived and were arranging to send a litter with Rosa's husband along a line up to the canyon rim. Danny walked a few steps away and radioed Carrie. "Get the paramedics down here," he said. "This baby isn't going to wait."

"It could take a bit to get them harnessed up and down to you," she said. "Can you handle it in the meantime?"

"I'll have to," he said. "She said this is her third child, so that should help." Maybe she'd even be able to tell him how best to assist her.

He returned to Rosa, who was moving restlessly.

When he touched her shoulder, she let out a scream. "Do something!" she shouted.

His radio beeped with a new transmission. "The paramedics won't come down," Carrie said.

"What do you mean, they won't come down?"

"They said they're not trained as climbers and it's too risky. That's a valid point. How is the woman?"

"Um...uncomfortable." Rosa let out a new string of curses.

"All right. Then, I'm on my way."

"You?" he asked. "Have you delivered a baby before?"

"No, but I've had two of them, so I know a few things. Tell Eldon he needs to climb up and take over on this end while I help you."

"Okay. And thanks." He probably could have remembered enough of his training to deliver the baby successfully—after all, Rosa would do most of the work—but knowing Carrie would be here made him feel a whole lot better.

He focused on his patient again and managed to get Rosa to calm down enough to tell him more about her contractions and about her other two labors. Apparently, her first child had arrived after only five hours of labor and her second had been born in the van on the way to the hospital. "The kids are with my mom," she said between contractions. "My husband and I were supposed to be going on a date, and then we hit a patch of ice and went flying. I've never been so terrified in my life, then we landed so hard—I think it jolted the baby on its way out."

Danny examined her again and thought he could feel the baby's head. He looked up at Rosa, over the mound of her abdomen. "Are you warm enough?" he asked.

"Are you kidding?" she asked. "The cold is the last thing I'm thinking about."

Right. He was sweating himself, though more from nerves than heat.

Carrie touched down beside him on the ledge and he rushed to help her out of her harness. "Am I glad to see you," he said.

"Here." She thrust a bag into his hands. "The paramedics said we might need this."

He opened the bag and recognized a birthing kit. Search and rescue even had one—somewhere in the supply closet back at headquarters. "Great," he said, and began laying out the contents of the kit.

Carrie moved to Rosa's head and took her hand. "Hi, Rosa, I'm Carrie," she said. "Let's see if we can get this baby into the world to meet you."

Carrie murmured to Rosa through the next round of contractions, her voice soothing and positive. The words were meant for Rosa, but Danny felt their effect, too.

"I gotta push!" Rosa said.

"Then, you go ahead and push," Carrie said.

Danny checked on the baby's progress. "I can see the top of the head," he said, and moved into position to ease the child into the world.

Five minutes later his hands were full of a warm, wet, very-much-alive infant. The baby squirmed and let out a loud cry. Rosa began to sob, reaching for her son. Danny swaddled the tiny boy against the cold and placed him on Rosa's stomach, then wrapped them both in every blanket available. "We need to get them both somewhere warm, right away," he said.

Carrie nodded and stood to bark orders. Shortly thereafter, mother and baby were strapped securely into a litter and fastened to a long line, being hoisted out of the canyon.

Danny and Carrie remained below, gathering discarded wrappings and equipment and packing everything away. When that was done, he felt together enough to turn to her. "Thanks for coming down," he said. "I think having a woman with her really helped Rosa." He put his hands on her shoulders. "And it helped me, too. I was feeling way out of my comfort zone."

"You did great," she said. "I never would have known this was your first."

She had switched off her headlamp, and he tilted his up so that it didn't shine in her eyes but gave enough light to illuminate her face. Her cheeks were pink with cold, and her eyes shone with excitement. "What was it like when you had your two?" he asked, truly curious to know.

"Dylan was born on a rainy night in October and my husband and I were both terrified. I was at the hospital twenty hours before he made an appearance and by that time I was too exhausted to appreciate the moment. Amber was born at three in the afternoon after only six hours at the hospital and I had an epidural right away, so I got to kind of enjoy the process more." She shrugged. "I don't think most women remember too many details about the delivery. They're too focused on the little miracle they produced."

"Yeah." Even Danny, a single man, could appreciate how amazing birth was, though he hoped not to have to experience it quite so up close and personal again anytime soon. He put his arm around her and pulled her to him. She didn't tug away. It was just the two of them here in the darkness, and he had never felt closer to her, or to anyone, really. They stood there for a long moment, until she began to shiver with cold. "You ready to go up?" he asked.

"Yes." She radioed Jake to let him know they were on their way.

Weariness dragged at Danny as he pulled himself up the canyon walls, but he forced himself to focus on carefully planting his feet, on maneuvering on the ropes, wanting to hurry but not letting himself.

He stumbled and almost fell as he climbed onto the canyon rim. Jake steadied him and helped him up.

"I sent the others back to headquarters," Jake said. "I told them I'd wait for you. Gage and Deputy Prentice got called away to a burglary, but they reopened the road."

"Are Rosa and the baby okay?" Danny asked.

"Mother and baby made it up top safely and are on the way to St. Joseph's," Jake said. "Dad regained consciousness before the ambulance left and he should be able to meet them at the hospital."

Carrie unclipped herself from her climbing ropes and joined him. "I'll give you both a ride back to headquarters as soon as we get the gear packed," she said.

The three of them coiled ropes and organized equipment and lugged it to the back of her SUV. "I'll get the car started and let it be warming up," she said. She took out her keys and started toward the front of the vehicle, but halfway there, she stopped and let out a cry.

"What is it?" Danny hurried to her side.

She shook her head, lips pressed tightly together and pointed toward the ground.

Jake joined them. "Someone slashed your tires," he said.

Danny stared at the deflated tires, gashes visible in the sidewalls of both front tires. It took a sharp blade and real force to make a cut like that. Force with anger behind it—the kind of hatred that motivated a killer, even.

Chapter Eight

Jake radioed the sheriff's department while Carrie waited with Danny beside her car. Those gashes in her tires had been such a shock. There was something so violent—so mean—about them. She hugged her arms across her chest and tried not to look at them, but they pulled at her gaze. It was too dark without her headlamp to see much, but just knowing they were there frightened her.

"Are you okay?" Danny asked. He stood very close, not touching her but his warmth and bulk comforting all the same.

Jake joined them. "Someone will be along soon." He frowned at the ruined tires. "I was up here the whole time, since we arrived, and I never saw anyone near your car who wasn't supposed to be."

"Everyone would have been in and out of it, getting equipment," Danny said. "I don't see how a stranger could have gotten near it."

"Not to mention Gage and Dwight were here, directing traffic. And the ambulance with the paramedics was here, too."

"One of the team could have done it." Carrie hated saying the words out loud, but there was no sense pretending they weren't true. No one would have thought twice about a fellow team member hanging out around her car, and they all carried sharp knives to cut ropes or seat belts or even tree branches that got in their way.

"Let's see what Gage has to say," Jake said. "He said he would leave Dwight to take the burglary call and come back here to deal with this."

Fifteen long minutes later, Gage pulled in behind Carrie's SUV. He left his sheriff's department's SUV running, its headlights flooding the area with harsh white light. "You okay?" he asked Carrie.

She nodded, and he moved on to examine the damage to her tires. He listened to Jake's brief explanation and studied the car, then returned to Carrie. "Has anyone threatened you?" he asked.

"No."

"Have you argued with anyone—a coworker? Your ex-husband?"

"No."

"Ted was pretty upset with you the other night," Danny said.

They all turned to look at him. He flushed. "Not that I think Ted would so something like this," he said.

"What was the argument about?" Gage asked.

"He couldn't keep up when we were jogging up a trail in search of a lost hiker," Carrie said. "I sent him back down. He was upset, but he had left by the time I got back to the trailhead and I haven't spoken to him since."

"Ted wasn't here tonight," Jake said.

"Who was here?" Gage asked.

Carrie listed everyone who was present, and Jake added the names of the two paramedics. Gage wrote them all down. "Even if we found fingerprints on the vehicle, they could have been made by a team member who had a legitimate reason to be here," he said. "The mud is all trampled down with no distinct shoe impressions. I'll have someone take a look at the tires, see if they can figure out what cut them, but I'm not holding my breath that's going to help us."

"I can take you home," Jake said.

"Take us back to search and rescue headquarters and I'll take Carrie home from there," Danny said. "If that's okay with you?"

"Sure," she said. At least she wouldn't have to make polite conversation with Danny all the way home, the way she would feel the need to do so with Jake. They were comfortable enough with each other for silence.

"We have to get the search and rescue gear out of my car first," she said. "If we get another callout, we might need it."

They filled the back seat of Jake's SUV with climbing and medical equipment, then unloaded it all at SAR headquarters. Carrie sent Jake home and she and Danny put everything away, working silently, each knowing what to do without direction.

When they were done, she took one last look around the room. "I guess that's all we can do for now," she said.

"Are you going to be okay?" he asked.

"My tires were slashed," she said. "That feels more petty than personal, at least right now."

"So you think this is related to the other attacks on search and rescue?" he asked.

"Don't you? Other than Ted, no one is angry with me, and we know Ted wasn't at the accident site tonight. There were too many people around who know him." She shook her head. "I think my car was there and it was an easy target for whoever is carrying this grudge against SAR. And the very worst thing is knowing it's probably one of us."

"I can't think of anyone in the group who's ever said

anything against us," Danny said. "Yeah, Ted is upset right now, but he helped found the group. I can't believe he would ever try to destroy it."

"We know Ted didn't slash my tires, and I know it wasn't you." She fished her keys from her pocket and held them, more for something to do with her hands than anything else. "You were down in the canyon from the first tonight. You were descending into the canyon beside Tony when he was hurt. Maybe you could have put that acid on the ropes, but then why be the one to point it out when none of the rest of us had noticed? And you were with me when the Beast was set on fire, and here when Austen was run off the road."

"We don't know Austen's accident was related to the other incidents," Danny said.

"Right." She leaned against the table at the front of the room. "I don't think Jake is responsible, either. He wasn't present for any of the other incidents before tonight."

"Sheri was out of town tonight," Danny said. "At least she said she was and we don't have any reason to doubt that. She knows more than any of us about climbing, so she might have heard that acid could damage ropes without it being noticeable."

"Sheri has had friends in the climbing community who died in accidents," Carrie said. "I can't see her deliberately arranging for someone else to be injured. And she likes Tony. She likes everyone."

"Hannah was sick tonight, but I suppose she could have faked that and sneaked over to the canyon. Anyone who saw her would think she was supposed to be there."

"Except she and Jake are engaged and he would have noticed her and known she was supposed to be home with the flu. And again, Hannah is a paramedic. Maybe I'm naive, but I can't see her deliberately hurting anyone."

"No one has a motive that I can see," Danny said. "Ryan gets along with everybody and so does Eldon. Search and rescue saved Austen's life and he's the most dedicated volunteer we've had in years."

"Yeah, and when Austen doesn't like something, he doesn't keep his opinion to himself," Carrie said. "His complaints annoy me sometimes, but now I can see that he gets things off his chest and moves on. I think we're looking for someone who is nursing a grudge we know nothing about." She stifled a yawn.

"We should get home." Danny suppressed a yawn of his own. "It's been a long day, and we aren't getting anywhere debating everyone's guilt or innocence."

"Yes, let's go." She straightened. She wanted to see her kids and her mom to reassure herself that they were all right. She seldom worried about her own safety, but the thought of anyone harming her family chilled her to the core.

Danny drove her through the silent town. Even Mo's Pub was closed now, the neon from its sign reflecting on the dirty snow banked alongside the street. He pulled his Honda to the curb in front of her house and shut off the engine. "I'll walk you to the door," he said.

"You don't have to do that,"

"Humor me."

She was aware of him looking around them, as if watching for trouble. "You're making me nervous," she said.

"Sorry." He shoved his hands in his pockets. "I didn't want to take any chances."

She stopped at the bottom of the steps. "My mom will still be up," she said. "I'll be fine. Thanks for the lift."

"No problem." He hesitated, then pulled her close in

a hug. His arms tightened around her as she leaned into him. The embrace felt so good. Safe and…right.

She tilted her head to look up at him, to tell him thank you again. Her attention was caught by the glint of light on the stubble across his jaw and the deep laugh lines on either side of eyes with purple shadows beneath them. She had forgotten that he had worked a full twelve hours today before coming out into the cold to rescue two strangers. "You were great, delivering that baby tonight," she said. "I never would have guessed you were nervous if you hadn't told me."

"You were the one who was great," he said. "Calming the mom down and telling her what to do."

"She would have figured it out," she said. She smiled, remembering the sight of that tiny infant cradled in Danny's gloved hands. "It was a beautiful baby."

"Yeah." His gaze met hers and held, and she felt the pull of it, drawing her toward him. She tilted her head up farther and focused on his lips. They looked soft, and she wondered what they would feel like against hers. It had been so long since a man had kissed her. So long since she had even wanted that. But she wanted it now. She wanted Danny to kiss her.

The porch light suddenly bathed them in a harsh white glare and Carrie squeezed her eyes shut and silently cursed her mother's timing. "Carrie? Why are you standing out in the cold?"

Danny took his arms from around her and stepped back as they heard the locks on the door disengage. "I'd better go," he said, and headed down the walk, long strides carrying him quickly to his car.

"Carrie?" Her mom looked out the door. "Who is that with you?"

"That was Danny." She climbed the steps and moved past her mother inside. "He gave me a ride home."

"Where is your car?" Becky asked. "Were you in an accident? Are you all right?"

"I'm fine. The car is fine, too." Or it would be, after she acquired two new tires.

"What's wrong? Why did Danny bring you home?"

"It's a long story. Let's make some tea and I'll fill you in." She would tell her mother almost everything. Except how Carrie was growing closer and closer to Danny Irwin—a man she had no business getting involved with. Danny was a fun, no-commitment kind of guy, but Carrie wasn't good at fun and frivolous. When she gave her heart, she went all-in. It was a bad habit she couldn't seem to break.

FRIDAY MORNING, Sheri called and invited Carrie to lunch. "Hannah is coming, too," she said. "She's feeling better and we want the scoop on what happened Wednesday night."

"It was no big deal," Carrie said. "We don't even know if it's related to everything else that has been happening."

"We're the only women with search and rescue," Sheri said. "We need to stick together. So let's have lunch and see what we can come up with if we put our heads together."

"Good idea." Carrie ended the call, feeling better than she had in weeks. She was pretty sure Hannah and Sheri didn't have anything to do with the attacks on SAR. And they were smart women with a lot of experience with search and rescue. Maybe they had realized something she hadn't, and together they could at least come up with some observations to share with the sheriff's department.

They met at eleven thirty at Kate's Kitchen, a short

walk from Carrie's office. "It's my off period and then I have an hour that's supposed to be free to meet with parents, only I don't have anything scheduled," Sheri explained. She taught at Eagle Mountain High School.

"And I'm off all afternoon," Hannah said. She was a paramedic, and she helped her parents operate the Alpiner Inn.

"I've got two hours free, if one of you will give me a lift to Butch's garage to pick up my car," Carrie said. Butch had called to let her know he had set her up with new tires.

"I'll take you," Hannah said.

They chose a booth near the back and ordered salads and iced tea, then Sheri leaned across the table toward Carrie. "We want to hear everything," she said.

"Not just about your tires," Hannah added. "I heard you and Danny delivered a baby."

"A little boy," Carrie grinned. The magic of those intense moments in the canyon still lingered. "Mom and baby—and Dad, too—are all doing well. The dad had a concussion, but seat belts and airbags, and the fact that their van slid and never rolled over completely before it landed on that ledge, saved them all."

"Details, please," Sheri said.

Carrie took them through the events of the night, from the call from the emergency dispatcher to the moment when she, Danny and Jake discovered her tires had been slashed.

"Jake told me it took a big knife and a lot of force to cut those tires," Hannah said. The server had delivered their orders and she stabbed at a piece of romaine.

"Jake was up top, not far from where we had parked, the whole time," Carrie said. "He and the paramedics and Gage Walker and Dwight Prentice all say no one went near my car except the search and rescue volunteers who were unloading gear."

"Could someone have cut the tires back at your house or at SAR headquarters and it took a while for them to deflate?" Sheri asked.

Carrie shook her head. "These were big gashes. The tires would have deflated right away. No way could I have driven even a few yards without noticing."

"So what do they think happened?" Sheri asked. "One of the volunteers who was there that night just crouched down, stabbed your tires and no one else noticed?" She scooped up a forkful of quinoa and arugula and frowned, as if the salad was guilty of some offense.

"I guess so," Carrie said. "It doesn't make sense to me. I mean, do you two think any of our volunteers would do something like that?"

"Until recently, I would have said no way," Sheri said. "But Ted is really angry with all of us right now. I saw him in the grocery store yesterday and he headed in the opposite direction as soon as he spotted me. He's never acted like that before."

"Ted wasn't there Wednesday night," Carrie said. "And I don't see how he could have showed up without someone spotting him."

"What does Danny think?" Hannah asked.

The mention of Danny startled Carrie. Had the other women picked up on Carrie's attraction to the man? That would be beyond embarrassing. "Danny?" she asked, hoping she sounded more curious than concerned.

"That's right," Sheri said. "Since you and Danny were delivering a baby when your tires were ruined, he couldn't have been responsible."

"And he was with you when the Jeep was set on fire," Hannah said. "Besides, Danny doesn't have a mean bone in his body and he loves search and rescue. It's just about the only thing he's serious about."

"You two dated for quite a while, didn't you?" Carrie asked. She had been dying to find out more about Hannah's relationship with Danny, and this seemed like the perfect opportunity to slip it into conversation.

"Five months," Hannah said. "He's a sweet guy and pretty much the perfect boyfriend, as long as you're not looking for serious commitment. I was, so we agreed to break it off. And then I met Jake." Her eyes took on a dreamy expression at the mention of her fiancé.

"Danny and I dated a couple of times, too," Sheri said. "But he said I intimidated him. He kind of made it into a joke. The thing about Danny, he doesn't really want to be challenged. If he had a motto, it would be No Stress, No Mess. I think it's why he's so good at rescue work. He never gets too excited about anything. He's the most Zen guy I ever met, but frankly, I like a little bit more adrenaline in my relationships."

"Is that why you married a cop?" Hannah asked.

"And why I remarried him." Sheri laughed. She had recently gotten back together with her ex-husband, Detective Erik Lester, when they reconnected during the search for a missing child in Eagle Mountain.

"So what does Mr. Zen think about whoever is going after SAR members?" Hannah asked.

"He's as baffled as I am," Carrie said. "Jake, Austen, Eldon and Ryan worked that accident with us on Wednesday and none of them have given any indication they aren't really happy with the group."

"Ryan was out for a while after that fall off Mount Baker earlier this year," Sheri said. "But he seems to be in a good place. He told me he plans to return to climbing competitively as soon as possible."

"Eldon always complains about the cold," Hannah said. "But he's from Hawaii. I think he mainly does it to remind everyone he's from the islands, when secretly he loves it. He's out with his snowboard every chance he gets."

"Austen always gets annoyed when we have to rescue people who get in trouble because of their own carelessness," Carrie said. "But I think we all resent that sometimes."

"Sure, but we rescue them anyway," Sheri said. "We're not about judging."

"I think he's getting better about his attitude," Hannah said. "He's really dedicated."

"He is," Carrie said. "We all are. We couldn't do this work if we weren't."

They turned their attention to their salads, and no one said much for a while. Then Sheri said, "Maybe we're looking at this all wrong. Maybe the person who's doing this isn't angry with SAR. They could be upset on the organization's behalf."

"What do you mean?" Carrie asked.

"Look at the things they've done." She held up a hand and began counting off on her fingers. "They put acid on the climbing ropes. Maybe they didn't intend for anyone to be hurt. Maybe they thought we would notice before anything bad happened. Maybe they did it to call attention to our need for more money to update our equipment."

"That's a pretty indirect way to go about it," Hannah said.

"Yeah, but hear me out," Sheri said. "Next, they burn the Beast. That was a huge loss to the group, but in our heart of hearts, were any of us really sorry to see the old thing go? It has been nothing but trouble in recent months. Something always needs fixing, it drinks gas and it's no fun to drive. By destroying it, the arsonist forces us to find a way to get a new vehicle."

"Okay, but what about the attack on Austen and slashing my tires?" Carrie asked.

"Maybe attacking Austen was just a way to keep our attention," Sheri said. "Or maybe it wasn't connected to the other incidents. Maybe it really was a careless driver. And by slashing your tires, our attacker calls attention once again to the need for a new search and rescue vehicle."

"It's a really twisted, mean way to lobby for a new vehicle and new equipment," Hannah said.

Sheri shrugged. "It's just another way to look at things."

"How are our fundraising efforts going?" Carrie asked, ready to change the subject.

"The *Eagle Mountain Examiner* has agreed to run an article about our need for donations," Sheri said. "We're going to have a booth at next week's Spring Carnival and sell T-shirts and solicit donations. Austen and Eldon are helping me and they have some good ideas. And the county has agreed to match the first $10,000 we raise."

"I'm going to ask Tony to come up with some specs for a new vehicle," Carrie said. "I wanted Ted to work with him, but I don't know now if that will happen."

"Give Ted a little time to calm down," Sheri said. "I think he'll come around."

"Can I get you ladies anything else?" Their server stood by the table.

Carrie checked the time. "No thanks. I need to get back to the office." Time to focus on those drawings—one of the few things in her life she could control.

Chapter Nine

Danny worked ski patrol Saturday morning, so was late to the regular search and rescue meeting that afternoon. As Carrie called the meeting to order, he settled into a folding chair at the back of the room and studied his fellow volunteers. Could one of these people, all of whom he had literally trusted with his life at one time or another, really be set on hurting this organization that had helped so many people over the years? He dismissed each person in turn. She would never hurt anyone, especially not a fellow team member, and he was devoted to the group and the last person in the world Danny would expect to resort to violence.

By the time Carrie moved to the front of the room to begin the meeting, everyone had assembled, except Tony, who had moved to a rehab facility to continue his recovery, and Ted, who Danny was beginning to believe had left the group for good.

"Let's get started, everyone," Carrie said, and the murmur of conversation slowly died out.

Danny thought she looked a little more tense than usual, a little paler, but maybe he was only projecting his own worries on to her. Seeing her tires slashed like that had really shaken him, as if for the first time he had realized they were all in danger.

"First up is a reminder about the course, Ground Search Awareness, hosted by Colorado search and rescue June 25," Carrie said. "Jake and Austen, you should definitely sign up for this, but it's a good refresher for everyone." She checked the notebook in front of her. "We also received a flyer from San Miguel County about a multiday course, Wilderness First Responder, they have planned for this summer, so be on the lookout for more information about that."

The side door opened and they all turned to look as Tony, leg outstretched in a wheelchair fitted for the purpose, rolled into the building, the chair pushed by Ted. "I figured I'd better show up to keep you all in line," Tony said.

Cries of surprise and welcome rang out as everyone rushed to greet the two new arrivals. "I called Ted and talked him into breaking me out of rehab for a couple of hours," Tony said as he shook hands and accepted pats on the back from everyone as Ted stood behind him, beaming.

Leave it to Tony to figure out a way to bring Ted back into the fold, Danny thought. The two might have argued in the past about Ted's role with the organization, but the older man wasn't the type to let down anyone who needed his help, especially someone like Tony, whom Ted had mentored as he came up through the organization.

"I didn't mean to interrupt," Tony told Carrie when some of the excitement over his arrival died down. "It took a little longer to maneuver this chair into the van Ted borrowed than we thought it would."

"That's okay," Carrie said. "It's great to see you." She smiled at Ted. "Both of you."

"Get back to conducting the meeting," Tony said. "I don't want to horn in."

"At the speed you're recovering, you'll be ready to teach that wilderness-first-responder class by summer," Ryan said.

Tony waved away the comment. "What's next on the agenda, Carrie?"

She glanced at her notebook. "Don't forget the search and rescue booth at next week's Spring Carnival," she said. "There's a sign-up sheet for everyone to take a shift. Anything you want to add about that, Sheri?"

"We got a new order of T-shirts in today—all sizes," Sheri said. "So tell your friends and relatives they all need one."

"Should have ordered sweatshirts," Ted said. "If it's like most spring carnivals, it will probably snow."

"It may say spring on the calendar, but not in Eagle Mountain," Hannah said.

"Snow is spring around here," Eldon said. "It's just wetter snow and you can ski in shirtsleeves."

"Any other fundraising news?" Carrie asked.

"Tammy Patterson with the *Eagle Mountain Examiner* is going to be calling you for quotes for the article she's doing highlighting our need for a new search and rescue vehicle, so just a heads-up," Sheri said. She turned to Austen. "I know she for sure wants to talk to you, since you are someone we rescued who became a volunteer."

"Sure," Austen said, "I can do that."

"That's about it for now," Sheri said. "Though if anyone else has a fabulous idea for how we can raise a whole bunch of money, really fast, let me know."

"Thanks, Sheri," Carrie said. "That's all I have for tonight."

"Wait a minute," Austen said. "Do you have an update on the attacks on SAR and our volunteers? I heard whoever this person is, they went after you."

"Someone went after Carrie?" Tony's voice rose over the others as everyone began talking at once.

"Someone slashed my tires," Carrie said. "That's not exactly a personal attack."

"When was this?" Ted asked.

"Wednesday night, after our rescue of the pregnant woman and her family," Carrie said. "She and her baby and her husband are all doing great, by the way. She called me at work yesterday to say thank you."

"Do the cops have any idea who did it?" Eldon asked.

"No," Carrie said. "All they could tell me was that the tires were slashed on the scene, with a big, sharp knife. There really isn't any evidence for them to trace, and apparently no one saw anybody suspicious near my car."

"There really isn't any kind of pattern to any of these things," Hannah said. "Tony was hurt when someone put acid on his climbing ropes. Then someone burned the Beast. Someone ran Austen off the road, and then Carrie's tires were slashed. It's so random."

"It's like whoever is doing this doesn't really plan," Eldon said. "He—or she—just sees an opportunity to do something to hurt one or all of us and takes it."

"There's one thing all these incidents have in common," Danny said.

The others stared at him. "What's that?" Sheri asked.

"The most likely suspect for all of them is one of us," he said.

"No!" Hannah protested.

"That can't be right," Eldon said.

"Why do you say that?" Tony posed this last question. He leaned forward in his wheelchair, frowning.

"No one else had access to our climbing ropes," Danny said. "Same with the keys to the Beast—they're kept in here, and someone took them and moved the Beast away from the building before they torched it. No one else really uses the road up to the headquarters building, which makes it unlikely anyone else ran Austen off the road. And everyone from the paramedics on the ambulance to a trio of sheriff's deputies say no one but SAR volunteers was anywhere near Carrie's car while it was parked on the side of the road Wednesday night."

This declaration brought another uproar from the room. But Danny wasn't sorry he had given voice to what they all had to be thinking. Despite their protests, he read the doubt on all their faces.

"What are we supposed to do now?" Ryan asked. "I know I haven't done anything wrong, but I'm not about to start pointing fingers at the rest of you. We can't help other people if we start doing that."

"I'm not saying we should accuse each other," Danny said. Even though, in a way, he had accused all of them. "I just think we all need to be extra careful."

"Like we hadn't already figured that out," Austen said.

Carrie moved over to stand beside Danny. "I'm as upset about this as all of you," she said. "But we need to remember that we have one really big thing in our favor."

"What's that?" Ted asked.

She paused to look at each of them. When her eyes met Danny's he felt the impact of that look. "We're a team," she said. "We're trained to work together and to take care of each other. If one person has turned against us, they're already outnumbered." Another pause as everyone digested this. "The group is always stronger than the individual. Whoever you are, you can try to pick us off but you can't defeat us all."

Danny studied the faces of the others in the room. Carrie's words made most of them sit up straighter, a new determination in their eyes. Some nodded in agreement. "She's right," Sheri said.

"You tell 'em, Carrie," Eldon said.

No one looked guilty or afraid. Did that mean the person who had made so much trouble wasn't one of them after all?

Or did it only mean the guilty person was very good at hiding their true feelings?

"CAN WE GET cotton candy?" Amber asked as she and Dylan skipped alongside Carrie on the way to the park where the Eagle Mountain Spring Carnival was being held. The week since the search and rescue meeting had been a quiet one, with no callouts and no more vandalism or other mischief. Maybe Carrie's speech about them all sticking together had made an impact. Or maybe all the attention was scaring off whoever was behind the mysterious misfortunes that had plagued the group.

In any case, she was going to focus on spending a fun morning with her kids, and doing her best during her shift at the search and rescue booth this afternoon to collect more donations toward the purchase of a new vehicle. In spite of Ted's predictions of snow the weather had turned almost balmy, with plenty of sunshine, and the first daffodils nodded their heads along the borders of the park.

"And I want to get my face painted," Dylan said. "A big bug, so people will think I have a tarantula or a scorpion crawling across my face."

"Cotton candy and face painting are definitely on the agenda," Carrie said. "But first I have to stop by the search and rescue booth."

"Mo-om," Dylan whined. "You don't have to go save someone today, do you?"

"I hope not," Carrie said. "I just want to check the volunteers have everything they need." Her own shift at the booth started at one, after her mom completed her volunteer stint with the Women's Club and could take over looking after the children.

A large banner across the front of the Eagle Mountain Search and Rescue booth proclaimed "Help Fund Our New Search and Rescue Vehicle! Donate Today!" in bright red letters. Below that, an assortment of search and rescue T-shirts swayed in the breeze, like bright cotton streamers or maybe oversize prayer flags. "How's it going?" she asked Hannah, who manned the booth with Jake, the engaged couple wearing matching green SAR T-shirts.

"We've only sold one shirt," Hannah said.

"But we've collected several donations." Jake held up the cardboard box designated for donations and shook it, change clinking inside.

"Let's hope there's more than coins in there." Danny spoke from directly behind Carrie. The sound of his voice sent a flutter through her chest and she turned to look, tilting her head up to meet his smile. He wore a bright yellow SAR shirt, one that, as it happened, matched her own.

"There's checks and bills in there, too," Jake said.

"You're not on duty today?" Danny asked Jake.

"I go on shift at eleven," Jake said. "My uniform is in the car."

"Do you rescue people, too?" Carrie looked down to see her son, head tilted way back to look up at Danny, who towered over him.

Danny crouched down so that he was eye level with Dylan. "I do," he said. He jerked his thumb toward Carrie. "Are you with her?"

Dylan nodded. "She's my mom."

"This is Dylan." Carrie rested her hand on her son's

shoulder. "And this is my daughter, Amber." She stroked the top of Amber's head. The little girl had moved in closer to lean on Carrie's legs, though she kept her gaze fixed on Danny.

"Hello Dylan and Amber. I'm Danny. I work with your mom on search and rescue."

"We're going to get our faces painted," Amber said.

"Yes, and we'd better go do that, hadn't we?" Carrie said. Not that she was anxious to get away from Danny, but she felt the children's impatience and their unasked questions. Lately, they were hyperaware whenever she was anywhere near a man. She didn't know if it was because they wanted her to date someone who might be a potential father—or they were afraid she would.

She glanced at Danny and immediately pushed away the thought. Danny Irwin was definitely not potential-father material.

He straightened. "Mind if I walk with you?" he asked.

"You can come with us," Amber said before Carrie could answer.

He fell into step beside them, relaxed, focused as much on the kids as on Carrie. Or maybe even more on the kids. "I'm going to get a bug painted on my face," Dylan said to Danny.

"Seriously?" Danny asked. "That's so cool."

"I think it's gross," Amber said.

"That's 'cause you're a girl," Danny said.

"No, it's because a bug on your face is gross."

Dylan grinned up at Danny, who grinned back, as if in silent celebration of successfully grossing out his sister. "Which do you think is scarier?" Dylan asked. "A tarantula or a spider?"

"They're both pretty scary," Danny said. "We once had a patient at the surgery center where I work who had to have surgery on his leg because he was bitten by a black widow spider and his leg started rotting around the bite."

"Are you a doctor?" Amber asked.

"No, I'm a nurse."

"Did the guy's leg really rot off?" Dylan asked.

"No, but he had to have a big chunk of his calf cut out."

Carrie and Amber exchanged looks of disgust, but Dylan hung on every word as Danny described the black widow spider and the damage from its venom.

At the face-painting booth, Carrie turned the kids over to a pair of high school cheerleaders. The girls were manning the booth to raise funds for a band trip to the Rose Bowl next year. "You certainly made an impression on my son," she said to Danny.

"Little boys like gross stuff like that," he said. "It's normal."

"So I've noticed. His favorite books are the *Captain Underpants* series."

Danny laughed. "I'd probably like them, too."

She turned to watch Dylan, who was apparently describing the *huuuuge* spider he wanted painted on his cheek. She smiled as he spread his hands wide.

"That was a great speech you gave at the meeting last week," Danny said. "The whole 'all of us against the one bad apple' thing. That was very moving."

She looked at him, wondering if he was mocking her. "Are you being sarcastic?"

"No, I mean it. It really turned the mood around. We stopped being afraid, or at least suspicious, of each other and started feeling like a team again."

The praise made her feel too warm, and she looked away. "Well, it's true. This is just one disgruntled person who doesn't even seem that focused," she said. "I mean, Tony being injured was terrible, and the fire was a huge blow, but since then everything has been so petty. Slashed tires? Really? It's getting harder for me to take this seriously."

"We don't want him doing anything worse."

"Well, no, but I wish he would make a mistake," she said. "I want him to do something to reveal his identity."

"That might be good, if he did it without hurting anyone else. Without hurting you."

She thought she must have imagined those words, and whipped her head around to face him again.

"Mom, look! I got the coolest black widow spider!" Dylan launched himself at her and she staggered back.

"Oh my gosh, that is a scary-looking spider," she said. The cheerleader had done a good job with the black widow spider crawling up one cheek toward Dylan's eye, a bright red hourglass glowing on its back.

"I pulled up a picture on my phone," the girl said. "It kind of creeped me out, painting it."

Dylan laughed with glee as Carrie paid for the artwork and included a generous tip.

Amber was next, a blue butterfly seeming to flutter on her cheek. "You look beautiful," Danny said, and Amber's cheeks pinked with pleasure.

"Do you like cotton candy?" Amber asked Danny.

"I do," he said.

"Then, you should come with us to get some."

He looked to Carrie. "Is that okay?"

"Sure." Though spending time with him that didn't relate to work still unsettled her, it wasn't necessarily in a bad way. They set off across the park. The festival was getting more crowded as the day lengthened, and there were lines at several of the booths, including the Elks Club refreshment tent. "Do you really like cotton candy?" Carrie asked as they waited to place their order.

"It's not my favorite, but it's not terrible," he said.

"No, it is terrible," she said. "Like eating sweetened fiberglass insulation."

He laughed. "I never thought of it that way, but I still like it."

He made a point to order a large cone of cotton candy—pink like Amber's. Carrie opted for a soft pretzel, while Dylan insisted on a strip of orange-and-white taffy half the length of his arm. Danny bit into his cotton candy and chewed thoughtfully. "Only a little like insulation," he said. "But tastier."

Amber giggled. "Do you really eat insulation?"

"I'm a bachelor," he said. "I eat everything."

"Let's check out the games!" Dylan pointed toward a section of the park set aside for various game booths.

"All right." They began walking in that direction. "When are you working the SAR booth?" she asked Danny.

"One p.m."

Another jolt of sensation shot through her. Excitement? "The same time as me," she said.

He grinned. "I may have arranged it that way."

"Wh…why is that?" She hated that she stumbled over the question, like some nervous teenager, even though that was exactly how he made her feel.

"I like hanging out with you." They passed a trash can and he tossed the half-eaten cotton candy into it. "I kind of thought you liked hanging out with me, too."

"Yeah, I do." Where was he going with this? She thought back to their almost kiss in front of her house last Wednesday night. Part of her really wanted to know where kissing him might lead, but the rest of her remembered Hannah's warning that Danny definitely wasn't interested in commitment. She had two kids. She couldn't afford a fling.

"What do you want?"

The question startled her. She stared at him. "Huh?"

He gestured toward the chalkboard set up in front of the games area. "You have to buy tickets for the games. Should we get a whole book, or just a few? My treat, but you know your kids best."

"You don't have to pay," she said.

He shrugged. "I was going to buy some anyway. I like to try my hand at the baseball throw and stuff like that."

They settled on splitting the cost of a whole booklet because, as he pointed out, that was cheaper than the same amount of tickets purchased separately. Then they spent the next hour trying their hand at knocking over plastic ducks with baseballs, tossing basketballs into hoops and watching Amber and Dylan try to knock themselves off a low beam by whacking at each other with pillows. The match ended in a draw, with both of them rolling around in a deep bed of wood chips, giggling.

From there it was back to the food booths, where they shared a lunch of hot dogs and curly fries at a picnic table under the shade of a towering cottonwood. They had just sat down with their orders when Danny's phone rang. He pulled it from the pocket of his jeans and frowned at the screen.

"Is everything okay?" Carrie asked.

"Yeah." But he continued to stare at the phone, the cheerful notes of the ringtone repeating.

"I don't mind if you answer it," she said. She stood. "I can move over to give you some privacy."

"It's okay. I'll call back later." He swiped to reject the call and tucked his phone away again. Then he picked up his hot dog and took a big bite—was he really so hungry or did he just not want to talk?

She kept glancing at him, but he didn't look her way. He sat hunched, drawn into himself. Who had called that had changed his whole demeanor so drastically?

At ten minutes to one, Becky texted to ask Carrie's location and arrived five minutes later, as everyone was finishing their meal, to take charge of the children. "Hello, Danny," she said, then turned a questioning look to Carrie.

"Hey, Becky," Danny said. He smiled, more his old self now, though Carrie still detected a shell of reserve.

Carrie made a show of checking her watch. "We'd better head over to the search and rescue booth," she said. She hugged each of the children, who were already showing signs of fatigue and overstimulation. "Be good for Grandma."

"Thanks for letting me hang out with you," Danny said, then offered a fist for each child to bump in return, which had them both grinning. The more delighted the two children were, the worse Carrie felt. *Don't get too attached,* she wanted to tell them. *He's not the type to stick around.*

But really, she might have been saying the words to herself.

"What's going on at the booth?" Danny asked as they drew nearer.

Carrie had been so lost in her thoughts that she had somehow failed to register the crowd milling around the search and rescue booth, including two uniformed sheriff's deputies. She and Danny broke into a jog. "What's happened?" Carrie asked a distraught-looking Sheri. Behind her, Austen spoke to Jake, his voice raised but his words indistinct in the clamor of the crowd.

"All the money we collected today," Sheri said. She waved a hand toward the counter where the cardboard box with its collage of search and rescue photos had sat. "It's gone. Someone just walked off with it. Who would do something like that?"

Chapter Ten

"The donation box was in the open, right by the counter," Jake said. He was in his khaki sheriff's department uniform now and had apparently responded to the report of the theft, along with Deputy Wes Landry. "Anyone could have walked off with the box."

"But we were watching it," Sheri said. "If someone had leaned over the table to get it, I know I would have seen them."

"When was the last time you know for sure the box was there?" Wes asked.

"A man who said he was from Texas bought a T-shirt and put an extra twenty in the donation box," Austen said. "I thanked him."

"When was that?" Wes asked.

"I don't know for sure." Austen rubbed the back of his neck. "Maybe fifteen minutes before Sheri noticed the box was missing."

"I remember the Texan," Sheri said. "I'm sure I saw the box after he left." She bit her lip. "I had my back to it for a few minutes while I talked to a couple of my students who stopped to say hello, but I'm sure I would have noticed if someone had leaned past me, into the booth."

"What did the box look like?" Wes asked.

"It's about eight inches square, with pictures from

search and rescue training exercises pasted all over," Jake said.

"Hannah's mom made the box for us a few years ago," Sheri said.

"We have it out every time we do a booth like this," Carrie said. "No one has ever bothered it before."

"But everyone would know the box had money in it," Jake said. "That's all the provocation some people need."

"How much was in the box?" Danny asked. "Any idea?"

"I don't know exactly," Sheri said. "But people were being really generous. The Texan wasn't the only one who left a twenty. I'm thinking at least a couple hundred dollars."

"I bet it was more than that," Austen said. "Maybe three hundred."

Danny may have been the only one to hear Carrie's low moan. "What are our chances of getting the money back?" she asked Jake.

Jake shook his head. "That money is probably long gone by now, but we'll do a search of the area. Maybe the thief still has the box."

"I'll help look," Sheri said. She looked to Carrie. "You and Danny are here to take over the booth, right?"

"Sure," Carrie said. "You go do whatever you need to do."

"I'll come with you," Austen said. He followed her out of the booth.

Carrie looked a little dazed. Danny glanced around them. Now that the sheriff's deputies had moved away, no one was paying much attention. Word of the robbery hadn't spread yet and they had the next two hours of their shift manning the booth to get through.

"We need something else to collect donations in," he

said. He dug around in a pile of plastic bins at the back
of the booth. Amid a stack of volunteer sign-up sheets,
old climbing rope and miscellaneous first aid supplies he
found a battered climbing helmet. "This should work,"
he said.

A further search unearthed a black marker. He wrote
Donations in sloppy printing around the opening of the
helmet and set it on the table at the front of the booth.
He studied it a moment, then pulled out his wallet and
extracted a five-dollar bill and added this to the empty
helmet. "I hear it's good to prime the pump, so to speak,"
he said. "Give people the idea."

She nodded and began straightening the stacks of
folded T-shirts on the table. "Do you really think this
was just some random thief?" she asked. "Or was it the
person who's been harassing us for the past few weeks?"

"I think someone saw a chance for quick cash and
took it," Danny said. "The money from the T-shirt sales
wasn't touched." He picked up the bank bag tucked into a
box of garments on the floor between them and unzipped
it. "There's a couple hundred in here, easy. Anyone with
SAR would know about the bag and where it's kept."

She nodded but didn't look convinced. "It seems like
too big a coincidence for these things to keep happening by accident."

A couple approached and asked about search and rescue, and Carrie moved over to talk to them. Danny joined
her a few minutes later when someone asked about the
shirts. After that, they spoke with a steady stream of
people. Before he knew it, his two-hour shift at the booth
was more than half over.

"That helmet is filling up," Carrie said, peering into
their new donation bucket. "Maybe we should take out

everything but a couple of smaller bills—just in case our thief makes another try."

"Good idea." Danny pulled out a handful of cash and began smoothing out the bills and laying them out in the table, sorted by denomination.

But before he was finished, shouting drew his attention.

"What is going on?" Carrie was already moving out of the booth, toward Austen and Sheri, who were shouting at a third person. Danny shifted over until he could see that the target of their wrath was Ted. And was that their donation box he was carrying?

Ted pushed past Austen and Sheri and set the box on the table in front of Danny and Carrie, who had moved back into the booth. "And before you ask, it's empty," Ted said.

Carrie stared at the box. "Where did you find it?" she asked.

"In the trash in the men's room. It was just sitting on top."

"I told him he should have left the box where it was and called the sheriff's office," Sheri said. "If there were any fingerprints, they're gone now."

"Maybe he wanted those fingerprints gone," Austen said. "Or he wanted an excuse for his own prints to be on there."

"I didn't know why the box was there until you told me someone had taken it," Ted said. "And by that time I was already halfway back to here." He scowled at Austen. "As for you—if you're accusing me of something, come out and say it to my face."

Austen folded his arms across his chest and glared at Ted. "It just seems mighty convenient that you just happened to find that box, when we all know you've got a grudge against search and rescue because you're not up to the challenges of the work anymore."

"I'm in better shape than you'll ever be." Ted lunged for Austen, but Danny intervened, pulling the older man back. "It's true," Austen addressed Carrie. "Ted could have pulled off every one of the accidents that have happened to us so far."

"He couldn't have taken this box right from under our noses," Sheri said. "We know Ted. We would have spotted him long before he reached the booth."

"Maybe he waited until we were distracted," Austen said. "We should search him. He might have the money still on him."

Ted let out a roar of rage and lunged for Austen again. This time it took both Danny and Sheri to hold him back.

"Stop it!" Carrie shouted.

Everyone fell silent, gaping at the woman who was, after all, their captain. Danny couldn't remember her ever losing her temper or even raising her voice, but right now her cheeks were flushed and she looked angry enough to spit nails. "No one is going to search anyone," she said. "If whoever is targeting SAR wants to destroy us, they're doing so by getting us to argue like this."

The others looked appropriately sheepish, though Ted and Austen continued to watch each other out of the corners of their eyes, like battling dogs circling one another.

"I'll get in touch with the sheriff's office and let them know we found it." Sheri took out her phone.

"I'm sorry if I messed up any evidence," Ted said. "I thought maybe the box had been thrown away because the bottom was busted out." He turned it over to show how it had been torn almost completely off. "I brought it back here to ask what had happened and to suggest that instead of just tossing it, we might try to repair it." He shook his head. "I remember when Brit made that box for us. She put a lot of work into it."

"It's okay." Carrie patted his shoulder.

"Whoever took the box probably tore it open to take the money." Danny picked it up and examined the damage. "It doesn't look cut or anything, just ripped open."

"It's just cardboard," Ted said. "Easy enough to tear with a little effort."

"Maybe we can tape it back up and keep it at the station as a memento," Carrie said. "We'll let the sheriff's deputies look at it, but I don't think it's going to help them find who did this. I think the money is just gone."

Sheri ended her call. "Jake says he'll stop by and collect the box. They still might find some prints that don't belong to one of us." She turned to Ted. "I'm sorry I went off on you like that. I overreacted."

"It's okay," Ted said. "At least you didn't accuse me of stealing from SAR." He looked around. "Where's Austen?"

"He left," Danny said, "probably because he didn't want to face you." Austen had looked almost furtive, slipping away while everyone else was focused on the box. He had likely realized how out of line he had been to accuse Ted. Sure, Ted had had an opportunity to put acid on the climbing ropes or burn the Jeep, but why would he? Ted might be afraid of losing his role in SAR, but he would never destroy it. The organization was too much a part of his identity.

The others left when a trio of women approached and asked about purchasing T-shirts. Jake arrived and took charge of the box. "We probably won't find anything useful," he said. "But we'll see if we can lift some prints, and we can ask if anyone saw a man going into that restroom with it."

At three o'clock Eldon arrived, followed by Ryan, and Carrie filled them in on this latest development. "We've been emptying the helmet every so often to keep the funds from building up too much," Danny said. "There's an envelope in the bank bag marked Donations, where you can put anything you collect."

"I think that's my old helmet," Ryan said. He pointed to a Patagonia sticker on the side and a large scuff in the surface. "From when that serial killer, Charlie Cutler, pushed me of Mount Baker. I had to retire it after that."

"It makes a cool donation bucket," Eldon said. "Especially when it's not empty, like your head." He laughed and dodged away from Ryan.

"Just keep a close eye on that money and bring everything to the station when you're done." The booths would shut down at five, when the light began to fade and temperatures turned cooler.

Danny walked with Carrie toward the parking lot. "What are your plans this afternoon?" he asked.

"Mom texted that she took the kids home about an hour ago," she said. "I plan to take it easy with them. What about you? Do you have a hot date?"

"No." The answer surprised him a little. He seldom spent a weekend without some female companionship. He had a list of women he could count on for a fun evening, even at short notice. He started to say he might call someone and go out, but stopped himself. He really didn't want to see one of those women. "I really had a good time with you and your kids today," he said.

"Oh. I had a good time, too." Her cheeks flushed and she jiggled her keys, as if suddenly nervous.

Her car lights flashed and he realized they were almost to her SUV. She stiffened as she looked toward it. "What is Austen doing by my car?" she asked.

"Hey, Carrie." Austen, who had been leaning against the side of her SUV, straightened. He glanced at Danny, then turned his attention back to Carrie. "I wanted to apologize for losing my temper with Ted," he said. "I was just so upset about that missing money. And I guess I feel guilty because that box disappeared while I was helping with the booth."

"You should talk to Ted," Carrie said.

"I will," Austen said. "But I didn't want to leave with you thinking bad of me."

"I don't think bad of you," she said.

She moved closer to the SUV, as if she wanted to get in, but Austen didn't move away. "What you said earlier, about all the things this person is doing tearing us apart, do you think that's true?" he asked.

"It could be, if we don't pull together more," she said.

"But losing that money is just a little setback," Austen said. "It won't take us down."

"No, it won't," Carrie said.

Austen studied the ground between his feet. Danny leaned forward, ready to suggest he move over so Carrie could go home to her family. That was what she really wanted. She didn't want to be here with either of them.

"Are you afraid?" Austen asked.

The question clearly surprised her. "Why would I be afraid?" she asked.

"This guy slashed your tires. And he tried to kill Tony. You're the captain now, so aren't you afraid he'll go after you?"

Was Austen trying to frighten Carrie, or was he too dense to understand the effect his words might have?

But Carrie's expression didn't change. "Whoever is doing this isn't powerful," she said. "He strikes me as more…pathetic."

"Pathetic?" Austen echoed.

"Yes. If the same person is responsible for all the things that have been happening to SAR, what he's been doing is so petty. Yes, Tony could have died from that acid on the ropes, but I'm not sure this guy didn't intend to just vandalize some equipment and things got out of hand. The Beast was a big loss, but we all know it was on its last legs. Since then everything's been schoolkid pranks—the equivalent of stealing lunch money and letting air out of bicycle tires. It's annoying, but silly, too. To me, that makes him pathetic, and we need to remember that." She touched his shoulder. "Go apologize to Ted and try not to worry about the money. I'll see you at the next SAR meeting if not before."

He stepped aside and she opened the door and got into her SUV.

"Maybe wait until tomorrow to talk to Ted, when he's had a chance to cool down," Danny said.

Austen scowled at him. "When I want your advice, I'll ask for it," he said, then stalked off before Danny could formulate a reply.

CARRIE GAVE HER mom credit for waiting until after dinner before she mentioned Danny. "I didn't realize you and Danny Irwin were such good friends," Becky said as Carrie helped her with the dishes. Amber and Dylan were in the other room watching television.

Carrie kept her expression neutral. "We work together on search and rescue," she said.

"Oh, I know that." Becky dropped a handful of silverware into the basket of the dishwasher with a sound like castanets. "But since when do the two of you spend the morning with the children—a regular family outing?"

"Mom!" Carrie sent a warning glance toward the living room. "It wasn't like that."

"The children seem to like him. He was all they talked about all afternoon. Amber even asked me if he was your boyfriend."

Carrie winced. "Danny isn't my boyfriend," she said. "We're just…work friends."

"There's nothing wrong with being more than work friends," Becky said.

"Mom, I don't want to have this discussion." She pushed in the chairs around the table. "And Danny isn't interested in me that way," she added.

"You mean romantically?" Becky asked. "Or sexually?"

"Mom!"

Becky laughed. "You know him better than I do, but you're an attractive young woman and he's a healthy young man. It usually doesn't take much more than that to get something started."

"I'm not interested in starting anything."

"So you say. I'm just not sure I believe you."

It wasn't a matter of belief, Carrie thought. She did find Danny attractive, and it mattered to her that Dylan and Amber liked him and he seemed to like them. But she had given her heart and had it handed back to her once already. She wasn't prepared to go through that again. Danny had never tried to deceive anyone about his nature—he liked relationships with low expectations. He was all about fun, not family. Carrie was the opposite—she wanted a love like her parents', one that lasted for a lifetime. Obviously, there were no guarantees in relationships, but the odds were better if both partners started out wanting permanence.

SHE WASN'T THINKING about permanence on Monday at
work, when Greg Abernathy called her into his office.
"Sit down, Carrie," he said, nodding to the chair across
from his desk. His office was easily twice the size of
Carrie's, with white carpeting and chrome and leather
furniture that looked out of place in the old Victorian
home. "I want to discuss the Cornerstone development."

Carrie sat up a little straighter. Cornerstone was a four-
office complex being built on the site of a building that
had burned last summer, on the edge of downtown. The
developer, Miles Lindberg, had specifically requested
Carrie as the architect. "I've gone over some preliminary
drawings for Mr. Lindberg and he seems very pleased,"
she said. So much so that he was talking about doubling
the size of the build.

Abernathy nodded, his expression grave. "That's good
to hear. I've decided to bring Vance in on the project," he
said. "I need you to bring him up to speed."

Vance Weatherby was an architect who had been hired
a year after Carrie, an amiable man who struck her as of
mediocre talent and low ambition. "Why are you bringing
in Vance?" she asked. "I thought I was going to handle
the project by myself."

"Since the customer has expanded the scope of the
build, we thought it would be a good idea to bring in an
additional person," Abernathy said. "And we want Vance
to get more familiar with all our major clients. That kind
of knowledge will be invaluable as he moves up the ladder at the company."

Up the ladder. Carrie translated this to *making partner*, something that had never been offered as a possibility to her, though she had hoped being given the
Cornerstone project on her own had been a signal that
the partners wanted to give her more responsibility. "I'd

like to be more involved with all our clients, too," she said, and sat up a little straighter. "And I want to move up the ladder as well."

She couldn't figure out the look he was giving her right away, then she realized he was puzzled. "I thought you were happy with your role here," he said. "You made your feelings about the job clear when we hired you and we think your situation has worked out well."

"What situation is that?" she asked.

"From the first you indicated that what you wanted most from the job was the flexibility to devote time to your family," Abernathy said. "We've been happy to support that, even if it has made things difficult for us at the same time."

"I always complete my work on schedule," she said. "My clients have been very pleased."

"Oh, of course. But you've never really taken on anyone demanding. That's why we'd like Vance to work with you on the Cornerstone build. He'll have the time to devote to it." He stood. "Get with him this afternoon and bring him up to speed. That's all."

Half a dozen replies whirled through her head, most of them things she would probably regret saying, so she merely nodded and returned to her office. How much of what had just transpired was Abernathy's fault and how much her own, for putting her family ahead of her job? But she shouldn't ever have to regret that, should she?

She didn't have much time to stew over the matter. She had barely settled back at her desk when Vance leaned into her office. "Greg said you'd bring me up to speed on the Cornerstone project. He said with your busy schedule, you could use a hand."

Why did a remark that could have passed for concern sound so much like an insult? But she shoved aside her annoyance and invited Vance in to go over the particulars of what had, until a few moment ago, been her biggest solo effort to date.

Three hours later, jaw aching from forcing so many smiles and temper frayed to the point where she was sure at any moment she would say the exact wrong thing, she left the office. If her bosses were going to view her as a slacker because she set her schedule around her family's needs why not take full advantage of that freedom?

She had an unsettling feeling of déjà vu as she approached her car and recognized the man leaning against it. "Austen? What are you doing here?" she asked.

He swept a fall of light brown hair out of his eyes and grinned at her. He looked particularly boyish today, dressed in a fisherman's sweater and dark jeans, and loafers without socks. "I didn't want to bother you at work," he said. "But I was hoping I'd catch you when you came out."

"What do you want?" The words came out brusquer than she had intended, but really, she was so tired of dealing with people today. Austen probably had some complaint about SAR. Despite his rookie status, he liked to point out things he thought they were doing wrong.

Either he didn't pick up on her foul mood or he chose to ignore it. "I wanted to ask you out," he said. "For dinner. Friday night."

She didn't do a good job of hiding her shock. She openly stared at him. "You're asking me on a date?"

"Yes. I mean, why not?" He shoved his hands in the front pockets of his jeans, his smile fading. "We're both single, we're almost the same age and I think we have a lot in common." He raised his head, chin jutted out. "I'll admit I'm a little rusty. I haven't gone out with anyone since my fiancée was killed, but did I botch this so badly?"

She immediately felt terrible. Of course it hadn't been easy for him to ask her out, after the tragedy he had weathered. She managed a genuine smile. "I'm sorry. I'm really out of practice, too. I haven't dated anyone since my divorce, several years ago." Did that sound too pathetic?

He shifted his stance from one foot to the other. "I thought maybe you and Danny were involved."

She felt the heat rise to her cheeks. "No. We're not."

"Yeah, well, when I saw him at Mo's Saturday night, I figured maybe I was wrong."

"He was at Mo's with someone?" The thought pained her, though really, why should it? Danny was free to see whoever he pleased.

"He said he was waiting for someone. I figured it was a woman. He has a different one every time I see him."

Yes, that was the Danny she knew. Time to move on. "I'm flattered you asked me, Austen," she said. "But between my job and search and rescue and my kids, I don't have time to date. But if I change my mind, I'll let you know."

"Don't think of it as a date," he said. "Just friends getting together. It would really be nice not to have to eat alone."

Was he trying to guilt her into going out with him? "No, I really can't." she said. She hit the button to unlock her car and it beeped.

But Austen didn't move. As she tried to push past him, he grabbed her arm. "I wish you'd reconsider," he said. "I really do think we have a lot in common."

She pulled away, her earlier annoyance returning. "No," she said, and yanked open her car door, forcing him to move. She slid in and slammed the door behind her, then started the engine. Out of the corner of her eye she could see him standing there, glaring at her.

Let him glare. She was so over dealing with men today.

Chapter Eleven

The spring thaw brought warmer weather, the first wild-flowers and spectacular waterfalls. It also delivered mud-slides, floods and accidents involving people anxious to climb peaks and hike higher elevations before it was safe to do so.

On a Sunday afternoon a week after the Spring Carnival, search and rescue responded to a report of a car swept off the highway by a slide of rocks and mud, into a flood-swollen river.

"Word is there's at least one person trapped in the vehicle," Carrie informed the others gathered at SAR headquarters.

"I'll get the Jaws," Ryan said. The Hurst hydraulic extraction tool, better known as the Jaws of Life, was a powerful cutting tool designed to free a person from a wrecked vehicle.

"I'll help," Eldon said, and the two headed for the storage closet where the tool was kept.

Danny inventoried his medical pack, deciding if he needed to add anything to deal with the potential injuries. "Do we know how many people were in the vehicle?" he asked.

"The 9-1-1 caller said he thought five or six," Carrie

said. Which could mean anything from two to ten. Danny added a few more cervical collars to his pack.

"I really miss the Beast," Sheri said as she hauled a litter out the side door. Larger equipment, like the litters, stayed packed in the rescue vehicle, ready to go without a volunteer having to remember to take it and figure out how to transport it. They were still short some items that had been burned along with the Beast.

"We can take my truck," Ted said. "A lot of equipment will fit in it."

"Thanks," Carrie said. She seemed to be making a point to welcome Ted back to the group, no questions asked.

"Carrie?" An agitated-looking Ryan approached their captain as she helped Austen stack coils of ropes in bins to be carried to a waiting vehicle. "Did someone move the Jaws?" he asked.

"The Jaws is in the closet, where it's always kept," she said.

"No, it isn't," Ryan said.

"We took everything out," Eldon said. "It's not there. And it's not like it's easy to overlook." The Jaws was over three feet long and weighed more than fifty pounds. Not to mention the blaze-orange reflective stripes across its case made it stand out even more.

Carrie and Austen followed them to the closet. Danny set aside the medical pack and joined them. The large space usually filled by the Jaws was empty.

"Do you think someone stole it?" Eldon asked.

"And did what with it?" Carrie asked. "It's not like you can sell something like that on the street."

"Maybe it's the same person who's been harassing us," Austen said.

"This is beyond harassment," Carrie said, her voice

rising. "This could cost someone their life." She looked at all of them gathered around her. "We don't have time to deal with this now. We need to get moving. I'll call the sheriff and see if they can find an extractor we can use if the need arises. Get going."

They formed a caravan of four vehicles headed to the site of the mudslide, on a county road east of Eagle Mountain. Danny loaded into Carrie's car, along with Austen and most of their medical equipment. Jake and Sheri had the rest of the medical gear they might need, while Ryan, Ted and Eldon carried the climbing tools in Ted's truck.

Barricades stopped them just ahead of the ten-foot-wide river of orange mud that covered the road, rocks suspended in the muck like nuts in fudge.

Sheriff's deputy Wes Landry walked over to Carrie's car. "You'll have to park here and haul your equipment out to where the vehicle went over." He gestured toward the middle of the mud where Sgt. Gage Walker stood with Deputy Jamie Douglas. "It's a minivan, with two adults and four kids," Wes continued. "They're stuck on a rock outcropping on the far side of the river, which is running high."

"Is anyone in the vehicle?" Carrie asked.

"No. Everyone is out, but they aren't really dressed for the weather. There are ice chunks floating in that water, not to mention tree trunks and other debris."

They climbed out of the SUV and stood at the edge of the mud flow, surveying the scene. The others joined them. "I wish I'd thought to bring muck boots," Sheri said.

"Nothing to do but wade through it," Ted said. He shouldered a coil of rope and started out, the mud rising above his ankles.

The others gathered equipment and followed, picking their way through the sludge and debris, every step making a sucking sound as they lifted their feet. The mud was cold and laden with sharp rocks that bit into Danny's ankles.

Thoughts of his own discomfort fled when they reached the shoulder of the road where Gage and Jamie stood and looked down into the river. Five people huddled together beside a crumpled van. A sixth person, a man, sat beside the van, head in his hands. Whitewater foamed around the rock, the roar of it drowning out all other sound.

"We're going to need to get a couple of people over to the other side to set up a traverse line." Sheri raised her voice to be heard above the thunder of the water. "Ryan, Ted, Carrie and I have taken the swift-water rescue course, so two of us should go."

"I'll go," Ted said.

Carrie shook her head. "No. Sheri and I will go. I want you here, as incident commander."

Ted glowered. "But I—"

"No arguments, Ted." She moved past him.

"All right," she continued. "Ryan, you and Austen set the line from this end. Danny, you get ready to go over on the traverse if they need medical assistance. Eldon, you and Jake help with the ropes."

"Where's Hannah?" Sheri asked.

"She's on shift with EMS today," Carrie said as she searched through the gear they had carried over for a helmet and life jacket. "She texted when the 9-1-1 call went out that she was on a run to the hospital in Junction and unavailable."

Sheri and Carrie donned helmets and life vests, then walked farther down the road to assess the situation, while Danny found a helmet and got into a harness, prepared to traverse down the rope line the others would set if any of the people in the canyon needed more medical attention than Carrie and Sheri could provide.

The women returned after ten minutes. "There's a couple of downed trees spanning the river farther downstream," Sheri said. "It looks like we can use them as a makeshift bridge to the other side and scramble down the shore to the outcropping where the family is stuck."

"If you fall in that water, you'll be swept away," Danny said. The idea made him a little queasy.

Carrie nodded. "Probably be sucked under, or caught on debris and drowned. So we won't fall in."

"It's a big risk," Danny said. He wanted to tell her she shouldn't go but figured she wouldn't listen to his objections and might even resist them. She was as well trained as any of them, he just hated the idea of her putting herself in danger. It was a new feeling for him, and he didn't especially like it, so he kept his mouth shut.

"Not that big a risk," Sheri said. "We can do it."

They roped up, in the hope that they might be pulled to safety if they did fall in. Danny stood with Ted and watched as first Sheri, then Carrie crawled out onto a massive cottonwood that lay on its side over the foaming water. Once on the trunk, Sheri stood and inched along to the jagged end and a gap of several feet they would have to clear to reach the second trunk, which formed the other half of the bridge.

Ted swore as Sheri made the leap to the second trunk. She turned and gave a thumbs-up signal, grinning widely, and Ted grumbled even more. "She's going to get in trouble, showing off like that," he said.

"You're just jealous you can't do it," Danny said.

"I'm too smart to take those kind of chances," Ted said. "You don't get to be my age by being foolish."

Sheri almost danced to the other side of the canyon and scrambled out onto the rocks and turned to watch Carrie complete the crossing. At the gap between the trees, Carrie hesitated. Danny could see Sheri's lips moving as she called to Carrie, but he couldn't make out her words from here.

Carrie nodded, gathered herself, then leaped. She hit the second trunk at an angle, and her back foot slipped into the water. Danny leaned forward, every muscle tensed as Carrie scrambled to right herself, then lost her balance and, arms flailing, fell backward into the water.

"No!" Danny shouted, and raced to where Ryan and the others waited with the ropes needed to rig a traverse line. He could hear Ted's feet pounding the ground behind him. Sheri had run back out onto the tree trunk and straddled it, both arms reaching for Carrie, who still clung to the trunk, most of her body in the frothing water.

"Someone should go help them," Austen said.

"Wait." Ted held up one hand and they all stared, no one making a sound as Carrie, with Sheri's help, hauled herself back onto the trunk. She lay there a long moment, water streaming from her body. "Is she okay?" Eldon asked.

"She'll be hypothermic if she doesn't get into dry clothes," Danny said. He cupped his hands to his mouth. "Carrie! Get back up here!"

Carrie pulled herself into a sitting position and looked back over her shoulder. "Come back!" Danny shouted again, and motioned for her to return to this side of the canyon.

Carrie stood and waved, but turned away, following Sheri to the opposite bank.

"I need to get down there and make sure she's okay,"

Danny said. He prepared to descend after the women, but Ted took hold of him.

"Wait for the traverse line," Ted said. "She looked like she's fine."

The two women picked their way along the opposite shore, moving along a narrow strip of slanted ground just above the water.

"Get ready to fire that rope across to the other side," Ryan said.

Eldon and Austen unpacked the line gun from its case. The gun used compressed air to send a projectile attached to stout rope across a distance of over two hundred yards, depending upon conditions.

Carrie and Sheri had reached the rock outcropping, and the family members crowded around them. Ted's radio crackled.

"We're ready to receive the line," Carrie said. "The driver of the car has a pretty bad head injury. I'd like Danny over here to assess him. A couple of the kids might be suffering from hypothermia, but we're going to get them wrapped up as warmly as we can."

"Roger that," Ted said.

Ten minutes later, with everyone standing well back from the target, Ryan fired the launcher and sent a ribbon of polypropylene unspooling across the narrow canyon. As soon as the projectile on the end struck the rock, Sheri was on it, fastening it to the anchor Carrie had already set. Eldon did the same on his end.

Danny moved into position and clipped onto the line, then rode down the line as if on a zip line. As he left, he heard Ted radioing for a couple of ambulances. Once on the other side, he moved to Carrie. "Are you all right?" he asked. "You must be freezing."

"I'm fine." She didn't even look at him, focused on

wrapping a blanket around a child who looked like the youngest member of the party. "You need to look after Mr. Hamilton." She nodded toward the dark-haired man who sat in the dirt beside the wrecked van.

Danny wanted to put his hands on her shoulders and look in her eyes for any signs of disorientation, to take her temperature and insist she change into dry clothing and drink something warm and take care of herself. Instead, he turned away to see to Hamilton, who showed signs of a serious concussion. "We need to get a medical helicopter on the way," Danny told Carrie when she joined him beside Hamilton. "And tell them to send over a litter to transport him."

While Carrie radioed this information to Ted, Danny and Sheri explained to the family how they were going to evacuate them. "Dad's going to go across first in this special litter," Sheri said. "Then the rest of you will ride over, kind of like being on a zip line, except we'll have people pulling you across on a pulley system. You'll be secured so you can't fall, and you'll all wear helmets and life jackets."

The two oldest children looked excited, Danny thought, while the youngest clung to mom, her thumb in her mouth. Mrs. Hamilton looked worried and exhausted. Danny couldn't blame her. As he helped get Mr. Hamilton secured into the sled, he kept sneaking glances at Carrie. She had to be freezing in her wet clothing, but she kept moving among the kids, wrapping them in blankets and helping fit them with helmets and life jackets.

Finally, they were ready to start across. The litter with Mr. Hamilton would go first, with Danny in line behind, holding on to it. They had learned the hard way that if someone didn't steady it, the litter could spin or twist, at worst tangling in the line and at best subjecting the occupant to a very uncomfortable ride. Carrie would come next with the youngest child, then the two older children and Mrs. Hamilton, and finally Sheri. Once everyone was taken care of, someone would repeat the river crossing Sheri and Carrie had made earlier, to unfasten the rope and retrieve the anchor.

The short trip across the narrow canyon took twenty uncomfortable minutes, with Danny steadying the litter until the muscles in both shoulders screamed for relief. He stumbled off the line onto solid ground and shook out his hands, then joined Ted in carrying Mr. Hamilton through the mud to the waiting ambulance, which would take it to the landing area a short distance away, where the medical helicopter was waiting.

Danny got back to the end of the traverse line in time to greet Carrie as she unhooked the youngest Hamilton child in her arms. Danny took the child from her. "Go get into some dry clothes," he said gruffly. "And don't pretend nothing is wrong. I can see you shaking, and your lips are blue."

She didn't even try to argue, which told him how much she was suffering. But he had to trust someone else would take care of her as he helped each of the children off the line and kept them together until they were reunited with their mother. "Is my husband going to be okay?" Mrs. Hamilton asked as soon as he handed off the youngest child to her.

"He's going to be on his way to the hospital soon," Danny said. "There are some paramedics waiting to check on you and your children, and then the sheriff's deputies will arrange for you to go to the hospital to see your husband."

"Is something wrong with my children?" she asked.

"It's just a precaution," Danny said. A couple of the

children had showed indications of hypothermia when he had examined them after he first arrived in the canyon, but they were already showing signs of improvement. For the fourth time that day he trekked back through the mud, leading the family to the waiting ambulance and turning them over to the paramedics.

He returned to the canyon where the others were already in the process of collecting their gear. "Where's Carrie?" he asked.

Sheri looked up from the pile of life jackets she was packing back into a plastic tote. "I don't know. I haven't seen her for a while."

Danny looked around. Ted was helping to haul the traverse line back up from the canyon. "Ted! Where's Carrie?" he called.

Ted looked up, frowning. "I don't know," he said. "I'm sure she's around here somewhere."

Had she become disoriented with the cold and wandered off? Heart pounding, Danny ran along the edge of the canyon, searching. He asked each person he passed if they had seen Carrie. "Maybe she went back to her car," Eldon said. "She said something about getting out of her wet clothes."

Of course. That had to be it. Danny set out toward Carrie's SUV, but running was impossible in the mud, though a county crew with a front end loader had finally arrived and begun scraping up the muck so the road could reopen to traffic. He reached Carrie's SUV, but felt as if he had swallowed rocks when he saw that it was empty. He looked around, panic rising to choke him. Deputy Jamie Douglas waved to him from her sheriff's department cruiser and he headed toward her.

"Are you looking for Carrie?" Jamie asked. The slim

dark-haired deputy was a familiar figure in town, currently the only woman on the force.

"I'm right here," Carrie said before he could answer.

He leaned down and relief flooded him as he spotted her in the passenger seat of the cruiser, a blanket around her shoulders and both hands wrapped around a steaming drink. "I figured the best thing was to warm her up fast, before she had to take an ambulance ride herself," Jamie said.

Jamie's radio crackled with a message that she needed to help with crowd control as they prepared to reopen the highway. "I need to go," she said.

"I'm good now." Carrie unwrapped the blanket from her shoulders and slid out of the cruiser. "Thanks," she told Jamie.

Jamie waved, climbed into the car and drove away. Carrie started to walk away, but Danny took hold of her arm. "Let me see," he said.

"I'm fine now. Really," she said.

He kept hold of her arm as he looked into her eyes, put the back of his hand to her cheek, then slid his fingers down to check the pulse at her throat. Her skin was satin soft and invitingly warm. He wanted to press his lips to that steady heartbeat just beneath her jaw, to lose himself in discovering every curve and velvety place on her body.

"Danny?" Her voice was scarcely above a whisper.

He pulled his mind away from the dangerous path it was taking, but he didn't lift his hand from her or shift his gaze away. "I don't think I've ever been so terrified as when I saw you go into the water," he said, his voice ragged.

"That makes two of us," she said, and tried to smile, but her bottom lip trembled, and he saw the flash of fear in her eyes as she relived the moment when the icy flood-waters had tried to claim her.

That trembling was his undoing. He bent and pressed his mouth to hers, stilling the tremor, pushing back the fear. She leaned into him, fingers clutching at his jacket, and he pulled her closer, as he had wanted to pull her from the water. He wanted to memorize the feel of her, to revel in the strength and softness and life in her.

She broke the kiss first but didn't pull away. "I'm okay, really," she said.

He nodded. "I know that now. But if anything had happened to you—"

"Shhh." She pressed fingertips to his lips and the gesture sent an electric current of desire through him. But this wasn't the time, or the place. He forced himself to release his hold on her and step back. Her cheeks were flushed, her eyes bright and she looked impossibly beautiful. "Just…don't do that again," he said.

She laughed. "I don't have any plans for it." She shoved her hands into the pockets of her parka. "You'd better go. I need to see that everything is wrapped up here."

"I can help," he said.

"Thanks, but I think it would be better if you go. Just for now." Her smile softened the words. "Okay?"

He nodded. "Yeah. Okay."

She turned and walked away and he tried not to focus on the sway of her hips, but he did. He wiped one hand across his face and took a deep breath, then turned around. Eldon was walking toward him, a coil of rope over each shoulder. "Can I catch a ride back with you?" Danny asked, taking one of loops from Eldon. "Carrie wants to finish things up here and I need to get back."

"Sure," he said. "I'm ready to go now."

He wasn't prepared to leave Carrie, but she was

right—they needed the space. He still felt shaky from the impact of seeing her go into the water, and shocked by his own strong reaction to her brush with death. He had always liked not being closely tied to anyone else. Could his whole outlook on life really change with one slip of a foot?

Chapter Twelve

"The theft from our booth at the Spring Carnival set back our fundraising efforts," Sheri reported at the next search and rescue meeting, the following Saturday afternoon. "We ended up with about $500 for the day, most of that from generous people who heard about the theft."

"We're never going to reach our goal at that rate," Austen said.

"It's just a setback," Sheri said. "Eldon and Ryan and I have been working on some other ideas to bring in funds." She nodded to Ryan, who strode to the front of the room, a single sheet of paper in hand.

"We're sending a letter to all our past donors, asking them to make a special contribution toward a new rescue vehicle." Ryan held up the paper. "This is the letter, and we want everybody here to sign at the bottom. Then we'll scan it in and print off a bunch to mail out." He laid the letter on the front table and returned to his seat.

Eldon took his place. He propped a poster on the table. Dinner Dance Fundraiser! the poster proclaimed. "Kate's has agreed to donate all the food if we do the serving and cleanup," Eldon said. "And Mountain Rose, a band over in Junction, will play for dancing afterwards. We're going to charge seventy-five dollars a person or a hundred dollars a couple."

"We're also going to have a silent auction to raise more money," Sheri added. She joined Eldon at the front of the room. "Every one of us will have to pitch in to make this happen, but we think it, along with the donor appeal, will be enough to meet our goal."

"Where are we going to hold this dinner and dance?" Ted asked.

"Right here." Sheri spread her arms wide to take in the big, concrete-floored space. "We'll need a decorating committee. We'll set up tables and chairs and a bar area, and leave space for a dance floor. We're working on getting businesses to donate everything else."

"You and Eldon and Ryan have done a terrific job," Carrie said. She led a round of applause. Sheri and Ryan grinned while Eldon flushed pink as everyone joined in with calls of "Thanks!" and "Way to go."

"Are we going to raise enough money to pay for a new Jaws?" Austen asked.

"One thing at a time," Carrie said. A search of all the equipment bays hadn't turned up the extractor, and everyone was certain it had not been in the Beast when the old Jeep burned.

"Do we have any idea what happened to it?" Eldon asked.

"None," Carrie said.

"Did you report the theft to the sheriff's department?" Sheri asked.

Carrie sighed. "I told them it was missing, but we don't know for certain that it was stolen."

"I did some checking, and nothing like that has come on the market," Jake said. "I looked around here, too. There was no sign of a break-in, and nothing else appears to have been taken."

The normally talkative crew fell silent, expressions

reflecting various degrees of anger, frustration or discouragement as this latest revelation sank in.

"We can't worry about that now," Sheri said. She began laying out sheets of paper on the front table, next to the fundraising letter. "I've got sign-up lists here for decorating, waitstaff, predinner prep and after-party cleanup," she said. "I expect to see everyone's name on at least two sheets."

"And don't forget to sign the donor letter," Ryan added.

Carrie stepped up to be the first to sign. She chose prep work and cleanup. As temporary captain, she felt the need to be here for the entire event, and she definitely wanted to make sure the building was locked up tight afterward. She couldn't take a chance on any more equipment going missing.

She was signing the fundraising plea when Austen moved in beside her. "Where's Danny?" he asked.

"He texted to say he had to go out of town." She hadn't seen or spoken to Danny since they had rescued the family from the mudslide last week—and shared that scorching kiss. His silence troubled her, though she didn't like to admit how much. Obviously, he had been caught up in the emotion of the rescue and the kiss they shared hadn't meant anything.

At least, not to him.

"Where did he go?" Austen asked.

"He didn't say."

"Huh. I figured he would tell you."

"Well, he didn't." She regretted the sharp reply as soon as it was out of her mouth. "I'm sorry." She massaged her forehead. "It's been a long day." Her morning had begun with another tense phone call from Vance, who had an objection to almost every design decision she suggested for the Cornerstone project.

"You work so hard." Austen put a hand on her shoulder, then slid it over and began rubbing her back. "This hasn't been an easy time for you."

A shiver rippled down her spine at his touch and she stepped back, out of his reach, and handed him the pen she had been using. "I need to talk to Sheri," she said, and hurried away.

She joined Sheri and Eldon at the back of the room. "You two have done a terrific job," she said. "Thank you again."

"We haven't raised any money yet," Eldon said.

"We will," Carrie said. "I'm sure of it."

"Is everything okay?" Sheri peered closely at Carrie. "You look upset about something."

She was upset—about her job, about Danny avoiding her, about the loss of the Jaws and the theft of the money, about Austen getting too familiar. She shook her head. "I'm just tired."

"I'll try to hustle people along," Sheri said. "We could all use an early night."

"These accidents and stuff going missing has us all a little freaked-out," Eldon said as Sheri moved away. "I mean, everything points to one of the volunteers being behind it all, but I can't make myself believe it."

Carrie nodded. "I know." She scanned the gathering, lingering on each familiar face. Every one of them had a very personal reason for being part of this group. She couldn't believe anyone would want to destroy it.

"All right, people." Sheri spoke from the front of the room. "If I don't see your name on these lists, I *will* come find you."

Half an hour later, lists completed, chairs rearranged and lights out, Carrie locked the door and said good-night to Sheri and Eldon. Everyone else had left ahead of them.

A few more minutes and she would be home. Maybe after she tucked in the kids, she would run a bubble bath and pour a glass of wine...

Her text alert sounded as she slid into the driver's seat of her SUV. Before she could read the message, her telephone rang.

"This is emergency dispatch," a pleasant woman's voice—Carrie recognized Darcie Davis—said. "We have a report of a vehicle off the road on Dakota Ridge, near Mile Marker 32."

Sheri and Eldon stood outside Carrie's car as she spoke to dispatch. She ended the call and lowered her window. "We got the page," Sheri said.

"We'd better unlock and go back inside," Carrie said. "The others will be here soon."

"Did dispatch have any details about what we might find at the accident site?" Sheri asked. "The text just said a car went off Dakota Ridge at Mile Marker 32."

"A motorist saw the skid marks and broken trees and called it in," Carrie said. She turned the key in the lock and shoved open the door. "They thought it must have just happened when they went by. No clue what kind of vehicle or how many people are involved."

"If I remember correctly, there's a drop-off there, but it's more gradual," Sheri said. "Still, we'll probably need climbing gear." She headed toward the area where the ropes were kept.

"I wish we had the Jaws," Eldon said. "It might come in handy if someone is trapped."

Carrie's phone rang and the screen showed a call from Ted. "Hello, Ted," she answered.

"I'm less than a mile from the accident site," he said. "I'll meet you there."

"There should be at least one deputy on-site," Carrie said.

Hannah and Jake were the next to arrive. She began assembling a medical kit, while Jake fetched a litter and helped Eldon load it into his truck. Ryan showed up and worked with Sheri on gathering the climbing gear. Austen and Carrie collected other items they might need, from signal flares to cervical collars and extra helmets. Everyone was calm and worked together smoothly. Less than twenty minutes from the initial text alerting them to the accident, they were headed toward the scene in three vehicles.

The red-and-blue strobe of the lights atop a Rayford County Sheriff's Department SUV guided them to the site, and they parked in a turnout just past it. Deputy Dwight Prentice met them in the road. "You can see where the vehicle slid off here," he said, and directed the beam of a flashlight over deep tire ruts in the soft shoulder of the road, then onto the broken brush at the lip of the drop-off. "I tried to look down there, but it's pitch-black and I couldn't see a thing."

"I'll get the portable spotlights," Jake said.

"I'll help," Austen said, and the two headed back to Jake's truck.

"Where's Ted?" Carrie asked the deputy.

She looked past him to Ted's truck, parked on the shoulder, just beyond the deputy's SUV.

"He said he was going to assess the situation." Dwight looked around. "I don't know where he went."

"I see a light down there." Hannah pointed into the drop-off. A beam, like a moving flashlight or headlamp, bobbed in the darkness.

Carrie cupped her hands to her mouth. "Ted!"

No answer. The light kept moving, away from them.

Carrie keyed her radio. "Ted, can you hear me?"

"I'm at the car." His voice came over the radio, a little breathless. "Looks like a Mini Cooper. On its side, roof of the vehicle pointed downhill. It's caught up in some brush. The driver is still inside. A young woman. I'm going to see if I can get closer."

"Ted, no!" Carrie's voice rose, so that the others turned to stare. "Let a team get down to stabilize the vehicle first."

No answer. "Ted. Answer me!"

He didn't reply. Carrie turned to see Jake and Austen carrying two pole-mounted work lights, the kind used by highway crews for night work. They set them up and in a few minutes the area just below was flooded in white light.

The car was at the very edge of the light's reach, lying on its side like an injured animal. Carrie didn't see Ted at first, then she spotted him, beside the car. She keyed the radio again. "Ted, back off and wait," she said. "That's an order."

The radio crackled and his voice cut through the static. "There's just the driver. She's caught up in her seat belt, bleeding from a head wound, unconscious."

"We'll have people down in a minute to stabilize the vehicle." To her left, she could see Sheri and Eldon gathering equipment, preparing to scramble down.

"Ted?"

But he either didn't hear or was refusing to acknowledge. Carrie walked over to where Jake and Austen had joined the others. "I'm going to set an anchor and uncoil some rope on the descent that we can use going up and down," Sheri said.

"I've got cable and anchors for the car," Ryan said, already looping the coiled cable over head and shoulder. "Lucky it's a Mini Cooper. It won't take much to hold it."

"If it was anything heavier, it might already have slid on down," Eldon said.

Carrie stared down the slope once more. She couldn't see Ted. What was he doing down there?

"Tell Ted we're on our way," Sheri said. She tugged at the rope, which she had tied to an anchor driven into the ground, then started moving down the slope. "It's going to take a few minutes. There's a lot of loose rock."

"Take your time," Carrie said. "Ted?" She tried the mic again, but her only answer was static.

A terrible screech cut through the night air. Austen swore. Everyone froze and stared as the Mini Cooper slid across the rock, tumbled onto its roof, then disappeared into the darkness.

"Ted!" Carrie screamed the word. It took everything in her not to start running down the slope.

The radio crackled. "It's okay." Ted's voice sounded harsh in the sudden stillness. Breathless. "I'm okay."

"What happened?" It was Jake who spoke. Carrie's heart hammered so hard in her chest she couldn't find her voice.

"It's okay," Ted said. "I pulled her out in time. She's going to be okay."

"I told you to wait," Carrie said. Anger helped her find her tongue again.

"I had to go in and get her out," he said. "I could see the car was going to go. I had to do it."

Carrie realized the rest of the team was waiting for her to tell them what to do. "Go," she said. "Hannah, you too. Eldon, take the litter. Take care of the driver."

"An ambulance is on the way," Dwight said.

Carrie nodded. She took three deep breaths, then lifted

the radio to her lips once more. "Ted, I want you up here with me. Now."

She cut him off before he could argue and turned her attention to the others.

The next half hour passed in a blur as the team stabilized the young female driver. She regained consciousness as they worked, and Hannah determined she showed no signs of a serious head injury and had no broken bones or internal injuries, though she would be transported to the hospital for a more in-depth assessment. Six people together brought the litter up to the road and loaded it into the ambulance.

As the vehicle drove away, Carrie pulled Hannah aside. "What Ted did—pulling her out of the car—did it cause any further injury?" she asked.

Hannah shook her head, her expression troubled. "It didn't," she said. "But it could have if there had been any spinal damage, or broken bones."

Carrie nodded and went in search of Ted.

She found him by his truck, sitting on the bumper, scraping mud off the soles of his boots with a stick. "Ted, you violated every established protocol for accident response," she said. "Protocols you helped establish."

He looked up, mouth in a stubborn pout. "I saved her life," he said. "You ought to be focused on that. That's what we're about here, not protocols."

"If she had had spinal injuries, you could just as easily killed or crippled her when you pulled her from that car," Carrie said. She couldn't keep the shaking out of her voice. "And the car probably would have been fine if you hadn't started climbing on it to get to her."

"I did what had to be done," he said.

"You disobeyed a direct order," she said.

He stared at her, slit-eyed, his face pale in the harsh white glow of her headlamp.

"We're a team," she said. "No one acts alone. You know that. I'm relieving you of your duties as of this moment."

He stood, and she was aware of how much taller than her he was. He topped her by at least a foot. "You have no right to do that," he said.

"I'm your captain. The team granted me that right."

"Tony is our captain."

"And Tony isn't here." She deliberately turned her back on him and saw the others, moving in a group toward them. "Go home, Ted," she said.

He saw the others, too. "I saved that girl's life," he said.

Ryan shook his head. "You'd better go home," he said, his voice gentle.

"Is that how you all feel?" he demanded. "You're taking her side."

"She's the captain," Sheri said. The others nodded.

Carrie bit the inside of her cheek, fighting tears—of exhaustion, and from a swell of pride and gratitude for their support. She didn't turn around, only listened as a truck door slammed, the engine roared to life, then Ted drove away, tires spitting gravel.

Sheri was the first to reach her. She put an arm around Carrie's shoulders. "You did the right thing," she whispered.

Carrie nodded. She believed that, but her belief hadn't made the decision any easier. She took another deep breath and raised her head to face them. "Good job tonight," she said. "Now, let's go home and get some rest." She didn't believe she would get much sleep tonight. Days like this had a way of replaying themselves all night long. As if living through it once wasn't enough.

Chapter Thirteen

Danny had signed up to wait tables and help with
cleanup at the dinner dance, and he arrived to find
search and rescue headquarters transformed by a jungle of plants, fairy lights and white-clothed tables. "The
dinner sold out!" Sheri informed him as she rushed by
with a tray of candles, which she began distributing
among the tables.

He followed her, lighting the candles and straightening chairs. All around the room, fellow volunteers hauled
in ice, arranged the bandstand and bar areas, and bus-
tled about. He scanned the room, searching for Carrie.
He hadn't seen her since the kiss they had shared on the
side of the road. She probably thought he was the biggest
coward ever, running away from her like that. He hadn't
been avoiding her, exactly, but he hadn't provided any
details beyond "family stuff" after his sister had sum-
moned him to deal with another setback involving their
mother. After spending ten days out of town dealing with
that situation, he had worked extra shifts at the surgery
center to make up for the time he had missed and had
continued to put off contacting Carrie. After all, maybe
she didn't even want to see him. As long as he had known
her, she had kept pretty much every man at arm's length,

so why should he be different? Maybe it was smarter to keep quiet about his feelings for her than risk rejection.

"You sure clean up nice," a woman said from behind him. He turned and smiled at Hannah, who was looking very pretty herself in a short, sparkly dress with a full skirt, a far cry from her paramedic's uniform.

"You look great," he said, and hugged her. He was glad he and Hannah could be friends now, and that she was happy. Over his shoulder, he spotted Jake, who, like Danny, wore a dark suit and well-shined shoes.

"If you're looking for Carrie, she's out back, talking to the caterers," Hannah said.

"I, um, just wanted to explain why I haven't been around much lately," he said.

Hannah sent him a questioning look. "She knows you were dealing with family stuff, right? I'm sure she said that. I hope everything is okay?"

The question invited an explanation, but he had a policy of not talking about his family. It was better that way. "It's fine," he said. "And I understand you only had one callout while I was gone?"

"A girl in a Mini Cooper slid off Dakota Ridge," Hannah said. She leaned closer and lowered her voice. "You heard about Ted, right?"

"Ryan filled me in. What was Ted thinking? He and that girl could have both been killed. As long as he's been in search and rescue, he knows that."

Hannah shrugged. "He says he didn't have a choice, but I don't really believe it. Maybe he was trying to prove himself, you know? Anyway, none of us have seen or heard from him. I'm worried about him."

"Maybe I'll get a chance to go see him," Danny said. "I wasn't there, so maybe it won't be as awkward as if someone else went."

"That would be great if you did that," she said. "Maybe you can find out what was going through his head." She glanced to the side. "Here's Carrie now. Talk to her. I know she feels bad about what happened."

Anything Danny had been prepared to say fled from his mind at the sight of Carrie making her way toward him. Her dress was a solid royal blue, of some shimmery material that slid over her curves, and a V-neckline showed just a hint of cleavage. She had caught her blond hair up in a sparkly clip, with a few loose strands framing her face. "Danny!" Her smile was tentative. Hopeful.

"It's great to see you," he said. "You look amazing."

Her smile brightened a few watts. "So do you!"

"I'm sorry I've been AWOL lately," he said. "I want to explain." He had no idea what he would say, but he owed it to her to try.

"Carrie! Where should we set up the table for the silent-auction donations?" someone asked from behind a cluster of potted palms on the other side of the room.

"I have to go," she said, and turned and hurried away.

Then Eldon called him to help move some storage totes to make room for another table, guests started arriving and the evening was off. Danny focused on greeting people, taking drink orders and serving the food, but all the while he was aware of Carrie, moving among the tables, talking to the guests. Why had he ever stayed away from her? He only hoped he would have a chance to get close to her again.

THIS MAY BE the best fundraiser we ever had," Carrie told Sheri as they stood at the edge of the dance floor after dinner, watching couples sway to a sentimental ballad from the band.

"It's certainly the most fun," Sheri said. "We've raised $2,500 from ticket sales, and should bring in more from the silent auction. And our letter-writing campaign is starting to pull in donations, too. I'm feeling more confident about reaching our goal."

Austen joined them. Like the other male volunteers, he wore a suit and tie, his complete with a black-and-gold brocade vest, which gave him the look of an Old West gambler. "Great turnout, isn't it?" he asked.

"It is," Carrie agreed.

"And no trouble from whoever has been harassing us," he said.

"Don't even mention that person," Sheri said.

He turned to Carrie. "May I have this dance?"

Carrie looked around. Several of the other volunteers were dancing—she spotted Hannah and Jake across the room, and Ryan with his girlfriend, Deni Traynor.

"Go on," Sheri said. "Enjoy yourself."

She walked with Austen onto the dance floor and took his hand. "You look especially beautiful tonight," he said.

"It's always a shock to see our fellow volunteers so dressed up," she said. "For instance, I never would have guessed you were the type to own a fancy vest. It's gorgeous."

He smirked. "There's a lot you don't know about me."

She could say the same about all her fellow volunteers. There was so much she didn't know about Danny, for instance, including where he had disappeared to for the last two weeks. He said he wanted to tell her, but she was half-afraid to hear his explanation.

"Carrie? Did you hear what I said?"

She shifted her attention back to Austen. "I'm sorry. What was that?"

"I said, do you have any more ideas about who might be making all this trouble for search and rescue?"

She shook her head. "I don't want to talk about that tonight."

"Sorry. I didn't mean to upset you."

"Excuse me." At the sound of the familiar voice she looked over to see Danny beside them. He smiled at her and she caught her breath. Since when could a smile make her feel this way? "May I cut in?" he asked. Then, not waiting for an answer, he took her hand and she moved into his arms.

"Hey!" Austen protested, but Danny whisked her away.

"Was that very rude of me?" he asked.

"Maybe just a little." She resisted the urge to look back at Austen. She wanted to keep her focus on Danny, on the feel of his arm at her back and his fingers entwined in hers.

"You looked like you might welcome an interruption," he said. "You were frowning."

"Was I? Austen wanted to talk about whoever is behind all the attacks on SAR. I told him I didn't want to think about that tonight."

"No," Danny said. "Not now. It's a night for celebrating."

"Celebrating all the money we're raising?" she asked.

"I was thinking about celebrating that we're still a tight team. It's taken every one of us to pull this off."

"That's a good thing to celebrate," she said. "And you're right. Everyone is working so hard."

"Especially you. We might have fallen apart after Tony was hurt, but you kept us all together."

She ought to have been elated by this compliment, but

regret dulled her happiness. "Ted should be here," she said. "This organization always meant so much to him."

"I heard what happened," Danny said. "You did the right thing."

"I did." She sighed. "But I hate it turned out this way. I know he's been fretting over his diminishing role with the team, but that wasn't the way to assert himself."

"I'm thinking of going to see him next week," Danny said. "Maybe I can get him to talk to me."

"That would be wonderful." She squeezed his hand. "Thank you." She glanced around them once more, as much to keep from staring at him as anything. Being here in his arms felt so intimate, yet she was conscious of everyone around them. "A night like tonight reminds me of how much support we really do get from the community," she said.

"I think most people realize any one of them might need us at any time." He grinned. "We could put that on a T-shirt—Search and Rescue, Not Just for Clueless Tourists."

She laughed, and felt the knot she had been carrying around in her stomach loosen a little. Maybe this wasn't the serious conversation she and Danny needed to have, but it was a step in the right direction.

THE DANCING LASTED until midnight, when the music stopped and Carrie and Sheri thanked the remaining guests for attending and announced the silent-auction winners. Then the cleanup work began. Almost everyone pitched in to help, including volunteers who hadn't signed up for the duty. Within half an hour they had the tables put away, the decorations taken down and the plants arranged by the door, ready to go back to the florist who had loaned them out for the evening.

Danny stayed near Carrie as much as possible, and lingered until they were the only two left.

"Leave the plants and I'll get them back tomorrow," Carrie said.

"I can help with that," he said.

"You don't have to," she said. "I know you're busy."

"I was busy, but I'm not now." He took her hand. "That's one of the things I wanted to talk to you about."

"You don't owe me any explanations," she protested, though she didn't pull away.

"I think I do." He led her to the old sofa, which had been moved back to its usual spot at the side of the room. "Just let me say this, okay?"

"Of course."

They sat, and he let go of her hand, aware that he hadn't prepared for this moment. "So, you know I left town to deal with some family stuff."

"That's what your text said, yes."

"It was true. I know I was vague, but it's not something I really talk about."

"You don't have to tell me—"

"I want to tell you." He wanted her to know this about him, something he didn't share with anyone else. "I went to see my mom, in Iowa. She has…well, she has mental health issues. Several different diagnoses, none of them pleasant or easy. She's fine when she takes her medication. That is, she's able to function pretty well. My sister is there and she helps look after Mom, but sometimes, Mom decides to stop taking the medication and bad things can happen." He paused, reflecting on all the ways that had played out over the years. No need to go into that. "Joy—my sister—can't handle Mom when it gets really bad, so she calls me. I'm usually able to talk her into getting treatment, going back on her meds."

"Oh, Danny. How awful for all of you."

The sympathy in her voice and her expression made his throat tighten. "It can be pretty awful, but we're used to it. It's just what we have to do." He had spent a lot of time when he was younger being angry that he didn't have a mother who did the things his friend's mothers did, or the kind of relationship children ought to have with a parent. Now he accepted this was the way things were. He told himself he didn't need anyone to lean on. He did fine on his own and always had. Most of the time he even believed it.

"Is she okay now?" Carrie asked.

"As okay as she ever gets." He met her eyes, letting her see that he was calm. He was fine. "She was in an inpatient treatment center for a week. She's home now and Joy says she's doing okay. She's upset with me for putting her in the hospital, so she isn't talking to me right now, but she'll get over it."

"I'm sorry." She took his hand and squeezed it and he had to fight not to pull her close.

"After I got home, I needed to make up a lot of shifts at the surgery center," he said. "And I didn't really feel like talking to anyone."

"I can understand that."

"But I wanted to talk to you," he said. He took a deep breath, the way he did before starting a steep descent into a canyon, or anything else that scared him. "That kiss we shared—that was really special. To me, at least. I thought about it a lot while I was gone. I thought about it when things got hard."

"It was special to me, too." She leaned in and touched his cheek, then stretched up and brought her lips to his.

He froze, afraid to move as her mouth pressed to his, afraid of the storm of emotion that threatened to over-

whelm them both. This is what he had thought of when
his mother was raging at him or weeping or flailing at
him with her fists as he tried to keep her from hurting
herself—of being here with Carrie. Of holding her and
her holding him.

She wrapped her arms around him, and her warmth
melted his last resistance. He groaned and returned the
kiss. He had so much he wanted to say to her, but he
couldn't find the words. So he tried to let the kiss convey
his emotions, all the pent-up longing and tender feelings
conveyed through the press of his lips and caress of his
hands. He slid his hands down her sides, shaping his fingers to her firm curves, pressing his body against hers,
letting her feel how much he wanted her.

She pulled him down on top of her, one leg wrapped
around his thigh, her tongue teasing the sensitive nerves
of his inner lip. It took everything in him to pull away—
just for a second. "Do you want to go back to my place?"
he asked, his voice ragged.

She smiled up at him, a wicked, sexy look that had
his heart racing even faster. "We could—or we could
stay here," she said.

"Good idea." The sofa was comfortable enough, and
the dim light lent an intimacy to the setting. And really,
what did it matter where they were? He didn't intend for
either of them to focus on their surroundings. "Give me
a second," he said.

He made himself get up and move to one of the bins
where they kept the medical kits. He fished out a foil-
wrapped condom and returned to the sofa.

Carrie laughed. "I wondered if anyone ever used
those," she said.

He eyed the gold packet. "I never have," he said. "But
the wilderness-medicine course I took emphasized that

you could use them to protect digits or as a makeshift tourniquet, so we keep a few on hand."

Smiling, she took the packet from him. "Why don't you make sure the door is locked? We don't want to be disturbed."

While Danny crossed the room to check the door, Carrie slipped off her dress and undergarments. The look on Danny's face when he returned to the sofa and found her naked was worth her slight self-consciousness. Danny wasted no time undressing, and she was happy to lie back and admire his muscular shoulders and legs and firm abs. All that training for rescue work had some definite physical benefits.

He retrieved a couple of blankets from the supply closet and joined her on the sofa once more. "This is nice, isn't it?" he said as he snuggled against her, then bent to kiss her again.

It had been a long time for her, but she was pretty sure sex was never this good before. Danny lived up to his reputation as a skilled lover, considerate and tender, making sure she enjoyed herself while clearly also enjoying himself. He took his time, touching and admiring her and encouraging her to do the same. Just the feel of him beneath her hands was exciting, and the easy way he laughed off the awkwardness of trying to arrange themselves on the narrow sofa was its own kind of foreplay.

By the time he knelt over her, condom in place, she was trembling with eagerness. She caressed his hips and lifted her own to guide him inside. She closed her eyes and let out a low moan as he filled her, the sensation almost overwhelming, but so, so good.

She felt the tension of him holding back, and urged him to move faster and go deeper, but he insisted on slowing things down, building the moment until, when her climax finally overtook her, she cried out and gripped him hard. When she opened her eyes, he was smiling down at her, and her emotions overwhelmed her so much she had to bite her lip to keep from telling him she loved him. She was sure such a declaration would send him running away. And really, what she loved was the way he made her feel right now, and that was something different, wasn't it?

Afterward, they lay in each other's arms with the blankets draped over them. She snuggled against him, and fought the desire to stay here all night, his arms wrapped around her, his warmth seeping into her. Instead, she forced herself to raise her head from his shoulder and brush the hair out of her eyes. "I wish I could stay, but I need to get home," she said. That was one reason she hadn't wanted to go back to his place. Leaving his bed would have been even harder than getting up off this sofa.

He nodded and sat up. "I meant what I said earlier— I'll help you with those plants tomorrow."

"If you really want to do that." She wasn't going to say no to help—or to seeing him again.

"I really want to see you again," he said as if he had read her thoughts.

"All right. But not too early."

"After lunch? I'll try to visit Ted in the morning and I can report back to you."

She kissed him again. A quick press of her mouth to his, then pulling away before she was tempted to linger. "Thank you."

"I'm the one who should be thanking you. I was sure my disappearing act had ruined my chances with you. I just… I tend to be cautious about relationships."

"Me too." So many emotions weighted those two words. She wanted to ask him where he thought things would go between them after tonight. But she didn't dare. She wasn't prepared to hear that he wasn't ready for a commitment, that a woman with two children was too much, that he was happy to be with her as long as she didn't take things too seriously.

Right. She could try that, couldn't she? Her heart ached at the thought, and she leaned over and picked up her dress from the floor. "I'll see you tomorrow," she said.

They dressed in silence, then put the blankets in the bin to be washed and fluffed up the cushions on the sofa. Danny walked her to her car and gave her the kind of kiss that made her think he wanted her to spend the next few hours thinking about him. No doubt she would do that, but she would try to focus on reliving what had been. She wouldn't let herself anticipate the future. She wouldn't allow herself to hope too much.

Chapter Fourteen

Danny woke far too early, wishing Carrie were there with him. Once she had decided to take a chance on him, she hadn't held back, and he loved that about her. He might even be falling in love with her—scary thought. He immediately pushed away the idea. No sense complicating a good thing with something as unreliable as love.

He rose and dressed and after coffee and a bagel, he got into his truck, made a brief stop in town, then headed out County Road 7 to the Lazy S Ranch. As far as he could tell, Ted didn't do a lot of actual ranching these days. He leased part of the property to a younger man who grazed cattle there some of the year.

Ted's truck was parked in front of the house, a long, low cedar-sided structure in need of paint. Ted opened the door when Danny was halfway up the walk. "What are you doing here?" he asked.

"I wanted to hear your side of what happened with search and rescue," Danny said.

Ted stepped aside and held the door open wider. He looked the same—freshly shaved, dressed in jeans and a button-up Western shirt. He didn't look like a man who was losing it.

"I brought donuts," Danny said, and held up the bag.

Ted took the sack. "I've got coffee in the kitchen." He

led the way through a darkened living room to a kitchen with faded, yellow-striped wallpaper and a metal kitchen table with mismatched chairs. He filled two white ceramic mugs with coffee—black—and sat at the table. "What did they tell you happened?" he asked.

"You were first on the scene and didn't wait for the others," Danny said. He took a donut and bit into it.

"Yeah, well, the car wasn't in a good position." He sipped his coffee. "I think it would have slid on down if I hadn't grabbed the girl when I did."

"What would you tell a rookie who did something like that?" Danny asked.

"I'm not a rookie."

Danny said nothing, but he didn't look away, either.

Ted shifted in his chair. "I've been with search and rescue longer than anybody else," he said. "That ought to earn me the benefit of the doubt."

"When I joined the group, you told me search and rescue isn't about individual heroes. It's about the team."

Ted stared down at the table. Danny was surprised to see that his scalp showed through his hair in places at the top of his head. "Carrie kicked me out," he said.

"She hasn't committed anything to record," Danny said. "There's been no formal report."

"Everybody knows what happened."

"Everybody still thinks of you as the founding member who stayed with the group the longest. You could keep that reputation."

"What am I supposed to do—just resign?"

"Isn't that better than being kicked out?"

The silence stretched so thin Danny could hear the warmer on the coffee machine cycling on and off. He finished the donut and sipped the last of the coffee. "Somebody will need to take the old climbing ropes to Luray

Elgin," Ted said finally, "if I'm not going to be around to see to it."

"Is she the woman who makes rugs out of climbing rope?" Danny asked.

"Yeah. You ever seen them?"

Danny shook his head.

"They're pretty amazing looking—all those bright colors. We give her the retired ropes that aren't safe for climbing and she donates 20 percent of her profits to Eagle Mountain Search and Rescue."

"I'll make sure she gets the ropes," Danny said.

Ted nodded and picked out a donut. "What do you think you'll do with all your free time?" Danny asked.

"I've been thinking of writing a book."

Danny tried to hide his surprise but was pretty sure he failed. "A book?"

"Yeah." Ted grinned. "I'm not an ignorant cowboy, you know. I read a lot. I'm thinking of writing a history of Eagle Mountain Search and Rescue."

"You're the perfect person to do that," Danny said.

"I am."

They made small talk after that, about the fundraising dance, Ted's ranch and stories he might put in his book. Before Danny knew it, it was almost noon. He slid back his chair. "I'd better go. I promised Carrie I'd help her return some plants we borrowed for the dinner dance."

"How did that go?" Ted asked.

"It went well. I think we raised several thousand dollars, and Sheri says more donations are coming in all the time."

"That's good." Ted shoved to his feet. "Tell Carrie I'll turn in my letter of resignation in a few days. She can throw a party."

"You deserve a party," Danny said. Yes, the older man

had made a mistake, but that didn't take away from all he had done before.

Carrie was waiting out front when Danny arrived at SAR headquarters. She moved into his arms and kissed him eagerly. He wondered what she would think if he suggested another session on the sofa. She must have been thinking the same thing, because she stepped back. "I only have an hour before I need to get back home," she said.

"Then, we'd better get the plants loaded."

It only took a few minutes to arrange all the pots in the back of Carrie's SUV. "Did you see Ted this morning?" she asked when they were done.

"Yes. And he's calmed down a lot." He shared the gist of their conversation, including the information about Luray Elgin and Ted's message that he would be resigning.

"We'll throw him a farewell bash," Carrie said. "And I'll make sure the newspaper knows all he's done for the organization over the years."

"He'll like that. And you're bound to still hear from him regularly. He seems serious about writing a history of SAR."

"That would be wonderful."

Danny checked his watch. "There's just one more thing. I want to take a look and see how much rope Ted has set aside for Luray," he said. "He keeps it all in the boiler room, so it doesn't get mixed up with the good rope."

"Sure. Let's take a look." She led the way to the back of the building, and a door marked Boiler. He opened it, then reached up and pulled the chain on the overhead light to illuminate a space that contained the dark metal boiler, a mop bucket and some gallon jugs of cleaners, and a large wooden crate overflowing with a tangle of multicolored climbing rope.

"Looks like it's been a while since Ted made a delivery to Luray," Danny said. He bent and tried to heft the crate, but it wouldn't budge.

"All that rope is bound to be heavy," Carrie said.

"It is." He straightened and frowned at the tangle "But not that heavy." He grasped a coil and tugged it out of the way. "Help me get some of this out of here," he said.

She helped him pull at the lines until a mass of them came free and tumbled onto the floor of the boiler room. He spotted a glimpse of orange beneath the rope.

"What is that?" Carrie asked, and reached in to clear more rope.

But Danny was faster. He leaned past her and pulled at the object at the bottom of the crate. He lifted the hydraulic extractor—the Jaws of Life—onto the pile of cords between them.

Carrie stared. "Did Ted put that there?" she asked.

"I don't know," Danny said. "But we need to find out."

TED GREETED THEM at the door to his house, coffee mug in hand. He slid his gaze over Carrie, then addressed Danny. "What are you two doing here?"

"We need to talk." Carrie said. "Please?"

"I already told Danny I'm sorry about what happened," Ted said. "I don't need you to lecture me about what I did wrong."

"No lectures," she promised. She wasn't angry with Ted, at least not anymore. Going after that girl on his own had been wrong, but no one had been hurt and she believed he regretted his actions. But hiding the Jaws from the rest of them was another story. She needed to understand why he would have done such a thing.

"We found the Jaws," Danny said. "The extractor."

"That's good," Ted said. "Where was it?"

"Can we come in?" Danny asked.

Ted turned and led them through a room that reminded Carrie of her uncle's place before he remarried—worn furniture, dust on the tables beneath a clutter of old magazines and books, and half-empty coffee mugs and glasses. A room that was a little neglected, just like the man himself.

On the wall by the door to the kitchen were a series of plaques—awards Ted had received over his years with search and rescue. Volunteer of the Year. For service as search and rescue captain. A state award for outstanding service. The plaques were dusted. Shiny. Loved.

"Coffee?" he asked, already filling his mug from an old-fashioned coffee machine beside the sink.

"No thanks," Carrie said.

"Nothing for me," Danny said. He lowered himself into a chair on one side of the vintage metal and Formica table. Carrie sat across from him and Ted took the chair at the end.

"You two look like you're getting ready to face a firing squad," Ted said. "Or maybe you're the ones who are going to do the shooting." He sipped his coffee. "What's this about?"

"We found the Jaws of Life," Danny said.

"Yeah, you said that. Where was it?"

"It was under the discarded climbing ropes in the storage closet," Carrie said.

"Huh." He set the coffee mug down with a thump! "Who put it there?"

Carrie looked to Danny. What had seemed so obvious when they had been standing in that closet together wasn't so clear now. Was Ted really this good of an actor?

"We thought maybe you did," Danny said.

Ted's shoulders slumped. "You think I'd put some poor person's life in danger with a stupid prank like that?" There was more hurt than anger in the words.

Carrie reached out and touched his hand. "I don't know what to think, Ted," she said. Not now, after seeing him here like this, and remembering all search and rescue had meant to him. "Do you know anything that could help us?"

He shook his head, and lifted the coffee mug to his lips once more. The fingers that wrapped around the handle of the mug were creased and scarred—hands that had gripped ropes and carried litters and cradled injured people in canyons and on mountaintops where most people wouldn't go.

"When was the last time you were in that storage closet?" Danny asked.

"I don't know," Ted said.

"Think," Danny said. "The Jaws went missing three weeks ago. Was it before or after that?"

Ted set the mug down again. "It was before that. After Tony fell, when we checked all the ropes. Sheri and Ryan and I went through the lot and pulled out a couple that were near their expiration date. I took them in there and added them to the pile. I remember thinking I needed to take them to Luray, but then it slipped my mind. I haven't been in there since."

"Have you seen anyone else in there?" Carrie asked.

"It's just a closet," he said, an edge to his voice. "Anybody could go in there. Somebody who needed cleaning supplies, for instance."

"The extractor was hidden under the coils of rope," Danny said. "Someone just looking in there wouldn't have seen it. We didn't see it until we picked up the rope."

"Well, I didn't put it there. But I sure don't belong with search and rescue anymore if you think I would."

His lips trembled and Carrie looked away. "I know you wouldn't do anything to hurt anyone," she said. "You've been the anchor of our organization for years and I'm going to make sure people don't forget that." She stood, and Danny rose also, but Ted stayed seated.

"I'm not the one behind all these things happening to SAR," Ted said. "But I hope you find the person who is. So far they've managed not to hurt anyone badly, but pretty soon our luck is going to run out. Someone is going to end up dead, whether it's someone from SAR, or a person we could have saved."

She nodded. It had been easy to dismiss most of their persecutor's actions as petty, but Tony had almost died from his accident, and hiding the Extractor could have had really serious consequences if they needed the equipment to get someone in distress out of a vehicle. "We're doing everything we can," she said, but even as she said the words, she knew that wasn't enough.

She waited until they were back in Danny's car before she spoke. "We can't just wait for the next bad thing to happen," she said. "We need to do more to find the person behind all these incidents."

"What else can we do?" he asked.

"I was hoping you had an idea."

"I have lots of ideas, but nothing to do with that."

She turned to him and he winked, which made her laugh in spite of everything. He took her hand. "Maybe if we put our heads together, and list everything we know about these incidents, we'll see some common thread," he said. "We'll notice some person who was involved every time."

"That's a good idea. But I have to be home." She

glanced at her watch. "In five minutes. My mom is going out with friends and I can't leave my kids alone."

"Why don't I take these ropes to Luray and bring dinner over in a few hours? After we eat, we can make a list."

She hesitated. Inviting him over was a big step—something that signaled he was more than just a fellow volunteer. Still, her kids knew and liked him.

"Is that not a good idea?" he asked.

"No. It's a great idea." She smiled, and hoped she was successful at hiding her doubts. "The kids will love it. And so will I."

It's just a casual dinner, she reminded herself. It didn't have to mean anything.

INCIDENT #1: TONY'S FALL
    People present: Carrie, Danny, Ted, Sheri, Ryan, Eldon, Hannah, Austen, Tony
    Incident #2: Beast burned
    People present: ???
    Incident #3: Austen run off road
    People present: Everyone was at the meeting. (Austen and Ted were both late)
    Incident #4: Money stolen from fair
    People present: Austen, Sheri (other volunteers were at the fair)
    Incident #5: Jaws goes missing
    People present: Everyone except Hannah
    Incident #6: Carrie's tires flattened
    People present: Everyone except Sheri, Hannah, and Ted.

Heads together, Carrie and Danny studied the chart they had made. Their take-out dinner of Chinese food had been cleared away, though the scent of cashew chicken and shrimp lo mein lingered. Dylan and Amber were in the other room, playing a noisy game of checkers, which Amber had only recently learned to do and was determined to never lose. The children had been comically blasé about Danny's arrival with dinner, though Carrie had caught them sending excited looks to one another. Whether because she had invited a man home or because she had invited this particular man, she couldn't be sure. She had chosen to ignore them, and Danny either hadn't noticed or was playing it cool also.

"Almost all the rescuers were at or near the scene at the time of most of the incidents," Carrie said. "Jake and Hannah and you were away for part of the time—but I never suspected you—or Sheri, Jake or Hannah, for that matter."

"That's the problem—we don't want to suspect anyone." Danny leaned back in his chair. "Ted still had the most opportunity, to my mind. And you have to admit, he hasn't been acting himself lately."

"I can't believe it," she said. She looked at the chart again. "I can't believe any of it, really."

"Maybe we should talk to Jake," Danny said. "Find out if the Sheriff's department has come up with anything they're not telling us. And we should tell them about finding the Jaws."

"You're right. I'll call tomorrow and set up a meeting." She stifled a yawn.

Danny slid back his chair. "I'd better go. Thanks for dinner."

"You bought the dinner," she said. He had refused to let her reimburse him.

"Then, thanks for your company." He kissed her cheek. "Your kids are great, by the way."

"They are." She walked him to the door, aware of a sudden silence in the other room. Danny shrugged into his jacket, gave her another kiss on the cheek and left. She waited until he was in his car, then turned toward the living room. Dylan and Amber both stared intently at the checkerboard. "Cut the act, you two," she said. "I know you were spying on us."

Dylan wrinkled his nose. "That wasn't much of a kiss good-night."

"What do you know about it?" Amber asked. She looked up at her mother. "I like him," she said, with such a sweet smile it made a lump in Carrie's throat.

Carrie held out her arms. "Come here, you two."

They came and let her hug them close—something Dylan was less and less inclined to allow. "Is Danny your boyfriend?" Amber asked.

Was he? "Maybe," Carrie said. "But whatever he is, the two of you still come first. Understand?"

They both nodded, solemn, and allowed one last hug before Dylan squirmed away. "Tell him he can bring over Chinese food anytime," he said.

The front door opened. "I'm home," Becky called. A few moments later, she came into the living room.

"How was your evening?" Carrie asked.

"It was good. You know Clara and Marie and I always have a good time. How was yours?"

"Danny came over and brought us Chinese," Amber volunteered.

"Oh, he did?" Becky sent her daughter a look full of questions. "Search and rescue business?"

"He kissed her good-night," Dylan said, then collapsed into giggles.

Carrie cursed her tendency to blush so easily. "I think it's time for a certain boy and girl to go to bed," she said.

She spent the next half hour getting her children off to sleep. Her mother was waiting in the kitchen when Carrie returned. Becky was studying the chart they had made. "Is this everything that has happened with SAR?" Becky asked.

"Yes. Danny and I were trying to see if there was any commonality among all the incidents that we had missed."

"It's good to have another adult to bounce ideas off of," Becky said.

Carrie sensed a question mark at the end of this statement, an invitation for her to say more about her relationship with Danny Irwin. "We're just...getting to know each other," she said. "It's early days. Don't read too much into it."

"I won't," Becky said. "But it's good to see you happy."

Was she happy? Sometimes, she was ecstatic. Also confused. And afraid. Nervous about messing this up. Hoping for more than was probably possible.

In other words, everything was proceeding in a perfectly normal way. The way life always seemed to do.

Chapter Fifteen

Monday morning, Danny was coming out of the coffee shop when he spotted Deputy Jake Gwynn across the street. Jake waved and Danny crossed over to fall into step beside the deputy. "Did Carrie call you?" Danny asked.

"She did. She told me the two of you found the hydraulic extractor in the supply closet."

"Yes, and we can't figure out who put it there. Has the investigation turned up anything?"

Jake shook his head. "No. These events are so random and seemingly unconnected, and so far whoever is responsible isn't leaving behind any evidence. I'm sorry I don't have better news for you."

"Do you still think a volunteer is behind all the harassment?" Danny asked.

"I don't see how someone from outside the organization could have committed those crimes," Jake said. "At least, the attempt on Tony's life and the arson to the Beast were crimes. A good defense attorney would probably argue that the extractor was just misplaced."

"It wasn't misplaced," Danny said.

"I know. I'm just saying what would probably happen in court," Jake said. "It's not enough to be suspicious about someone. We have to have a lot of proof in order to make an arrest."

Danny sipped his coffee, wishing he had some kind of proof to offer, but there was nothing.

"Whoever it is hasn't done anything recently," Jake said. "Maybe they're tired of it. Or something happened to scare them off."

"It doesn't feel good knowing someone I have to depend on in a bind could be behind this," Danny said. "And that they've gotten away with it. Tony could have died. That's attempted murder."

"If we find the person responsible, we'll charge them, but right now we just don't have evidence."

They reached the public lot where Danny had parked his car. "I have to get to work," he said. "It was good talking to you, even if the news wasn't what I wanted to hear."

"We'll let you know if we turn up anything new," Jake said. "We're not going to give up."

Danny's mood didn't improve as he drove to work. He couldn't shake the feeling that he was letting Carrie down. This was what he hated about getting too close to other people—this feeling that he wasn't doing enough to help. He had spent his whole life feeling that way with his mom and though he knew it was wrong, he could never completely lose the guilt.

He was in the employee locker room, about to begin his shift, when his supervisor, Helene, leaned around the doorway. "Danny, can I see you in my office a minute?" she asked.

He doubted anyone heard those words and didn't feel a clench in their stomach. He shut the door to his locker. "Sure," he said, and followed her to the cramped space that served as her office. Helene, a cheerful, round-faced woman with a mass of short blond curls, settled into the worn desk chair.

"Don't look so worried," she said as he sat in the chair across from her, his knees pressed against the metal front of her desk. "This is good news."

"What is it?" he asked, still wary.

"A supervisory position has come open and I want to recommend you."

"What supervisory position?" Usually, the rumor mill broadcast this kind of thing for weeks before any official announcement.

"Actually, I'm leaving to take a position with the hospital in Junction." She smiled. "I want you to take over here."

Both of these statements—that she was leaving and that she wanted him to replace her—surprised him. "You know I'm not interested in supervising anyone," he said.

"That's what you always say, but Danny, you've got more experience than everybody else. And you're good with people—patients and coworkers. You could do this. It would mean more pay, a step up the ladder."

He shook his head. "I'm not interested."

"At least think about it." She smiled in a way he thought was meant to be encouraging. "You're not getting any younger."

"You're not getting any younger" was code for "Isn't it about time you grew up?" Stepped up. Took responsibility. But all being responsible had brought him was more disappointment. Why take the risk when he didn't have to?

CARRIE'S PHONE CONVERSATION with Jake Monday morning left her frustrated. If the sheriff's department, with their access to forensic testing and computer databases couldn't come up with anything that even pointed to a suspect in all the crimes that had been committed against search and rescue, what chance did the rest of them have of stopping whoever was responsible before someone was seriously hurt?

This was still on her mind when she sat at her desk later that morning. A large yellow sticky note on her computer screen said "See me about the Cornerstone project!" in bold letters printed with a marker. The note wasn't signed, but she didn't have to wonder who it was from. Bracing herself for the worst, she rose and went to Greg Abernathy's office.

"You wanted to see me?" she asked.

Abernathy looked up from his monitor. As usual, he was dressed straight out of a Ralph Lauren ad, his leather vest too uncreased and his boots too unscuffed to pass for authentic. "Miles Lindberg isn't happy with the plans for his new building," he said.

She waited, refraining from pointing out that those plans weren't the ones she had originally drawn up for Lindberg. The ones he had been enthusiastic about when she had shown him the preliminaries.

"You need to redo them," he said.

"What, exactly, does he want changed?"

"He wants a walled courtyard connecting the new and old construction."

"That was in my original drawings." She should have stopped there but couldn't help herself. "The ones Vance changed."

"No, it wasn't," he snapped. "You don't know what you're talking about."

She drew in a long, slow breath. "I'll call Mike and find out exactly what he wants," she said.

"No!" Abernathy rose, both hands flat on the desk,

leaning toward her. "I'll have Vance do it. You don't need to talk to Mike."

"Part of getting the plans right is consulting with the client," she said. "I need his input to do a good job."

"Vance will tell you what to do," Abernathy said. "This is his project now. You're his assistant."

It was my project until you gave it away, she thought. Her stomach hurt, and the tension at the back of her neck foretold an imminent headache—one that probably wouldn't go away as long as Abernathy and Vance were in this office.

Or as long as she was.

The truth of that thought came into her head with blinding clarity. Yes, this was the only architectural firm in Eagle Mountain. The only employer who would give her the flexibility she needed to be with her children. But what was stopping her from changing that? There was no law saying she couldn't open her own firm, and make her own rules. She held her breath, letting the idea sink in. It was ridiculous. Foolish. She had a family to support. A reputation to protect.

Abernathy wasn't doing her reputation any favors, though. Not as long as he refused to give her more responsibility and blamed her for other people's mistakes. She met his gaze directly. "You'll have my letter of resignation within the hour," she said, surprised at how calm she sounded.

"What?" The word emerged as the squawk of a startled rooster. "You can't resign."

"I can, and I will." Not waiting for more, she turned and retreated, not to her desk, but to the ladies' room, the one place she could be sure Abernathy wouldn't follow. Once sure she was alone, she pulled out her telephone and called her mother.

"Carrie? Is everything all right?" Becky sounded alarmed—probably because Carrie almost never called her at work.

"I just quit my job," Carrie said.

"Good for you."

Her mother's reaction surprised her. "You don't think I was being too rash?"

"I think it's long overdue. Those chauvinists are never going to give you the credit you deserve."

"You never said anything."

"It wasn't my place, but now that you've done it, I think you made the right decision."

"I think I'm going to open my own business," she said. "Try to find some clients."

"That's an excellent idea."

"It will probably take me a while to get off the ground and make any money."

"I have savings. We'll be fine."

Her mother sounded so calm and confident. She made Carrie feel that way, too. "Thanks," she said. "I just wanted to let you know. I have to go write my resignation letter now."

"Don't let them talk you out of this," Becky said. "It's really for the best."

Abernathy didn't try to talk her out of it, and Vance didn't even bother to stop by her desk to say goodbye. Carrie left her letter of resignation on Abernathy's desk, then packed her belongings in a box that had once held copy paper and left under the curious eyes of a few clerks and the receptionist. "Good luck," the receptionist, Lynn, said, and flashed a brief smile.

Carrie loaded the box into the back of her SUV, then sat in the driver's seat, shaky and a little light-headed. She was elated and terrified, mind spinning with plans for the future. She would need to find office space, but it didn't have to be anything big or fancy. She could contact the local real estate companies and contractors, and let them know she was available to design new construction or additions. She would need to register her business, open a bank account, maybe take out an ad in the paper. She needed a business plan and a budget. Should she talk to the bank about a line of credit?

She dug a notepad from her purse and began making a list, energized by all the ideas flooding her brain. She was so lost in her plans she didn't register her ringing phone at first. The call was from emergency dispatch.

"Hello, Carrie," Rayanne's pleasant voice said. "We just received a call about a climber fallen in Horse Thief Canyon. Near Mile Marker 6, where County Road 31 parallels the gorge."

Carrie made note of the location on her pad. "Who called it in?" she asked. "What did they say?"

"They didn't leave a name and they weren't on the line long enough for our system to register the number. Either that or they were calling from a phone with blocking software or something. Sorry I don't have more for you. The sheriff's department is responding, so there should be an officer to meet you there."

"Thanks, Rayanne." Carrie ended the call and immediately started typing a text to the other volunteers. As many as were available would respond. As she entered the location information, she realized this was very close to where they had been training the day Tony was injured. A shudder went through her at the memory.

She hit Send, then turned the key in the ignition, intending to drive to search and rescue headquarters. But before she could pull away from the curb, her phone rang again, with a call from Austen.

"Hello, Carrie?" Austen sounded out of breath. "I need your help."

The real fear in his voice startled her. "Austen, what's wrong?"

"I got the text about the fallen climber and I realized I was right here," he said. "I mean, I was less than a mile away. Now I'm here at the location and I don't know what to do. I can hear someone down there. Someone screaming." His voice broke. "I think they're really hurt. I don't know what to do."

"It's okay," she said. "Just…calm down. Wait for the rest of the crew to arrive. Remember, we're a team. Wait for the team. We'll be there soon."

"Can you come right now?" he asked. "I don't have enough experience to handle this. It's freaking me out."

"I'm on my way to SAR headquarters now." She shifted into gear and checked her mirrors before pulling out into the empty street.

"Please, could you come now? The rest of the team will get the supplies we need. I'm sorry to be so much trouble, but I'd really appreciate it if you'd come."

He really did sound desperate. She thought back to her own early days with SAR. Being alone at the scene with a hurting person would have shaken her up, too. "All right," she said. "I have to change clothes, then I'll be right there."

DANNY WAS THREE hours into his shift when he got the text about the fallen climber. Helene saw him checking his phone. "Is it a search and rescue call?" she asked.

"A climber has fallen in Horse Thief Canyon," he said.

"We're slow today," Helene said. "You should go."

It was true they didn't have a full schedule today, and he had an informal agreement that allowed him to respond to SAR calls if there was enough staff to cover for him. "Thanks," he said, and headed for his car. He hit his emergency flashers and set out. He would need to stop by SAR headquarters for his full medical pack, which would eat up more time, but he would still arrive in time to back up Hannah for any needed medical care.

The drive from Delta took twenty-five minutes. He was surprised to find the parking lot at SAR headquarters full of vehicles when he arrived. He recognized Hannah's Toyota and Sheri's Subaru, along with several other volunteers' cars. Most of them should have left for the accident scene by now. He hurried to the side door and tried to open it, but it refused to budge.

He pounded on the door. "Hey! Somebody let me in."

Moments later, he heard footsteps approaching. Sheri's face appeared in the small window at the top of the door. "The door is jammed," she said. "Or there's something wrong with the lock. Can you open it from the outside?"

He tried again. "No. What's going on? Why is everyone still here?"

"There's something wrong with the doors," Sheri said. "We got in okay, but now we can't get out."

Was this the work of the person who had been targeting them? "Did you call for help?" he asked. Did they need a locksmith? Or the sheriff?

"Our phones aren't working, either," Sheri said.

Danny pulled his phone from his pocket. The screen showed No Signal, which didn't make any sense. Was a transmitter down somewhere?

Ryan took Sheri's place at the door. "We think something is jamming the phone signal," he said.

This was sounding more sinister by the second. "Where's Carrie?" Danny asked.

"She went straight to the scene." Sheri again. "She said she was meeting Austen there."

"Why didn't Austen come here first?" Danny asked. As a trainee, he wasn't going to be able to do much at the scene by himself.

"I don't know," Sheri said. "Carrie just texted that she was meeting him there."

"So Carrie is alone at the scene with Austen?" Fear was quickly overtaking confusion.

"The sheriff's department was sending a deputy," Sheri said. "I'm so glad you showed up. You're going to have to go for help."

"I'll call someone," he said, and turned away. But he'd do it while headed for Horse Thief Canyon. He had a bad feeling about this.

Chapter Sixteen

The flashing lights of a sheriff's department cruiser marked the location of the accident on County Road 31. Carrie slowed and parked behind Austen's truck in the pullout a short distance from the cruiser. She had stopped at her house long enough to change into technical pants, boots, and a fleece top. Austen was dressed much the same as he trotted toward her down the roadside. "Thanks for coming," he said. "The poor guy is still carrying on down there. I'm really worried about him."

He took her arm and tugged her toward a wider pullout, beyond the cruiser, where she could see ropes beside an anchor, and other climbing gear. "Some of this is my stuff, but most of it was already here when I arrived," Austen explained. "I guess it belongs to the guy who fell."

She looked around them. "Where's the deputy?"

"He walked up the road a ways to try to get a better phone signal." Austen pointed down into the canyon. "I can't see the guy who fell, but from the sound of him, I think he's just below us."

Just then, a scream of agony sent every hair standing up on the back of Carrie's neck. "Has he been doing that since you got here?" she asked.

"Yeah. It's just terrible. I tried shouting down that help was on its way, but I don't know if he can hear me."

"Was he climbing by himself?" She studied the ropes. There were two sets arranged twenty feet apart, but Austen had said one of them belonged to him.

"I don't know," Austen said. "There was only one set of gear when I got here, but maybe whoever he was with panicked and left. Maybe that's who called in the accident."

"You would think he would stay with his friend," she said.

"I guess everyone reacts differently in a crises," Austen said.

The man down in the canyon screamed again, the sound echoing off the rock walls. Carrie cringed. She told herself it was a good sign that he still had the strength to cry out that way, but he must be terribly injured to be in so much pain. "One of us should go down there and see if there's something we can do to make him more comfortable until the others get here," Austen said.

"We don't have any medical supplies," she said. "Hannah or Danny should be here soon." She looked down the road, hoping to spot someone approaching. But the pavement was empty, the only movement the flashing lights of the cruiser. "Who was the deputy who responded?" she asked. If it was Jake, he was one more trained person she could count on.

"A reserve officer, I think," Austen said. "Nobody I know."

Carrie pulled out her phone as the man in the canyon let out another strangled cry. "Help! Won't somebody help?"

She checked the time—11:30 a.m. Half an hour since she had texted the call to SAR volunteers. Headquarters was only about fifteen minutes away. Say, five or ten minutes there to assemble their gear. Ten or fifteen minutes before that for people to start arriving at headquarters. "The first volunteers should be here any second now," she said.

"If you go on down to the injured man, I can watch from up here," Austen said. "The deputy should be back soon, too, and he can help."

"I'm not going to be able to do anything when I get down there," Carrie protested. "And one of our more experienced climbers, like Sheri or Ryan, will be able to get down there much faster."

Another wail, primal in its terror, cut off her words. "We can't just let him suffer," Austen said. He picked up the pack next to the coils of climbing rope. "I have some medical stuff in here—bandages and splints and a neck brace. Warming packs and stuff like that. He's probably going into shock. At least you could get him warm and stabilized." He slipped on the pack. "If you're too scared to go down there, I'll do it."

"I'm not scared. It's just not proper procedure."

"I think alleviating someone's pain—and possibly saving their life—comes ahead of any procedure," Austen said. "Especially when the others will be here any minute."

She turned away from him, toward the sound of an approaching car, spirits lifting. The gray SUV slowed for the curve, then sped up, past the sheriff's cruiser, on down the road. Not one of the SAR volunteers. Carrie's stomach twisted as the man below began sobbing and pleading with them again. "All right, I'll go down." Anything to stop that poor man's crying. And Austen was right. Shock was a real danger with injuries like these. Getting him warm now might make the difference between him living and dying.

"Use my gear." Austen handed her a harness and climbing helmet.

Carrie stepped into the harness, then put on the gear. She fastened her personal anchor system to the anchors drilled into the rock, double-checking that it was secure. Austen handed her the climbing rope and she tied an overhand knot in one end and clipped this to her harness with a carabiner. Then she threaded the other end of the rope through the rappel rings on the anchors and pulled until the center of the line was in the rings. She gathered the ends of the rope together and tied a stopper knot, pulling hard to make sure it was secure. She clipped her belay device to the rope and to her harness, then unclipped and untied the overhand knot she had made earlier.

"That all looks good," Austen said. "You're ready to go."

She glanced toward the road once more. "I don't understand why no one else is here yet."

"I'm sure they'll be here soon," Austen said, his last words almost drowned out as the man below screamed again. "You'd better get going."

She nodded, then took a deep breath and tossed the rope into the canyon. It uncoiled gracefully, falling free of obstacles. She leaned back to make sure her harness and anchors were secure, checked that the rope below her was even, with stopper knots in both ends. So much of climbing safety was about double-checking and triple checking. When she was satisfied everything was as secure as she could make it, she unclipped her personal anchoring system from the fixed anchors and took her first step backward into the canyon. She kept firm hold on the prussic loop, using it to provide friction to slowly lower herself down. At the same time, she was listening for the arrival of anyone overhead.

"You're doing great," Austen called when she was about ten feet down. "But hurry. Our climber has gotten awfully quiet down there."

It was true there was no longer any noise from the canyon below. Had he lost consciousness, or worse, was he dead? She pushed the thought away and focused on descending into the canyon. For her, that was the only way to get through this task. She needed to concentrate on doing everything exactly as she had been taught. She had to keep herself safe in order to reach the bottom safely, where she could help the person who needed her.

She lowered another ten feet, then some noise at the canyon rim, or maybe some movement of the rope, made her look up. She couldn't see Austen anymore. Had he moved away, or was he simply out of sight because of the angle of her body now? "Austen?" she called.

No answer. A chill went through her. She told herself she was being foolish. Maybe the others had arrived and he had gone to greet them. She couldn't hear anything, but all this rock around her was probably blocking noise.

She continued her slow descent. She wanted to look down and see if she could spot the injured man, but she knew from experience that looking down was a bad idea. She had never been the first to rappel into a canyon before. Every other time she had done this, someone had been waiting at the bottom to steady her as she arrived and help her unclip. She looked to her left, to gauge how much farther she had to go, and was dismayed to see that she was only about halfway through her descent. She had always envied other climbers, like Tony and Sheri, who seemed to float down, descending rapidly and easily. For her, every rappel was an exercise of physical and mental will.

"How are you doing?"

She looked up and was relieved to see Austen, leaning over to look down at her. "I'm good," she called up. "Halfway there."

"It's a long way to fall," he said.

Was that his idea of a joke? "I'm not going to fall!" she shouted up at him. "Is anyone else there yet?"

"They won't be coming," he said. "It's just you and me."

"Of course they're coming!" she said. Why was he behaving so oddly? "Quit making stupid jokes."

"It's not a joke. Not a joke at all." He held something out in his hand. "I'll say goodbye now, Carrie. I have to leave soon."

"What are you talking about? Austen, stop it!" He was frightening her now.

"This is a bottle of acid," he said. "I'm going to pour it on the ropes. The whole thing, not just a little, like I did with Tony. You might be able to climb a little farther down before the ropes give way, but I doubt it."

His words had the effect of drenching, icy water. She couldn't breathe, and she couldn't move. *He* was the one who had tried to kill Tony? The one who had destroyed the Beast and hidden the Jaws and everything else that had plagued them. "I thought you loved search and rescue!" she shouted. "Why would you do this?"

"I loved Julie," he said. "Search and rescue was supposed to save her, but you didn't. I can't bring Julie back, but I can make you pay for her death."

She wanted to argue that they had done everything in their power to save his fiancée. She had simply been too badly injured to recover. And they had worked to save Austen's own life. But she knew there was no sense trying to reason with a man who would pour acid on a climber's ropes. "Austen, don't do this!" she said instead.

"Goodbye, Carrie," he said, and moved the container of acid closer to the ropes.

DANNY SCROLLED THROUGH the directory on his phone until he found Jake's direct number, then hit the call button as he started the engine in his car. The call didn't go through on his first attempt, but as he sped back toward town, his cell signal returned and the phone began to ring. "Hello?" Jake answered.

"Jake, it's Danny. Someone rigged all the doors at search and rescue headquarters, and the other volunteers are trapped inside. Their phones won't work, either."

"Where are you now?" Jake asked.

"I'm on my way to Horse Thief Canyon."

"I got the text about a climbing accident there," Jake said.

"Right," Danny said. "The others had reported to headquarters to get their gear to respond to that call when they ended up trapped inside. I was coming from Delta, so I arrived after everyone else. But Carrie got a call from Austen asking her to meet him at the scene, so she bypassed headquarters and drove straight there. She's alone at the scene with Austen and that has me worried."

"Because you think Austen might be the person behind the previous attacks on SAR?" Jake asked.

"I don't know," Danny said. "But the whole situation is wrong—the other volunteers being trapped at headquarters and Carrie and Austen alone at the scene of an accident. Maybe both of them are in danger."

"I'm patrolling in the southern part of the county," Jake said. About as far from Horse Thief Canyon as he could get, Danny thought. "Hang on a minute," Jake said. "I'm going to contact the deputy we sent to the accident site."

Danny focused on driving, one hand clutching the steering wheel, the other his phone as he waited, trying not to think of all the things that could be happening with Carrie and Austen. Was Austen the person behind all the attacks on SAR? He and Carrie had both thought he was too dedicated, and too new to the group to have developed any grievances. "Danny?" Jake asked.

"I'm here."

"I can't raise the deputy. He's not responding to the radio. I'm going to head over there, but it's going to take me at least twenty minutes to get there."

"Could you send someone to get the other volunteers out of search and rescue headquarters?" Danny asked. "I should be at Horse Thief in a few minutes."

"Wait for law enforcement," Jake said. "If Austen or someone else on the scene is behind all of this, you shouldn't confront them."

Danny nodded. What Jake said made perfect sense. Except that Carrie was in danger. He wasn't going to sit on his hands and do nothing if that was the case. "I'll be careful," he said. "But I'm not going to let anyone hurt Carrie." He ended the call and tossed the phone into the passenger seat. It rang again almost immediately, but he ignored it.

He thought back over the events of the past month. Austen had been one of the people helping with the climbing gear the day Tony was injured. Could he have poured acid on the ropes without anyone noticing? He could have come back to headquarters that night and burned the Beast. They had dismissed him as a suspect because he had been attacked himself the next day. But what if he had faked that accident to deflect suspicion? His injury wasn't that bad, and it would have been easy enough to let his truck slide into the ditch and bang his head against the door frame. Austen could have hidden the Jaws in the boiler room. He could have even slashed Carrie's tires.

Danny slapped his hand on the steering wheel as yet another realization hit him. Austen had been working the booth at the fair when the contributions went missing. All he had to do was wait until Sheri was busy talking with someone and he could have taken the money.

They had been so fixated on Ted as the most likely culprit he hadn't considered the rookie. Ted was angry and didn't hide his feelings. What if Austen had come into the group with a grudge and bided his time until he could get his revenge? Maybe his dedication was only an act.

What was the best way to approach this? If he roared up in his car, he might startle Austen—or someone else, if Austen was innocent—into doing something stupid, something that would hurt Carrie. What had happened to the deputy? Was Austen planning another prank, like hiding the Jaws and slashing Carrie's tires, or did he have something more dangerous in mind? The man was clearly unpredictable. Danny would have to be smart, and careful.

He spotted the emergency lights of a sheriff's department cruiser ahead and slowed, then pulled to the side of the road, several hundred yards from the cruiser. He pocketed his phone, then searched for some kind of weapon. Nothing. The first aid kit probably had scissors, but he didn't plan to get close enough to Austen for them to be effective. The only thing in his favor was that he was a lot taller and maybe stronger than the other man. And he wasn't unhinged by whatever motive had led Austen to want to hurt the organization that had first saved his life, then welcomed him as one of their own.

Maybe he was wrong. Maybe Austen was innocent

and there was nothing going on here but two search and rescue volunteers trying to save an injured climber. If that was the case, Danny wouldn't need to do anything but pitch in and help. But being cautious wouldn't hurt anything.

He crossed the road and moved into the cover of trees, trying to assess the situation. The sheriff's cruiser sat empty, the red-and-blue lights silently flashing. He couldn't see anyone inside or near the vehicle. Just past it, Carrie's SUV sat behind Austen's truck in a pullout. And past that, there was Austen. He crouched on the ground next to the rim of the canyon. What was he doing down there?

Heart in his throat, Danny watched from behind a scrubby piñon. Where was Carrie? His gaze fixed on the lines coiled next to Austen, and anchors sticking up from the rock, and with a sickening plummet of his stomach, he realized Carrie must be on the end of the rope. Austen was doing something to them. Was he going to cut through them? No, that wasn't a knife in his hand. It looked like a bottle.

"No!" The word tore from Danny's throat, and he hurtled from the trees and crossed the road at a run.

Austen looked up, then half rose. "Stop right there!" he shouted. "Stop now, or I'll dump all this acid right on top of her."

Danny skidded to a halt, sending a shower of gravel into the canyon below. "Get away from her!" he shouted.

Austen shook his head. "It's too late for that. And don't think you can stop me. If you try to tackle me now, you'll send us both into the canyon. I don't think you want that."

"Danny, no!" He recognized Carrie's voice, from deep in the canyon.

"Are you all right?" Danny called, then decided this

was a stupid question. How "all right" could she be with Austen threatening her?

"You need to leave," Austen said.

Danny glared at him. "You poured that acid on Tony's climbing ropes," he said.

"I didn't use enough," Austen said. "I won't make that mistake this time." He tilted the bottle over Carrie's ropes.

"No!" But it was too late. The acid cascaded over the twined fiber, sending up an acrid stench. Danny knotted his fists, shaking with rage and the frustration of not being able to do anything to help.

The sound of a car door slamming echoed around them like a gunshot. Austen's head jerked in the direction of the sound and he swore.

Danny took advantage of that brief distraction to act. He rushed forward, but instead of pushing Austen, he grabbed him and dragged him away from the canyon rim. Austen fought like a wildcat. He had dropped the acid bottle, but he scratched at Danny's face, kicked him and tried to gouge his eyes. Danny dodged the blows and succeeded in punching the shorter man in the stomach, hard, knocking the wind out of him. Then he forced him to the ground and began pummeling him, determined to beat him into submission.

Strong arms pulled Danny off the now-subdued Austen. "It's okay." Jake patted Danny's back. "Calm down."

Danny nodded and drew in a shaky breath. Austen lay on his stomach on the ground, Deputy Dwight Prentice fastening his hands with flex-cuffs.

"You okay now?" Jake asked.

"Yes."

Jake released him, and Danny immediately turned toward the canyon. "Carrie!" he shouted, and ran to kneel beside the ropes. "Austen poured acid on her climbing ropes." He stared at the spot where he could see the acid had eaten into the rope, weakening the fibers.

"What's going on up there?" Carrie called up, her voice taut with fear.

Danny lay on his stomach and extended head and shoulders over the edge until he could see Carrie. She stared up at him, white-faced beneath an orange climbing helmet. "Is there a ledge, or any kind of hand-and-foot-hold?" he called. "Anywhere you can take some weight off the rope?"

She looked around. "There's a little tree growing out of the rock."

"Do you think it will hold your weight?" Danny asked.

"Maybe."

"Get over to it and tie off on it," Danny said. "I'm going to come down and get you."

A second set of ropes was tied into a pair of anchors twenty yards to the left. He pulled at the rope and it came up easily. Jake moved to help him, and together they brought up the rope. "Is there an injured climber down there?" Jake asked.

"I don't know," Danny said. "But we've got to get to Carrie."

"You don't have any climbing gear," Jake said.

Danny looked down into the canyon. Someone like Ryan or Tony might have been able to free climb down, but he didn't have that kind of experience. "How are you doing, Carrie?" he called.

"I'm tied off on the tree," she said. Was it his imagination or did she sound calmer? "I think it's going to hold."

"We're going to get to you as soon as we can."

A horn honked and he whipped around to see Sheri's Jeep pulling in behind Carrie's SUV. Sheri, Eldon, Hannah and Ryan spilled out of the vehicle. Danny stood. "Did you bring climbing gear?" he called.

"Of course," Ryan said, and turned to pull ropes and harnesses from the vehicle.

"What's the situation?" Sheri jogged up to join them. She stared at Austen, still prone on the ground, a grim-faced Dwight standing over him.

"Austen poured acid on Carrie's climbing ropes," Danny said. "She's tied off on a tree about halfway down the canyon, but we've got to get to her."

Sheri nodded, then turned to Ryan, who had approached, coils of rope over his shoulder. While the two of them conferred, Danny turned to Eldon. "How did the rest of you get out?"

"Gage Walker showed up and busted in the door." Eldon grinned. "It was like something out of a movie."

A movie Danny wouldn't have wanted to see. Eldon nodded to Austen. "What's with him?"

"He's the one who tried to hurt Tony and burned the Beast and everything else," Danny said. "He tried to kill Carrie."

Eldon's eyes widened. "Why did he do that?"

"I don't know." Danny closed his eyes. He didn't even care why Austen had acted the way he had. All he wanted was for Carrie to be safe.

But for the next half hour, all he could do was wait while Sheri, Ryan and Eldon worked to descend into the canyon to where Carrie waited. Long minutes later, she emerged on top once more. "I'm okay," she said as the others swarmed around her. "It was terrifying, but I'm okay." She smiled at Danny and his knees felt weak. He held out his arms and she came to him and he pulled her close, not even caring that the others were watching.

But their moment of closeness lasted only a few seconds. She pulled away and resumed the role of captain. "Someone needs to get down into the canyon and see about the injured climber," she said.

"Sheri is headed down," Ryan said.

"Are you sure someone is down there?" Danny asked.

"Someone was down there, screaming in agony." Carrie bit her lower lip. "They haven't said anything in a long time. We may be too late."

More cops arrived, along with an ambulance and a newspaper reporter. Austen was put into Dwight's cruiser and driven away. "He blamed us for his fiancée's death," Carrie said. "He wanted revenge on all of us for her dying. Joining SAR was just a way to get back at the team."

"That doesn't even make sense," Eldon said.

"These kind of things usually don't." Jake said.

Sheri radioed from the bottom of the canyon. "There's no one down here," she said. "But there is a big tape recorder with speakers."

"I guess that's what I heard," Carrie said. "A recording of an injured person."

"Austen must have been the anonymous caller who reported the fallen climber," Jake said. He gestured to the ropes in the anchors. "He set up all this with the recorder in the canyon to fool you."

"The pleas for help on the recording were so awful," Carrie said. "Anyone would have wanted to help a person who was suffering that much."

"That's what he was counting on." Danny put his arm around her again and she leaned against him.

"The locks on all the doors at search and rescue headquarters had been tampered with," Gage said. "And he probably planted some kind of cell phone signal blocker in the building. You can buy them off the internet."

"He sure went to a lot of trouble," Ryan said. "It's like something out of a spy thriller—jammed door locks and cell phone signal blockers. And he had to climb down into the canyon to set up that recorder, then climb back up on his own."

"I think he had been planning all of this a long time," Jake said.

"What happened to the deputy?" Carrie asked. "The one who first responded to the call?"

"Austen hit him on the head, probably with a rock, and probably when his back was turned," Gage said. "Then he tied him up, gagged him and locked him in the trunk of the cruiser. He's on his way to the hospital to be checked out, but he should be okay." He put a hand on Carrie's shoulder. "What about you? Do you need to be examined?"

"I'm fine. Just…a little shaken up."

"You should go home," Ryan said. "The rest of us can finish up here."

She straightened her shoulders. "I'm still captain. I'm not going to leave the rest of the team behind."

"You should let them mop up here," Gage said. "We need you and Danny to come to the sheriff's department and give a statement." His eyes met Danny's over Carrie's head. "The sooner, the better."

Carrie insisted on driving herself to the Rayford County sheriff's office. Danny followed, his gaze continually returning to the back of her head, his mind bouncing between relief that she was all right, and the terrible image of what might have happened.

CARRIE GOT THROUGH the next hour on automatic pilot. She had no memory of the drive to the sheriff's department, and couldn't have told anyone later what she said in the interview with Deputy Dwight Prentice. She told him everything that had happened from the moment she received the call from the emergency dispatcher until she arrived safely at the top of the canyon, the events playing out in her mind like a movie trailer—the way Austen looked so normal as he encouraged her to help the man in pain at the bottom of the canyon, and the wild edge to his voice as he talked about pouring acid on the climbing ropes and sending her plummeting to her death. "He always seemed so ordinary," she said. "He wasn't angry or resentful or anything like that. I trusted him."

"There was no reason you shouldn't have," Dwight said. "For what it's worth, none of us suspected him, either. He did a good job of not leaving evidence behind."

Finally, they released her and she found Danny waiting for her in the little lobby of the sheriff's department. He pulled her close and she rested her head against his shoulder and closed her eyes. She could have stayed there all afternoon, but after a few minutes, she began to feel awkward. She looked up at him. "Want to hear something funny?" she asked.

"What's that?"

"I quit my job this morning. I thought that would be the thing I remembered most about this day."

"Let's get a cup of coffee," he said.

She followed him to his car and she thought he would drive to a coffee shop. Instead, he drove to his apartment. They climbed the stairs to the four rooms over a T-shirt shop and he fed coffee pods into a machine and poured two cups. Then he sat at his small kitchen table across from her. "How are you doing?" he asked.

"I'm okay." She took a sip of coffee and felt its warmth spread through her. "Getting better every minute."

"Yeah." He stared at the tabletop, both hands wrapped

around his mug, but made no move to drink. "I'm still shaking inside," he said. "I've never been so terrified in my life."

"Oh, Danny." She leaned over and put a hand on his. "It's okay."

He squeezed his eyes shut and nodded. Alarmed, she thought she saw tears. She wanted to reassure him again, but she couldn't find her voice, so moved by the depth of his emotion.

He drew in a deep breath, then finally took a sip of coffee. When he set the cup down again, he looked calmer. Able to look her in the eye. "I don't do commitment," he said. "I can't. I always end up holding back, and hurting people I don't want to hurt."

Was he telling her this as a prelude to breaking up with her? She didn't read it that way. "Is that because of your parents?" she asked. A mother who was mentally ill probably hadn't been able to be there for her children. And it sounded like he spent a lot of time taking care of her now.

"It doesn't take a genius to figure that out," he said. "I guess if you find out at an early age you can't count on the people who are supposed to look after you, it warps you somehow."

"I don't think you're warped," she said. "You spend your life looking after other people. You risk your life to take care of people you don't even know as part of search and rescue." And he dropped everything to take care of the mother who had never really taken care of him.

"Yeah, well, I guess we all try to fill in the gaps in our lives."

Was rescue work her way of filling the gaps—of trying to redeem her failed marriage and her stifled career? "Why are you telling me this?" she asked. It was the kind of intimate confession she wasn't sure she would have had the courage to share.

He took another deep breath, and let it out slowly, like a weightlifter preparing to hoist a heavy burden. "I'm telling you because you make me think about the long-term—sticking with you. That maybe this time I could do it." His eyes met hers. "I'm warning you, I guess. It feels like a big risk."

Her heart pounded, a dull ache in her chest. She rubbed at the spot, trying to massage away the sensation. To push down the mix of fear and elation. "You know how much I don't like climbing," she said. After today, it certainly wouldn't be any easier.

He nodded, eyes questioning.

"But I do it anyway," she said. "Because I know it's important. And I believe it will make a difference." She wrapped both her hands over his. "Some risks are worth taking, no matter how scary they are." She leaned closer. "I think we're worth the risk, don't you?"

His lips met hers in a crushing kiss, equal parts desperation and passion. She stood up and wrapped her arms around him and tasted salt, and didn't know if the tears were hers or his. She was alive. She was with the man she loved, who loved her in return. Everything else seemed minor compared to that reality.

He broke the kiss and stared into her eyes. "Do you really think we can do this?"

"Yes," she whispered, then more firmly. "Yes."

He kissed her again. Somewhere a phone rang. His? Hers? "Do you need to answer that?" he asked, his lips still pressed to hers.

"In a minute," she said. She was going to enjoy this a little bit longer. Right now she was exactly where she needed to be. Where she wanted to be, maybe even for the rest of her life. The thought wasn't as scary as she expected. Maybe finding the right person was like that—like a secure anchor you could count on to never let you down.

Epilogue

"It's time, everyone!" Sheri stepped forward and raised a beribboned champagne bottle. Smiling for the cameras, she brought the bottle to rest against the hood of the bright yellow rescue vehicle parked in front of the search and rescue headquarters. "I hereby christen you Beast Two!"

Carrie joined the crowd in cheering. Two months had passed since the terrible day in the canyon, and search and rescue had rebounded from that near tragedy. In addition to a new Beast, they had three new trainees. Tony was back on limited duty, and even Ted had moved into the new role of historian. He was working on his book, combing through the archives and interviewing past and present volunteers for stories of rescues.

Sheri had been elected the new SAR captain after Carrie had declined to continue in the role. She had a new business to get off the ground, and a new relationship to tend to. She looked across at Danny, who was opening bottles of champagne to distribute among the attendees. Things were going so well with the two of them. She had thought it would be difficult to adjust to having someone in her life constantly, but Danny and she had meshed so easily. The two of them were looking for a house together, while Becky planned to get her own place nearby. His new supervisory position at the surgical center had given him a new enthusiasm for his work as well as an increase in pay that would help them afford a mortgage. Dylan and Amber were excited, too, about the new house, and about Danny being a part of their lives.

"You look happy." Danny joined her, and handed her a glass of champagne.

"I am happy." Happier than she could remember being.

"I talked to Jake just now," he said. "He says the judge has finally set a trial date for Austen."

"That's good." She sipped the champagne. Austen had been charged with two counts of attempted murder and one of arson as well as theft of funds from a nonprofit. He had relocated to Denver while he awaited trial, but the sheriff's office seemed to think they had a solid case against him. Files on his computer showed he had been planning the crimes for months.

"We'll probably both have to testify," Danny said. "Are you okay with that?"

"A little nervous, but it's nothing I can't handle." That was her approach to life these days. Instead of avoiding things that felt scary or uncomfortable, she was forging ahead. She had been climbing three times since the accident, each a little less nerve-wracking than the time before. And she had worked up the nerve to approach contractors and real estate agents, resulting in almost more business than she could handle. She had been able to hire an administrative assistant and was thinking of taking on an intern.

Danny put his arm around her shoulders. "You inspire me," he said.

This wasn't the first time he had said this, and as compliments went, she thought it was her favorite. She had come a long way from the woman whose voice shook the first time she had to address a search and rescue meeting. With Danny by her side, they would both go a lot further.

* * * * *

BISCAYNE BAY BREACH

CARIDAD PIÑEIRO

Chapter One

John Wilson's internal alarms were ringing louder than the warning sirens in a nuclear power plant.

Someone had tried to get into the servers, and he had no doubt why: they wanted to steal the new software he was developing, which made him worry for multiple reasons, other than the obvious attempt at theft. First and foremost was that even he had concerns about what this software could do and what would happen if it fell into the wrong hands. Secondly, because it meant either someone inside the company was behind the attempted hack, or had blabbed to someone outside the company about what was supposed to be a top-secret project.

Regardless of the reason, he had to act to protect his code. But he wasn't sure he could do it alone and there was only one group of people he could think of that could help: South Beach Security.

He had no doubt they would assist if he asked since he'd helped them in the past, but involving the Gonzalezes' family-run agency meant having to deal with one prickly and beautiful family member: Mia Gonzalez.

Their relationship, if you could even call it that, had started off clumsily and ended even more awkwardly. Mia and her cousin Carolina, affectionately nicknamed "the Twins," were well-known social-media influencers and also regularly helped the family with their personal and professional connections to gather valuable information for the agency.

Despite that, he knew he had no choice but to call the Gonzalez family for their assistance. This project was just too important to risk.

But first, he had to take steps to make life more difficult for whoever was trying to hack his company. A scan for malware on all the end points and servers; making sure his cybersecurity programs were working properly; checking for any and all targeted attacks; and finally, changing passwords across his different access points in case any of them had been compromised.

"What's up, bro?" his brother, Miles, asked as he strolled into John's temporary office. Since he'd sold off his tech start-up several months earlier, he and the half dozen or so employees who had come with him were in a small, leased space in a Brickell Avenue building, just a couple of blocks down from the South Beach Security offices.

John swiveled in his chair to face Miles. His brother was dressed casually, like so many Miamians. He wore a pale yellow *guayabera* shirt that hung loosely over sharply pressed khakis. His dark blond hair was cut short on the sides, but longer on top, where strands were ruthlessly plastered in place with gel against the Miami heat and humidity.

It made John feel a little—no, make that a lot—underdressed since when he'd rolled out of bed this morning, he'd jerked on one of his many graphic T-shirts and well-worn jeans. As for his hair, he nervously ran his hands through it to tame the rumpled waves.

"Not much," John lied, wary of mentioning his concerns to anyone in the company, even his brother.

Miles narrowed his hazel eyes, which were so much like his own it was like looking into a mirror. Although sometimes John didn't like what he saw. Like now.

"You sure?" Miles pressed.

"I'm sure. Just a little wonkiness with some code I'm trying to figure out. What are you up to today?" John asked, swiveling back and forth in his chair.

"Heading over to the Del Sol to finalize plans for Friday night's party," Miles said as he tucked his hands into his pockets and tottered back and forth on his heels.

John was so done with Miles's party scene, but his brother enjoyed the attention and the women. He suspected that Miles knew that, hence his slightly guarded reaction. But since the parties were important to Miles, he went along with it.

"Sounds good. Do you think they could add some Cubanos to the menu?" He had a hankering for the tasty pork-ham-and-Swiss-cheese sandwiches he'd shared with Mia when they'd gone out a couple of weeks earlier.

Mia, he thought again with a rough sigh. "Do you think the Twins will be coming?"

Miles shrugged and narrowed his gaze again as he said, "I can invite them if you want but I thought you were done with Mia."

He did a little lift of his shoulders and swiveled to and fro in the chair again. "I am. Just wondering is all."

Miles nodded and flicked a finger in the direction of his computer. "Are you sure I can't help?"

Miles was a decent enough programmer, but John wasn't letting anyone near this software project. He waved him off. "No need. Just doing some routine security checks," he said and nearly bit his lip since it was a different reason than he'd given before. He hoped Miles wouldn't pick up on that.

Miles opened his eyes wide. "Someone hacking us?"

He shook his head and waved his hands again. "Like I said. Routine checks. I'd let you know," he said even though he wouldn't. He'd already been stung once before when leaks about a problem had made his old company's stock price dive. He suspected someone had done it intentionally to short the company's stock.

With a quick salute, Miles said, "I guess I'm off to the Del Sol then. Let me know if you want anything besides some tasty Cubanas."

"Cubanos," John corrected, uncomfortable with how Miles was referring to Mia and Carolina, two Cubanas who would also not appreciate his joke.

"Chill, bro. Just kidding," Miles said with a laugh and left the office, but John saw he was immediately on his phone, and he hoped it was just to coordinate with the hotel about the party.

He hurried to his door, closed it and returned to his desk. After unlocking his smartphone, he checked it out to make sure it hadn't been hacked. Satisfied, he dialed Trey Gonzalez, the current second-in-command at South Beach Security. He'd gotten to know Trey quite well since he and his fiancée, Roni, had investigated him about a month ago when John had been a suspect in one of their cases.

A few weeks after that, right when he'd first started seeing Mia, he'd also helped Trey with a different case involving an abusive ex-husband attacking his ex and bribing building inspectors to ignore dangerous construction issues.

"*Hola*, John. Good to hear from you," Trey said.

John clenched his lips as he said, "I'm not so sure it's a good thing you're hearing from me."

Trey was silent for a moment. "If you need help, we're here. We help our friends."

John was grateful that Trey wasn't doing it solely out of a sense of obligation because John had helped SBS in the past. He'd had few friends in his life, since he was always too busy, first with putting food on the table and later, building his business. But his gut told him that Trey and some of the other Gonzalez family members could actually be friends.

Well, except for Mia, of course. The last thing he wanted was to be in her friend zone.

"Thanks, Trey. I'd like to keep this as quiet as I can," he said, worried that another leak would hurt his new venture.

"Totally understand. Why don't we meet at Versailles at noon? It'll be just two friends having lunch," Trey said.

"I'd appreciate that." John swiped to end the call.

He had several other checks to run so that he could give Trey as much information as he could about the possible hacks during their lunch.

MIA POPPED INTO Trey's office and held up the bag with the *café con leches* and Cuban bread toast she'd picked up at a nearby restaurant to surprise him.

But as she walked in unannounced, it was impossible to miss her brother's brooding look that told her something was up and that it wasn't anything good. When he saw her, however, he shuttered that worried expression, grinned and clapped his hands. "Please tell me that's breakfast."

"It is, *hermano*," she said, and quickly added, "Everything okay?"

He nodded, tight-lipped. "Totally, how about you? What brings you to the office so bright and early, and without Caro?"

"Carolina is doing a short mom-daughter getaway with *Tia* Elena. I didn't feel like being a third wheel and remembered you still had some things to unpack," she said and gestured to the corner of his office, where a few boxes still lingered.

Trey dipped his head to acknowledge it. "I haven't had a chance with everything that's been going on."

Her older brother had definitely had a lot happening between almost being killed during a police investigation, leaving the department, getting engaged and a dealing with a case involving their younger brother, Ricky, and the woman who was now his fiancée, Mariela.

Trey rose and strolled to a small conference table at one side of his office. She followed, laid down the bag and pulled out the breakfast she'd brought. As she did so, her smartphone chirped a message notification.

She pulled out her phone and grimaced as she saw it was from Miles Wilson, inviting her to the Del Sol for a Friday night party.

"You don't look happy," Trey said as he sat at the table, slipped the top off the *café con leche* and took a sip.

She held up the phone for Trey to see. "I gather you're not a fan," he said.

She wrinkled her nose as if she was smelling a dirty diaper because that's how Miles made her feel. Dirty. "Not a fan at all," she said and sat down to have her coffee and toast, although the text had diminished her appetite.

"Is that why you and John—"

"No, it's not, and when did you become such a gossip?" she teased and elbowed her brother playfully as he sat beside her.

Trey chuckled. "When my *hermanita* starts dating an eccentric multimillionaire tech guru."

"He's not all that eccentric and we were never 'dating,'" she said with air quotes for emphasis.

"You were 'going out.' What happened?" Trey kidded with similar air quotes, but despite his lighthearted tone, she sensed there was more behind his question.

She deflected. "Not much. He was nice. We had fun," she said with a slight lift of her shoulders as she sipped her coffee.

"Sounds…boring," Trey replied and wolfed down a big piece of toast.

Surprisingly it had been anything but boring. Too many men treated her as if she was a piece of arm candy to make them look better. To his credit, John hadn't. He'd been respectful and had seemed genuinely interested in finding out more about her as a person. And there had been some sparks, only…

She didn't enjoy the parties, like the one to which she'd just been invited. Or the flashy red Lamborghini he drove. Those things screamed "lack of confidence," and in her mind, there was nothing sexier in a man than confidence.

Like her brother Trey. He had confidence in spades, which was just what was needed to become the next head of South Beach Security. She asked, "You getting settled? *Papi* okay?"

"Yes, and yes. I know *Mami* and he are happy I left the force. *Papi's* doing what he can to make me feel welcome here, even going business-casual," Trey said as he finished the last of his toast and hungrily eyed the half she hadn't touched.

"Take it," she said and pushed the piece toward him.

As he devoured it, she shook her head and said, "You are never going to fit into your tux for the wedding."

He grinned, a boyish relaxed grin that had rarely happened when he was on the police force. "I'll work it off, don't worry."

She didn't. She had never seen her brother as happy as he was now, working with the family and engaged to Roni Lopez, her closest friend aside from Carolina. It made her heart ache with joy for them, but also hurt a little for herself.

Trey was truly happy with Roni.

Her younger brother, Ricky, was seriously in love with Mariela.

And she was…still busy hitting the social scene with Carolina. Not that she didn't like spending time with her cousin. It's just that lately, with her biological clock inching toward thirty, she wanted more in her life. Someone who would be there for her like Trey and Ricky were for Roni and Mariela.

Maybe even a bigger role in her family's business and not just the occasional help that she and Carolina regularly offered. She had a degree in business administration, after all.

As for John Wilson... He wasn't the kind of guy who could give her what she wanted.

You probably weren't a Miamian if you hadn't eaten at Versailles at some time in your life, John thought as he found a parking spot on *Calle Ocho* near the restaurant. There were a number of people lined up at the take-out window—*La Ventanita,* as it was known to locals. If you wanted to know anything about what was happening in Cuba, Little Havana, Miami, or Washington involving Cubans, all you had to do was hang out around *La Ventanita* to find out.

He hoped the restaurant wouldn't be quite as busy as the take-out window.

John got out of the nondescript BMW sedan. He had thought it better to take that than the flashy red Lamborghini Veneno. While it was an amazing vehicle, he didn't really like calling attention to himself, but Miles thought John had to maintain a certain image in order to attract investors for their new venture.

John thought that if anyone was stupid enough to invest money based on the car someone drove, they were asking to be fleeced.

He walked to the hostess podium to ask for a table, but realized Trey was already sitting at one in a back corner of the restaurant. Trey flagged him down and he excused himself and walked to meet the other man.

"Good to see you, John," Trey said and rose to bro-hug him.

"Thanks for agreeing to meet me." John took a seat opposite Trey, his back to the crowd of diners. It occurred to him then that Trey had picked the table and John's seat to provide the highest privacy possible in such a public place.

"Anytime," Trey said and picked up his menu to take a look.

John did the same although he knew what he was going to get. He was hooked on Cuban sandwiches and the teeth-achingly sweet shakes the restaurant made.

When the waitress came over, they ordered, and Trey quickly got to business. "You said you needed help."

John hesitated and bit his lip, but then blurted out softly, "I think someone is trying to steal my new software."

"I'm assuming you don't have a clue who is trying to do that," Trey said nonchalantly.

"I don't. I'm running a bunch of scans. I've beefed up security on the servers and supercomputer—"

"Like beefed-up security technology-wise, not like security guards and alarm systems to keep people out?" Trey asked.

The waitress came over with their shakes and placed them on the table. When she stepped away, John said, "We have some security like that. We hired Equinox ages ago, before I knew about SBS."

Trey picked up his glass to take a sip. "They're a good company. I can call and ask what they're doing and, if you don't mind, add anything I feel may be necessary."

John held up a hand in a go-ahead motion. "It's why I'm hiring you."

Trey shook his head. "We owe you for all the help you gave us with Ricky and Mariela. Not to mention not outing Roni during that earlier investigation. Besides, we're friends."

Friends. There was that word again and John wasn't going to argue with him. He needed friends, especially loyal ones like Trey. "I appreciate that."

"No problem. As for the tech side of things, I know you're a smart guy, but Sophie and Robbie are really good at what they do. Would you mind if they helped out?"

So far John had kept any access to his new program to himself and he really wanted to keep it that way. "I'll give them as much access as I can, but my new code... It's really important to keep it secret."

The waitress walked over and placed their sandwiches in front of them and a plate of ripe plantains in the middle of the table. Trey picked up his sandwich and took a big bite. After he swallowed, he nodded and said, "I get it. We'll respect any boundaries you set, but if you don't mind my asking, what exactly does this program do?"

In truth, even John was having trouble defining just that because the program was proving to do so much more than he'd ever imagined it could. He kept it simple because he was sure that he'd have to explain again once he met with Trey's tech-guru cousins. "It's a program that reviews data, finds trends and makes...predictions," he said, hesitant to use a word like that because it created all kinds of expectations in people's minds.

As expected, Trey arched a dark eyebrow. "Predictions. Like who'll win the next Super Bowl and stuff like that?"

"In theory you could, if you fed those stats into the system, but you could also use it to analyze what your competitors are doing, facial recognition, weather, customer churn—"

"What is customer churn?" Trey asked with a puzzled look.

"How many customers you lost during a specific time frame," John said and took a bite of his own sandwich, enjoying the tasty combo of the meat, cheese, pickles and mustard. He chased down the bite of sandwich with the super sweet mango milkshake and smiled.

"Sounds like it can do a lot," Trey said and snagged a ripe plantain from the plate in the middle of the table.

"It can. You can even use it to predict possible crimes and their victims," he explained, which made Trey perk up.

"Really. How does it do that?" he asked, but John waved him off.

"How about you set up a meeting with your cousins and anyone else you think needs to be in on this case. I can tell you more about how the software works, and we can decide what to do to stop whoever is trying to break in."

"I think that sounds like a plan. Can you come by the office in the morning?" Trey asked and, with a slurpy sip, finished the last of his shake. He ordered another one with a shake of the empty glass in the direction of the waitress.

"Diabetes, much?" John joked.

"I know. For some reason, I've had this horrible sweet tooth lately. Hungry, too," he admitted and forked up another sweet plantain.

"Boredom, maybe? I imagine working at SBS is quite different than what you were doing as an undercover detective."

Trey shrugged his broad, muscular shoulders. There wasn't an ounce of flab on them, or anywhere else on Trey, from what John could see. "Different for sure but in a good way. I like spending time with Roni and my family. You know how it is."

"Actually, I don't. My family life, it was kind of dysfunctional so being around you all... It's really different for me," he admitted.

"Sorry to hear that, John. No matter what happened with Mia—"

"Nothing happened with Mia. I respect her too much to treat her like that," he said to shut down whatever Trey was thinking because he did want this man as a friend.

"Glad to hear that," he said and accepted the second shake

from the waitress as she brought it over. After a healthy sip, he said, "Mind if I come by on Friday to make sure?"

John narrowed his gaze, not understanding, but when it hit him, he muttered a curse. "Miles. He invited Mia and Caro to the party."

"He did. Let's say Mia was less than pleased," Trey admitted.

"I'm sorry. Miles has his own way of keeping both me and the company in the limelight. You can tell Mia she's free not to come," John said and polished off the last of his sandwich.

Trey laughed heartily. "Tell Mia? Did you forget what my little sister is like?"

John smiled. He hadn't forgotten, which was a big part of his problem with Mia. He just couldn't forget her.

"I'll see you tomorrow," he said and motioned the waitress for the check, but when she came with it, Trey snagged it and tucked several bills into the leather wallet.

"Cash is king, John. Remember that. Until we figure out what's going on, no credit cards. Have you checked your phone to make sure it's clean?" Trey said and handed the waitress the wallet.

"As far as I can tell," he admitted.

"Good. We'll have Sophie and Robbie double-check it tomorrow during the meeting," he said and rose, but when John started to stand, Trey signaled for him to sit.

"Wait a few minutes and then go. No sense risking that anyone sees us together until we have more info on what's happening," he said and, without waiting for a reply, he left.

John sat there, running his straw through the runny remains of his shake. He hungrily eyed the last ripe plantain on the plate before giving in and eating it. Impatient, he looked at his phone and figured it had been at least a few minutes since Trey had left.

He got up and walked out, satisfied that he'd taken the

right steps to protect himself and his new software. He hoped that being with the Gonzalez family might give him another chance with Mia.

CLACK, CLACK, CLACK went the fake shutter on his digital camera.

He zoomed in with the telephoto lens to get a better look at the man who had been sitting with Trey Gonzalez, and as he zoomed in, he sucked in a sharp breath.

"John Wilson," he murmured. He recognized the man from some news reports on a recent charity event Wilson's new software company had sponsored.

Interesting, he thought, wondering what the tech multi-millionaire had to do with Trey. As far as he knew, it was Mia who had been hanging out with the man. Maybe that's what this little meeting had been about: what Wilson's intentions were toward Mia.

The Gonzalez family was a little old-fashioned that way. They stuck together. Protected their own.

Too bad they hadn't cared at all about what had happened to his family. How his family had suffered over the years while the Gonzalez family had achieved the American Dream.

He intended to make sure that they'd pay for that suffering when the time was right, and his gut told him that would be soon.

He'd been patient after the last attack, waiting for them to let down their guard. It had dropped…a little. That was obvious from what he'd seen of today's lunch meeting.

Trey had done his best to hide in that back corner and not be seen with John Wilson, but he didn't know who he was dealing with. Trey and his family had underestimated the danger for months now, but soon he would give them what they deserved: the same kind of pain and loss he and his family had endured for over sixty years.

Soon, he thought, and snapped off a few more photos.

Chapter Two

When John returned to his office, his brother was there. His feet were up on his desk and the chair was leaning back precariously. Miles was thumbing through the latest issue of a tech magazine, but when he saw John, he casually tossed it on John's desktop and sat up.

"Where have you been, bro? I came to get you for lunch," Miles said, a broad smile on his face.

"I had a…date," he said, wishing he didn't feel so unsure of his own blood, but until he got to the bottom of this, everyone was a suspect.

"That Gonzalez girl again?" Miles asked with the lift of an eyebrow.

"A business lunch," he said but then wished he hadn't.

"Why didn't you ask me to come along?" Miles asked, touchy as always about his role in the business.

With a shrug, and to keep Miles from getting angry, he said, "I didn't think anything would come of it. Just someone trying to talk me into looking at their building for our new office space."

"And?" Miles said and shot out of John's chair.

"No interest. It was in South Beach, but way too small for what we're planning," he said, making sure to emphasize the *we're* when he spoke.

That seemed to mollify Miles a little. With a shrug, he said, "It would be nice to be in South Beach."

Miles loved all the glamour and partying in the area, but John wasn't convinced that was the kind of impression they'd want for potential clients. He favored a location in downtown, like the one they had for the start-up he'd sold, but he didn't say.

"Do you want to do dinner tonight?" he asked, changing the subject to avoid having the same old argument with his brother.

Miles was too smart not to see what he was doing, but didn't challenge him. "I'd like that, bro."

"Great," he said and mentioned one of Miles's favorite places along the Ocean Drive strip in South Beach.

"How does eight sound?" Miles said.

"Sounds good. It'll let me get some more work done on the program," John said, and Miles perked up at the mention of the software.

"Is it going better than this morning?" Miles asked, his sandy-colored eyebrows raised in question.

"Still giving me some issues, but I hope I'll get the kinks out. How are the other projects going?" he said, referring to the apps and programs he'd assigned others to code and which Miles was supposed to be overseeing.

"Okay. We should have more for you to look at soon."

"Great. We'll need those projects bringing in money until I can do more on this program," he said and jerked a thumb toward his desktop.

"We have lots of money," Miles said, and John didn't correct him to say that he was the one with the money. He'd only allocated a set amount for this new start-up, and as for his personal finances, a lot of Miles's "suggestions"— like the parties and the Lamborghini—were eating into his savings.

"We need to have some income to show investors," he said, and Miles reluctantly nodded.

"I'll have updates for you by the end of the week," he said, then turned and left the office without waiting for John's reply.

When John was sure that Miles was gone, he did a quick check to make sure there wasn't anything like a key logger or other malware in place. He hated doing it, hated not trusting the only family he had left, but he couldn't take a chance.

This software was too important and too dangerous to fall into the wrong hands.

CAROLINA WOULDN'T BE back for another day, so Mia decided to go into the South Beach Security offices the next morning and finish unpacking Trey's boxes. They should have been able to do it the day before. There had only been three boxes, but somehow, they'd started chatting about all the changes that had happened in the last few months. They'd barely gotten through one box when their father had come in to haul away Trey for a meeting and then her brother had left for lunch with a client.

Having no desire to be alone, she'd left to run some errands, visit with her mother and then attend the opening of a brand-new club on Ocean Drive. But that sense of restlessness for more had lingered all day and night. She'd woken with it and, feeling like she had to do something, she'd gone back to the SBS offices to finish what she'd started the day before.

Trey was clearly surprised to see her as he walked into his office, carrying a paper bag that matched the one she'd brought with her. "I'm sorry. I should have let you know I planned on coming in."

"It's okay. I just wanted to grab a bite before…a client came in," he said and placed his bag beside hers on the table.

"I can go if you want," she said and gestured to his door, sensing he was uneasy about the upcoming meeting.

He stopped her with a raised hand. "No need. I have some time before the meeting," he said as he sat down at the table and took out his *café con leche* and toast.

She joined him and did the same, removing the contents from both bags. "Anyone interesting?" she asked.

Her brother hesitated, surprising her. Seeing his discomfort, she said, "I understand, Trey. I get that the company has to keep some things confidential."

"You know I would share if I could," Trey said and held the coffee cup between his hands as if warming them.

"I understand, but if you need my help with anything—"

"I know I can count on you," Trey said and took a sip of his coffee.

"I can leave once we're done or finish unpacking. Whatever you want," she said and nervously tore off a small piece of her toast to dunk in her coffee.

"We're meeting in the conference room, so feel free to stay, and thank you. I've hated staring at those boxes for the last couple of weeks," he said, finishing his cup of coffee. Then he reached for the one she'd brought, along with the toast.

Feeling even more restless than she had the day before, she said, "I've been thinking that maybe I could do more around here. Help out with things."

Trey lifted an eyebrow in surprise. "Really? What about Carolina?" he asked, clearly shocked that it seemed like she intended to break up the Twins.

With a little shrug, she said, "She knows I want to do something different, but that doesn't mean we can't continue to do a lot together."

Trey nodded in understanding. He tapped his chest on

a spot over his heart. "You'll know in here when it's time for that change."

She suspected that more than anyone, Trey would know. *Change* had been his middle name lately.

"You'll be the first to know," she said with a smile and squeezed his hand.

Trey's office phone rang and he answered. "Please put Mr. Smith in the conference room and let my father, Sophie and Robbie know as well."

When he returned the receiver to the cradle, he pushed to his feet. "Duty calls."

"Mr. Smith? Not very original. What's next? Jones?" she teased.

With a grin, he jabbed a finger in the direction of the boxes. "If you're serious, once you finish that, I have other work for you to do."

Mia bobbled her head from side to side, considering his offer, and finally said, "I think I'm serious."

JOHN PULLED THE ball cap low and hunched down into the collar of his jacket, hoping to avoid being recognized by anyone in the office. He'd been careful coming over as well, walking quickly and keeping his head on a swivel to make sure no one was following him.

After Trey strolled into the conference room, he walked to some switches by the door and hit a few buttons, and the glass wall on the reception side of the room went opaque. He gestured to the wall of exterior windows and said, "Those have a privacy film. No one can see in."

"Thanks," he said and ripped off the ball cap and denim jacket, since he'd been sweltering in it with the heat and humidity of a Miami morning.

A second later, Trey's father and tech-guru cousins walked in. His father was in a bespoke suit while Trey and his cousins were casually dressed.

"I think you know everyone," Trey said.

John nodded. "I do. Mr. Gonzalez. Sophie. Robbie. Thank you so much for any help you can provide."

"Trey has told us that you're worried that someone is trying to steal the new software that you're developing," his father, Ramon, said.

"I am," John replied and opened his knapsack to remove his laptop. He set it on the table, intending to demo it, but Trey motioned for him to wait.

"Before you tell us about it, I just want to fill you in on what we've done so far," Trey said.

John nodded and sat down at the table, eager to hear, and Trey continued.

"As I mentioned yesterday during our lunch, I reached out to Equinox to discuss with them what security they had in place at your temporary office and the location for your supercomputer. I had them increase how often the guards did rounds, and I also asked them to install a few more CCTV cameras on the interior of the building with your supercomputer. Finally, I verified that they were using a top-notch alarm system on all the entrances to the super-computer location, so we're set that way."

"That all seems good," John said, but Trey looked toward his dad, obviously still concerned.

"We have another suggestion to make, if you're willing to listen," Ramon said.

"I am. It's important to safeguard this software," John confirmed.

Trey nodded. "Good. Where security is a little lacking is at your temporary office space. They don't have 24/7 guards in the lobby and other areas and you're using the internet the building provided."

"I'm waiting for a dedicated line to be dropped for our internet access," John explained. Because his venture was so new and there were delays with installing the line, he'd had no choice but to use the building's cable to be able to work.

Trey nodded. "We have a dedicated line into this building and better security. The floor below this one is empty if you want to use it. No charge."

"That's very generous of you," John said, wondering at that kindness.

Trey must have seen his reticence. "You're a friend and you helped us in the past without hesitation."

"Okay. I appreciate that. I can make arrangements to move in whenever that's good for you," John said, thinking it wouldn't be that difficult since he only had about half a dozen employees in his new start-up.

"Great. We'll make arrangements to activate the connections on that floor and you can work with Sophie and Robbie to make sure you're happy with that and with the security we use on our network," his father said.

"I guess it's time for me to explain what I'm working on," John said.

"We'd love to hear," Sophie said, and Robbie nodded excitedly.

With a quick dip of his head, he began. "It's a new kind of AI predictive software that uses a neural network—"

"What is that exactly? In layman's terms, please," Trey asked, raising his hands to ask him to slow down and explain.

"It's a series of algorithms that mimic the actions of the human brain. You feed data into the network, and it processes it the way a human brain would," Sophia said, trying to simplify the concept for her cousin.

John nodded. "Exactly. But here's where my network might be a little different—normally a user collects and feeds in the data."

"Garbage in, garbage out," Robbie offered.

"Very true. Feed in inaccurate data and the result is

suspect. Plus, it may not be all the data you need to make a truly accurate prediction," John said and continued with his explanation.

"I've created this kind of digital vacuum that can suck in data from dozens of sources. Social-media accounts. News articles. Credit reports. User-provided data. You name it. It's probably 10 times, if not 100 times, the amount of data that a user typically feeds into a program to prepare a report," he said, popped open his laptop and Sophie handed him a piece of paper with SBS's network password.

He logged in using a VPN for security reasons and pulled up a very rudimentary dashboard. "Sorry if this looks a little wonky, but I'm still working on the front end and some of the reporting features."

"Can you show us how it works? Predict something," Trey asked.

"What do you want to know?" John asked because Trey's question had been so open-ended.

With a boyish grin, he said, "How long will Roni and I be married?"

"Forever, hopefully," Sophie said with an eye roll, obviously exasperated.

John typed in Trey's real name—Ramon Gonzalez III— and ran the program. "This may take several minutes."

"Minutes? To process that much data? How fast is your supercomputer?" Sophie asked.

With a shrug, John said, "Not as speedy as Summit at the Oak Ridge National Laboratory, but I'm hoping to expand it and do some optimization to make it faster."

"Wow, that's fast," Robbie said with a low whistle.

"Aren't you worried about garbage in from all these different sources?" Ramon said while they waited for the program to spit out a result.

"It is possible you'll get some junk, especially if you're

dealing with someone who normally generates a lot of trash news stories, like some celebrities," John clarified.

"What do you do in a situation like that?" Trey asked.

John didn't get a chance to answer because his computer dinged to let him know he had a preliminary report, but as he looked at it, he felt the blood drain from his face and a chill fill his core.

"Something wrong?" Trey asked, his sharp blue gaze picking up on John's discomfort.

"Something wonky. Let me tweak something here," he said. He looked at the code to confirm all was in order and then commanded the program to run the analysis once more.

"I'm just going to do it again. It may still be glitchy," he said, not wanting to believe the result the program was providing.

He sat there staring at the screen but didn't fail to miss how the family members gathered around the table were leaning forward, anxiously awaiting the result.

When it came, it wasn't very different, and he slumped back in his chair, his body feeling almost boneless.

"John. What is it?" Trey pressed.

With a shaky hand, John pointed in the direction of the monitor on the far wall. "Can I cast to that?"

Sophie nodded and picked up a remote. After pushing a few buttons, she said, "It's ready."

He did and a collective gasp went up around the room at the risk-assessment table.

"This report says we'll be married less than a month? It's got to be wrong," Trey said, shifting his head vehemently back and forth in denial.

"It's worse than that, Trey," Sophie said, and at his questioning look, she added, "It says you'll be dead in a month."

Chapter Three

Mia was walking past the conference room when she heard the ruckus going on inside. It was loud enough to draw the attention of the SBS employees with cubicles close to the room. They were poking their heads above the panels like meerkats coming out of their dens. The receptionist at the nearby front desk was trying to act as if she hadn't noticed something was up.

Since the privacy glass had been engaged—meaning they didn't want any attention being drawn to the conference—she knocked on the door to let Trey know they were achieving the exact opposite with their noise.

Her brother jerked open the door violently and almost jumped back when he saw Mia there. "What is it, *hermanita*?"

She looked back over her shoulder to draw his gaze to the people who were now mightily trying to appear as if they hadn't been interested in whatever was going on in the conference room.

Trey looked toward their employees, and she rose on tiptoes and whispered in his ear, "You were a little loud."

Her brother grasped her arm, gently tugged her into the conference room and closed the door. "I'm sorry. We've just had a nasty surprise," he explained.

As she looked around the room, she was stunned to see

John Wilson sitting there. The mysterious guest. Given the media interest in anything he did, visiting South Beach Security was bound to cause unwanted rumors and possible damage to his new start-up.

"People were noticing with all the noise," she said and jerked a thumb in the direction of the door.

"Like I said, a nasty surprise, and John was just trying to explain it," Trey said.

John started tapping away on his keyboard and while he did, he muttered, "Just taking a look at some of the data."

Mia shot her brother a questioning look and he said, "John's new software just predicted that I'll be dead in a month."

She jumped, startled, and said, "That's crazy."

"It is, but the prediction is based on existing data and that includes all that's happened in Trey's life so far. His military service. Work as a cop. The data from those roles will weigh heavily in any calculation, but now Trey's life is different, which hopefully means a different outcome," John said, nodding his head as he worked as if he was trying to convince himself of the inaccuracy of his program's prediction.

"Prove it," Mia said.

John whipped his head in her direction. "Prove it?"

She nodded. "Yes. Make a prediction about someone else. Our dad. Me. Soph. Rob. Yourself."

He stared at her hard, his hazel eyes probing as he assessed her suggestion. With a nod, he said, "Makes sense. But not your dad. His background is too similar to Trey's."

"Your software isn't 100 percent accurate?" she said, crossing her arms and cocking a hip in challenge.

A flush of hot color swept across his cheeks and guilt slammed into her. She liked John and she hadn't meant to cut him down at the knees, but she also didn't like his software's stupid prediction about Trey.

"It's been right on everything else so far," he defended.

"Like what?" Sophie asked and stepped around to watch John as he worked.

"FOOTBALL GAMES. STOCKS. Various local elections," John said, and Sophie handed him a piece of paper with everyone's full names and dates of birth. Glancing down at the paper, he typed in Sophie's info. He sat back in the chair, his heart pounding as he waited for the results, but the program predicted the same outcome for Sophie.

"That makes no sense," he muttered and then quickly returned to the keyboard to enter Robbie's data.

Unlike the earlier noise in the room, it was deathly silent as the program ran its routine, but the prediction remained the same.

"There's got to be a bug," Sophie said, but John shook his head defiantly.

"There isn't. I've tried it over and over, including some older celebrities, and it worked," John said.

"How? Where does it get the information for life longevity?" Robbie asked and came over to stand behind him and next to Sophie.

"It accesses various actuarial tables. I even did it for myself," John explained, which prompted a chorus of questions.

"What did it say?" Sophie asked.

"How old?" Robbie said.

"When did you do it?" Trey asked.

"A ripe old age and I did it several weeks ago," John answered while his mind raced for explanations as to why his program had suddenly gone awry.

"Try it again," Mia prompted, and he peered up at her. Her blue-eyed gaze was dark and intense, and she still stood there in that defiant stance. He understood. His program had just decided to decimate her family without any apparent reason.

"I will," he said, certain of what the program would say. But if it did, he worried what that meant for the various Gonzalez family members.

He plugged in his details and waited, fingers drumming on the table. When the program spit out the answer, he sucked in a surprised breath.

"Doesn't look like a ripe old age to me," Robbie said glibly, earning a sharp elbow from his sister, Sophie.

"It's got to be a glitch," John said and opened up the source code, uncaring of the fact that Robbie and Sophie stood behind him, because if the coding wasn't wrong...

"Maybe it isn't a glitch. What's the one thing that's changed in your life since you did it?" Mia said as she relaxed her stance and began pacing back and forth by the table.

He wanted to say "Her." Nothing in his life had been the same since the day they'd first gone out together and since he'd become involved with the various members of South Beach Security. That was the connection.

"SBS," he said, which made Mia whirl to face him.

"SBS? Could that really be the connection?" she said and walked back to his side to write down her information on the piece of paper. She also added the details for Trey's fiancée, Roni, whom John understood was one of Mia's best friends.

He plugged in Roni's name first and waited, his body stiff to match the tension radiating from the trio who now stood behind him, watching. When it came, the answer was not unexpected.

He repeated the analysis with Mia only to arrive at the same conclusion several long minutes later.

Something else occurred to him then. Something possibly more sinister than the connection to South Beach Security. "We need benchmarks. Someone who isn't a family member who works for SBS and a Gonzalez family member who doesn't work with you," John said, his mind whirling as he ran through other possible permutations if these didn't work.

"Pepe never works with us," Ramon said and wrote out his nephew's information on a piece of paper he handed to John.

Trey held up a finger, picked up the phone and dialed out. "Julia. Would you mind sharing your full name and birth date?" He jotted down the info their receptionist supplied and handed the slip of paper to him.

"Here goes nothing," John said as he entered the receptionist's information.

The Gonzalez family members had drifted away to quietly chat among themselves, and John understood. But even though he did, their actions made him feel the way he had so much of his life: like an outsider.

But then Mia hurried over, laid a hand on his shoulder and gave a reassuring squeeze. He glanced up at her and her blue-eyed gaze was understanding, but worried. Despite that, she said, "Whatever it is, we will handle this."

He didn't know if the *we* included him. He wanted it to. He wanted that and more, especially with Mia, but she had rabbited after their last time alone, needing space, she said.

"We will," he said, but it sounded almost robotic, and she clearly picked up on that and more.

"It is a *we*, John. We will do this together," Mia stressed.

He nodded and reluctantly pulled his gaze from hers back to the screen. This time the response was quite different, luckily for the receptionist. But that also raised a very scary possibility: that this was directly related to the Gonzalez family working with SBS.

His fingers felt as heavy as an anchor as he typed in the information for Pepe Gonzalez. Mia stayed by his side, her hand on his shoulder, the weight of it comforting. Welcome, especially as she swept it across his back, soothing him even though he imagined she was feeling her own kind of torment wondering if his program was right.

Every breath he took was measured as he tried to control the turmoil making his gut clench. As the seconds flew by, he closed his eyes, waiting for the telltale ding that warned of a prediction.

The slight tightening of her hand coincided with the damning ding.

"He's fine. Pepe is fine," Mia said with delight, which was short-lived. "What does that mean?" she asked, although he suspected she knew.

Peering around the family members gathered in the conference room, he felt as if he was the executioner on judgment day, but he had no doubt about what his program results now meant for them and for him.

"We're all in danger. Someone is going to end our lives unless we can figure it out."

MIA'S STOMACH WAS in knots as the team sat down at the table to consider John's ominous warning.

It just didn't make any sense to her as John ran the names of the other Gonzalez family members who were involved with SBS and got the same dire results. Luckily, other family members were spared.

"*Tia* Elena and *Tio* Jose are fine. So is Pepe, but not Carolina. Why is that?" Mia asked.

"Maybe because you and Caro are intimately involved with SBS even if not officially employed by it," her father said.

"What about the *abuelos*?" Trey said, worried about their grandparents, especially since *Abuelo* Ramon had been the founder of the business.

John ran them through the program but shook his head

at the response. "They're fine, only... I was, too, a few weeks ago."

"Meaning?" Trey asked, a dark eyebrow raised in challenge.

"Meaning that if we fail to stop this current danger, their outcomes could change. They're only safe if we're safe," John said.

Trey muttered a curse and raked his fingers through his hair. Mia understood his frustration. Family was a priority in their lives, and they would all do whatever it took to keep their family safe.

Her brother paced back and forth while the rest of them sat around, lost in their own thoughts, until Trey whirled and said, "The last investigation with Ricky and Mariela. I thought there was something off about the attacks on them."

Mia had only been tangentially involved in that case and needed clarification. "Care to explain?"

Trey nodded, walked to the table and gripped the top of the leather executive chair. "There was a drive-by at Ricky's house that didn't connect for me because whoever had attacked Mariela the night before couldn't have possibly known to go there."

"There was a drive-by at the Del Sol when you and Roni were investigating your partner's murder," Mia pointed out.

"But drive-bys are a common gang tactic," Sophie said, adding to the discussion.

"You're right, Soph. When gang members do that, they have a specific target in mind," Trey explained.

"But they could have been targeting Mariela even if it was at Ricky's. I mean, it doesn't seem like gang members care very much about collateral damage," Mia said, sadly familiar with it since there had been quite a few of them in Miami over the years.

"What if Mariela wasn't the target? And what if whoever shot at Roni and me wasn't a member of that human-trafficking ring?" Trey mused.

Sophie glanced over at John and said, "Could your program tell us the probability that those two drive-bys were related?"

"I'd have to make a few changes to feed in just data from those two events, but, yes, it could," he said and immediately got to work on it.

Trey looked at his watch and clapped his hands. "Hard to believe, but it's almost lunch and I think we need a break so we can have fresh eyes on anything John pulls up. I'm going to have Julia order some lunch."

"Tux, tux, tux," Mia teased, ignoring that if John's predictions came true, they wouldn't be dressing for a wedding in a few months. Just funerals.

Trey ignored her jibe, picked up the phone and asked Julia, the receptionist, to order sandwiches from a nearby Jewish deli. "Tired of Cubanos," he said in response to the look she shot him.

"I never get tired of Cubanos," John muttered, fully aware of what was happening around them despite his intense attention to his laptop.

"Is there anything we can do to help?" Robbie asked as both he and Sophie sat there, itching to hit the keys on their laptops.

"Not right now, but maybe in the future," he said, and Mia was grateful that he was willing to trust them with his code. Which made her wonder… "Why did you come see us this morning?"

He shot her a brief intense look and said, "Someone's trying to steal the program."

"Is there any chance that the same person is responsible for our less-than happily-ever-afters?" Mia asked.

With a shrug, John said, "We can run that through the program as well."

By the time the deli sandwiches had arrived, John had the program pull in the data for the drive-bys from various news accounts and the reports the police had provided to SBS. While they waited for an answer, they snagged food from the platter loaded with assorted sandwiches with brisket, corned beef and pastrami, along with side dishes of coleslaw, various salads, and several types of pickles.

Mia grabbed a brisket sandwich and layered some coleslaw on it. With a laugh, John said, "A brisket po'boy."

Mia chuckled and smiled. "I guess you could call it that, especially if you're from N'awlin," she teased, mimicking what a native would call that city and hoping she might be able to learn more about him.

"Not from New Orleans," John advised and grabbed a pastrami sandwich and a sour pickle.

On their few dates, if they could be called that, he'd never really said where he was from and his bio had omitted that info, probably deliberately. Plus, he had no discernable accent to give it away. "Flyover country?" she asked because of the lack of accent.

"Nope," he said and bit into his sandwich.

Scrutinizing him, he had the kind of preppy looks that she could picture in an Ivy League school, but his bio had said nothing about that either. "New England?" she asked.

That noncommittal "Nope" came again, challenging her to try again.

There was nothing surfer-dude about him, so she eliminated California, but before she could ask, the program warned it had an answer.

John cast the answer onto the large screen for all to see. "75-percent probability the two attacks are related."

"I knew it," Trey said. "My gut told me something was off about that drive-by."

"I'm sorry we all dismissed your gut. What else did you think was off?" Sophie asked and put down her sandwich, seemingly ready to start gathering information for their next prediction.

"Mariela's husband supposedly committed suicide, but I wasn't buying it. It just tied everything up too neatly when it was anything but neat," Trey said.

"What else?" Robbie challenged, also eager to tackle the problem.

Trey tapped his palm with his index finger, delineating the various points he was making. "If those two drive-bys were connected and had nothing to do with Mariela's ex—"

"Did whoever was behind them have something to do with her ex's death?" Sophie interrupted, connecting the dots he had laid out.

"And what does it have to do with the family and with whoever is trying to steal John's program?" Robbie said.

"John? What do you think?" Mia asked, since he'd remained silent during the discussion.

He sucked in a deep breath, held it for a long moment and roughly blew it out. "I think we need as much data as we can get about all those events and you two—" he pointed at Sophie and Robbie "—need access to the program."

That statement sent Trey, her cousins and John into a flurry of action, leaving her father and her waiting for them to work their magic.

Her father's face was set in a deep glower, full of worry and anger. She walked over and laid a hand on his arm, much as she'd seen her mother do so often when he'd come home bothered about something at work. As her mother had done more than once, she said, "I know you're worried, but we'll figure it out."

His rough grunt wasn't reassuring, so she tried again. "What are you worrying about, *Papi*?"

"Everything," he said and shook his head. "It's all too much to believe. Predictions. Software."

"But it's real, *Papi*. AI can even help doctors diagnose

schizophrenia," she said, recalling a recent article she had seen when she had been trying to understand what it was that John did to earn his millions.

Her father harrumphed and pointed first to his head, then to his heart and finally to a midsection that was still surprisingly flat for a sixtysomething. "Trey's gut said something was wrong weeks ago. I should have listened."

"*We* should have listened, *Papi*," she said, wanting to lift some of the weight he carried off his shoulders. It was one of the reasons she'd been happy that Trey had decided to join SBS. It was time to share that burden and pass it on to someone younger to handle.

It also reminded her of the discussion she'd had with her brother earlier. It wasn't fair for Trey to have to shoulder that burden alone and hopefully she could help him.

"Sit down and have something to eat. Let them do whatever and then we can decide how to proceed," she said, hoping to ease his worries.

"*Gracias, mi' ja,*" he said and offered her the flicker of a smile, confirming that she had successfully channeled her mother to tame the bear.

She walked back to grab her sandwich and soda, and moved to her father's side, offering him her support while they waited for the others to work their magic. They had finished their sandwiches and brought in coffee when Sophie got the first ding from the program.

As John had done before, she displayed her result on the large screen. "70-percent probability that Mariela's husband didn't commit suicide."

"I don't need to have a program to tell me that whoever attacked Ricky and Mariela is responsible," Trey said, and from beside her, his father grunted his agreement.

Barely a minute later, a second ding burst from Robbie's computer with an answer, and he immediately popped the image onto the screen. "Whoever killed her ex…the probability is 85 percent that they'll be responsible for our deaths."

"So we solve her ex's murder—" Trey began.

"We stop our own," Mia said, finishing for him.

Another ding sounded from John's laptop, but he muttered a curse when he saw the answer.

"What's the matter?" Mia asked.

John shook his head and finally displayed the response. "Only 50-percent probability that it's the same person who's trying to steal the software."

"That's okay, John," Trey said. "It just means we have two cases to investigate. Are you all ready? Mia?"

She knew why he had singled her out. It wasn't just their earlier conversation to work more at SBS, it was because John was involved. But just because she had her doubts about any kind of relationship with the tech millionaire, even a friendly one, when family was involved, there was only one answer she could give.

"I'm ready."

Chapter Four

He had to get this right because he wasn't sure they'd have another chance to do it, he thought.

John Wilson hadn't noticed the tracking software loaded on his phone.

He was barely two blocks away and on the move. That meant he'd be in the office in no time.

Great.

He sent out a short text to warn his hired muscle that he had to be ready to move.

Looking at the phone again, he held his breath, counting down until he saw the blip on the phone turn toward their building.

It wouldn't take more than a few minutes for John to take the elevator to the floor. He texted his accomplice to tell him to get on the move.

Sucking in a deep breath, he prepped himself for the attack.

JOHN WAS SURPRISED when Mia slipped her arm through his as they took the short walk to his temporary office space.

"Try not to look so grumpy," Mia said and faked a bright laugh, as if he'd said something funny.

John forced a smile he wasn't feeling and leaned his head close to hers. They'd shown up in some tabloids and gossip sites when they'd first been spotted together, so it made perfect sense to fake it in case someone was following them.

"Better?" he said, and this time Mia laughed for real.

"Seriously, John. You look like the crazed clown in those *It* movies," she said and playfully tugged on his arm to urge him to loosen up.

"Pennywise?"

She furrowed her brow, obviously confused. "Pennywise? I didn't know that was his name."

"That is the crazy clown's name. I guess you're not into horror movies," he said and shot a quick glance at her.

She wrinkled her nose and shook her head. "Too scary for me."

He had to remember that because it was too tempting to picture her curled beside him, watching a movie. But not a scary one. Maybe one of his black-and-white classics.

"I'll keep that in mind," he said, but she immediately shut him down.

"Just going to your office to help you assess what it'll take to move," she said, but with a smile, in case anyone was watching.

"A shame. I have a really nice entertainment system at my house," he said.

"We never went to your house. Why is that?" she asked, that furrow on her brow marring her flawless skin again.

He paused to look at her and smooth a finger across the crease. "Do you really want to know?"

She nodded and he dipped his hand down to swipe his thumb across her cheek. "I'm a very private person."

She smirked and arched her perfectly manicured eyebrows. "Really? The Del Sol parties. The Lamborghini? They don't scream *private* to me."

He blew out a harsh breath and shook his head before resuming the walk to his temporary office space. "Those are all Miles's doing. He thinks I need a certain image."

"Really? Like, 'I need to show I have a bigger—'"

"Yes, like that. I'm not a fan of it, but he's my brother," John admitted as they walked into the building, and he badged them through the security checkpoint.

"Isn't he your half brother?" she asked, and he shrugged.

"He's my only family, so as far as I'm concerned, he's my brother," he said and her gaze grew dark, almost troubled.

"I guess that's something else you want to keep private. You don't say much about your family," she said and shot him a quick look from the corner of her eye.

With another, heavier shrug and a frown, he said, "Not much to tell. We're not like your family."

To her credit, she left it at that, sensing it was a topic that not only troubled him, but also probably caused him pain.

As soon as they walked into their temporary offices, the young woman who was manning the reception desk smiled at them. "Good afternoon, John."

"Good afternoon, Rachel. Could you please send an email blast to everyone—"

The loud bang of a door slamming against a wall jerked his attention to the end of the hall.

A masked man rushed out of the stairway entrance and raced toward them, gun drawn.

John shoved Mia behind him and shouted at Rachel. "Call 911."

John braced for the attack, but barely a breath later, Miles rushed out of his office and threw himself at the masked man.

Muttering a curse under his breath, John rushed forward to help his brother, who was grappling with the intruder. But a second later the man pistol-whipped Miles, threw him off and scrambled to his feet. The man backtracked toward the stairway, seemingly surprised that it hadn't gone as planned, and then sped away, passing by several of their workers, who were standing at their office doors, immobilized by shock.

John reached Miles, who had sat up and was leaning against the wall, dazed. A thin trickle of blood ran down the side of his face from a cut on his brow.

Mia was there a second later as John kneeled by his brother. "Are you okay?" he asked.

Miles shook his head as if trying to clear away the shock of the attack. He reached up, his hand shaky, touched his brow and winced. When Miles pulled back his fingers and saw the blood, his face paled.

John laid a hand on his shoulder as Mia handed him a small handkerchief to staunch the blood. John gently placed it on Miles's brow, but his brother winced again.

"Sorry." John looked up at Mia and said, "Could you ask Rachel to call for an ambulance?"

Miles waved his hand. "No. I'm okay. Just a little shaken."

"Can you stand up?" Mia asked.

Miles did a wobbly nod and when John offered his hand, he grasped it and unsteadily got to his feet.

"Let's get you cleaned up," Mia said just as a pair of security guards rushed through the front doors, followed by two Miami police officers.

John glanced toward the door. "Can you help Miles while I talk to the police?"

Mia nodded. "I can."

MIA WATCHED AS John went to speak to the authorities, and after, helped Miles back into his office, where he sat on the couch. Seconds later, a pale and flustered Rachel rushed in. "Here's a first-aid kit."

"Thanks. Could you please get us some water?" she said. Giving the young woman something to do would hopefully make her calm down.

"Sure. I'll be back in a second," Rachel said and rushed from the room.

"Smooth move," Miles said and smiled, but then winced, the movement obviously bringing him pain.

As much as she disliked Miles, she respected what he had done to protect his brother. "That was a brave move. The man was armed."

She sat on a coffee table in front of the sofa where Miles was and laid the first-aid kit at her side. She opened it, took out some alcohol pads and ripped them open.

"This might sting," she said and dabbed at the cut to wipe away the blood that had trailed down his face.

Miles grimaced and sucked in a breath, but then said, "He's my brother. I had to protect him."

She didn't correct him the way she had John before. She sensed being more than half brothers was important to them, but she also sensed something else. Something that was troubling her, but that she couldn't really put a finger on.

"You could have been shot." She grabbed some butterfly bandages to apply to the small cut on his brow.

"I wasn't really thinking about that." He shrugged, and the movement was so much like John's, it was impossible to deny they were related by blood. But as his hazel gaze locked with hers, he rubbed her the wrong way again. His eyes might be the same color as John's but there was a deadness there that worried her.

A knock on the door drew her attention to John and two police officers, one female and one male, standing there.

"The police have some questions for you, Miles. You, too, Mia," John said, his handsome face all hard lines.

She nodded, not that she had much info to provide. But she sat there patiently as the police questioned Miles, jotting down anything he remembered. But as he had before, something struck her as off about his testimony. Almost as if it was too pat. Rehearsed, which was impossible considering how quickly the situation had all gone down.

"Miss Gonzalez?" one officer said. She was a twenty-something that Mia had seen patrolling the area more than once when she'd visited her family's agency.

"I'm sorry. Did you ask me something?" She'd been too focused on Miles and hadn't heard the young woman's question.

"What can you tell us about what happened?" the officer asked.

Mia took a moment to mentally run through the incident. With a nod, she said, "A masked man raced out of the stairway access. He must have come in through a service area to avoid lobby security. There's hopefully CCTV footage from that area."

She jotted down the info and said, "Thank you. Anything else?"

Mia nodded. "He was hunched a little as he ran at us, but based on the height of the doorframe, I would say he was at least six feet tall, maybe a little more. A little heavier than medium build. Right-handed. He held the gun in his right hand. I think it was a 9mm Glock and he was either white or white Hispanic."

As the male officer narrowed his gaze as if in challenge, Mia circled her index finger around her eyes. "The mask exposed the area around his eyes. Brown, I think."

His gaze narrowed even more and in an accusatory tone the officer said, "You seem to have seen a lot in a really short time."

The female police officer elbowed him. "That's Detective Gonzalez's sister," she said and that seemed to explain everything to the other officer.

"Sorry. I didn't mean to offend," he said.

"That's okay, Officer Johnson. I guess I've hung out with my brother too much."

"We know him well. He was a great detective and is missed on the force," the female said.

"Thank you, Officer Puente. I'll let him know," she said with a slow dip of her head.

"I think we have all we need, but we'd recommend you going to the hospital to get that checked out. It looks like he hit you pretty hard," Officer Puente said and gestured to the makeshift bandage Mia had applied to Miles's brow.

"I agree," John said and looked at her.

"Why don't you take your brother to the hospital? I'll take care of things here," she said.

"I'd appreciate that, Mia. Thank you," he said, then helped Miles to his feet and walked out with him, followed by the police officers.

Mia waited until they were gone before dialing Trey. When he answered, she said, "We have a problem."

JOHN PACED BACK and forth in the waiting area for the emergency room, anxious for any word from the doctor on his brother's condition. The knapsack containing his laptop dragged at his shoulder, but since it was the only machine that could access the full code for his program, he took it with him everywhere unless he locked it up at home.

In his mind's eye, he ran through what had happened and what else he could have done during the attack. His first concerns had been for Mia and Rachel until Miles had rushed out of the office and engaged the intruder.

That was when he'd sprang into action, but by the time he'd gotten there, Miles had already been hurt and the intruder had been on the run.

Clearly, the masked man hadn't had a taste for more violence, but if that was the case, why break into a crowded office at midday, armed and masked?

As someone who was supposedly a genius and a problem solver, it bothered him that he couldn't wrap his head around the motivation behind what had happened. That made him feel even more useless considering how little info he'd been able to provide the police.

Not like Mia. He had been impressed with all the observations she made in the space of scant seconds. Hopefully enough for the police to move their investigation along.

A doctor in a standard white jacket approached him. "Mr. Wilson?"

John glanced at the man's nametag. "Dr. Castillo. Thank you for taking care of my brother. How is he?"

The doctor motioned to his brow. "Small cut that someone very capably butterflied. No signs of a concussion, but sometimes it takes hours for symptoms to show up."

"Nothing's broken, right?" John said and peered toward the ER, where he could see his brother resting on a bed.

"Nothing broken from what I can see, but I think we should take Miles down for some X-rays to confirm and I'd like to keep him overnight to watch for those concussion symptoms. You can see him now before we send him for the X-rays," the doctor said and pointed the chart at Miles.

"Thanks, I will," John said and hurried in to see his brother.

Miles's eyes were closed, but as John laid a hand on his arm, he opened them, almost sleepily, making John worry that he might have a concussion.

"How are you feeling?" John said.

"Tired. Sleepy."

"Doctor doesn't think there are any internal injuries but they're going to do X-rays to confirm and keep you overnight in case you have a concussion," John explained.

Miles nodded and offered him a weak smile. "I'll be okay."

"That was a stupid thing to do," John said and squeezed Miles's arm.

"He was heading for you. I had to do something. Mom

always said I had to protect you," Miles said, rousing memories of the two of them huddled in a closet, hiding from John's dad as he beat on their mom.

"I know and I can't thank you enough." John knew his brother wouldn't appreciate what he was about to tell him.

"I'm moving our offices to a more secure location."

Miles jerked back, clearly surprised. "Is that really necessary?"

"I think it is," he said and watched the slow rise of color creep up his brother's neck.

"And I guess what you say goes," Miles said. For as long as John could remember, Miles had hated John being the one calling the shots, especially since Miles was the older brother and presumably the one who should be in charge.

"I appreciate all that you've done for me, but when it comes to the company—"

"It's your baby. I get it," he bit out, his anger impossible to miss.

"Let's not fight, Miles. All I care about right now is knowing that you're okay." John squeezed his brother's arm again in reassurance.

With a few abrupt nods, Miles said, "Sure. I'm fine. You go take care of things. I'll be okay."

"I'll see you later. Try and get some rest," John said, rose and bro-hugged him before walking out the door.

As he exited the emergency room and flagged down a cab, he dialed Mia.

"How is it going?" he asked.

"People have packed their personal items and computers. Trey has a truck waiting for us in the delivery area. We'll be waiting for you at the SBS building so you can direct people on where to go," Mia advised.

"I'll be there in about a half hour. Thank you for taking care of things," he said.

"Of course. I hope Miles is okay," she said, and in the background, he could hear the hushed murmur of people talking.

"He is. I'll go back later to check in on him. See you soon," he said, then leaned forward and provided the address to the cabbie, who had been patiently waiting for him to end the call.

The cabbie whipped out of the emergency-room area and headed for the highway to take them to downtown Miami.

John bounced his legs up and down, anxious to get to the building so they could finish the move and get settled. He was sure his people would need an explanation for what was happening, and he needed to figure out what were the necessary next steps they had to take to find out who was behind the attacks on his servers and on Miles.

Miles, he thought, recalling his fear as the gunman had rushed in and his brother had challenged him.

But what could the gunman have expected to do? Kidnap me? he wondered.

If they had him, they could force him to give up the code, and then what? Was his code worth such a risk? he asked himself, but the answer was clear.

Yes.

He had no doubt that if the code got into the wrong hands, it could be used for all the wrong reasons. Stock manipulations that could take down companies and exchanges, destroying people's livelihoods and national economies. Warfare games that would lead to real-life conflicts and deaths.

John's mind whirled with the many ways lives could be changed by the misuse of his code, and more than likely not for the better, like the predictions that his software had made for himself and the various Gonzalez family members.

Dead in a month.

It boggled his mind, which was why he had to get to his

people and the Gonzalez family and work on stopping the threat to the family and to his software.

As the cab pulled up in front of the building, he threw open the door, tapped his card to pay for the ride and handed the driver a generous tip in cash. "Thank you," he said and met the driver's eyes in the rearview mirror.

The driver offered him a sympathetic nod, obviously aware that all was not well, since he'd picked up John at the hospital.

With an abrupt nod in response, John rushed toward the doors of the SBS building, but as he hurried inside, it occurred to him that he didn't have a badge to clear security. But when he looked toward the desk with the security guards, Mia stepped out of an elevator and walked toward the guards.

Although *walk* was a tame way to describe the way she moved. Confident. Sexy as hell in those impossibly high heels that made her long legs look even longer. She was focused on her phone, but when she looked up and saw him, she smiled.

That smile did all kinds of things to his insides. Joy. Something he'd rarely experienced in his early life. Need. And not just sexual need. It was a soul-deep need from a man who was tired of being alone. Tired of being seen as something he wasn't.

That smile stayed on her face while her eyes darkened and narrowed, as if reaching inside him and finding that need.

"You okay?" she asked as she walked up to him and tenderly laid her hand on his arm.

That touch, so freely given and full of concern, gentled the turmoil in his soul.

I am now, he thought but didn't say, afraid to reveal too much to her given their unsettled relationship.

"Thank you for everything," he said, which made her

purse her lips with annoyance as she realized he was shutting her out.

With a nod, she reached into the pocket of her jacket and handed him a building badge.

"I hope you don't mind that we took some liberties for your photo," she said.

He examined the picture and realized it was a cropped version of a selfie that Mia had taken on one of their dates. It kindled memories of that date and how much fun they'd had. How happy he'd been.

"I don't mind," he said, although the photo would remind him every day of what he wanted with her and didn't have. *Yet*, he thought hopefully.

She flipped an elegant hand toward the security desk and the gold bangles at her wrist jangled musically. "The badge clears you for your new floor, the SBS floors and the penthouse suite."

He inched up an eyebrow in question. "Penthouse suite?"

She nodded and pushed the button for the elevator. "We have a space for family and guests to use if they need to stay overnight. I can show it to you later."

"Thanks, although I'm not sure I'll need it. I have the suite at the Del Sol—"

She wrinkled her nose at the mention of that since it was clearly distasteful to her.

"I'm not a fan of it either," he said as the elevator arrived. They stepped into it and she inserted her badge.

"If you're not a fan, why do you do it?" she pressed.

With a careless shrug, he said, "Miles thinks we need to keep ourselves in the public eye."

"I guess that explains the Lamborghini, too?" she said with a quick side-glance.

He offered up another shrug. "The Lamborghini, too. It's an amazing ride, but I'd rather not call so much attention to myself."

The glance she gave him this time was longer and more thoughtful. Her voice was a touch softer as she said, "Then why don't you say no?"

"It's important to Miles and he's always been there for me. I feel like it's the least I can do."

The ding warned them they had reached their destination and they stepped out of the elevator and into a beautifully appointed space, where Rachel was already at a curved reception desk that could easily sit another person. The base of the desk was the rich color of Cuban coffee and topped with a frosted white glass counter. The wall behind the desk was covered in colored stones that enhanced the deep hues of the wood and at its base were matching storage cabinets.

"Are you doing okay?" he asked Rachel, certain the young woman might be rattled by all that had happened in the last few hours.

Rachel offered a weak smile and shake of her head. "I am. How is Miles?"

"He's fine, thank you. If you're all set up, why don't you take the rest of the day off. I'm sure you could use some time to relax," he said, but Rachel shook her head.

"I'm fine, really. But if you want, I could help you or some of the others unpack," she said.

"That would be nice. Why don't you check with the others to see if they need your help?"

The receptionist shot him a strained smile, rose and walked down the hall to assist their other employees.

Mia leaned close and whispered in his ear, "She's got a crush on you."

"Does she?" he asked and looked back over his shoulder at Rachel before she ducked into one of the other offices.

"She does. Who wouldn't?" Mia bit her lip at what she'd said and waved her hands to stop him. "I mean, a young girl like her is bound to be impressed by someone like you."

"But not a sophisticated older woman like you," he teased and loved the flush of color that swept up her neck to her face.

She ignored his comment and led him to the farthest point of the hall, where there was a space for another desk and, beyond that, an immense corner office. The door was open, but as they walked in, Mia said, "This door is also controlled by the badge in case you want to lock it."

He nodded, walked to the wall of windows and let his knapsack gently slip to the floor. Sucking in a deep breath, he almost inhaled the beautiful panorama of the parks and marinas along the waterfront, the assorted causeways and bridges leading to Miami Beach and, in the distance, Biscayne Bay and Brickell Key.

"This is really nice. Thank you," he said and faced her.

"Whenever you're ready, we're on the next floor up," she said and pointed her perfectly manicured index finger toward the ceiling. "Trey is reviewing the police reports for today's attack and Sophie and Robbie have been working on some things as well."

"Let me just give my people a heads-up and then we can go. I'll unpack later," he said, then picked up his knapsack, slung it over his shoulder, approached her and laid a hand at the small of her back to gently urge her out.

"Sure. That probably makes the most sense. This way you can visit Miles as well before it gets too late."

They walked back toward the front lobby and the reception area. Just to the left of the stone wall behind the reception desk was a large conference room. "Why don't you wait for me there?"

She nodded and he walked down the hall to where a number of employees were unpacking their areas. He rounded them up and herded them to the conference room.

When they were all seated there, he offered them a smile

that he hoped would reassure them. "I know what happened today was scary. Luckily no one was seriously hurt."

"Is Miles okay?" Rachel asked, wringing her hands together.

"He is, thank you. And moving here, into this more secure area, will make sure all of you will be okay as well. But as you can imagine, it's important we keep what happened and this move confidential so as to not hurt the company," John said and was pleased to see the nods of everyone seated around the table.

"Good. I'm glad you're all on board. Since you may need a little time to deal with this change, feel free to take the rest of the day and tomorrow off."

"No need, John. At least not for me. If you don't mind, I'm going to finish unpacking and get back to work," said Oliver York, one of the programmers who had been with him since day one.

The murmured agreement of the others around the table filled John with hope and satisfaction. "Thank you, all. I truly appreciate it," he said and laid a hand over his heart in emphasis.

When his employees had drifted out of the conference room and back to their offices, Mia walked over to him.

"They are all so very loyal. That's impressive," she said and slipped her arm through his.

"I'm lucky to have them," he said. *And you*, he thought.

Together they strolled to the elevator. Once inside, Mia slipped in her badge and pressed the button for the floor above them.

In no time they were there, and as they entered, a young Latina receptionist greeted them with a warm smile. "Good afternoon, Mia. Mr. Smith," Julia said with almost a wink since she had obviously realized who he was.

"John, please, Julia," he said and smiled.

"John. Mia. Everyone is in the conference room," Julia

said and motioned behind her to the room where the opaque window glass was still in place. It was clear when they entered that Trey, Sophie and Robbie had news for them.

Chapter Five

Mia hurried to the table, where Trey was hovering behind Sophie and Robbie as they worked, his large hands resting on the backs of their chairs as he leaned forward to look at their laptops.

"Looks like you found something," Mia said and ambled to a spot at the table where she had earlier left her purse.

Trey flicked a hand in the direction of the large television on the far wall of the conference room. "Why don't you put up that analysis, Sophie," he said.

With the push of the remote and a few clicks on her keyboard, Sophie cast her laptop to the television.

Mia recognized the financial summary and chart for the start-up that John had recently sold. The mountain-style chart was appropriate considering that the peak of it was as high as Everest at the time John had sold it. But even she could see that in the midst of that growth there was one big chasm where the stock's price had bottomed.

She gestured to it. "What was going on there?"

John walked up to the TV and pointed to the drop. "The press got hold of bad news about a problem we were having with one of our important programs."

"Do you know how that happened?" Trey asked and tucked his arms across his broad chest.

With a shrug, John said, "I'm not sure, but I always suspected someone leaked the news to a reporter."

"To short the stock?" Mia asked, thinking someone could have made quite a bit of money from selling the stock at its high at the time and buying it back when it bottomed out.

"And if it was someone in the company, they could face charges for insider trading," John said, lips in a tight line that communicated so much to her.

"You think what happened today was done for the same reason?" She had earlier thought that there had been something wrong about the attack and about Miles's answers to the police.

"If it hasn't already hit some online news services, I expect it might hit the local news later tonight," John said.

In response, Robbie tapped away on his keyboard. A second later he said, "There's nothing in the news so far."

Trey added, "I reached out to some friends on the force and asked them to keep it low-key. Just a random break-in and I asked them to keep your names out of it."

"Can they do that?" John asked and dragged a hand through the waves of his light brown hair, tousling it messily.

She wanted to go over and smooth it out as she had more than once when they'd been going out, but resisted the urge.

"They can for now. If someone starts pressing, they may not be able to," Trey admitted.

If someone started pressing, Mia thought, but then something else came to her. "What if someone did the attack for another reason?"

Trey moved away from their cousins and toward the conference-room table. Leaning on a chair there, he eyeballed her. "Like to cover something up?"

With those words, John hurried back to the table and his knapsack. He yanked out his laptop and sat down in front of it. "Like if something had been stolen?" he said and started tapping away at the keys.

"Or if they wanted to hide what they were doing. Are you going to run it through your program?" Mia asked.

"I am," he said and nodded.

"Robbie and I are going to try and see what we can find out about the kinds of transactions that went on during that short-selling period," Sophie said as she got to work on her laptop.

"If it was an insider, they probably did it through a hold-ing company to avoid filing a Section 16 report with the SEC," Mia said.

Trey chuckled and shook his head. "I always knew you were more than just a pretty face."

A beautiful face, she thought she heard John murmur under his breath, but as she glared at him, he appeared to be buried in whatever he was doing on his laptop.

"The one thing they most likely wanted to steal is your program, but from what I can see, you always take your laptop with you," Mia said and glanced toward the battle-scarred leather bag that John took virtually everywhere.

"I usually carry it with me except when I lock it up at night, but you're right. It goes everywhere because it's the only way to fully access the code," John confirmed with a bop of his head.

"But that would be a really low-tech way to steal some-thing very high-tech," Sophie said, her brow heavily fur-rowed over her deep blue eyes.

"They would still have to hack your password to get in," Robbie said.

"It takes multiple passwords to log in and on top of that, they'd need to know how to piece together everything to have the full work of code. Not likely a run-of-the-mill bur-glar could do that," he said and closed his laptop. Barely a beat later, he added, "Based on local crime data, the nature of the crime and other variables, the program rules out that it was an actual robbery or attack."

"Which means it was planned to hide something," Trey said.

"Like who might be working for you who wants to short the stock," Mia said.

"Or who wants to steal the code. That's why you first came to us, after all," Trey added to the discussion.

"Or someone who wants to do both," Sophie said, earning an agreeing grunt from Robbie.

Trey sat down and gestured for Mia to join him, the cousins and John at the table.

Mia did, but her mind was running through all the variables of who would fake an attack and why. Miles's face immediately came to mind. She kept that thought to herself as Trey said, "If you had to short-list who might want to do this—"

John waved his hands to stop Trey. "Short-list? For real? I trust them. It's why I kept these particular people for this new venture after I sold my start-up."

Mia leaned over and laid a hand on John's as it rested on the surface of the table. "I know this must be hard for you."

"You can't imagine. They've been with me for years, and Miles… He's my brother," he said and drove his fingers through his hair in agitation.

"It's obvious this is difficult for you so why don't we take emotion out of this," Mia said and peered at his closed laptop.

It was obvious what she wanted him to do, but he shook his head, as if in disbelief. "You want me to use the program?"

"It calculates probabilities, doesn't it? Let the program tell us who is on the short list," she said, and Trey murmured his agreement.

"She's got a point, John. The program takes any and all feelings out of the decision."

John looked between the two of them and then over to Sophie and Robbie, who nodded, almost in unison.

With a heavy sigh, John opened his laptop, but paused with his fingers over the keys. "This may take a while. There's Miles and about half a dozen employees."

"We'll wait. In the meantime, we'll get to work on some other investigations about the stock transactions and I'll reach out to the police to see if they have anything else on today's attack," Trey said.

John nodded, but his face was set in harsh lines, his lips in a knife-sharp slash. His hazel eyes had grown muddied, almost lifeless, as he entered in the information.

Needing something to do because it was distressing to see how pained he was by the possibility of one of his people being a traitor, she got up and got him paper and a pen in case he needed to jot something down. She also went out to grab some of the menus that the receptionist kept, since she suspected they'd be working right through dinner.

John had said that he wanted to go visit Miles at the hospital—maybe it would make sense to take a break before dinner and visit before it got too late.

When she went back inside, John was writing something down, while Sophie and Robbie were seated on the other side of the table, busy working. Trey had left the room through a side door, probably to call his friends at the police department.

She sat beside John again, but took a moment to swipe through her social-media accounts as well as some other sources she followed that carried local news and events.

There was no mention of what had happened earlier and beneath her breath she thanked Trey's connections for doing as they had promised.

As she swiped through her various accounts, she caught

John's actions as he added names to the paper along with a number. She suspected the numbers were for the probability of their being on the short list.

The list grew longer until there was only one name left to add, but she noticed John hesitating.

She leaned close and in a soft whisper, she said, "I know you don't want to do it."

"I don't," he said and muttered a curse beneath his breath. "He's my brother."

Half, she wanted to remind him, but didn't because she understood the importance of family, especially to him since he seemed to have lacked it in his life.

"Isn't it better to rule him out instead of having doubt eat at you?" she urged.

He laid his fingers on the keys, clearly conflicted. But then he started typing away and said, "You're right. It's better to know."

As he finished and sat back to wait for the response, she held her breath and prayed for the answer that she knew he wanted.

Chapter Six

Mia had been stuck to his side like white on rice ever since the program had provided its damning accusation.

Miles had come out as Suspect #1 on their short list with a seventy-five-percent probability.

But he reminded himself of how he'd considered seventy-five a failing grade when he was in school.

So why trust that kind of number when it came to Miles? His brother. His only remaining family. Really his best friend as well, not that he had many friends, as he'd told Trey.

Trey, who held back from saying anything when John had revealed the results. He'd been almost too businesslike as he'd asked John if Sophie and Robbie could run their own analysis of those on the short list.

What could I have said or done? John thought. To reject the results was to reject that his software worked, but accepting it…

"I know you're bothered," Mia said softly as he drove the Lamborghini to the hospital to see Miles.

"Wouldn't you be?" he replied, angered by the results but also because in the back of his mind he'd had his doubts over the last several months. Ever since the stock had tanked, Miles had been different. That sense of Miles being off had only intensified in the last couple of months since he'd sold his start-up and begun this new venture.

"I would. Family is important to me, and I know it is to you as well," she said and, in a supportive gesture, stroked a hand down his arm.

As it had before, her touch gentled the riot of emotions that had pretzeled his gut into a painful knot.

"It is. It's just Miles and me," he admitted. He normally didn't like to talk about his personal life and had kept it from Mia in the past, but now it seemed almost useless to keep secrets. After all, if his program was right, they might be dead in a month.

"We had a tough life," he said and faltered, not sure how to continue.

"I understand," she said.

He laughed and shook his head. "You? Come on, princess. Don't play games with me. You've got a Cartier Tank watch on your wrist. If I'm not mistaken, that's a Prada bag and a Carolina Herrera dress."

"Judgy much?" she snapped, the heat of anger on her face.

"If the Louboutin fits—"

"I've earned my money but in case you care to know, things weren't always easy for my family either. Not when my grandparents came from Cuba or when my dad was a cop or in the marines. I don't know how my mom did it sometimes, but we always had food on the table and a roof over our heads," she said, her tone sharp and filled with pain.

He hadn't known that and wouldn't have guessed because of the current success of the family.

"I'm sorry," he said and pulled off the highway and onto the road leading to the hospital.

The silence in the car was as heavy as a thousand-pound boulder as he finished the drive to Jackson Memorial. They parked and walked in silence into the building. After checking in at the lobby, they hurried up to Miles's room only to find that it was empty.

"Wait here," John said and headed to the nurses' station to find out where Miles was, but as he neared the station and heard a very feminine giggle, he knew.

Miles was in a wheelchair and chatting up a twenty-something nurse who was clearly eating up the attention.

The young woman looked in his direction, which also drew Miles's gaze to him. The broad, welcoming smile that had been on his face a moment before faded slightly.

"Bro. I wasn't expecting you," Miles said.

"I promised you I'd be back," John reminded him as he walked over, then took hold of the handles of the wheelchair. As John swiveled the chair back in the direction of his room, he leaned close to Miles and said, "Good to see you're feeling better."

Miles laughed and shook his head. "I told the doctor I wanted to go home, but he insisted I stay the night."

"No sense taking chances. I'm glad you're feeling okay," he said and wheeled him into the room, where Mia was patiently waiting.

"You're looking well," Mia said when they entered and Miles scooted up from the wheelchair into the bed, one hand tucked behind him to keep the hospital gown in place.

"Thanks. I can't wait to get out of here," Miles said and pulled the sheets up to his midsection.

"I guess we can come get you in the morning," Mia said, surprising John given their earlier silence in the car. He hadn't figured she'd help him because of their argument.

"I'll be waiting for you first thing," Miles said and looked from Mia to John and back to Mia. Jerking his finger between them, he said, "The two of you—"

"Just friends," Mia said with a wave of her hands.

Friend-zoned, which John hadn't expected, so he supposed he was lucky to have that at least. But it also re-minded him of the reason she was here with him in the first place.

"That was a brave thing you did," John said, recalling the moment when his brother had rushed out to tackle their intruder.

Miles shrugged. "I had to do it, bro. I couldn't let him get to you."

John narrowed his gaze as he considered that comment, but Mia beat him to the next question.

"Why do you think he wanted to get to John?" she asked, gaze narrowed as she peered at Miles.

Another careless shrug came as Miles frowned. "Why would they want me? I'm nobody important."

John didn't fail to miss the bitterness there. It wasn't the first time that he'd heard it, but given the prediction the software had made earlier, that tone took on an entirely new meaning.

"You are important, Miles. You're a valued member of the team and you're my brother," John said, hoping to re-assure him.

"Right," Miles said, but he was clearly unconvinced. He quickly added, "I'm feeling a little tired. Would you mind going?"

"Sure. We understand," John said, although he didn't. He'd always looked up to Miles and kept him close. He'd brought him into the company and given him a leadership role even though he'd lacked the experience. On a personal level, he'd done whatever Miles had wanted, from the par-ties to the Lamborghini. What more could Miles want?

Respect, maybe? was the answer that came immedi-ately. Could that be the reason for what the software had suggested?

"I'd say a penny for your thoughts, only I suspect they're a lot more costly," Mia said as they stepped onto the elevator.

"They are. You could say it's a multimillion-dollar question," he said and shook his head.

"Your software could be wrong, you know," Mia said and as the elevator door opened, she slipped her arm through his and they stepped out to find one of the local news reporters waiting for them in the lobby.

"Mr. Wilson. Is it true someone attacked your offices earlier today?" the young woman said as she chased after them, notebook in hand.

When they hurried past her without answering, she added, "Ms. Gonzalez. Has your family been engaged by Mr. Wilson or is this a personal relationship?"

John glanced at Mia from the corner of his eye, and in response, she brushed a kiss across his cheek and whispered, "Ignore her. She has no right to invade our personal lives."

The reporter was tenacious, however, and followed them out of the hospital, chasing after them in their dash to his car. To make a quick getaway, he hit the button for the remote start.

A fireball erupted, lifting the body of the Lamborghini into the air.

John threw himself in front of the two women as the force of the blast, the heat of it, threw them back against the doors of the hospital. Bits and pieces of metal and glass rained down on them. The chassis of the car hit the ground in flames with a resounding crash.

His ears were ringing from the concussion of the blast and the nearby car alarms blaring their complaints into the air. Luckily, most of the debris had seemed to go upward and not at them.

He helped Mia to her feet. "Are you hurt?" he said and could barely hear his own voice from the alarms and ringing in his ears. He realized there were also alarms going off inside the hospital and that the fire from his car was quickly spreading to other nearby vehicles.

"I'm okay," she said, the sound muffled to his ears.

Facing the reporter, he inspected her, but she seemed fine, if a little dazed. Still, he asked, "Are you okay?"

The reporter nodded and, not missing a beat, she said, "Can I get a comment from you now?"

TREY HUGGED HER so hard that she worried he might crack a rib. "Trey, I'm okay. Really," Mia said and wiggled to get some breathing room.

Her brother finally released her and jammed his hands on his hips as he inspected the mess in the hospital parking lot.

Mia tracked his gaze to where two firetrucks and assorted firefighters were pouring water on the remains of the Lamborghini and the other cars that had surrounded it. Off to the side, two patrol cars sat at the curb next to a fire marshal's truck and a CSI van.

Mia and the reporter had already provided what little information they could to the police officers. It hadn't been much. Only that John had hit his remote start button, triggering the explosion. Since his car had caused the conflagration, John was still with the police, answering even more questions.

As if reading her thoughts, Trey said, "The bomber probably didn't count on John doing a remote start. Thank God, he did."

Her insides chilled at his comment. If John hadn't done that, the two of them would be dead right now. The reporter, too, if she had continued to dog after them. Her determination had probably saved them since it had pushed John to start the car before they got anywhere near it. But even as she thought that, another idea took hold and refused to leave.

"This wasn't intended for John, was it?" she said, voice choked with fear and emotion.

Trey wrapped an arm around her shoulders and drew her tight to his side. "If it was intended for you, someone is tracking you and brazen enough to plant the bomb right here in the parking lot. But no matter who it was directed at, we'll find a way to keep you safe."

She wanted to believe that, but only luck had saved them tonight. She had never been one to solely rely on luck.

Before she had a chance to reply, an unmarked car with lights flashing jerked to the curb in front of them. Roni rushed out of the car and up to them.

She hugged Mia hard. "Thank God. When I heard the news, I had to come over and make sure you were okay."

"I'm okay, *amiga*. Shook up. Scared, but okay," she admitted to her best friend.

Roni glanced up at her fiancée. "Have you had a chance to talk to anyone about what they have so far?"

Trey shook his head. "Not yet. Now that you're here, maybe you can go over while I take Mia and John home."

"That's a good idea. They'll probably be more willing to talk to me since you're 'retired,'" Roni said, air quotes reminding him that he was no longer officially one of the men in blue.

"Stay safe and watch your six, *mi amor*. I'm worried this attack was directed at the family," Trey warned and dropped a kiss on Roni's cheek.

"You, too," Roni said and marched toward the first responders while John walked to join her and Trey. But before John could reach them, Miles came running out of the hospital, fully dressed, and raced to his brother's side. He hugged him hard, and John returned the embrace.

Mia and Trey shared a look and together they hurried over to where the two brothers stood.

"I heard about the explosion, and they couldn't keep me

inside. I had to make sure you weren't hurt," Miles said and kept an arm around John's shoulders.

"I'm fine. We're fine," he said and shot a look at Mia.

"Right. Mia. You're safe, too," Miles said, almost as an afterthought. It made her wonder if he'd truly forgotten she had been with John, or if there was another reason, like jealousy.

Over the course of their few dates, if you could call them that, she'd gotten the sense that Miles almost resented the attention that John had been paying to her even though Miles had been the one pushing them together at first.

"I am, thank you. But you really should stay the night to make sure you're fine," she said and gestured toward the hospital.

Miles shook his head. "No. I'm AMA and staying that way," he said, referring to his decision to leave against medical advice.

"We can take you home," Trey said and whipped out his phone to call for the SBS Suburban that had brought him to the hospital.

Miles peered all around them, as if searching for something, and then gestured toward the twisted and soaked mess of steel many yards away. "Oh, no. Please tell me that's not the Lambo."

"It's the Lambo," John said and didn't seem quite as upset about it as Miles was.

"Like I said. We'll drive you home," Trey said as the Suburban pulled up to the curb.

They all piled in and once they were seated, Trey said, "Where can we drop you off, Miles?"

In the dim light inside the SUV, Miles peered at John, obviously confused. In response, John said, "Mia, Trey and I have some things to go over. You should go home and get some rest. Take tomorrow off as well."

Miles's earlier happiness that his brother was okay dimmed, and a hard set slipped over his features. "Of course. I'm sure the three of you have important things to do."

"What's important is that you get the rest you need. I'll fill you in on things tomorrow," John said and that seemed to mollify his brother, but only a little.

The silence that settled over all of them weighed heavily on Mia. She felt the confusion, worry and tension in that false quiet and it only lifted the slightest bit after John walked Miles to the door of his South Pointe condo building and returned to the SUV.

When he slipped back in and took a seat beside her behind the privacy screen that had been added to the SUV, he said, "You think this had something to do with him?"

Mia shook her head. "No. I'm worried that explosion was meant to take me out. You and anyone else were just collateral damage."

"Luckily there was no collateral damage besides a few other vehicles," Trey added from the seat behind them.

"That explains the change in my life expectancy. Becoming involved with you is the risk," John said and surprised her by cupping her cheek. "I'm not going to let anything happen to you."

She offered him a weak smile. "I'm sorry I got you involved in this."

"Can we keep the pessimism down a bit, please? I'm not ready to buy the farm just yet," Trey said, lightening what had become a maudlin moment.

John shook his head and, while looking at her, he said, "I'm not either. I've still got too many things to appreciate."

Mia ducked her head, his gaze just too intense. His words offered hope for things she wasn't sure were possible. But even though someone had possibly tried to kill her tonight, she wasn't about to roll over and make it easy for them.

She was going to fight them every step of the way. "Let's go. We've got crimes to solve."

Chapter Seven

He'd expected Wilson to park his fancy car in a less crowded area of the parking lot. That's what a lot of jerks with fancy cars did to avoid door dings. Parking the car close to other vehicles had made it easier for him to hide while he wired the car with the bomb. But he hadn't expected Wilson to use the remote start, something he did because that stupid reporter had been chasing after them.

And since Wilson had parked close to other cars, those vehicles had deflected almost all of the blast upward, keeping Wilson, Mia and the reporter from being injured.

He raised the binoculars and peered down at the smoking remains of the Lamborghini and the vehicles surrounding it. Firefighters were still pouring water to douse the last of the flames and hopefully the water would wash away a lot of evidence as well.

Not that he'd been careless. He'd been gloved when he'd built the bomb and when he'd connected it to the spare wires he'd installed when the car had been in the repair shop a week earlier. A real shame to lose the car. Now there were only four of them left and way too many of the Gonzalez family. He'd been patiently watching Wilson in the hopes that Mia would be with him when the car exploded.

They'd been lucky this time. He vowed to make sure they wouldn't be as lucky the next.

"I CAN'T SOLVE crimes on an empty stomach. Besides, I want to hear what Roni has to report from her talks with the local LEOs, fire marshal, and the CSI unit," Trey said and picked up one of the menus Mia had laid out on the table earlier that night. They had all decided on a late dinner, which had enabled John and Mia to visit Miles.

Before getting to know Trey, John might have doubted the sanity of his actions considering all that had happened that day. But a break for food and rest might help all of them get some distance from the events and think more clearly.

Especially since things were getting so convoluted and intertwined. Mia might think that the car bomb—he had no doubt that's what it was—had been intended to take her out, but the bomb had been placed in *his* car when they'd gone to visit *his* brother.

Coincidence or more? he thought.

Mia handed him one of the menus. "I know you like Cubanos."

His gaze met hers and he realized that like her brother, she was trying to draw him out of his thoughts about all that had happened that day. The attack on the office. The bomb at the hospital. *What else could come next*? he wondered.

"Thanks, but I suspect you're probably tired of eating those," he said with a chuckle.

She shook her head. "Never, but a change of pace might be nice."

He handed her back the menu for the Cuban restaurant. "Whatever you'd like, Mia. To be honest, I'm not really hungry."

"I get it, but trying to keep some routines normal helps," Mia said, reached across the table to grab a few more of the menus, and handed them to him.

"Got it," he said with a nod just as Mia's brother Ricky and his fiancée, Mariela, hurried through the door of the conference room.

"We got here as soon as we could," Ricky said and hugged Trey, Sophie and Robbie. There was no mistaking that he was Trey's brother, since they looked alike, but Ricky had a lean runner's build while Trey was slightly taller and more muscular.

Ricky's fiancée was a beautiful woman, with sun-streaked caramel hair, emerald eyes and a voluptuous, centerfold body.

Like Ricky, she hugged her future relatives and then the couple worked their way over to Mia.

When Ricky reached her, he embraced Mia tightly and rocked back and forth with her. "I was so worried."

"We're okay," she said and playfully ruffled the thick waves of his mahogany-brown hair.

Ricky nodded, released her and rushed to his side to shake his hand as Mariela hugged Mia. "John. Good to see you again, although I'm sorry it's under these conditions. How are you doing?"

"Okay, considering we came this close to being toast," John said and brought his index finger and thumb together to emphasize his statement.

At his words, Mia's face paled, but she bucked that fear by pulling her shoulders back and glaring at him. "But we're not toast and we're going to find out who's behind this."

"We are," Trey said and clapped his hands. "Let's get going with dinner. Roni texted to say she'll be here soon."

"Pizza. It'll let us work while we eat," Mia suggested, and when everyone nodded in agreement, she slipped her phone out of a pocket and made the call.

Barely fifteen minutes had gone as they got settled around the conference room when a ding sounded from Trey's phone. He took a quick look at it, did a little nod and then swiped his screen. With a look at Sophie and Robbie, who were stationed at their laptops at the conference-room table, he said, "Local PD just sent over some videos from the hospital's CCTVs. I just forwarded them to you."

"We'll see what we can do with them," Sophie said.

Robbie nodded in agreement and said, "They might need enhancement, but hopefully we can make them clear enough to compare them with the videos from the drive-by shootings."

"Would you mind sharing them with me?" John asked as Mia sat beside him.

She glanced at him. "Do you think your program can get something from them?"

He nodded. "We've already linked both those drive-bys and believe they're connected to your family. I can analyze if it's the same individual involved."

Mia lifted a perfectly plucked eyebrow. "And if it is?"

"If it is, it's worrisome," Ricky said, a dark glower on his face.

"Why do you say that?" Mariela asked from beside him and grasped his hand, as if to comfort him.

Ricky shook his head and blew out a breath. "These other attacks... They were more personal. They targeted the family for the most part. This one... He could have taken out a lot more people. Innocent people."

"But why our family? That's the key to finding this person. And let's not forget we have to figure out who's trying to steal John's code," Trey said.

John nodded. "I appreciate that, but no one's tried to kill me."

"What about today in the office?" Mia said, surprised by his comment.

With a shrug, he said, "That attack rubs me all wrong."

Mia narrowed her gaze. "You think it was planned to do something else."

"I do. Probably to throw us off the scent. To make us

think someone else is behind the hack, when it's really someone in-house," he explained.

"Did your software tell you that?" Trey asked.

John pointed to his midsection. "My gut tells me and you more than most know how important that is. You thought there was something wrong with the attacks and Mariela's ex's death."

That seemed to shock the young woman, who sat up in her seat and opened her eyes wide to look at him. "What do you mean?"

"I'm sorry, Mariela. We meant to talk to you beforehand, but I've always thought there was something off about Jorge's supposed suicide. It just tied things up way too neatly," Trey explained.

"I'm sorry, too. I didn't mean to spring it on you like that," John said, feeling awful about Mariela's shocked and pained reaction.

"You think Jorge was murdered?" she said in a choked whisper and laid a shaky hand at her throat.

Trey nodded. "I do and I always suspected that it was someone who was trying to hide other crimes, like the drive-bys. Possibly the bombing of Jorge's construction site now that I think about it. Two bombs is just too much coincidence."

"Which means you have someone skilled with weapons and bomb-building. Who would have those kinds of skills?" Mia asked.

"Normally I'd say someone in law enforcement or the military," Trey said and stood as the sound of activity in the lobby area grabbed his attention.

He was going into fight mode, John guessed, but Trey immediately relaxed as Roni waltzed through the conference room door carrying four pizza boxes.

"A little help here," she called out and Trey rushed over

to grab the boxes and take them over to a credenza on one side of the conference room.

Roni walked with him and once he'd put down the boxes, she embraced him and Trey slipped his arms around her. They kissed and John had to look away because the obvious love there, and the possibility it might be lost before it could grow, was too painful.

He busied himself by reaching into the knapsack sitting at his feet and pulling out his laptop. "You'll give me access to those videos?" he asked Sophie and Robbie.

Robbie nodded. "Just finished uploading all of them to our cloud server. I'll email you a link so you can get them."

"Thanks," John said, then checked his email and followed the link to the videos.

"Can I get you some pizza?" Mia asked.

"Thanks. I'd appreciate that," he said with a smile, before immersing himself in analyzing the videos.

FEELING USELESS, Mia turned her attention to setting out the various pizza boxes on the credenza, and with Mariela's help, they raided the office pantry for plates, cups, napkins and sodas from the supply they kept for SBS employees.

They returned with them to the conference room to find Robbie flipping open box tops to check the pizza selections.

"Don't worry. I got you your Hawaiian pizza," Mia said with a chuckle and shake of her head. Arms full of the paper goods, she dropped them on the free space on the credenza while Mariela wheeled over a cart with assorted sodas, snugged it close to the furniture and then returned to the table to sit beside Ricky.

Robbie rubbed his hands together with glee, grabbed a plate and snagged a couple of slices of his favorite pizza. Then he prepped a second plate, probably for Sophie. As he started to walk away, Mia shoved napkins against his chest, feeling way too much like a mom even though Robbie was the same age as her.

Trey and Roni walked over next and loaded their plates before returning to the table where Ricky and Mariela were sitting, heads tucked close. Mariela's distress was impossible to miss, and Mia understood. It had been a shock that her ex had possibly been murdered and hadn't committed suicide.

Sophie was just a few feet away, head buried in her laptop as she worked on the videos that had been sent over by the police department. Robbie laid a plate beside her, and she glanced up and offered her older brother a grateful smile.

Sophie often lost herself in her work, much like John, Mia thought as she glanced back at him. He had his game face on—his brow was creased and his hazel gaze was focused on his laptop.

It yanked a smile to her face since it reminded her of how intense he'd been when they'd been gaming in his penthouse at the Del Sol. She'd been surprised when that was all that he'd wanted when he'd first invited her to come into his private area in the penthouse. She'd worried he'd ask for more, which she had not been prepared to give, and had been determined to find out something—actually anything—about the reclusive multimillionaire.

She hadn't found out much. John Wilson was very much a closed book about his past.

It had intrigued her even more, but also saddened her because it was impossible to miss there was hurt buried there. Hurt that had shaped him, but also kept him from moving on, she suspected.

She muttered a curse since she'd always been one to bring home injured animals and John was very much that: injured.

Shaking that thought loose from her brain, she grabbed

a plate, two slices of pizza, a diet soda and a napkin, and took it over to him.

He immediately looked up and smiled. "Thank you. You didn't have to do that."

With a quick lift of her shoulders, she said, "Have to do something. I'm feeling a little…"

"Challenged?" he said sympathetically with a half smile when she struggled for a word.

"Thanks for that," she said and glanced at his laptop, which was running a video while a program shot all kinds of weird lines, dots and numbers across the image.

She pointed to the screen. "What's it doing?"

He jerked his head in the direction of the credenza. "Why don't you get some food and I'll explain."

With a nod, she did as he asked and grabbed herself a couple of slices, since she was feeling famished, and a regular soda because she'd never acquired a taste for the fake stuff. When she returned to sit beside him, he gestured to his laptop.

"Those lines and things are my program doing an analysis of the person in the image. Hopefully it'll be able to tell us his approximate size and weight," John informed her.

"They're grainy, aren't they?" she said and took a bite of a slice.

"They are. Makes it hard to identify features like race and eye color. But you can tell other things."

"Like age? No senior citizen is going to be able to hop up on the edge of the car window like that," she said and circled her finger over the image of the shooter from one of the drive-by videos.

"And he's right-handed," she added as she examined the photo.

"He is. You're very observant. You were able to tell the police a lot about the man who attacked the office earlier," he said.

She did a slight lift of her shoulders. "Like I said, I've hung out with Trey too much. Roni, too. She's a great cop."

"I heard that," Roni teased from across the way, a bright smile on her face.

"Super cop that you are, do you have anything for us from your fellow LEOs at the hospital?" Mia teased right back.

"I do. CSI was able to find some bomb pieces and I asked them to compare those pieces and the explosive used to the bombing at the construction site. ATF is probably going to get involved as well," Roni said.

"Any fingerprints?" Trey asked.

"None so far," Roni said, a frown on her face.

"I'm not a car expert, but aren't the ignition wires under the hood?" Mia said, thinking about her own car and the few times she'd had it serviced.

"Good point. Ignition wires are generally not accessible without lifting the hood," Sophie said and leaned forward to examine her screen. "In this video, he just walks up to the car and slips underneath. He's there for at most a minute or two."

"Which means he had another way to get to the ignition system," Trey said and peered at John. "Have you had the car serviced recently?"

"A little while ago. It was overheating," he said and shook his head. "If he knew that—"

"He's been following you. Maybe because of me. You could have been killed because of me," Mia said and laid a hand against the tightness in her chest.

"But we weren't killed, and he won't get to us again," John said and squeezed her hand to soothe her concerns.

"Can you give us the name of the company that did the servicing? If we're lucky, they'll have CCTVs at their location and we'll be able to get a visual on a suspect," Roni said.

"I should have the info in my emails. I'll send it to you," John said and returned his attention to the laptop.

"What else can you tell us, *mi amor*?" Trey said and got up to grab another slice.

"That I'm the one who should be eating for two, not you," Roni said with a grin and shocked silence filled the room.

Chapter Eight

A second later, a chorus of congratulations erupted from everyone gathered around the table.

"That's wonderful!" Ricky said and hugged his older brother's fiancée. Mariela popped up to hug Roni and Mia did the same, rushing over to embrace her best friend.

"Why didn't you tell me?" she said as she clasped Roni tight.

Roni looked over at Trey as he returned to the table with another slice and accepted a hug from Mariela.

"We only just confirmed it today and with everything that's been going on... We had only told the parents just before Trey got the call about the explosion. We'd talked about when was the right time to tell you—"

"And I guess you decided now was the right time," Trey said facetiously, but bent to drop a kiss on Roni's cheek and Mia hugged him.

SOPHIE AND ROBBIE got up and walked over as well to congratulate the couple, leaving John sitting there, wondering what to do.

Happy family gatherings had never been a common occurrence in his life, but that was his past and as he glanced across the table at the family gathered there, he realized this was his promise for the future. He pushed away from the table and walked over to shake Trey's hand, and as the women stepped away from Roni, offered his hand to her as well. But Roni hauled him in for a tight embrace.

"Congratulations," he said, his voice slightly hoarse from the emotion he was feeling.

"Thank you, John," she said and as she released him, she whispered, "Treat Mia right."

He nodded and hurried back to his laptop, more determined than ever to discover who was behind the attacks on the Gonzalez family. As for his own issues, he'd set them aside for now and would work on them later. It wouldn't be the first time he'd spent late hours on a problem, and it wouldn't be the last.

When he sat, Mia came to his side and said, "Can I get you another slice?"

He glanced at his empty plate. He'd been so involved in what was happening on his laptop that he'd eaten both slices without thinking. Despite that, he was still hungry.

"I'd like that, thanks. Plain, please," he said with a smile.

She returned the smile, ran a hand across his shoulder in a fleeting caress and walked away to get his pizza. He returned to watching his program do the analysis and just as the results came in, Mia returned with his slice and another diet soda.

"Did you find something?" she asked, then sat beside him and nibbled on her pizza.

"Based on the new video info, the program says the probability of it being the same shooter in both drive-bys is 90 percent. On top of that, it estimates he was about six-foot-two, and about 180 pounds."

"And he was either white or white Hispanic," Ricky added, having overheard what they were discussing.

"And right-handed, which makes him sound a lot like the man in the office today," Mia chimed in.

It actually did, John thought, recalling what Mia had

told the police earlier that day. Too much coincidence, even though the general characteristics of the man were fairly average.

Looking across at Trey and Roni, he said, "Did the police ever get any CCTV footage from the service areas of the other building?"

"Not as far as I know, but I can reach out to them to confirm," Roni said and stepped away from the table to make the calls.

"What else can we see from the videos?" Mia asked from beside him.

"The program's analyzed—"

"I mean us," she said and gestured between them.

"Us. As in we'll look at the videos?" he asked, just to confirm.

"Yes. Let's look at the videos. Maybe we'll see something that will give us a lead," Mia said and pointed at his laptop.

It made sense to give it a shot the old-fashioned way, but not on his smaller laptop screen. With a flip of the hand in the direction of the big television, he said, "Let's watch them on that."

"Mind if I join you?" Trey said.

"Maybe it'll jog something in our memory," Ricky said, and Mariela nodded.

With a few keystrokes, he cast the videos from the first drive-by that had happened in front of the Del Sol hotel while Trey and Roni were investigating the murder of Trey's partner and a human-trafficking ring.

Unfortunately, the driver hadn't exited the vehicle to shoot and had been both masked and gloved. Except for possibly confirming the shooter's height and build, that video didn't provide any new information.

He pulled up the videos snatched from Ricky's video

doorbell as well as those from some of his neighbors during the second drive-by.

"Better quality," John said as he brought up the videos. They were much clearer than the grainier ones from the hotel CCTVs.

They ran through the videos and as they finished, Mia said, "Could you rerun it? I thought I saw something."

He nodded and did as she asked and a few seconds later, she said, "Freeze it. There."

She jumped up from her chair and hurried toward the TV, where she bent slightly to view the screen. As she did so, her designer dress lovingly caressed her curves, pulling his mind from anything having to do with the investigation and forcing him to tame his body's reaction to hers.

Pointing to the screen in the general direction of the shooter's right hand, she said, "His shirt rode up his arm. There's something there on his wrist. Can you zoom in?"

John zoomed in, but as he did so, the video grew more and more pixelated. Despite that, when Mia circled one area on the image, it was clear there was something besides shadows in the space she'd identified.

"Is that a tattoo?" he asked, squinting to try and make sense of the shape that was visible.

"I think so," Ricky said, and Mariela echoed her agreement. "Definitely a tattoo."

Turning his head to the side, he tried to figure it out, but couldn't.

"Beads," Mia said and popped up from where she had been peering at the screen. "Rosary beads. I've seen tattoos like that," she said and motioned to her forearm. "The beads start here and wrap down and around. Sometimes the cross is in the person's palm—"

"Or higher up on the forearm," Mariela said.

"What do they mean?" John said, totally unfamiliar with what you did with a rosary.

JOHN WASN'T CATHOLIC, Mia realized and explained. "Rosary beads are used when praying, usually when you're doing penance. You say the Hail Mary to ask for forgiveness for any sins you've committed, but you can also say the rosary for reflection."

"Our attacker is religious?" John said, clearly unable to link someone wanting to commit murder with a religious type.

"Or a gang member. The rosary has become popular with some Latin gangs," Trey added with a disgusted shake of his head at the perversion of the symbolism.

"We have more clues then. The attacker is a Latino and possibly a gang member," Sophie said.

"And the attacks started happening in the last three months. Maybe this person just got out of prison," Roni suggested for consideration and continued. "I'll run that through our databases in the morning and see what I get. We can compare that to the other evidence we've noted, like knowledge of bomb-making and expertise with weapons."

"But the program now says there might be some connection to John's program. Minimal, but possible," Mia reminded them.

John nodded. "Maybe whoever is behind the hack hired this guy not knowing about the connection to your family?"

"Maybe. I have some friends who are undercover in the gang scene. I'll reach out to them to see what they can say about anyone looking to hire some muscle," Roni said.

"I still have some connections there as well," Trey added.

"Robbie and I will keep on looking at those stock transactions and if John is willing to give us access, maybe we can look at the server activity to see if someone left any fingerprints that will lead us to them," Sophie said.

"Fingerprints?" Mia asked, eyeing her cousin in puzzlement.

With a shrug, Sophie said, "Hackers use certain things

to try to break in. It may give us an idea of how sophisticated they are."

"And we can look at security policies and other things to see if access was changed," Robbie added.

"That makes sense. With all that's happening, I haven't really had a chance to delve into any possible hack, just to try and prevent it again," John explained.

"I can see Roni's getting a little tired, so maybe it's time for us all to go our separate ways and work on all these things," Trey said, but then pointed to her and John. "Except for you two. Someone is clearly out for you so it may be best for you to stay in the penthouse suite. At least for tonight."

John tossed his hands up in the air. "I hadn't planned on that."

"Me either," she said and smoothed her now very wrinkled dress.

"There is some new clothing up there for emergencies like that. Roni can bring you some things in the morning and if you don't mind, John, let me have your house keys. I can check it out and arrange for security there and pick up some clothes for you," Trey said, his tone making it clear that disagreement would not be permitted.

"Yes, sir," Mia said with a salute and a smile. Trey only wanted what was safest for them, but she worried about him and the rest of her family.

Trey seemed to have read her thoughts. "Roni and I can take care of ourselves. Ricky and Mariela are still with *Mami* and *Papi* and it will be hard to get past the security guard at the gate. Same for Sophie and Robbie's condo building, with its doorman and security systems."

John reached for his knapsack, pulled out his keys and tossed them to Trey. "I'll text you the code for my security system."

Trey nodded. "I'm sure it's a good one, but I may beef it up with some other things, if that's okay."

John nodded. "It's okay. Whatever you think we need to keep Mia and me safe."

Mia and me? *Did I hear that right*? Mia wondered, but as she met his gaze, it was obvious she'd heard correctly.

Somehow that didn't bother her. With every hour that she spent with him, she was growing more and more intrigued by him, attracted to him.

Trey looked her way and when she didn't protest, he nodded. "We'll be going then. See you in the morning."

"Carolina is supposed to be back tomorrow, but I think I should call her and let her know that she and *Tia* Elena should extend their girls' getaway," Mia said.

"I think that's a great idea," Trey confirmed and then he and Roni rose as one, followed by Ricky and Mariela. They came over to hug her and John, and then went to Sophie and Robbie, who were still sitting in front of their laptops.

At a questioning lift of Trey's brow, Robbie said, "We're just going to work a little longer."

"Not too long," Sophie said, which was unusual since she was the one who usually lost track of time when she was on the computer.

With a nod, the two couples walked out, leaving her with her cousins and John. She pointed up and said, "Let me show you to the penthouse suite."

Chapter Nine

The elevator doors opened into a luxuriously appointed penthouse suite.

John strolled in, the weight of his knapsack seeming heavier than usual. Considering all that had happened that day, he was surprised it didn't drag him to the floor, but having the support of the Gonzalez family had made a world of difference.

Especially Mia. Having her beside him…

He tried not to think of that too much because he didn't want to have to deal with the disappointment. He'd already had too much of that in his life.

"Let me show you to the guest bedroom," she said and flung a hand in the direction of a far wall.

He glanced that way and realized the space had a central living-and-dining-room area with a kitchen off to one side and what looked like another bedroom on the opposite wall. The bedroom he followed her to was the one farthest from the kitchen.

The entire wall opposite the kitchen and a centrally located fireplace was made of glass, providing amazing views of downtown Miami, Miami Beach and the waters beyond.

"You don't need to worry about the glass. Like downstairs, it's all privacy-protected," she explained.

"There should be an assortment of robes and things in

the closet and drawers as well as fresh toiletries and towels in the bathroom," she said.

"Do you have overnight guests often?" he asked, wondering why the family would have included such a space in their building.

With a lift of her dainty shoulders, she said, "Occasionally. Usually, people who don't want other people to know they're in the area or need to be safeguarded. Trey and Roni had to stay here during their earlier investigation. More often it's a family member who's working late."

"Like Sophie and Robbie?" he asked, feeling bad that the two tech gurus were still at work downstairs when he had left.

"Like Sophie and Robbie. I don't know how they do it sometimes," Mia admitted with a roll of her blue eyes.

Shrugging, John admitted, "It comes with the territory. I often get so lost in the code that I don't realize I've been at it for hours."

Mia narrowed her gaze and peered at him. "If you want to work on something, why not get comfortable and have at it."

Have at it? No woman had ever said that to him about his programming. What few women he'd ever been involved with had resented the time he'd spent on his laptop while enjoying the financial benefits it brought.

"I think I will. Feel free to turn in if you want to. I imagine you're tired," he said and laid his knapsack on the bed.

"I am but wired, too. Still trying to wrap my head around all that's happened," she confessed and wrapped her arms around herself, as if trying to keep herself from falling into pieces.

He walked over and cupped her cheek, admiring the strength she had shown. "Weren't you the one who told me we'd figure this out?"

She offered him a fragile smile. "I am."

Her cheek was so soft beneath his thumb, he had to stroke it gently. "Why don't you get comfortable as well. Maybe we can share a drink to relax before I start working."

She nodded and her smile brightened. "I'd like that. I think I'm going to take a shower first."

"Sounds like a great idea. I'll meet you out there," he said and waited until she was out of the room to scrounge through the drawers to find an assortment of comfy T-shirts and sweatpants with the tags still on them.

He grabbed a University of Miami T-shirt and matching sweatpants and headed for a quick shower.

When he exited into the living-room area, he heard the whoosh of the water running in Mia's shower. He opened the refrigerator to see it was fully stocked with an assortment of sodas and food items. The cabinets beside the fridge held plates, glasses and snacks.

He walked to the side of the kitchen where there was a bar with an assortment of liquors and glasses. Remembering what Mia had ordered on a couple of their dates, he popped some ice cubes into highball glasses and added a couple of fingers of a single-malt scotch. After picking up the glasses, he walked with them to the sofa, placed them on the coffee table and, feeling the chill of the air-conditioning, went over to the glass fireplace and lit it.

"Being decadent, are we?" Mia teased as she walked out of the bedroom, fluffing her wet, shoulder-length hair with her hands. Her face was devoid of makeup, but if anything, she was even prettier in her natural state. Her cheeks bore the kiss of the sun, and her skin was flawless even without the benefit of foundation or whatever women put on their faces. Impossibly long lashes framed those amazing blue eyes that could be as bright as the sunniest Miami day, or as deep and blue as the ocean during a storm.

"John?" she asked at his prolonged perusal.

"Yes, being decadent. Not something I'm used to, I must

confess," he admitted and handed her a glass as she curled up into the corner of the sofa, tucking her legs beneath her.

Like him, she had slipped into a T-shirt and sweats, making her look like a young coed and not the sophisticated woman he was used to seeing.

"You look…nice," he said, coughed and looked away as he noticed how the chill of the AC had tightened her nipples beneath the soft cotton fabric.

From the corner of his eye, he caught the rush of color up her neck and to her cheeks, and how she untucked her legs and drew up her knees to provide some protection from the chill, or maybe his gaze.

"Silly," he said and flinched as he realized he'd said it aloud.

"It is," she admitted and the color across her cheeks deepened. "I mean, we're both adults. Consenting ones at that. We should be able to deal with being attracted to each other."

He jumped with surprise at that admission. "You're attracted to me."

She muttered a curse beneath her breath and took a bracing swig from her drink. Finally, she said, "I am. But it's not just physical. You're a puzzle."

"Wrapped in an enigma and covered with a paradox," he teased to hopefully get them past the awkwardness of the moment.

She laughed, as he'd hoped she would, and shook her head. "Seriously. We're a pair, aren't we?"

"We are. Tell me about yourself, Mia. Tell me about the girl who didn't have everything," he said, recalling her words from earlier that day.

"I can't say I was like most little girls. Being in the middle of Trey and Ricky was a challenge," she admitted.

John could understand. They were very different men.

Trey was an all-action guy while Ricky was quieter and more cerebral, which actually explained a lot about Mia.

"I see now why you can kick ass as good as any marine, as well as fix hurts like you did with Miles," he said.

She chuckled, shook her head and took another sip of her scotch. "I had to learn to survive."

She had not only survived, but she had also probably exceeded her own expectations. "You've done very well for yourself, Mia. I'm sure your family is proud."

She nodded without hesitation. "They are."

He wished he could be as sure of how his family would have felt about him and she seemed to sense his uncertainty. "What about your family? What you've done is amazing."

Peering down at his glass as if it would have the answer, he delayed, unsure of what to say. But then Mia reached over and laid a hand on his, offering comfort.

"It's okay if you don't want to share," she said, her voice husky with emotion much like what he was feeling.

For so long he'd kept it all to himself and it had become the proverbial albatross around his neck, dragging him down. Maybe finally letting it free would lessen that burden.

Slugging down a gulp of scotch, he winced as it burned down his throat. Slowly lifting his gaze, he met hers, the color of a stormy sea, reflecting the pain in his.

"My dad was abusive. He used to beat the heck out of my mom. Miles and me, too, sometimes if we didn't hide fast enough."

She said nothing, only twined her fingers with his to offer support.

"Luckily, and I can't believe I'm using that word to talk about someone dying," he said and shook his head in disbelief. At another gentle squeeze on his hand, he continued. "He was killed in a bar fight. I guess he decided to beat on the wrong person. With him gone, we were safe, but it was really hard on my mom to keep the family going. She had to work long hours so we wouldn't go hungry, but she did it and somehow made sure we could go to college. Unfortunately, she died of cancer right after I graduated."

"That must have been so rough on you—" she paused briefly "—and Miles." And it was obvious she didn't have as much sympathy for his brother as she did for him.

"He's not as bad as you think, Mia. He's always protected me and had my back," John said and took another sip of his scotch.

"I'd be lying to you if I said he didn't rub me the wrong way," Mia said.

"All I ask is that you give him a chance."

A chance? To a man she worried was behind the attempted hack of John's program? But even as she thought that, it occurred to her that she didn't see Miles as being involved in the attempt to kill them. Because of that, and because she wanted to explore whatever this was between her and John, she would do as he asked.

"I will try, John," she said and raised her glass as if in a toast. "To new beginnings."

His smile was carefree as he tapped his glass to hers. "To new beginnings."

They both took a sip of the scotch, but then sat there in companionable silence for long moments until Mia shifted closer and cupped his cheek.

Beneath her palm, his skin was rough with his evening beard. She leaned close and breathed in the scent of him, the eucalyptus-and-mint body wash he had used. "You smell good. Feel good," she said and brushed her lips across his cheek.

He locked his gaze on hers, and being this close, she could see the shards of gold and green in his hazel eyes. See the desire darken the color to an almost molten gold.

He tunneled his hand into the damp strands of her hair, but didn't urge her closer, letting her make the next move. She didn't hesitate, but she didn't rush either.

Even though they'd gone out a few times before, she'd had her doubts about him. Some of those doubts had disappeared in just a day as she'd seen him deal with all that was happening. How he'd protected her during the office attack and again during the explosion. The admission that the parties and over-the-top car weren't his choices, but his brother's.

Narrowing her gaze, she examined his face. A strong and handsome face.

"I don't know what to make of you," she admitted and stroked his cheek again.

"Do you have to? Can't we just see where this goes?" he said and ran the back of his hand across her cheek, his touch tender. Achingly restrained.

Considering what he'd told her, it occurred to her that maybe he wasn't used to gentleness. Gentleness like what she'd grown up with in her loving and very giving family.

Wanting to give that to him, she shifted the last final inch and kissed him. A soft, fleeting kiss, offering tenderness. Inviting him to take the lead and let her know what he wanted. If he wanted her.

JOHN'S BODY SHOOK as she kissed him, and he barely contained his moan of need.

She smelled so good, tasted even better, he thought as he sampled her mouth with his. The kiss, tentative at first, was growing deeper, needier, when she answered his demand, meeting his mouth with hers over and over, opening her mouth to him and slipping from the corner of the couch to ease into his lap.

Her center cradled his hardness as she straddled him and this time he couldn't hold in his moan. But he tempered his need because it was too soon. Especially with all that had happened that day.

She must have felt his pullback because she sat back on her haunches and peered at him, but she laid her hands on his shoulders and stroked them, the touch gentling. Comforting.

"I know it's maybe too soon for...you know," she said, and a telltale flush swept up across her cheeks.

He loved that for all her sophistication, she could still be flustered about something so basic.

Smiling, he swept his finger across that color. "Too much has happened today and maybe you're vulnerable," he said, earning a roll of her eyes.

"Maybe *I'm* vulnerable," he teased, prompting her to laugh and run a hand through his shower-dampened hair before she leaned forward again.

"Maybe I just want to kiss. Just kiss," she said and did just that, opening her mouth on his.

He kissed her back, took her breath into his as if he needed it to survive. She was life and love and so much more than he'd ever had before. He cradled her back with his hands, keeping her close until the kisses slowed, and they shifted away from each other.

"I like kissing you," she said, grinning, her blue eyes dancing with laughter.

"I like kissing *you*," he said, feeling a lightness in his heart that he'd never felt before and it all had to do with the amazing woman in his arms. A woman who was strong. Caring, and yet had her own hurts as well.

It couldn't have been easy being sandwiched between Trey and Ricky. Surviving those early family hardships to watch them become near legends in Miami. Becoming her own legend and millionaire with her hard work as an influencer. But that only made him remember that someone wanted to hurt her family because of that success, which made him even more determined to find whoever was behind it.

"I won't let anyone hurt you," he said and brushed back a lock of her dark hair that had fallen forward when they kissed.

"*We're* going to stop him and we're going to find out who's trying to steal your software," she said.

He frowned at the mention of his program. "Sometimes I'm sorry I ever wrote it."

She startled a little, surprised. "Why? It seems like it could be really helpful."

"Or really hurtful, like the Manhattan Project. I can't imagine what those scientists thought when they realized how what they had created would be used," he said, once again thinking about how much harm could be done if his software got into the wrong hands.

She cradled his cheek again and then ran her finger across his mouth in a fleeting caress. "We won't let that happen."

It was his warrior speaking and he told himself to believe it because she believed it.

"We won't," he said to convince himself, and with a final kiss, she slipped off his lap and stood.

"Did you want to work at the dining-room table?" she asked and nodded her head in the direction of the dining section of the open-concept room.

He shook his head. "A little tired of sitting at a table. I'll just get my laptop and work here," he said and patted the comfy cushions of the leather sofa.

"Can I make you some coffee?" she said and wrapped an arm across her chest, suddenly uneasy.

"I'd love that." He shot to his feet and went to get his knapsack.

In the bedroom, he heard the distant whir of the coffee machine as it ground the coffee beans and the earthy smell of the brew hit him when he returned to the sofa. The gurgle and hiss of the coffee machine filled the quiet as he unpacked his laptop and power cord, then settled onto the sofa, feet resting on the coffee table.

As he logged on to the network, Sophie's earlier words about fingerprints slammed into his consciousness. She was right that whoever had tried to hack in may have left little clues behind and if it was someone in-house, maybe he could recognize who by how they'd attempted to do the hack. After all, he knew the strengths and weaknesses of each of the programmers he'd kept on after selling his start-up. When looking at a project, he could tell who had coded what section because each of them had a unique way of approaching a program.

It was with that knowledge in mind that he started looking at the security logs and other information available on the servers, as well as on the logs of the desktop computer that he sometimes used.

The desktop computer Miles had been sitting near when John had returned from lunch with Trey the other day.

Thankfully, Mia came over at the moment, snapping him from going to that dark place of distrust with regard to his only remaining family.

"Light and sweet, right?" she said as she placed a mug on a coaster on the coffee table.

"Yes, thanks," he said, but was surprised as she placed a second mug on the table and snuggled into the corner of the couch.

"You don't have to keep me company," he said, guilty that she felt she had to stay.

She smiled, but it was a tired smile. "Not a problem, plus I have to catch up on some of my own work, too," she said and held up her smartphone.

"Got it." For someone who was likely on social media daily, probably multiple times a day, she'd been too caught up with everything else to post anything. But he trusted that she wouldn't post anything that would compromise their safety.

Focusing on his laptop, he searched for clues as to who had done the hacking, taking sips of his coffee as he did so. He hoped the rush of caffeine and sugar would give him the energy he needed to check the various logs. He went through every line meticulously until his eyes were glazing over with fatigue.

A soft thud drew his attention. Mia's smartphone had fallen to the floor, and she was sound asleep beside him. The barest snore escaped her, dragging a smile to his face.

A quick glance at the clock on his laptop warned it was nearly three in the morning and the day's events had taken their toll on him.

Time for both of them to get some sleep.

He rose and carefully slipped his arms beneath her to carry her to her bedroom. At his touch, she smiled sleepily, wrapped her arms around his neck and tucked her head against his chest.

Grateful for the strength training he had been doing for years, he easily lifted her and carried her into the bedroom, but as he laid her on the bed, she refused to let go.

"Stay with me," she murmured softly.

It would be torture to lie beside her for what little remained of the night, but what pleasant torture. And maybe lying beside her would drive the niggling worry from his head about what the logs might be revealing: that one of the attempted hacks had come from his desktop computer.

He slipped beneath the sheets beside her, and she snuggled into his side, her arm wrapped around his midsection and her head pillowed on his shoulder. That soft snore came again, reminding him that she wasn't perfect.

But maybe perfect for me, he thought as he lay beside her, the weight of her comforting, creating peace to drive away the concerns that had crept into him as he'd searched for those telltale fingerprints.

Fingerprints that were leading him in the direction of someone quite dear to him. Someone he would have trusted with his life. *Had* trusted with his life when his father would go on a rampage.

She stroked her hand across his chest, as if sensing his unrest, and it calmed him.

But as he drifted off, those troubling thoughts tangled into his brain like a noxious weed, digging their roots deep. Warning him that his life might not ever be the same again.

Chapter Ten

Mia woke against the delicious warmth of John's body. She'd gotten a surprisingly good sleep despite going to bed late and rousing when John had carried her to bed.

His presence had helped tame the fear created by all the dangers of the day.

When he sucked in a deep breath and stretched, she shifted upward to drop a quick kiss on his lips.

He awakened more fully and rolled to trap her under him, his body hard against hers. He kissed her more deeply and she responded, savoring the feel of him. Savoring the peacefulness of the morning as the sun was barely cracking the horizon, and the first fingers of purple and pink were creeping over the darker blues of the ocean.

She lay there, enjoying that peace. Embracing the calm that filled her because she sensed today might be trying.

"I don't want to get up," she said with a sigh against his lips.

"I don't either. This just feels...wonderful," he admitted and rolled onto his back once more but kept her close to his side.

She settled in again until the annoying ringtone of her phone warned that it was time to get up. The phone was still in the living room, and she let the alarm finish its ringing. Its warning chime would come again in ten minutes, interrupting their peace again.

But barely two minutes had gone by when the phone chirped that a call was coming in.

Fearing the worst, she scrambled from the bed and rushed to the coffee table to answer her phone. Trey was calling.

"What's up?" she asked and plopped onto the couch.

"*Papi* and I are at the office. Ricky, Sophie and Robbie are on their way. We thought we might order in breakfast so we can get an early start. Roni has clothes for the two of you if it's okay for her to come up," he said.

She'd been hoping for some quiet time with John that morning before reality intruded. With a sigh of frustration, she said, "It's okay for Roni to come up. I'll let John know."

Trey must have sensed her frustration. "Everything okay?"

"Sure. Why wouldn't it be? I mean, it's not like someone tried to kill us yesterday. Maybe twice," she said facetiously, not ready to face the real world quite yet.

"I get it, *hermanita*. It's not easy to handle this kind of stress on a daily basis," Trey said.

He was only trying to commiserate, but it made her feel incredibly guilty as well, since both Trey and her father had regularly dealt with it, first as cops and then as part of the SBS. It only strengthened her determination to become more involved and help alleviate some of that stress.

"Thank you and *Papi* for all that you do," she said and hung up.

When she looked up, her gaze clouded by tears, John was standing there, peering at her sympathetically. "We can stay here for a little longer if you want."

She shook her head. "No, I'm fine. Roni is on her way with our clothes and I'm sure you have things to share with them."

His features tightened at that mention. "Not much," he said but it was obvious to her he was keeping something from her.

Because she trusted him, she'd let him keep that secret for now.

She bolted to her feet just as the elevator dinged to warn that Roni had arrived. As her friend came off the elevator, Mia hurried over and hugged her hard.

"Thank you and congratulations again, even if you didn't tell me first," she said, rocking Roni from side to side joyfully.

"I wanted to, believe me. We had planned to ask Ricky and you over for dinner, but then we got the call about the explosion, and everything got crazy," Roni said and handed a bag to John. "Trey picked some things up for you."

She handed Mia a second bag. "Casual clothes since I thought you might be running around today."

"Thanks. Are you staying for the meeting?" she asked as Roni walked with her to her bedroom while John went into his to change.

"Only for a little bit. I'm heading into the office to do those searches we discussed last night. Hopefully it will give us a good pool of possible suspects," Roni said and sat on the bed.

Roni placed the small duffel bag on the bedspread and pulled out the clothes her friend had packed for her. Comfortable faded jeans, a short-sleeved light blue blouse, soft fleece hoodie and assorted underthings. Another few changes of clothes and, beneath them, her favorite sneakers.

Mia slipped out of the T-shirt and sweatpants that she'd taken from the guest supplies and left them on the bed for their housekeeping staff to launder. As she slipped into her underthings and socks, she said, "Do you really think someone is targeting SBS?"

Roni shrugged uneasily and dipped her head. "When Trey first told me his concerns, I had my doubts, but now..."

Now those doubts were gone, Mia thought as she stepped into her jeans and tugged them up. They were buttery soft against her skin and sat low on her hips. The blouse hung loosely around her midsection and just kissed the waistband of the jeans. She wasted no time slipping on her sneakers and grabbed the hoodie.

Facing her friend, she said, "Thank you again for bringing this."

"What are friends for?" Roni said with a smile and stood.

Mia hugged her friend hard. "I'm so happy for you and Trey."

Roni's smile grew even broader. "I'm happy, too."

Mia slipped her arm through Roni's. As they walked toward the door, Roni said, "What's happening with you and Wilson?"

"He's a good kisser," Mia said with a laugh.

With the arch of an eyebrow, Roni said, "A good kisser, huh? Is it serious?"

Mia pursed her lips and shrugged. "Is it serious? I can't say. Could it be serious? Maybe," she admitted.

"Fair enough," Roni said, and Mia stopped short, surprised by her friend's response.

"Really? That's all you've got to say?" Mia asked, staring at her.

With a hunch of her shoulders, Roni said, "I spent a little time with him during an investigation. I didn't know what to make of him at first, but once I got to know him, he seemed like a nice guy."

A nice guy. Mia couldn't deny that, but was it enough?

Mr. Nice Guy was waiting for them out in the living room, his ever-present knapsack slung over his shoulder. Like her, he was dressed casually in a pale yellow, linen *guayabera* and faded jeans. His feet were clad in brightly colored sneakers that made her think of the boyish side of him that often emerged when he was video gaming.

The sneakers dragged a smile to her lips and invited her to go over and drop a kiss on his lips, not fazed by the fact that Roni was there to witness it.

John seemed a little taken aback by the openness of the affection and gazed between her and Roni, who said nothing about it.

"Let's go," Mia said and hurried to the elevator.

JOHN WAITED FOR the two women to enter the conference room, where the South Beach Security patriarch, Ramon, stood chatting with his two sons. Ramon's head was downcast as he listened to something Ricky was saying while Trey was immobile, arms across his chest, a stern set to his face.

Ricky stopped talking as they walked in, and Ramon and Trey looked their way. The hardness on Trey's face melted away as he caught sight of his fiancée and he smiled and walked over to greet them.

"Good morning," Trey said as he shook his hand, then hugged the two women.

Ramon and Ricky both came over and greeted them, but it was impossible for John to miss that Ramon remained troubled by whatever Ricky had been sharing earlier.

"I should get going and run those searches. I'll send the information over as soon as I have anything," Roni said, then hugged Mia and Trey, and kissed them both before rushing out the door.

Ramon swept a hand in the direction of the credenza, where an assortment of breakfast pastries, bagels and spreads sat along with carafes with a trio of juices, coffee and tea. Creamers and sweeteners completed the breakfast offerings.

"Please help yourselves while we wait for Sophie and Robbie. They'll be here in a few minutes," Ramon said.

"Thank you," John said, hungry despite his concerns about what they would do today to stop the possible attacks on the Gonzalez family and the theft of his program.

He apparently wasn't the only one since Mia was immediately at his side, following his lead as he grabbed a bagel and cream cheese and prepped himself a coffee.

By the time he sat down at the table, with Mia at his side, Sophie and Robbie were walking in and setting up their laptops to work.

"Good morning," Sophie said with a smile, looking none the worse for wear even though she and Robbie had stayed late the night before.

Robbie echoed her greeting and while the two of them went over to get breakfast, Trey took control of the meeting.

He stood to the right of his father, who was at the head of the table, leaned his hands on the top edge of one of the executive leather chairs and began. "As promised, I reached out to some friends for information on what's happening with local gangs. There were rumors a couple of weeks ago that someone was looking to hire a gang member to put the hurt on someone."

"And you think that gang member attacked my brother in our office?" John said, trying to wrap his head around Trey's report.

"It seems probable, which is why your program somehow made the connection between your possible hack and the attempts on the SBS," Sophie said.

But there was something niggling in his brain. "Someone in my office paid for that attack to either have time to steal something—"

"Or to hide something," Mia said, repeating the idea that had been tossed out the day before.

The attack played out in his mind from the moment the

intruder had rushed in, to the short minutes when Miles had fought off the man. Shaking his head, he said, "Most people were standing at their office doors, shocked by what was happening."

From the corner of his eye, he caught how Mia's hand shook as she put down her cup of coffee. She was upset, holding back, and he suspected why.

"No one would have been in a position to steal anything during the attack," Robbie said.

"No," he answered without hesitation and met Trey's gaze. He was clearly troubled, his blue-green gaze as turbulent as the ocean during a hurricane.

"Eliminating theft, that leaves deception, and the most likely suspect would be whoever is trying to hack your software. They used the attack to hide what they're doing or mislead anyone investigating the hack," Trey said.

"He wanted to throw off any suspicion that might come his way," John said, and it was impossible not to run with that thought, especially after the research he had done the night before. "He paid a gang member to do the attack. Stood by as it happened or maybe even tried to be a hero."

His hands tightened into fists of rage, not wanting to believe Miles had had a hand in it, but as someone who dealt with logic all the time...

"Occam's razor. The simplest explanation is usually the right one," Mia whispered from beside him.

"You remembered that," he said, recalling one of their dinner dates and how he'd tried to explain to her how he developed some of his ideas.

"I did, but maybe this isn't one of those times," she said and laid her hand over one of his clenched fists.

"But Miles *is* the simplest explanation," he finally said aloud.

"If he's the one who has access to your desktop," Sophie chimed in and shot a quick look at Robbie to continue.

"Our search of the logs and other things shows some unexpected activity coming from that computer, but also a small DDoS attack—"

"Denial-of-service. An attacker will create excessive traffic on a website or server to overwhelm it. I noticed the increased traffic when I did my first review, but it didn't seem to last long enough," John explained to Mia.

"It didn't," Sophie confirmed and continued. "Whoever tried it was either worried they hadn't hid their trail enough or didn't really know how to execute the DDoS."

"Or maybe they had second thoughts. Maybe they felt guilty about doing it," Mia suggested.

John wanted to believe that was the reason. That Miles had had second thoughts, maybe even about the attack if he was behind it. *Had that been the reason he'd rushed the intruder to stop him*? he wondered.

"That kind of guilt is possible," Ricky said from across the room and peered at Trey, who nodded, prompting him to go on.

"Trey asked me to do a possible profile on who might be responsible for the attacks on the family, but first let's discuss whoever paid for this gang member. You're right that they might be experiencing guilt, especially if they had felt loyalty to you, John."

"Like one of my employees?" John asked.

"Like one of them. I'm assuming you've made them all quite well off. You trusted them enough to go with you on this new start-up—"

"Or left them behind. Isn't it possible it's someone who resents not being asked to join the new start-up?" Mia suggested.

John appreciated that she was playing devil's advocate even though he was well aware of her dislike of Miles.

"Someone that I left behind would have been capable

of executing a DDoS. Whoever did this wasn't a sophisticated hacker," he said.

"Like Miles?" Trey said, arching a dark eyebrow.

"Like Miles," John finally admitted out loud as he relaxed his fists, the admission washing away his rage and replacing it with sadness. Mia immediately slipped her hand into his, offering comfort.

"We can make that assumption, but let's not rule out other possibilities," Ramon warned from the head of the table.

"*Papi* is right. We have to keep all options open to not avoid missing something," Trey said.

"Like the fact that the gang member knew when you would be there," Sophie said and held out her hand. "Please let me have your cell phone."

Puzzled, he said, "I already checked it when I first thought there was a hack."

Despite that, he unlocked it with his fingerprint and handed it to her. It took her only a few swipes, then she said, "The locate function was enabled the night before the attack. Who had access to your phone?"

Miles did during dinner, he thought, and while he didn't say it, everyone around the table knew who might have possibly done it.

"I don't know why Miles would do something like that or why someone wants to attack your family," he said, trying to divert attention away from his brother while he wrapped his head around Miles's possible betrayal.

"Whoever it is may see a family that he believes did something wrong that warrants punishment," Ricky said.

"Like what? We try to help people," Mia said in defense of the Gonzalez family members.

"But maybe someone thinks we didn't do enough or did too much or accused one of their loved ones," Ricky pointed out.

"If it is a gang member, he could have a gripe if I helped arrest a fellow gang member," Trey said with a dejected drop of his shoulders, as if burdened by guilt.

"Not just you, Trey," Mia said quickly, also sensing her brother's change of mood.

Trey shook his head and blew out a disgusted sigh as Ricky said, "Mia's right, Trey. It could be any of the cases we've worked on with the SBS."

Trey nodded, but it was obvious he wasn't convinced. "Maybe we'll be able to find out more once Roni sends over a list of recently released gang members."

Ricky peered at John and said, "The person trying to steal your code… It could be just simple theft motivated by greed."

John didn't fail to hear what Ricky was implying. "But it also could be more."

With a shrug, Ricky continued. "It could be someone who's jealous of what you've accomplished, resents it, or feels they're not getting enough credit for what they do."

Once again, the warning bells were going in his head that Miles fit those criteria. "Miles resents that I don't let him make important decisions at the company," John admitted.

"But you let him do a lot of things for you," Mia said, trying to be supportive.

"I do, but…it's because I feel guilty," he said and tapped at a spot above his heart. "I feel guilty because he always protected me, and I feel like I owe him for that."

"If he senses that guilt, it could make him even more resentful, John," Ricky said, his tone filled with compassion and not condemnation.

John nodded. For too long he'd wanted to clear the air with Miles, tell him how he felt. But he'd worried about how Miles would react. Worried that he'd lose the only family he had.

"Maybe it's time to talk to him," Mia said with a tender squeeze of his hand and a reassuring smile.

With another nod, John said, "Maybe." He shot a quick look at his watch and said, "If there isn't more right now, I should really go down and make sure my employees are okay. Get to work on trying to find out more about that DDoS and the other hacks."

"We'll keep working on that as well," Sophie said.

"That makes sense, John. We can reconvene once I have Roni's info and have a chance to review it," Trey said.

"Great," John said and shot to his feet, and Mia joined him.

At his questioning look, she offered him another smile and said, "I can help you unpack. I'm good at unpacking. Just ask Trey."

Her older brother chuckled and shook his head. "She is, John. I'd take her up on it unless you want boxes sitting in your office for weeks."

John peered at him and then Mia. Seeing they were determined, he nodded. "I'd appreciate the help."

Chapter Eleven

He laid the tripod for the rifle on the coping along the roof of the skyscraper and peered through the scope toward the South Beach Security building.

The glass sides of the building gleamed aqua in the bright morning sun, reflecting the almost blinding rays and the silhouettes of the nearby structures.

He knew where the family hid in the building. The two floors where they housed their business, John Wilson's start-up on the floor below the SBS and the penthouse suite.

Focusing on those floors with the scope, he tried to see through the glass, but the film on the windows made it impossible.

Luckily, he'd planned for that option and had slipped an AirTag into Miles Wilson's knapsack. Pulling out his phone, he went to his cloud account for the location information. The tracker was working just fine. Miles wouldn't even know he was being tracked since he was using an Android phone, but he only had three days before the provider might fry the device for suspicious behavior.

Based on the tracker's signal, Miles was right in front of the building. He turned the scope in the direction indicated by the signal and, sure enough, there he was.

He watched as Wilson walked into the building. He guessed it would only take a few minutes to clear security, get an elevator and reach the floor for the start-up. Would Miles drop his knapsack in his office and head for a coffee? If he did, it would be a waste of time for him to be up here.

But if he went straight to the boss's office…

MIA PLACED THE box on John's desk while he unloaded an assortment of books into a bookshelf at the far side of the room. Being a tech guy, she hadn't expected him to have so many physical books, but there were at least two boxes of them on diverse subjects. She itched to go over and see which ones in the hope they would reveal even more about the man who was increasingly owning a bigger piece of her heart.

She unloaded the first of the items from the box: a red stapler. Laughing, she laid it to the side as she took out the rest of the desktop accessories. She'd leave the placement of everything to John because the layout of the desk was such a personal thing.

She was about to walk over to the bookcase to help John when Miles walked into the room, his knapsack slung over his shoulder. He dipped his head in greeting and then sauntered to John's side. As they stood there, it was impossible to deny they were related, but John was slightly taller and leaner. John's hair was wavy, and more brown than blond, unlike Miles, who had a high fade haircut where the longer strands were ruthlessly gelled into place.

"How's it going?" Miles said and let his knapsack slip to the ground, as if he intended to stay for a while.

A *plink*, like that of two marbles colliding, made her half turn toward the window. A slight crack in the window confused her until the *plink* came again. Suddenly a hole appeared in the glass and needles of pain erupted in the hand she had leaned on the desk.

Stunned, she froze, but a second later John rushed at

her, wrapped his arms around her and hauled her around the protection of the desk, drawing her down beside him.

In a burst of motion, Miles joined them as shot after shot broke through the skyscraper's glass wall and slammed into the heavy wood of the desk.

John whipped out his smartphone, but Mia stayed his hand. It was then she noticed the blood on her hand and the splinters from the wood of the desk. "Call Trey. Maybe he can get eyes on whoever is firing at us."

"Are you crazy! Dial 911, John," Miles said as he cowered beside them. With each bullet slamming into the wood, he jumped, and all color had fled from his face.

John called Trey, who immediately answered. "Someone's shooting at us. We're pinned down in my new office."

"Stay down. I'm calling 911," Trey said and hung up.

A salvo of shots hit the desk and then silence. Blessed silence.

Mia released a sharp breath of relief and melted against the back of the desk. Her body was shaking from the adrenaline rush and John wrapped her in his arms.

"It's over," he said and kissed her temple.

This incident was over, but the threat to them, all of them... It was still there and just as deadly as John's program had predicted.

"You're hurt. We need to take care of your hand," John said and started to rise, but she urged him to stay down.

"We need to wait for the all-clear from Trey," she said.

Miles said, "I'm not going to be a sitting duck here." He got on all fours and crawled out of the office and into the hallway.

When Miles had gone, she said, "How did someone know we were here?"

"We'll figure it out, Mia. The most important thing now is to make sure we're all safe," John said.

A second later, John's phone rang. "Trey," he said and put the call on speaker.

"Are you all okay?"

Mia waved her uninjured hand to stop him because Trey would lose it if he knew she was hurt.

John understood and said, "We're okay. Is it safe?"

"It's safe. Police chopper caught sight of someone on a roof two buildings over. They lost him when he used the rooftop access to enter the building. Officers are headed there now. They're coming here, too. I'll be down in a couple of minutes."

"We'll be waiting for you," John said and ended the call.

He held his hand out to her. "Let's get out of here and tend to your hand."

She rose on shaky legs, wobbly until John slipped an arm around her waist to offer support.

He walked her toward a conference room where the windows faced in a different direction. Miles was at the front desk, standing by Rachel, who was on the phone, presumably with the police.

"Are you okay?" Miles asked and ran a hand through his hair, creating sharp, erratic spikes in the strands.

"Can you track down a first-aid kit? Mia's hand needs some cleaning and patching," John said.

Mia looked down at her hand where the blood was starting to dry around a few large splinters of wood and several smaller ones. Her knees weakened, but she forced herself straight, determined to be strong.

"It's okay to lean on me," John said and increased his support at her waist. She was wan, her skin almost translucent, as the enormity of what had happened sank in.

She nodded and together they walked into the conference room, not that he felt safe now in any room with a glass wall. Except his house, since the prior owner—whom he had suspected had been involved in a less-than-legal venture—had installed bulletproof glass in all the windows.

He sat her down and Miles hurried into the room barely seconds later, a red first-aid box in his hand. Miles placed it on the table beside him. His gaze skipped across his brother's and there was no missing the worry there. That and a nervous tic along his jaw and his general jumpiness as he ripped his gaze away and started to pace by an inside wall of the room.

Mia glanced his way, watching his nervous back-and-forth, while John took out an alcohol pad.

"This may sting," he said.

Mia only nodded—all her attention was focused on Miles. She barely moved as he wiped away the dried blood. She flinched, her body doing a little jump, when he pulled out the biggest of the splinters. Blood immediately leaked from the small hole, and he dabbed at it, but then quickly yanked out the other splinters so he could clean the entire area and bandage it.

Luckily, he had just finished when Trey rushed into the room, but his eagle eyes immediately zeroed in on the bright white bandage on Mia's hand.

He hurried over, kneeled before his sister and took hold of her injured hand. "You're hurt."

"It's nothing really," she said weakly and braved a smile.

"When I get the bastard, he's going to be sorry," Trey said and brushed a hand across her cheek.

"How did he know where we were? We haven't been out of the building in well over a day," Mia said, then glanced in John's direction and then over at Miles.

John tracked her gaze to where Miles continued to pace like a caged tiger, back and forth, back and forth, in front of the inside wall of the room.

"Miles?" John said to draw his attention.

His brother stopped short and faced him but remained

silent. His fists were clenched and that nervous tic jumped along his jaw.

"Did you notice anyone following you?" John asked.

Miles immediately shook his head in denial, but then seemed to reconsider. Tossing his hands up in the air, he said, "I don't know, okay. I don't know."

John wanted to shout at him. Ask him how he could be so careless, but bit back the angry words. It would only add even more tension to what he was already sensing between them. Tension that was palpable to everyone in the room.

"Did you notice anyone following you?" he asked again, carefully tempering his tone in the hopes that Miles would reconsider his earlier statement.

Miles shrugged and shook his head. "I don't think so. I left the condo, drove here and parked down the street. I didn't see anything out of the ordinary."

"Have you seen any strangers around lately?" Trey asked as he straightened to stand behind Mia, his hand on her shoulder in support.

Miles jammed his hands on his hips, pursed his lips and then blurted out, "Besides the attacker I stopped yesterday?"

The hard line of Trey's jaw warned that he didn't appreciate the sarcasm. "Besides that intruder."

"Nothing. No one," Miles confirmed with some bite.

But despite his assertion, John was convinced that the shooter had to have some connection to Miles. As his gaze locked with Trey's and then drifted down to Mia's, it was obvious they felt the same way.

Trying to give his brother some rope, but not so he would hang himself, he said, "Even if Miles was followed, that would only lead them to the building and not to this floor."

Trey nodded. "You're right."

Rachel came to the door of the conference room at that moment. "There are some officers here to see you."

"Would you come with me, John? Miles, would you mind staying with Mia? She doesn't look like she's up to being interrogated right now," Trey said, and John didn't miss the silent communication between the two siblings.

Miles nodded and John followed Trey out of the conference room. Officers Puente and Johnson from the day before were in the lobby alongside two officers from the CSI unit.

"Officers. Thanks for getting here so quickly," Trey said and motioned to John. "I believe you know Mr. Wilson from yesterday's…incident. If at all possible—"

"We understand this requires…discretion," Officer Puente said with dip of her head and gazed at the other officers, who likewise acknowledged the request.

"The bullets came in through my office window. We didn't see anything because we were too busy trying not to get shot," John said and took the lead, directing the police to his office. At the door, he hung back, understanding the importance of not contaminating the scene.

The two beat cops stayed with him while Trey entered with the CSI officers.

But as he waited there for them to do their job, he wondered what was going on with Mia and Miles in the conference room.

Chapter Twelve

Miles sat across from her, his gaze focused on his hands, which were clasped before him tightly. He rested his elbows on his thighs and bounced them up and down.

Everything about him grated on her, but she held back from attack mode. It would be better to try and reach him in other ways, not to mention her head and hand were throbbing.

"Is there any aspirin there?" she said and lifted her chin in the direction of the first-aid kit.

"Let me check," he said, then fumbled as he tried to open the kit, but once he got it open, he searched through it and found a small packet of aspirin. He handed it to her and said, "I'll get you some water."

He hurried from the room and returned a few minutes later with a bottle of water.

"Thank you," she said as she tore open the packet, then tossed back the aspirin with some water.

"We're lucky no one was seriously injured," Miles said as he resumed his seat and his bouncing. "It seems to me this all started as soon as John got involved with your family," Miles challenged and glared at her.

Wow, talk about the pot calling the kettle black. She was not about to let him turn the tables on her, however.

"Seems to me there have been problems for a while.

Someone leaking news. Possibly short-selling the stock," she replied and carefully watched for his reaction.

The bouncing stopped and he splayed his hands on his knees, locked his gaze on hers. He had hazel eyes, like John, but they lacked the warmth and caring of his half brother's eyes.

"I had nothing to do with that," he said, voice as chilly as a glacier, hands tight on his knees.

"I didn't say you did. Why would I think that? Especially since you were so brave to confront that intruder yesterday," she said, forcing an almost cajoling tone into her voice.

"I had to stop him. John is the only family I have left," Miles said, but he said it in a practiced tone, as if he'd rehearsed it over and over in order to sound convincing. Much like he had sounded yesterday when speaking to the police officers.

Only he didn't sound convincing. At least not to her.

"Family means everything to me, Miles. Make no mistake I will do whatever it takes to protect them and John."

What little color remained on his face drained, as his skin turned a sickly green.

She hated to be pleased at his discomfort, but was happy that he'd recognized that her words weren't only a promise. They were a threat. If he was involved with whatever was going on, he would pay for that.

Satisfied he'd gotten the message, she sat back to wait for Trey and John to return.

"YOU WERE VERY LUCKY, Mr. Wilson," one CSI officer said as he dug out a bullet from the side of the desk while Trey hovered nearby.

Mia's brother was in worried mode, arms across his muscled chest and his blue gaze focused on whatever the CSI officers were doing.

John watched from across the room as the cop held up what he assumed was the bullet.

Trey leaned forward to peer at it, gaze narrowed. "50 cal?"

"50 cal. Like I said, lucky. The glass slowed the bullet—a little—and the downward trajectory kept the bullets from ripping through the desk."

And into Mia, Miles and me, John thought and his heart stopped for a beat before pounding so hard the sound echoed in his ears.

"There's blood here," said the other CSI agent, a young blonde woman who seemed barely out of her twenties.

John motioned to his hand. "Mia had some wood splinters in her hand from the first bullet."

"She was lucky she didn't get hit directly," the officer said and swabbed the blood to preserve a sample for evidence.

Trey gestured to the bullet holes and cracks in the glass. "This pattern indicates it was a high-speed bullet, right? 50 cals are usually slower."

The CSI agent nodded, raised his camera and snapped several photos of the bullet holes and cracks in the glass before he motioned to them. "You're right that the faster the bullet, the more cracks. 50 cals are usually slower unless—"

"It's a 50 BMG," the female agent said.

Puzzled, John peered at Trey, who was clearly not happy with the officer's comment.

"50 BMG means this person is possibly a sniper with a pretty pricey gun," Trey said.

The female officer nodded. "Even a cheaper gun, like the Serbu or ArmaLite, will run you a few thousand."

"What doesn't make sense is why they would blindly shoot at this office. They can't see through the film," said the male CSI officer, who was still inspecting the window glass.

No, they couldn't, but maybe it didn't matter to whoever was shooting. Maybe they had been willing to take out everyone in the room. Including Miles, but was that only coincidence or an intentional attempt to tie up any loose ends?

"No, they can't," Trey admitted and glanced in his direction. "We should round up everyone and get them to safer locations until we can get a handle on this."

John nodded. "I'm going to send my people to work remotely."

Trey arched an eyebrow. "Including Miles?"

John shook his head. "I assume these officers will want to interview everyone who was in this room and afterward... I think we need to have a talk with him."

"I agree," Trey said and turned to the officers. "We're ready whenever you are for the interviews."

"Officer Johnson and I can handle that," Officer Puente said, and the other officers confirmed that was in order.

"We'll send the information on any evidence we gather here or in the other building to Detective Lopez," the female CSI officer advised.

"We'd appreciate that and if we dig up anything, we'll be sure to reciprocate," Trey said with a thankful nod.

As Trey walked toward the door, John turned and returned to the conference room, where Mia and Miles were waiting. Undeniable tension simmered between them, creating an uneasy feel in the room.

The strain didn't lessen once Trey and the police officers walked in. Trey went straight to his sister. "How's the hand?"

"Fine," Mia said, even though she was pale and cradling her hand gingerly, obviously in pain.

"Would you mind answering a few questions?" Officer Puente asked.

"Not at all," Miles said, almost too eagerly. He sat up in the chair straighter and faced the two cops.

Officer Puente began questioning Miles about his earlier movements, much like they had done barely an hour earlier, and the answers remained much the same.

"You went straight to Mr. Wilson's office when you arrived. You didn't stop for coffee or talk to anyone else?" Officer Johnson said.

Miles shook his head. "I said hello to the receptionist and then went straight to my brother's office."

"Is that what you normally do?" Johnson asked.

"Sometimes. Sometimes I go to my office first. Get a coffee. That kind of thing," Miles said and peered between him and the officer. "Tell them, John. It wasn't anything out of the ordinary."

Officer Johnson looked in his direction, seeking that confirmation.

"Miles sometimes comes right to my office. Sometimes he doesn't," John said, thinking that wasn't unusual. But the timing of it coupled with the shooting worried him.

"Where were you standing when the first shot occurred?" Puente asked, pen poised above her notepad to record his answer.

"John was at the bookcase, emptying boxes because we'd just moved. Supposedly because we'd be safer here," he said and glared at Mia and Trey. "How'd that work out?" he added in challenge.

Trey gritted his teeth, biting back a response, but nothing was holding Mia back.

"How is it that you were conveniently present at yesterday's attack and again this morning?"

"So were you, Mia. You *and* John. Whatever is going on has nothing to do with me," Miles argued, but there was a waver in his voice that worried John.

"Mia and I had been together for at least an hour," he

said, avoiding any mention of breakfast and how that might be misinterpreted by the officers. "But the shooting started right after you came in," John challenged.

Miles shot to his feet and whirled to face him. Agitated, he tapped his chest with both his hands. "You're accusing me, your blood, instead of virtual strangers," he said and wildly flung an arm out in the direction of Mia and Trey.

John forced calm into his voice and posture. "I didn't mean to accuse you. You're my brother. But maybe someone was following you—"

"I already told you that I didn't see anyone following me," Miles said and lifted his hands in a pleading motion.

"But maybe you're being tracked," Trey said in a calm tone. *Deadly calm*, John thought.

Miles glared at the siblings, and for a second, John thought Miles might accuse them again, but then he said, "Fine. Search me. Here, let me help."

Miles reached into his pockets and tossed his wallet, keys and phone onto the conference-room table. Then he ripped off his smartwatch and placed it there, too.

Puente gave her partner a go-ahead command and the male officer walked over to Miles. "Please place your hands on the wall and spread your legs."

Miles assumed the position and the officer patted him down.

"Nothing here, Puente," he said.

The female cop motioned to the phone and watch. "CSI will want to take those for analysis."

A knock on the doorjamb drew their attention to where the CSI officers stood holding a knapsack.

Miles's knapsack, John realized, and a sick feeling oozed through his gut like an oil slick on water.

"Does this knapsack belong to one of you?" the female officer asked.

MIA'S HAND THROBBED PAINFULLY, but it was nothing compared to the pain visible on the faces of the two brothers. She felt for them, even Miles, as much as she distrusted him.

"It's my bag," Miles said, his voice barely above a whisper.

Mia glanced at the officer's badge and asked, "Is something wrong, Officer Maxwell?"

The young woman walked to the table, laid the knapsack on it and reached into one of the small side pockets. She removed something and placed it beside Miles's belongings. It was a small black-and-silver disk, just slightly larger than a quarter.

"An AirTag?" she whispered in surprise.

"That's not mine," Miles immediately said, shock obvious on his features.

"It's small enough and light enough to slip in without anyone noticing," John said, offering his brother an out.

Way too easy to do, Mia thought. "Aren't there safeguards—"

"He's using an Android phone and watch. They won't pick up that he's being tracked. If the service provider sees anything funky going on, they'll disable it," John explained.

"But not for a couple of days, right?" Trey asked.

"Three, I believe," John said.

"That means we have three days to use it to find whoever planted it," Mia said.

Chapter Thirteen

Her brother had had to pull in all kinds of favors for the CSI officers to leave the tracker with the SBS so they could attempt to draw out whoever had slipped it into Miles's knapsack.

If it had even been someone else, Mia thought, gazing at Miles as he sat in one of the interior conference rooms they had on their floor. For safety's sake, SBS had sent everyone with glass-walled offices to work at home.

"Did anyone else have access to your knapsack?" Trey asked as he angrily paced back and forth across the room.

Miles pursed his lips and shrugged. "Just me as far as I know."

As much as she didn't want to give him another out, Mia said, "Anyone get too close or bump you in the last day or so?"

He shook his head. "Not that I can recall."

Trey nodded and looked at his cousins. "Can you do anything with the tracker?"

"We can get the serial number and contact the authorities to try to get the provider to reveal the identity of the person who owns the account," Sophie advised.

With a sarcastic smile, Robbie added, "Good luck with that but maybe there are other things we can do."

"Like what?" Mia asked.

"Like things you might not want to know," Sophie admitted with a half smile and laugh.

Mia held her hands up in a don't-tell-me gesture. "What about drawing them out?" she asked.

"And risk having someone shot or worse?" her father challenged from across the width of the table and peered at the white bandage on her hand.

"I'm fine," she said even though her hand still throbbed.

"Mia's right, *Papi*. We can't just sit here and wait for another attack," Trey said as he stood beside her and rested his hands on the top of the leather chair.

THE TWO SIBLINGS were determined, John thought, but like their father, Ramon, he was worried about another possible attack.

"I don't want to risk anyone's life," he said.

"Too late. This person is already after the family and now, after you and Miles. I'm sure your program would tell you that if you ran the data," Mia challenged, her dimpled chin tilted up defiantly.

"She knows about the program?" Miles said, accusation ringing in his tone. He looked all around the table and his eyebrows raised as the truth of the situation sank in. "They all know. You told them all about the 'top-secret' program," he said, emphasizing the words with bunny-ear fingers.

"It was necessary, Miles," he defended.

Miles laughed with derision. "Yeah. Sure."

Trey's smartphone rang, saving John from having to say anything else to ease his brother's wounded pride.

"Mi amor," Trey said and turned his back on the room as he walked to the farthest wall to listen to Roni, he guessed.

Trey murmured his agreement at whatever his fiancée reported. "I get it. Thank him for the info. Please copy Sophie and Robbie when you send the video. See you later and watch your six. We've got a psychopath here."

A psychopath. Not an understatement, John thought and his gaze was drawn to Mia's hand again. His heart constricted with the thought that he might have lost her earlier that day. If she had been standing just a few inches over, the bullet would have struck her.

Trey returned to the table. "Roni has a list of recently released gang members for our review. They weren't able to get any prints or casings from the rooftop, but the chopper got some video of the shooter. So did the building's CCTV cameras. Like he did at your old location, he got in through the service area."

"It's someone who's familiar with those areas," Mia offered.

"Contractors. Inspectors. Delivery people. Garbagemen. Mail persons," John said, thinking of all the possible workers who would have regular access to those areas.

"We can cross-reference that list of gang members with current employment to see if anything clicks," Sophie said.

"If you can send me the videos, I'll run it against the earlier ones to see if the physical characteristics are the same," John said.

"Mia and I can review the list the old-fashioned way and see what we can come up with," Trey said and laid a hand on Mia's shoulder.

Miles did a quick toss of his hands. "And what do I sit here and do?"

An uncomfortable silence filled the room.

John sucked in a deep breath, then released it and said in a rush of words, "It's not that we don't trust you, Miles."

"But you don't, John. I've had those vibes from you for months, ever since…the leak," Miles said and looked away from him, which only heightened John's unease.

"That leak really hurt the company, but benefitted someone, Miles. Was it you?"

Miles continued to look away, but then with a resigned

shrug and shake of his head, he said, "You don't understand, John."

Mia rose and said, "Maybe Miles and John need some privacy."

Sophie and Robbie snapped their laptops closed, stood and followed Ramon, Trey and Mia out of the room. But as she walked by, Mia offered John a supportive smile and pass of her injured hand across his arm.

He offered her a strained smile and once they were gone, he closed the door and leaned against it. Staring hard at his brother, he said, "What is it that I don't understand, Miles?"

Shaking his head, Miles shot to his feet and paced, still avoiding his gaze. "It's not easy being your brother."

"And that's the reason you leaked the info? Sold our stock short? *Our* company stock, Miles," he said, almost shouting the words.

"*Your* company," Miles shouted back. "*Your* company, *your* ideas. Me, I'm just along for the ride," Miles said and pounded his chest in frustration.

John shook his head and tempered his anger, seeing Miles's pain. "That's not true. You're an important part—"

Miles slashed his hand to silence him. "Would you have hired me if I wasn't your brother?"

He couldn't immediately answer, in part because the truth would be too painful. But if there was a time to cause pain in the hopes of fixing whatever had gone wrong in their relationship, it was now.

"You didn't have the qualifications for the job, but I knew you could do it," he confessed.

Miles dragged a hand through his hair in frustration and finally faced him. "But I haven't, have I? I'm nothing more than a glorified administrative assistant because you don't trust me with anything valuable."

"This software is too important to share," he said, but Miles raised his eyebrows and held his hands wide.

"Everyone who just left this room knows about it. I'd bet that the two tech dweebs even have access to it. Am I wrong?"

"They do know, but, no, they don't have access to it. But I would trust them with it," John said.

Miles thumped his chest once again with his fingers. "But not your flesh and blood."

"Are you responsible for the leak? Did you sell the stock short?" John pressed, needing to know.

Miles's shoulders slumped and he looked away as he said, "I did."

John's chest hurt so much he almost couldn't breathe. Throat constricted with emotion, he drew in an anguished breath and was barely able get out the single word. "Why?"

With a little shrug, Miles said, "I wanted to be rich enough that I wouldn't have to rely on your charity."

"Charity? It's not charity—you're my brother," he said and walked toward Miles, but his brother held up a hand to stop him.

"Half brother," Miles reminded him.

John couldn't believe what he was hearing. "I've never thought of you that way."

"But that's what I am and a bastard son at that. Your father reminded me of it often enough," Miles said, the tone of his voice slipping from his earlier antagonism into a well of darkness and pain.

"My father... He was an evil man. You kept us safe from him," John said, then walked over and embraced his brother.

Miles remained stiff in John's arms at first, then shook him off and took a step away.

"I brought this danger to your doorstep," Miles said softly.

"You know who he is?" John said, saddened that what he and the others had suspected all along was proving true.

Miles shook his head. "Not really. I didn't get a name."

"But you saw him?" John pressed.

Miles did another small shake of his head. "No. I asked around and he called me. Asked me what I wanted. Told me what it would cost and where to leave the money."

And he'd obviously done just that. "What was he supposed to do?"

With a stiff jerk of his head, he said, "Come into the office and act scary. Run off when I confronted him."

"Nothing else?" John asked.

"Nothing else," Miles admitted.

"And you did this to scare me?" John asked, needing to have the entire story.

"Sometimes when you looked at me lately, I could tell you didn't trust me. I figured that if I was a hero all of a sudden, you might think differently," Miles confessed with a little shrug.

Because if he thought differently, John might trust him enough to give him access to his new project. "You already were a hero to me, Miles," he said sadly, then walked to the door of the conference room and opened it.

He didn't need to say anything else. Couldn't do anything else as Miles walked to the door and paused. "You know where to send my stuff," his brother said and hurried down the hall toward the reception area.

John watched him turn the corner to go to the elevators and he wondered if that was going to be the last time he ever saw his brother.

He was standing there when Mia stepped into the hall and looked down his way, worry etched on her beautiful features.

What he wanted most was to crawl into a hole somewhere and hide, but he couldn't. Straightening his spine, he walked toward her. The Gonzalez family needed him right now. Mia needed him and he wasn't about to fail her.

As he neared, she held out her uninjured hand and he slipped his hand into hers.

"Are you okay?" she said and tucked herself into his side, offering comfort.

I will be as long as you're here, he thought, but kept it to himself. It was too new and complicated between them.

"I have something to tell you," he said and recounted what Miles had said, but kept some things to himself, still unable to share everything because he was processing it himself.

She accepted that was all he was willing to share at that moment. That intuition was probably what made her so good at dealing with the people she met at her various social events and he was grateful that she didn't press for more when he finished.

JOHN WORE THE hurt of his brother's betrayal the way a priest of old might wear a hair shirt, with grace and elegance even though it was causing great discomfort.

Mia raked her fingers through a lock of his hair that had fallen forward, leaned close and whispered, "I'm here if you need me."

He smiled, but it didn't reach his hazel eyes, which were flat and a darker brown with his upset.

He said nothing and she didn't press.

She walked him into the unused office they had grabbed to leave him and Miles alone in the conference room. It belonged to a marketing manager who was on maternity leave and wouldn't be back for several months.

Sophie and Robbie were at a small table at one end while Trey sat at the desk, reviewing the list Roni had sent over. Mia had been working with him, going over the police files in search of anyone who might have the telltale tattoo, or had access to buildings in the downtown area.

She gestured to the desk and said, "Trey and I have a

number of possible suspects, but we still have quite a few to review."

"Too many," Trey said, exasperation in his voice.

"Why don't you send me the list to run through the program?" John said.

"Aren't you going to do the videos?" she asked and shook her head as she realized. "A supercomputer. I bet it can do multiple things at once."

"Like you can if you want to keep me from getting hangry," Trey teased.

"Sexist much?" she teased right back.

"Not sexist at all," Robbie said. "You know all the best places to eat in the area. If you left it up to us it would be the same old, same old."

"Good save, Rob," Sophie said with a laugh.

A save, but true, she had to admit. "I'll order food and set it up in the conference room again. Is *Papi* still around? Should I order for him?"

Trey shook his head. "He's gone home to deal with *Mami* before it hits the news."

Mia understood. Mama Bear Samantha would go into full protective mode once she'd heard, but they needed her to stay out of it and safe at home. She didn't ask about Miles since he'd bolted after his talk with John.

"I'll go order," she said and hurried from the room to call a local Thai restaurant. A warm meal would keep them because she suspected that it might take some time to get any results, analyze them and decide on a course of action.

She selected a variety of items and, using the alias they'd created for deliveries to the SBS, she placed the order. The security guard downstairs would make the payment on their behalf from a cash drawer and send another guard up with the food. It was how they kept confidentiality when dealing with certain clients, and in this case, maybe kept their killer from tampering with their food.

While she waited for the delivery, she set out plates, napkins, cups and soda, and also took a moment to grab some aspirin to dull the ache in her hand. As much as it hurt, it chilled her to think that it could have been much worse.

"How are you doing?" John asked as he walked into the room and set his laptop on the table. Assorted lines and numbers flashed across the screen as the programs continued to run.

"I should be asking you that," she said and wrapped her arms around him when he approached.

"I'll…survive," he said, and she didn't press for more. There would be time enough for that after their late lunch.

They stood there, wrapped together in the comfort of the embrace until Mia's phone rang to warn the delivery had arrived.

"I have to get that," she said.

"Let me help," he said but she shook her head.

"Better no one sees you're up here," she warned and raced off without him.

Julia had accepted the delivery and helped her carry the bags to the conference room. "Do you need help setting it up?" the young Latina asked as she placed the bag on a credenza.

"I can help," John said and waved off her assistance.

"Don't let me keep you from work," Mia said, and John smirked. Again.

"Supercomputer. I get it. Too bad it has us all getting killed soon," she joked, then removed the take-out dishes from the bags and placed them on the credenza.

John did the same and soon the enticing smells of lemongrass, various chilies, garlic and ginger wafted into the air.

Almost on cue, Trey strolled into the room along with Sophie and Robbie. Her cousins placed their laptops on the table and walked over to look at the various dishes Mia had ordered.

"Looks good, Mia," Robbie said and grabbed a plate.

"It's one of my favorite places. You've got pad Thai, *som tam,* which is a green papaya salad, fried rice, stir-fried water spinach and that omelet is called *kai jeow.* I didn't forget about your sweet tooth, Trey. That roti has bananas and condensed milk."

"You're the best, Mia," Trey said and playfully hugged her.

She waited off to one side as Trey, Robbie and Sophie prepared plates for themselves.

John stood beside her, waiting for her to take some food. "After you," he said and she smiled in thanks, grabbed a plate and served herself some pad Thai, spinach and a slice of the *kai jeow.*

John followed suit but grabbed a second plate, where he loaded a couple of pieces of the roti.

"I guess Trey isn't the only one with a sweet tooth," Mia teased.

JOHN WANTED TO say that he was sweet on her, but knew she wouldn't appreciate it in front of her family. He'd keep it for what he hoped would be another kissing session that night. Maybe even more, but not in the penthouse suite, he realized. That was no longer a secure area.

Once he was sitting at the table, Mia beside him, he shot her a quick look before he said, "I was thinking that since Mia and I seem to be his primary targets right now, it would make sense for us to move somewhere safer tonight."

Trey narrowed his gaze and a puzzled look slipped over Mia's features.

"Your place in Indian Creek? The one on the water with all the glass?" Trey asked as he forked up some rice.

John held his hands up, asking for a chance to explain. "You've had your guards there for over a day. It is on the water, but all the window glass is bulletproof."

"Bulletproof?" Mia said, her doubt obvious.

With a sheepish shrug, he said, "I don't know what the prior owner did, but he valued his safety."

"Drug lord," Robbie said with a fake cough and earned the now almost familiar elbow from his sister. The shot was so hard, it shook loose a piece of green papaya on Robbie's fork.

"Maybe, but lucky for us since John's right that they can't stay in the penthouse tonight," Trey said.

"Do I have any say in this?" Mia asked and forked up some of the egg dish.

"Of course, but do you have any better suggestions?" John pressed, pausing with a forkful of spinach halfway to his mouth.

"I don't, but I'd like some say in what to do," she said and relented. "It makes sense to go there. We won't be safe here or at the penthouse at the Del Sol."

"What about your brother? Seems to me someone was taking a shot at him as well," Trey said and finished the last of the food on his plate.

Peering at the tabletop, he ran an index finger across the wood grain in an uneasy gesture, but then forged ahead, revealing the explosive information he'd kept to himself earlier. "Miles is…out of the picture."

Mia shook her head, her gaze shuttered as she said, "What does that mean?"

"He confessed he was responsible for the leak so he could short the stock. He also admitted to hiring the goon who attacked us yesterday," he said, feeling not only the anger and pain again, but also stupid that he hadn't listened to what his gut had told him.

Mia reached out and took hold of his hand, drawing his gaze to her. He had expected to see pity there, but instead he saw righteous anger on his behalf. Armed with that, he said, "He told me he didn't see who he hired. He made the arrangements over the phone and was told where to leave the payment."

"This gun-for-hire may have been following Miles even if he hadn't realized it. He probably slipped the tracker in his bag," Mia said and gave his hand a reassuring squeeze.

"Maybe when we have our list of suspects, we can get Miles to come back and look at the photos to see if any of them look familiar. Maybe he saw the attacker and didn't realize it," Trey suggested and stood to get more food.

Considering how it had ended with Miles, John wasn't sure his brother would be cooperative, but he didn't say. Instead, he returned his attention to the meal, even though the food was tasteless from his upset. The others around the table weren't as fazed, and seemed to be enjoying the meal Mia had selected.

"Don't like it?" Mia asked.

"It's very good, I'm just not really hungry," he lied and was spared from continuing the conversation when his laptop pinged to warn that one of the operations had finished.

He examined the results and smiled.

Chapter Fourteen

"The program finished the analysis on the videos from the chopper and CCTV. There's a 95-percent probability it's the same person from the drive-bys and the attack in our office," John said and swiveled his laptop around so the others could see.

Mia stared hard at the results, heart pounding. There was no doubting any longer that whoever was after her family had managed to weave himself into the lives of John's family, and despite her anger at Miles, she worried about his safety.

"We're together, but Miles doesn't have any protection," she said.

"He doesn't and whether Miles knows it or not, he may be able to lead us to this killer," Sophie said and picked up the tracker that had been sitting in the middle of the table.

"I don't think the killer would be stupid enough to let us find him via his cloud account," Mia said, puzzled by what her cousin was suggesting.

"That's true, but if he's actively tracking, his phone is accessing that cloud account regularly," Sophie said.

Robbie immediately jumped into the discussion. "But the location of the tracker is being sent using Crowd GPS and those transmissions are encrypted."

"Crowd GPS?" Mia asked, not as familiar as her cousins or John about how the tracker worked.

John picked up his phone as he explained. "The tracker connects to your phone using your Bluetooth, and when it does, it sends the location to the cloud account."

"Wouldn't someone notice that the tracker was connecting to their phone?" she asked.

"The connection is very quick and uses little data so unless you set up your phone to warn you or use some kind of scanner or app on an Android phone, you wouldn't know," John advised and set his phone back on the tabletop.

"And the data being sent is encrypted, which makes things a little harder, but not impossible," Robbie said.

"If I'm hearing you right, you want to try and monitor where those signals are being sent to find the cloud account?" Trey said, finally piping up from where he had been sitting silently, finishing his meal, but clearly following the discussion.

Sophie and Robbie nodded in unison. "We do," Sophie said.

"Miles said he got a call from the killer. Maybe he has a phone number," Mia offered.

"It's likely a burner phone," Trey countered.

John immediately responded, obviously onboard with her and her cousins. "But it could be a burner app on the phone he's using to access the cloud account. If it is, he's leaving digital information all over the place. If we reach out to the phone provider—"

"We'll get information on the cell towers and other things, which may give us his location or a connection to our list of suspects," Trey said, finishing for him.

"Will Miles help us?" Mia asked, realizing that John's half brother's cooperation might help them move a step closer to catching the killer.

John splayed his hands on the table, hesitating, but then with a heavy sigh, he said, "I hope he will."

JOHN DROVE THE nondescript black BMW that Trey had offered him from SBS's pool of vehicles. Mia was in the car beside him, and he hoped that with her people skills she might be a help in what was likely to be another painful discussion with his brother. As observant as she was, he also hoped she'd be able to pick up on anything unusual going on in the area.

It didn't take long for them to go from downtown Miami to his brother's South Pointe condo. The tall building was within walking distance to South Beach and adjacent to South Pointe Park and Biscayne Bay.

John pulled into the underground garage and parked. He hesitated because he wasn't sure of what kind of reception he would get, or how he would respond, for that matter. His gut churned with anger and pain every time he thought about what his brother, his only family, had done to him.

Mia's reassuring touch came on his hand. "It's going to be okay."

He met her gaze and plastered a tight smile on his face. "I used to tell myself that as a kid when my dad…" His throat choked up and he couldn't continue.

Mia brushed the back of her hand across his cheek, leaned across the narrow distance in the car and whispered a kiss across his lips. "You have us now, too."

He nodded. "Thank you. I guess we should go."

With a dip of her head, she exited the car and reached into the back seat to grab Miles's knapsack with the tracker tucked back into the side pocket, just like the killer had left it.

He got out of the car and grabbed his own knapsack. As he did so, he noticed an SBS guard off to one side of the garage. From his position, the guard would have a view of anyone entering through the garage entrance or going to the elevator and stairs into the building. Trey had clearly arranged for protection and he was grateful for that.

Placing a hand at the small of Mia's back, he applied gentle pressure to guide her in the direction of the building entrance and once they were in the lobby, he waved at the building security guards who let them access the elevators to Miles's condo. With each floor they climbed, John's tension increased until he was almost bouncing on his feet in anticipation. Much like she had done before, Mia slipped her hand into his and with that comfort, some of his apprehension eased.

He wasn't surprised when Miles yanked open his door even before they reached it.

He stood there, arms across his chest, his face as hard and cold as a death mask.

"I didn't expect to see you so soon," Miles said, voice flat and chilly.

"May we come in, Miles?" Mia said in a stern voice.

He almost sneered at her, but stepped aside to let them enter.

When John walked into the condo, it was dark, since every window shade and blind had been pulled low to block any view into the rooms. Normally there would be a vast expanse of Fisher Island, Miami and Biscayne Bay visible from the panoramic windows.

In his mind's eye, he recalled what other buildings were nearby and could understand his brother's fear. There was another tall tower to the north and quite a number of tall residential buildings on Fisher Island across the way although only homeowners could access that private island.

"What do you want?" Miles said as he followed them into his living room, but hung back, away from the windows.

Mia held his knapsack out to him, but Miles hesitated,

eyeing it dubiously. To his surprise, Mia said, "Yes, the tracker is in there. We need your help."

Miles almost recoiled, but then shook his head and laughed. "Gotta give it to you, Mia. You've got brass. Not sure what I can do," he said, then grabbed the knapsack from her and tossed it on the granite breakfast bar.

John motioned to the knapsack. "The tracker will probably stay active for a couple of days. We want you to hold on to it for now."

"So I can be a sitting duck?" Miles said with a haughty lift of a sandy-colored eyebrow.

"My brother has arranged for extra security around the condo, and he's talked to building security as well," Mia explained.

There was a visible release of the tension in his brother's body until he gestured to the windows.

"Not much we can do there, Miles. But I ran the probability of the killer—"

"Killer?" he said in surprise.

Mia nodded. "We think the man you hired accepted the job to get closer to my family and we think he already murdered Jorge Hernandez."

Miles traced his finger through the air, as if connecting the dots. "Wasn't that the developer who blew up his own building and killed himself?"

"One and the same," John confirmed.

Miles shook his head roughly and blew out a harsh breath. "I really messed up bad. I'm so, so sorry, John."

For too long he'd accepted his brother's various excuses for the things he did carelessly, but maybe it was time for some tough love. "*Sorry* isn't going to cut it this time, Miles. Like Mia said, we need your help."

He detected something in Miles's gaze as he narrowed it to peer at him. Admiration maybe. When Miles nodded, he said, "What do you need me to do?"

"Hold on to the knapsack and act like you didn't find it. Stay home," John instructed.

"You mentioned that you spoke to the killer on the phone. Do you have his number?" Mia asked.

"He hid his number when he called," Miles said. He reached into his back pocket, pulled out the phone the CSI team had returned and handed it to John. "You know the security code."

He accepted the phone and unlocked it to scroll through the calls. "The number's hidden, but we may still be able to trace the origin of the call."

"Did you notice anything about the caller's voice? An accent or anything?" Mia asked.

With a shrug, he said, "He sounded kind of like you."

Eyes wide with surprise, Mia said, "Like me?"

Miles nodded. "Yes, like you and some of the other Cubans I've met in Miami. It's just…something. An accent, I guess."

"It's a start, I guess. It could mean he's a Cuban-American," John said.

"You never saw him, but he had to get close enough to slip that tracker in your bag. We're working on a list of suspects. Would you mind taking a look to see if any of them look familiar?" Mia asked, taking the lead on the discussion.

"I'll do whatever you need me to do. I never meant for any of this to happen. You've got to believe that, John," Miles pleaded.

"I do believe it, but actions have consequences," he said, not wanting his brother to think that he could wheedle his way out of this problem.

Miles nodded. "I get it. There's no get-out-of-jail-free card this time."

"No, there isn't," he responded.

To his relief, Mia stepped in to ease the growing discomfort. "Thank you for your help, Miles. Know that we are doing what we can to keep you safe. We'll let you know when we need you to do anything else."

"Whatever you need," he said and walked them back to the door.

Mia exited and John followed, but he stopped to face his brother. "Thank you, Miles."

His brother's grim smile confirmed that he understood. It was a thank-you for the past and possibly a goodbye as well.

That Mia had sensed the undercurrents as well became clear as she wrapped her arms around him in the elevator and held him tight, silently offering comfort.

They rode the elevator down to the parking structure, but before they exited, John peered out to confirm the security guard was still there.

He escorted Mia to the car for the drive to his home, anxious about what she would think of it when she saw it. Unlike the Lamborghini and the Del Sol penthouse that Miles had favored to make a statement, he had chosen the Indian Creek home because it had appealed to him with its stunning views of Biscayne Bay and all of Miami to the south.

He'd actually bought the place for just the location, since he'd gutted most of the interior, which had been a style he might have described as Versailles meets Broadway. He'd wanted a calmer, more natural vibe to have a retreat away from his high-tech world. He hoped she'd see that and appreciate it.

"You said you live in Indian Creek?" she asked, breaking the initial silence in the car as he drove up A1A in the direction of the exclusive community.

"I bought the place just after I sold my start-up," he said while keeping a close eye on traffic and the rearview mirror to make sure they weren't being followed. As he did so, he realized that Mia had pulled down her visor even though it was dusk. She was also diligently watching his six.

"Did you really buy it from a drug lord?" she said with a laugh, recalling Robbie's comment.

"If he was, he didn't admit it. The closing was done electronically so I never got to meet him," he said, imagining what the owner of the home with the over-the-top decor might look like.

Mia read his thoughts. "I imagine that he might have been…unique."

"Tactful, very tactful. The house took a lot of work," he said, but he didn't get a chance to explain as Mia's phone rang through the car's speakers.

She waved the phone in the air so he could see it. "It's Trey," she said and when she answered, his voice filled the interior of the BMW.

"How did it go?" Trey asked.

"Miles is going to cooperate. Unfortunately, the killer hid their phone number, but I'm assuming we can still use Miles's phone number to try and track things," Mia said.

"Roni is asking the provider to give us the call detail records. I'm almost done making my list of possible suspects from the report Roni sent over. I should have it by the time you get to John's," Trey advised.

In the background Roni called out, "I've flagged my favorites on the list."

"My program's analysis is done as well, but I haven't had a chance to review it. Once I do, I will send it along," John said as he stopped at a light near North Beach Oceanside Park.

"Sounds good. Roni and I are investigating a few other leads and if we have anything new, we'll call. Hopefully Sophie and Robbie will have something soon as well," Trey said and hung up.

There was a moment of silence again as they waited for

the light to turn green, but when they were moving again, Mia said, "Do you think my cousins will be able to get anything on that cloud account?"

John sighed and shook his head. "That's tough to say. It's probably going to be almost impossible to hack into the user's cloud account to get any info. I'm sure the company has major defenses."

MIA HAD WORRIED about that as well, but if anyone could get in it would be Sophie and Robbie. They had inherited their NSA parents' computer smarts and she trusted not only their abilities, but also their ethics. As people who used their hacking skills, understanding the balance between what they could do and what they should do made all the difference in the world. Which reminded her of the conversation she'd had with John just the night before about the Manhattan Project and his concerns about how his program could be abused. But she kept silent about that since there were so many other worries to think about.

In no time, John was turning onto 91st Street to cross over to Indian Creek Island Road. By now dusk had completely fallen, and only the faintest rays of sunlight crept above the horizon while the deeper blues and purples of night colored the darkening sky. There were no streetlights along the road, just the lights coming on in homes set close to the water. In the areas surrounding Indian Creek and to the south, lights flickered on like fireflies on a summer night.

John continued until he was almost at the dead-center point of the island and then turned into a driveway. As he did, she caught sight of the SBS security guard sitting in a car parked near the mouth of the driveway, nose pointed toward the road in case he had to move quickly.

When John parked in front of his home, there was another car with a security guard in a ready position. As they got out, Mia grabbed the overnight bag Roni had packed for her that morning from the back seat. When they approached the door, the guard stepped out of the car, and John positioned himself in front of her in a protective gesture, his body tense.

"Mr. Wilson. Ms. Gonzalez. Ted Masters," he said and pulled out an SBS photo ID.

John relaxed, stepped aside and shook the man's hand. "Mr. Masters. Nice to meet you."

Mia greeted the man as well, recognizing him as one of Trey's older, former colleagues. "You used to be with Miami PD."

He acknowledged it with a dip of his head and a warm smile. "I was. Trey made me an offer I couldn't refuse."

"Thank you for being here," Mia said, appreciating that he was there to protect them.

With a wave of his hand toward the house, Masters said, "We have another man in the back and the guard at the gate and me will take turns checking the grounds. We have replacements coming in the morning."

"We appreciate anything you can do, Mr. Masters," John said and with another handshake, they left the guard and walked into the house.

When they entered, John stepped away from her, a sheepish look on his face.

"Welcome to my home," he said.

Chapter Fifteen

John held his breath, waiting for her reaction as she sauntered into the open-concept space that held his living and dining areas and a large gourmet kitchen. The lights he'd programmed had come on automatically, casting warm light at various spots throughout the room.

She almost twirled around like a ballerina as she took in his home, and when she faced him, her smile was brilliant.

"This is lovely. It's so...peaceful," she said.

It pleased him that she had gotten the vibe he had been hoping to create. He walked toward her and slipped his hand into hers when she held it out to him.

"I wanted it to be...zen is what the designer called it," he admitted, and also looked around his home as if seeing it for the first time.

Mia shook her head. "This is all you, not just the designer's."

The heat of a blush swept up his face. "I think she got a little frustrated with me at times, but this was going to be my home." A home that he had thought about sharing with her more than once even though they'd only dated a few times. She'd made that kind of impression on him and in the two days that had passed, she'd only cemented her place in his heart.

"Thanks. Let me show you to your bedroom so you can

get comfortable," he said, and with gentle pressure on the small of her back, he led her to a bedroom that was on the opposite side from his wing in the house.

She strolled slowly, taking in his home the way a foodie sampled a fine meal. She paused to examine a painting and side table tucked into a small niche in the hall. A wrought-iron candlestick and fragrant eucalyptus candle sat on the table beside a palm-leaf-shaped tray holding an assortment of local shells and rustic balls made with twigs and rattan.

"It's a beautiful landscape," she said and then leaned forward to peer more carefully at the artist's signature. "Wilson? Any relation?"

He smiled. "My mom. She used to paint."

"She's a wonderful artist," she said, then asked, "Is that where you used to live?"

"Determined, aren't you?" he teased because of her continued attempts to find out more about his past.

She held her hands up in a why-not gesture and gave him a flirty grin. "It would be easier if you just told me."

It would be easier, but not as much fun. "Maybe later after we get some work done."

That seemed to satisfy her for the moment since she did that little ballerina whirl again and walked down the hall to the two guest bedrooms.

"You can have either, but I'd suggest the room to the right. It has great views of the water," he said, gesturing toward the room.

"Thanks. I'll only be a few minutes while I unpack. Where should I meet you?" she said.

"Take your time. I have an office in the other wing, but I like working at the dining-room table," he said. While he'd built the office to have everything he could need and to be comfortable, he preferred the wide-open spaces and views from the dining room.

"I'll meet you there," she said, and he left her to also slip into his usual at-home sweats and T-shirt. Better she see the real him and not whatever ideas she'd gotten from the various articles about him or their encounters at the Del Sol parties. He had hoped that he'd let her see that real him on their few dates, but then she'd suddenly stopped seeing him. *Maybe she hadn't liked the real you*, he wondered as he hurriedly changed and returned to the dining room to set up his laptop and print out his program's analysis of the possible suspects along with the report that Trey had sent.

In the distance came the whir of the printer in his office as it spat out the pages. He went to pick up the papers, and as he did so, the opening and closing of cabinets in his kitchen caught his attention. After the last page came out, he grabbed them and returned to the dining-room table.

Mia was in the kitchen, searching through cabinets. She faced him and said, "Not snooping. Just trying to find the fixings for some coffee."

"Not a problem," he said, then walked over and pointed out where everything was in the kitchen. *"Mi casa, su casa."*

"Gracias, mi amor," she said with a teasing light in her blue gaze, but the words still made his privates tighten as he imagined her saying it while they made love.

He rushed away, then immediately sat to hide his very obvious reaction and busied himself with placing the two reports side by side so they could compare them. As he began his review, the whir of the burr grinder intruded as she milled the beans. He looked over to watch her. Appreciate the sight of her in leggings that hugged luscious Cuban curves. The soft fabric of her T-shirt was tight against her generous breasts, but looser around her middle.

He dragged his gaze away from her to quell his desire and buried his head in the report.

Scant minutes later, the earthy aroma of coffee wafted over. Just the smell alone was enough to lift some of the tiredness he was feeling from the very taxing and emotional day. After all, how often was it that a sniper tried to take you out and you found out your brother had betrayed you?

He'd been so distracted by those thoughts and her presence, he realized he hadn't processed anything on the page he'd just finished reading.

Flipping back to the first page of his program's analysis, he was about to start again when Mia came over with mugs of coffee. She placed his in front of him, and he took a sip. It was perfect.

"Thanks. I need a boost of energy," he said and set down the mug, away from the papers.

"You'll get it with that much sugar and caffeine," she said and cradled the mug in both hands as she sipped her coffee.

"Can I help?" she asked.

"Sure," he said and laid the report on the table between them. They went through the report together line by line, only stopping so he could run into his office for paper and pens to take notes.

By the time they'd finished, they had made a list of the highest probability suspects identified by his program and it was an eclectic mix from young one-time minor offenders to hardened felons.

"Do you know why the program chose these men?" Mia asked as she looked at her list and did another flip through the pages of the report.

"I wish I did, but there are so many paths in the neural network I programmed that it's hard to say why it made those decisions," he confessed.

HIS WORDS REMINDED Mia again about some of the materials she'd read when she was trying to find out more about John and what he did for a living. It was when she'd seen the article about programs that identified schizophrenia.

She'd learned more about what he did, but not who he was, which she'd found frustrating because he intrigued her. Even more so with all that had happened in the weeks since she'd first met him.

"This is what Trey and Roni came up with," he said and placed that report on the table between them. As they had before, they carefully examined each of the suspects and the notes that Trey and Roni had made for each one. They had apparently focused not only on the past crimes of the suspects, but also on things like whether they had tattoos, jobs in downtown buildings, or relatives who had also been in trouble with the law.

"They did a lot of work in a short time," Mia said.

"And there's quite a few points that overlap," John said as he laid out his pad with his notes and gestured to several suspects that had made it to both of their lists.

"That's amazing," she said, impressed by what her brother and his fiancée had assembled in just a couple of hours and how it had produced results similar to those from John's program.

"Looks like Trey and Roni's police guts are as good as your computer," she said.

"Reminds me of that Hepburn-Tracy movie where the librarian outsmarts the computer," John admitted.

"*Desk Set*," Mia said.

"Huh?" he said, puzzled.

"That's the name of the movie. *Desk Set*. I love those old black-and-whites," she admitted.

He smiled and said, "So do I. I've got a collection of them if you want to watch one later."

She grinned, happy to find out that one little tidbit about him. "I'd like that."

"Let's make a list of these suspects and add my computer's probabilities for each one," he said.

They got to work on the final list, identifying the most

likely candidates to discuss with Trey and Roni. When they were done, John scanned the list with his phone and sent it to Trey with a request that they call when they were ready.

While they waited, Mia refreshed their coffees and he pulled out some menus from the kitchen junk drawer so they could think about dinner before it got too late.

She had barely laid out the menus on the table when Trey video-called them. He cast the call to his laptop and motioned for Mia to join him.

"Looks like we all agree on a number of people," Trey said and held up a copy of the list.

"We do, but that's assuming the information we started with was reliable," John cautioned.

"Garbage in, garbage out," Mia chimed in, but she quickly added, "But I trust what Roni did to produce this list."

"If our basic premise was right, namely, that he was a gang member," Roni cautioned, and the earlier optimism Mia had felt dimmed with Roni's warning.

John must have sensed it since he reached out to offer comfort, covering her hand with his. "We have to start somewhere, Mia. It's a good start and if it isn't...we'll start again."

Roni nodded. "It's a solid start. I'd bet my badge on it. But if we're going to be able to charge whoever it is, we're going to have to follow the official route."

"Meaning?" Mia asked.

"An official photo lineup. I'll have to head over to Miles eventually to see if he can identify any of them. If he does, we'll have to call in the DA and see what they have to say about getting a warrant," Roni explained.

"Is the lineup alone enough for a warrant?" John asked.

"Possibly not. But we're still waiting for the additional review that Roni's colleagues are doing into the evidence from the Hernandez suicide. If we're lucky, maybe we'll have more. Same with what the bomb squad and ATF are reviewing from the two bombings," Trey explained.

"Seems like there's still a lot to cover," Mia said with an exasperated sigh.

"There is, but don't lose hope," Roni said, and her best friend's words brought comfort, as did John's gentle touch.

"What do we do now?" Mia asked.

Roni jerked her thumb in Trey's direction. "The bottomless pit beside me is hungry again. I swear he's going to waddle down the aisle."

"Eating for two," he said and playfully nuzzled Roni's neck.

She scrunched her neck and said, "Get serious."

Trey swept his hand down his face and did just that, forcing a more thoughtful look on his features. "Get some rest while we wait for whatever Sophie and Robbie can dig up for the cloud account. Hopefully our police contacts will have more soon."

"I've reached out to Miles's phone provider to get his cell-phone data. Talk to you as soon as we have anything," Roni said in closing.

The video call ended, leaving Mia staring at John over the assorted papers on the table and the take-out menus.

"I know you're upset," he said and twined his fingers with hers.

"How did you guess?" she bit back sarcastically, but then shook her head and apologized. "I'm sorry. This is all so much to absorb."

"But you can do it. You always struck me as the kind of woman who could handle most anything," John said, attempting to reassure her.

She appreciated his words. "Thanks," she said and, as her stomach rumbled, she added, "I guess I'm more like Trey than I thought."

When John's stomach did a similar little noise, he

laughed. "I guess we all are. Let's order something, eat and maybe take a break to watch a movie."

It sounded like a plan. While John organized all their papers and cleaned off the dining-room table, she flipped through the various menus and picked out one from a local Cuban restaurant that she recognized, since it wasn't all that far from Carolina's Surfside condo. Plus, she remembered that John loved his Cuban sandwiches so why not.

She placed the order for them and also got sandwiches for the guards on the property. Stepping out to Masters, she let him know to expect the delivery, and gave him the cash to pay for the meals. "If you need sodas or water, just let me know," she said and went back in to wait for the food.

HE HAD BEEN surprised when the tracker had begun to move from the SBS offices and toward South Beach. He had expected the cops would find it during their investigation of the shooting scene, but apparently, they hadn't.

Stupid cops. Typical, he thought, thinking of how he had avoided the MPs during his time in the army and after, when the cops had chased him and his gang members.

Was Miles heading to the Del Sol again? he wondered, hoping he was. He'd cased that place before when he'd tried to shoot Trey and his cop girlfriend.

But the tracker stopped well shy of the luxury hotel. From what he could see, the new location was in the South Pointe area, below Fifth Avenue and close to the park and water. Probably one of the high-end condo buildings in the area.

Determined to find out, he hopped into an older Mercedes he had "borrowed" from his cousin's used car lot the night before. Victor wasn't a big fan of his borrows, but since he often used his muscle to get car payments that were too far behind, his cousin couldn't complain too loudly.

He drove away from his mom's cinder-block home in

Little Havana to the highway, racing to reach the location for the tracker in the hopes of discovering where Miles might be. Hoping John and Mia would be there also, so he could get rid of three birds with one stone.

Traffic was heavy, but moving nicely, and in no time, he was speeding across the causeway. His hands clenched the wheel in anger as he recalled messing up the attack on Ricky Gonzalez right by Jungle Island. Less than a mile or so up the road, he peered toward Palm Island, where the Gonzalez family had their gated home. He'd failed there, too, when their security guards had chased him away from the dock.

Fail, fail, fail, he thought and smacked the steering wheel in frustration. It had been the story of his life, from dropping out of high school, to his military service, and even the time in the gang and a local militia group. He'd never succeeded at anything unlike the Gonzalez family members, who seemed to be able to spin gold from whatever junk they touched.

But then again, he and his family hadn't had the advantage of being treated like heroes the way the Gonzalez patriarch had been. Every year they'd parade the eldest, Ramon, with the other Bay of Pigs heroes while his grandfather had rotted in a Cuban jail.

He was so lost in his angry thoughts he almost ran the red light at the end of the causeway and came to a screeching halt. Not good, especially since there was a police car parked across the way, hoping to catch anyone speeding off the causeway into South Beach.

The cop behind the wheel even looked his way, but he just played it cool and slowly turned down Alton Road and toward South Pointe once the light turned green. He kept an eye on the tracker as he inched closer and closer to its position until he was finally in front of the Portofino Tower.

Not bad, Miles. Being his little brother's gofer had

clearly paid off, he thought. From what he could tell, Miles was about ten or so floors up, and even though there was another tower nearby, taking a clear shot from that other building would be tough. Fisher Island was across the way, but getting on that private island was impossible. Only those invited by residents could board the ferry to get there.

It would have to be close and personal, he thought, smiling. There was something very rewarding about doing a kill that way. Bombs and bullets did the job, but watching the life fade from someone's eyes...

He pulled into the parking garage for the condo building, but as he entered, he caught sight of the SBS security guard positioned by the area for the elevator and stairs. The guard was armed and had his back to the wall, so he wouldn't have any element of surprise. He suspected that once he got past that one guard, there would be another inside.

Driving around the parking area, he tried not to attract too much attention as he pulled back out and found a spot in the visitor parking area of the nearby South Pointe Tower.

An hour passed and then a second and a third. Night had fallen hard with a bright full moon bathing the glass of the towers and making them glisten in the night sky.

Beautiful, but not good for any kind of sneak attack. There was just too much light and Miles was clearly not going anywhere.

He'd have to wait for a better time. He was good at waiting. After all, his family had been waiting over sixty years for any kind of justice.

Chapter Sixteen

Mia's life was usually a whirlwind of activity revolving around her and Carolina, and the various events they attended. It was an exciting life and had proved to be financially rewarding once their lifestyle social-media accounts had taken off. "The Twins" as she and Carolina were affectionately known, were invited to most anything of importance in the Miami area. Those connections had also helped her assist her family on assorted cases, like the one that had first introduced her to John.

Now here she was, stomach full and feeling a little sleepy, tucked into his side while watching one of the movie classics he had in his collection. Not her usual nightlife.

With his high-tech existence, she hadn't figured him to be a black-and-white kind of guy, or have a home that made her feel like she was in a spa. The colors were calming, the furniture inviting. The moonlight shimmering on the pool outside cast patterns into the home, enveloping her with relaxing vibes. There was even a scent, clean and crisp, spilling from a diffuser in a far corner.

"This is nice," she said, snuggling deeper against him and closing her eyes.

"It is. I'm not used to just lying around," he said.

She half opened her eyes to peer at him. His head rested against the soft cushions of the leather couch. His eyes were closed, and a peaceful smile graced his lips. Those lips that had provided such pleasure the night before.

She inched up and dropped kisses along his jaw until she reached the side of his mouth. He half turned, met her mouth with his. Kissed her, his touch light at first, tender, but it wasn't enough. *Not nearly enough*, she thought and slipped into his lap, cradling his center with hers.

Heat built as he hardened beneath her and she did a roll of her hips, caressing him.

He gripped her hips hard with his hands, stilling the motion.

She drew away slowly to meet his gaze, questioning.

"I want you, Mia. Don't mistake why I'm stopping," he said as he brushed back a lock of her hair that had fallen forward and cupped her cheek.

"Why?" she pressed, wanting to understand.

"There's too much going on. Emotions are running high."

She laid her pointer finger against his lips, silencing him. "I'm not vulnerable, John. I know exactly what I'm thinking. What I'm feeling. What I want."

John blew out a breath and shook his head. "You're making this hard, Mia."

Grinning, she dragged her hips across him. "I hope so."

HIS BODY SHOOK from the force of the desire that blasted through his body with that sexy shift of her hips. But it was about more than passion for him. He wanted all of her. Wanted her, heart and soul, and while making love to her now might be putting the cart before the proverbial horse, he couldn't stop denying her or himself.

He surged to his feet and carried her to his bedroom, where he laid her on the bed and pushed a button by the bedside to engage the privacy film on the wall of windows. The film dimmed the moonlight, but it was still bright enough to see her. See the crystalline fire blazing in her sky-blue eyes, and her lips, those lips…

Bending, he kissed her, and she wrapped her arms around his shoulders and drew him down to rest against her on the bed. They kissed over and over. Touched, her hands mobile along his back, holding him close.

He slipped his hand beneath the hem of her soft T-shirt to find even softer skin there. Trailing his hands up her body, he cupped her breast and she urged him on with soft cries of need.

He gave her what she needed, but took as well, savoring the pleasure of her loving.

He didn't know how they got naked as clothes almost flew off by themselves, but when skin hit skin, it was impossible to stop. He couldn't deny that he needed her more than he'd ever needed anything in his life.

Fumbling in the nightstand drawer, he yanked out a condom and tore it open to fit it over himself. But as he did so, Mia pushed him to his back to finish the task. She covered his body with hers and took him into her warmth. But she didn't move. She just straddled him and gazed down at him, searching his features.

When she finally moved on him, he hoped that she had found what she was looking for.

Each shift of her hips drove passion ever higher, until her body tightened above him, and she arched her back, calling out his name. But he wasn't done. He wasn't sure he'd ever be done with her and as she fell back to earth, he shifted her beneath him and started the rhythm of their lovemaking again.

HER BODY WAS still trembling from her climax as he drove into her once more, slowly at first, but then with more command. Demanding, wanting her to join him as he fell over.

She cradled his shoulders and answered him, feeling the

pull of his need. A need that she suspected was more than just physical, just as it was for her.

Passion grew ever more intense. She climbed with him, higher and higher. Grasping his shoulders, she inched up to rain kisses across his face. Urged him on with tender words. *"Mi amor,"* she said.

His body shook and he called out her name, on the edge of his release. With a few final strokes, he took them over the edge, calling her name.

"Mia. You're mine, Mia. Forever mine," he said as he kissed her and took her breath into him.

It slipped from her then. *"Te quiero."*

His body stilled and he leaned a hand on the mattress to lift off her slightly. "You love me?"

She silently cursed, sorry that she'd lost her control. It wasn't something she normally did, especially when she wasn't quite ready to admit it to herself.

Backtracking, she said, "I think I do. I mean, like you said, there's so much going on and emotions—"

He stopped her with a kiss, and she was grateful for that because it kept her mouth from saying any more stupid things.

When he finally broke away, he said, "I understand. You don't need to say more."

And yet she felt like she had to say more, especially as he rolled to his back, gathered her into his arms and pulled the sheets up over them. She tucked herself tight to his warmth and against the chill of the AC.

Even though the world was in turmoil, comfort and peace filled her in his arms, and little by little, sleep claimed her.

JOHN WASN'T USED to sleeping with women. It wasn't his kind of thing to sleep around no matter what the tabloids intimated about him.

Mia wasn't just any woman. She was beautiful, intelligent, brave… He could go on and on, but that would only make it harder when she left.

And she would leave despite the words that had slipped out of her mouth. He was just a nerdy computer programmer with too much money. Not the kind of man someone as vibrant and social as Mia would want.

But he'd accept this loving for now, short-lived as it might be.

Her body relaxed against him in little pieces, growing heavier as she drifted off. Long minutes later that soft little snore sounded in the quiet of the night, confirming she was fast asleep, but he couldn't join her. There were too many thoughts and ideas flitting through his head about what they had uncovered so far.

Too many thoughts that made him gently move away from her side, easing a pillow in his spot so she'd be less likely to notice his absence.

He searched the floor for his clothes, slipped into them and crept from the bedroom, closing the door behind him as not to wake her.

His laptop sat on the table, calling to him to get back to work, as it did so often. Other than Miles, the laptop and his code had been his constant companions. But now he had Mia as well. At least for now, and he had to do whatever he could to protect her.

He sat and powered up the computer, then considered what else he could do and a vague memory came to him about some cell-network providers being hacked, possibly by the Chinese. Immediately a result popped up in his search engine and he read through the various articles, until he reached one that discussed that the hacks had obtained years' worth of call detail records. That information was exactly what he wanted and, digging deeper, it seemed various tech journals explained how the hackers had broken into the system to get the information.

But the article also mentioned how the National Security Agency had been collecting similar call detail records for millions of Americans. If they were still running the program, they might possibly have the information that Roni was trying to obtain from Miles's cell-phone provider.

Hacking the NSA would have way too many consequences if he was caught, but if that turned out to be his last resort, he'd do it to protect Mia and the rest of the Gonzalez family.

For now, he started off by hiding his own information with his VPN and other tools. Feeling safely screened from discovery, he repeated the steps done by the most well-known hackers to try and break into Miles's phone provider, searching their network for certain types of non-Windows servers that had more lax security and monitoring solutions in order to access the server. If he was successful, he'd use a password-spraying protocol he'd developed to break into the servers or maybe even find one of the back doors the hackers had left to let them reaccess the servers. But as he tried and tried again, it seemed as if this cell provider may have taken steps to protect against the hacks.

He was about to try another avenue when the snick of the door opening drew his attention to the bedroom. Mia stood there in only a T-shirt, her hair sleep-tousled and her blue gaze assessing as she glanced in his direction.

She walked over, stood behind him and wrapped her arms around him. When she saw what he was doing, she said, "Please, tell me you're not—"

"I am," he admitted. "I feel like I have to do something."

Hugging him tight, she said, "You're doing more than you know and you can't compromise all that you've worked for like this."

He put his hands on the table and stared at his screen. With a shrug, he said, "I haven't been able to break in."

"Good. Come back to bed and get some rest. We need to be fresh in the morning when we have more information," she said and smoothed a hand across his chest.

He glanced over his shoulder and met her sleepy gaze. "I wish I could be as optimistic about what we'll have in a few hours."

She whispered a kiss on his forehead. "Come back to bed."

Smiling tightly, he shut the laptop, rose and encircled her in his arms. "Let's go to bed."

DESPITE HER ASSERTIONS to John that they needed to get some rest, it had taken her a very long time to fall asleep. Once he was in bed beside her, he'd been sound asleep in only a few minutes, and she wondered if he'd trained himself to do that. She could picture him doing long hours at his computer and then dropping off to get some *z*'s before going back to work.

In a way she was used to it as well, thanks to the late nights she often kept with Carolina at their various social events. But she normally didn't end her nights with a very handsome man in her bed, contrary to what some might think.

She sighed as she recalled their lovemaking and the accidental slip of the tongue that was bound to complicate things beyond their already complicated state.

Shaking her head in chastisement, she busied herself with making coffee and rummaged through his cabinets and refrigerator to see what she could make for breakfast. She located some granola and yogurt, as well as eggs and cheese. *Enough for a healthy parfait and an omelet*, she thought.

She had just finished the parfaits and was whipping up

the eggs when John strolled out of the bedroom, raking back the errant locks of his hair with his fingers.

"Good morning," he said. He walked to her side and hesitated for a second before dropping a tentative kiss on her cheek.

She understood his caution since she was feeling it, too, after the eruption of passion from the night before. But she didn't want that restraint between them. She wanted to see where this could go, so she leaned into him and kissed him without hesitation.

This time he answered her eagerly, meeting her mouth with his until they broke apart, breathless and staring at each other. "I'm not sorry about last night," she said.

"I'm not either," he said, but they didn't get to explore it further as the phone rang, warning that reality was intruding.

Chapter Seventeen

John hadn't been feeling optimistic the night before, but as Roni detailed the updates she'd gotten from her colleagues that morning, he finally felt some relief.

"The bomb squad and ATF have confirmed that similar materials and methods were used in the bombing at the Hernandez construction site and the car bomb," she said. "Both bombs contained fertilizer and gasoline. In the car bomb, the gasoline in the gas tank amplified the blast."

"If there is that connection, what about Hernandez's supposed suicide?" Mia asked, leaning forward to peer at her best friend on the video call.

Roni smiled. "We caught a break there as well. CSI found a partial print on the casing of one of the unfired bullets in the revolver. It will take them a few hours to clean up the print enough to run it through AFIS. Once they do, that may take another couple of hours to see if we have a match to anyone in the system."

The mention of the bullet prompted John to ask a question. "What about the bullets from the sniper?"

Roni shook her head. "Too damaged from impact and the shooter policed his brass on the rooftop. No prints on the rooftop door either."

One step forward, two steps back, he thought.

Trey's fiancée noticed his frustration and said, "We're closing the noose around him, John. You have to believe that."

He nodded. "What about the tracker? What do we do with that for now?"

It was Sophie who popped in with a report. "We're getting close to identifying the cloud account using the serial number on the tag and trying to reach it with fake location pings."

"Won't that alert the provider and make them disable the tag?" John queried.

Sophie and Robbie shared a look. "It might. That's why we're being very careful with how we're doing it."

It was ingenious and he admired their creativity. "If you ever want to leave SBS, let me know," he teased, earning smiles from the two siblings.

"What can we do in the meantime?" John asked, feeling useless because he had exhausted what he could do, absent illegally hacking into the cell-phone provider or the NSA. It also didn't escape his notice that he'd made it a *we* and not an *I* because Mia and he were partners in so many ways.

"We should have the call detail records in the next hour or so. It may be a lot to process manually, especially plotting the cell-tower locations," Trey said.

John nodded. "I'll process that data as soon as you send them," he said, paused and added, "What about Miles? What do we do about him?"

At the mention of his brother, Mia laid a hand on his shoulder to offer comfort, understanding it was still a raw wound.

Roni and Trey shared a look and Roni's lips tightened into a harsh line. "I'm not sure we'll be able to protect him if the DA wants to press charges for what he's done, both the insider trading and the attack in your offices."

"I understand," John said with a dip of his head.

"If he reaches out to you, or if you reach out to him, tell

him to sit tight and not to move the tracker," Trey said, and his cousins confirmed it by nodding.

"I'll let him know."

WILSON HADN'T MOVED from the night before. Or at least the tracker hadn't moved.

He'd done surveillance off and on until midnight, carefully driving around the area as not to draw too much attention to himself. He'd even passed a police car patrolling the area, but the cop hadn't blinked an eye as he drove by.

He scanned the tower and noticed the floor where the window shades and blinds were still drawn against the late-morning light. They'd been closed last night as well.

The snake was hiding in his hole, but for how long and why? he wondered. Had John Wilson caught on to the fact that Miles couldn't be trusted? Is that why he was still at home on a workday, or were the brothers afraid of another attack on their offices?

Regardless, Miles had to come out eventually, and when he did, he'd be ready.

RONI HADN'T BEEN kidding when she'd said that the call detail records would be too much to review manually, Mia thought. It had all seemed like gibberish to her until John had explained each item and what it meant. With little else to do, Mia was determined to get something useful from the information.

Wanting quiet because she'd realized that even a sitting John was like a teakettle about to boil, sometimes nervously bouncing his legs or tapping his feet, other times mumbling beneath his breath, she escaped to his office. However, she couldn't get to work right away since the photos, awards and other ephemera of John's life called to her from the wall units to the side of his desk. She laid down the call detail record reports they'd printed and casually strolled from one item to the next, taking in those tidbits from his life.

A framed photo of John with Miles and a woman she assumed was their mother. Miles had her sandy-colored hair, but John was almost a spitting image of the beautiful woman. She had a button nose that softened a face dominated by a strong chin and square jaw. It looked like the picture had been taken at some kind of graduation—college, she guessed.

In another photo, Miles and John stood in front of the door to the start-up John had sold several months earlier. Awards from charity organizations, mostly ones helping women in need, were mixed in with an assortment of books and technical manuals.

Returning to the desk, she set the report with Miles's call records in the center of the desk, grabbed a pen and highlighters, and started reviewing it. After barely an hour, her eyes were blurring from looking at the data, but she focused and decided to keep her attention on the columns with the cell-site data.

The same three cell sites seemed to be popping up for Miles and she wrote them down on a pad of paper and highlighted them, assuming that they were for things like the offices in downtown and the two brothers' homes. When she looked at the phone numbers being dialed from those cell sites, there seemed to be a lot of communication between John and Miles at the various locations. Not unexpected, since the two were working together.

Frustrated, she leaned back in the comfy leather executive chair and gazed out the wall of windows across the way. They faced the lush gardens that had been planted around the home and at the edges of the road, a well-manicured lawn and a central courtyard, where water spilled down tiered basins into a large pool. Flashes of gold and orange hinted that there were fish in the large lower basin.

Much like in the rest of the home, there was a decided zen feel to the room, what with the views of the garden and fountain, and the colors of the furniture, floor and walls in the office. It created a peaceful and relaxing feel that chased away some of the frustration raging inside her.

Returning to the papers, she flipped the pages until she got to the date and time when the attack had happened at John's old offices. She flagged it and noted something interesting: the cell site for the incoming call and Miles's phone at that time were the same. On top of that, the number hadn't been hidden.

The intruder had been close to the office, which made sense. Miles must have tipped him off as to when to fake the attack.

She wrote down the number reflected on the report, not that it would do much good. It was likely a burner phone. But she still went through the rest of the report, noting that there had been at least two other calls from that number to Miles prior to the attack, but none after.

"Bingo!" She heard John's voice from the other room and hurried out to where he was staring at the laptop.

"Good news?" she asked and peered at the laptop screen, which appeared to show a map of the area with clusters of dots in various areas.

He grabbed a remote, flipped on the television and cast his screen there.

Using a laser pointer, he highlighted the various areas and explained.

"I programmed the locations of the various cell towers and analyzed how many phone calls were made in the vicinity of those towers. You can see the larger circles, which indicate the volume of calls," he said.

"I eliminated calls that Miles and I made to each other," he said, and with the tap of a few keys, the circles diminished substantially, but there were still quite a few calls emanating from the downtown area with even more scattered circles in South Beach and Little Havana.

Holding her hands out in question, she said, "There are still too many other calls."

"THERE ARE, SO I used my program to eliminate commonly called numbers, like ones to Versailles and other restaurants. The Del Sol, of course," John said and issued another command to the laptop.

"Wow. That got rid of a lot of them," Mia said with a breathy sigh.

"It did. I'm going to have the program make a list of the addresses for the remaining locations and compare it to the last known addresses for our various suspects," John said, and at that statement, Mia held up a finger and rushed off to his office.

She returned a few seconds later with the printed reports, where she had highlighted various items and a pad of paper with her notes.

"These are the cell-tower sites for calls made from what I think was the attacker to Miles. You should be able to confirm that against your data. I wrote down the dates and times as well and one of them matches up with the attack on your office," Mia explained.

"Good work. Once we have that, we'll send the analysis to SBS and see if they have any new info," he said. As he started to type, a knock came at the door.

"I'll get that," Mia said and raced off to answer the door.

A few seconds later, Mia's surprised gasp traveled across the room. "What are you doing here?"

John turned in his seat to look past Mia to where Miles stood at the door, the security guard at his side. Mia half turned to face him, her gaze questioning.

He joined her and jerked his head to let the guard know

he could go back to his car. "Mia's right. We asked you to stay put."

Miles ran a shaky hand through his hair. "I was going stir-crazy. Let me help, John."

John looked past Miles and down the driveway to see if there were any other cars in the area. "Did you make sure you weren't being followed?" he asked.

His brother looked back toward the road and with a shrug and shake of his head, he said, "I don't think so."

"Dude, you need to be careful. Go home and stay put," John urged.

Miles looked from him to Mia and back to him. "You won't let me stay?"

His brother had stayed with John dozens of times after late nights of programming or partying, but that had been before, and things were different now. "I won't. We're working on things—"

Angrily, Miles jabbed a finger in each of their directions. "We're working? The two of you? What can she possibly do?"

He wanted to say "More than you've ever done" but that wouldn't be fair. His brother had done a lot for him, possibly even saved his life from his abusive father. Because of that, he tempered his response.

"I'm not sure you can help right now. Please go home. When we need you, we'll call. Text me when you get there," John said.

Miles looked between the two of them, and with an abrupt nod, he marched away to his car.

They stood there, watching the car drive down to the road and almost disappear from sight behind the thick foliage along the edge of the road.

Mia slipped her hand into his. "It'll be okay, John. *He'll* be okay," she urged.

Miles might be okay, but John wasn't sure he could ever trust his brother again and that filled him with sadness.

With a quick dip of his head, he squeezed her hand and said, "Let's get back to work."

HE HUNG FAR back from Miles's Lexus, not wanting to let the man know that he was being followed. It was relatively easy along A1A, with enough traffic to let him hide behind other cars as they drove northbound. But as they got into the Surfside area and he realized Miles was turning off to head to Indian Creek, he slowed considerably.

The island only had about forty or so homes and a golf course, so it would be tough to stay out of sight. But he wanted to know where John had his home. Where Mia would be hiding out with the tech multimillionaire and likely more vulnerable than the other family members in their gated and protected residences.

He slipped onto a side street as Miles continued across the bridge onto the island, then doubled back and onto the bridge, creating a good deal of distance from Miles. But he could still see that the Lexus had driven in the direction of the golf course.

He did the turn as well, moving slowly and surveilling the area to get a feel for it, so he would know the best way to make an escape.

Barely fifty yards ahead of him, Miles pulled into a driveway and excitement raced through him.

He contained himself, moving at a normal pace past the driveway, so as not to draw attention.

A few homes down, the land on either side of the road opened into grassy areas that signaled the start of the golf course.

He kept on going and turned into the parking lot for the country club, where he parked and yanked out his phone to get a map of the area. He muttered a curse as he realized the only road on the island dead-ended at either end and the bridge was the only way on and off the island.

Any attack would take a great deal of planning, he thought and drove away, his pace measured again, especially as he neared the driveway where he had seen Miles turn in.

There was heavy foliage all along the area by the road, but he thought he caught sight of a car near the mouth of the driveway and two other vehicles parked by the front door. They screamed of being cop cars, at least two of them, so it might not be easy to get up close for a kill, the way he liked it. But there was also a lot of open space that might give him a clear shot from the golf course.

If that was all he could get, he'd take it.

It was impossible to miss the dejected set of John's shoulders and the misery in his gaze.

Mia understood. She didn't know how she would handle it if one of her siblings had behaved like Miles. But then again, she couldn't imagine that anyone in her family ever would.

She left John at the table working on his computer and walked into the kitchen to make some coffee. As she did so, her phone chirped to say she had a message.

How r u holding up? Carolina texted.

Guilt filled her that she hadn't really kept her cousin and best friend in the loop. Because of that, she called Carolina.

"Hola, amiga," she said as her cousin answered.

"Hola, prima. Mami and I saw the news about the explosion, and we were so worried."

"I'm so sorry that I didn't call, but things have been too crazy," Mia said in apology.

"I know. Besides we have that twin thing, so I knew you were okay," Carolina teased, helping to ease her guilt.

"Gracias. I'm glad you and *Tia* Elena are away and safe,"

she said, and in the background, she could hear her aunt calling out a greeting.

Carolina blew out a sigh that carried across the line. "I wish there was some way we could help."

"Me, too, but for now staying away is a big help," she said, and it made her think of Miles's visit. Worry filled her that he hadn't been careful and that the killer may have tracked him to John's home.

"We'll stay at the spa as long as you need, but if that should change—"

"We'll let you know," Mia said and ended the call. But no sooner had she hung up than her phone was ringing again with a call from Trey.

His voice was excited as he said, "Sophie and Robbie think they may have gotten the cloud-account name."

"Let me put you on speaker so John can hear," she said and hurried over to John's side. She tapped on the speaker key, set the phone on the table and said, "What can you tell us?"

"I've got Sophie and Robbie here as well," Trey said.

A second later, Sophie came across the line. "We only had it for a second before the system's security shut us down, but we got it. *JMMADDTRAX.*"

"JMADDTRAX?" Mia said, wanting to make sure she had understood.

Sophie spelled it out so there would be no confusion and after she did so, Mia peered at John to see if it made sense to him because it didn't mean anything to her.

He shook his head. "Not a clue," he said but immediately jumped on his laptop.

"It didn't mean anything to us either and an internet search didn't get us any hits," Trey advised.

John gestured to his laptop so she could see that he was also drawing a blank.

With a shrug, she said, "Could it be initials? Some kind of nickname?"

"Or tracks as in motocross, or lay down music tracks or even racks for something," Robbie mused.

"We'll have to play around with it. Can you guys do that as well?" Trey asked.

"Will do, but in the meantime…have you heard from anyone about the partial print?"

"Not yet, but we hope to have it soon. What about you? Any progress on the call detail records?" her brother said.

John and she shared a look and then John said, "I've plotted where all the calls either originated or terminated, and I'm working on eliminating as many as I can. Mia put together some info as well and we'll hopefully have something for you in another couple of hours."

"Great. Let's touch base again before dinner. I'd love to get together to share ideas, but I don't want to clue anyone to where you might be," her brother said.

The look she shared with John this time was troubled. "We already had a guest today. Miles came by, but we sent him back home and told him to sit tight."

A long silence drifted across the line. "That worries me," Trey said calmly. Too calmly.

"We have the guards here, Trey. No need to worry," Mia said, trying to dispel any fears he might have.

"If he was followed—"

"He wasn't, we don't think," Mia said.

Another awkward silence followed but then Trey said, "I'll make sure the guards are on high alert. We'll talk to you later."

Once he'd hung up, Mia sat beside John, who met her gaze, clearly troubled. "Trey's right. What if someone followed Miles?"

"You have a security system that goes to a central station, right?" she said and gestured to the keypad by the front door.

When he nodded, she said, "We have three armed guards on the grounds and bulletproof glass."

"But he's a sniper who knows how to make bombs," John replied quickly.

She didn't argue with him because she couldn't. But they were safe for now and so was Miles, who had texted to confirm he had arrived at his condo.

Turning the conversation away from that, she said, "If *JMMADDTRAX* stands for something else, what could it be?"

"Like you said before, it could be a lot of different things," John said with a shrug.

"Too many combinations," she said.

"92,378, if we start rearranging all ten letters," he said nonchalantly, but at her surprised look he shrugged and added, "I'm kinda good with math."

"I should have figured you were some kind of genius," she said.

He grimaced. "You don't know how I hate that word. Besides, we don't want to look at all the combinations. Just ones that maybe mean something."

Because he obviously didn't want to talk about his genius skills, she said, "I guess we start searching for those combos."

He nodded. "Let's start searching for any references to 'mad tracks.'"

"Two real words that someone may have changed for their username?" she asked.

With another nod, he said, "Maybe 'mad tracks' was already taken. Sometimes people add numbers but other times they just add letters."

If anyone would know about the behavior of computer users, it would be John, Mia thought.

The first search got immediate results, returning dozens of hits for a very popular video game. "The gang member is a gamer?" she said, speculating.

"If he is, maybe it's also his gang-member name. Roni can probably have her people run that," John said, and Mia jotted it down with their notes.

They kept at it, thinking of possible word combinations and variations, and searching on the internet for anything that would point them in the direction of one of the possible suspects they had previously identified.

As they were about to try another set of variables, Trey phoned again.

"You have news?" Mia asked.

"I do, but it isn't good."

Chapter Eighteen

John watched the faces of the various Gonzalez family members on the video call as Roni ran through the information she'd been given about the partial print.

She screen-shared a rap sheet for a possible suspect. "AFIS spit out Jaime Cruz based on the partial print. Cruz was on my list of favorites and high on John's list of possible suspects."

"That's a good thing, isn't it?" John asked and looked at the report his program had produced based on the information Roni had provided. According to his program, there had been an eighty-percent probability that Cruz was involved in the attacks.

"It is except for one problem—Cruz was killed six months ago in a gang-related shooting," Roni advised.

Silence filled the air and the faces of the family members turned stony with that revelation.

From the corner of his eye, he caught sight of Mia's worried features. "He's been dead for six months but somehow his fingerprint is on a bullet casing?"

"Can you say 'bizarro'?" Robbie said.

"The gun must have gone to someone who knew Cruz," Trey said and brought up the photos of a few of their other suspects on the screen. "These are other gang members who may have known him and were on our list."

John skimmed his finger down his report, checked the probability numbers and shook his head. "These are all low probability."

"It's what we have to go on so far," Roni said with a frown and continued. "I was waiting to ask Miles to come in for a lineup until we had the result from the partial print, but I think it may be time to have him take a look at these other suspects."

John wasn't so sure about that. "I trust your judgment, but…can we hold off until tomorrow? We're still working on this cloud-account info, and I should have more for you on the cell-site locations soon."

Roni slipped an uneasy glance at Trey, but then reluctantly nodded. "Okay, tomorrow. I'm going to reach out to my contacts and see if they know who Cruz's friends in the gang were. Relatives also. If I get anything, I'll pass it on."

"Sounds good and thanks for everything, Roni. We appreciate it," Mia said, and John ended the call.

"Dead." John sighed in frustration. "Our one and only suspect is dead."

Mia understood how he felt. She'd experienced the same emotions more than once when she'd been involved in one of her family's investigations. But this was worse because this was way more personal.

She slipped her hand into his. "Let's take a break. I'll make us dinner."

He raised his hand in a stop gesture. "Let me. I like to cook."

"Really? A liberated man. I like that," she said and playfully tugged on his hand to pull him from the table and into the kitchen area.

Mia took a spot by the counter as John opened the fridge, pulled out several things and walked over to the counter.

"Stir-fry, okay?" he asked and laid an assortment of vegetables and a skirt steak on the granite.

She nodded. "I'd like that. Want me to make some rice?"

"Sure," he said and got to work, cutting and chopping while she rinsed the rice and got it cooking.

While he did the stir-fry, she set the table, and opened a bottle of white wine. After pouring them each a glass, she returned to John's side and set the glass by where he was working. Leaning against the counter, she watched as he added the carrots and broccoli to the wok and gave a stir.

He stopped to take a sip and smiled. "Tasty," he said and raised the glass to clink it against hers.

She grinned. "You have an excellent wine cellar. Did you pick the wines yourself?"

With a self-deprecating smile, he shook his head. "No way. I wouldn't know Moët from Mad Dog, but I'm trying to learn."

"You get an A for this one," she said and turned down the heat on the rice as it started to boil, setting it to a low simmer. The rice would finish cooking and steam so it wouldn't get sticky.

"That's praise coming from you, princess," he said, dampening her mood a little.

"Not a princess, remember. There are things I had to learn, too," she admitted.

He set aside his wooden spoon and peered at her. "I'm sorry. I know you haven't always had it easy. Maybe we can learn together," he offered an apology.

Grinning, she said, "I'd like that. How about I stir while you keep on chopping?"

He nodded and together they cooked the meal like a well-choreographed ballet, and in no time, they were sitting at the table, eating the delicious meal they'd prepared.

She must have been hungry since she devoured her first plate and so did John. She served them the last of the rice and stir-fry, and after, they cleaned up and loaded everything into the dishwasher, then settled onto the couch to finish their wines before returning to work.

They sat there quietly, lost in their thoughts and their company as they sipped the wine.

The ideas in her brain were like a kaleidoscope, whirling and twirling, multicolored, as she tried to slip all the different thoughts into seemingly logical categories. But there were just too many loose threads that refused to be woven into any kind of pattern, so she focused on one.

"What if the *JM* aren't the initials?" she suggested and finished off her wine.

"You're saying the initials are *JMM* and we should search *ADDTRAX*?" he asked.

She shook her head. "No, I mean what if the start of the name is actually *JMMADD*? I know it's weird—"

"No weirder than *MADDTRAX* and that's gotten us nowhere. Stay here," he said and hopped off the couch to grab his laptop.

She tucked herself close as he placed his computer on his lap and did the search on *JMMADD*.

"I'll be damned," he said as the results came up.

"Wow, what are the odds that's not a coincidence?" she said as she saw result after result. *JMMadd* had been the code name of a secret CIA airfield in Guatemala used as part of the Bay of Pigs invasion.

"Didn't your grandfather take part in the Bay of Pigs?" John asked.

She nodded. "He was a member of the brigade." Pointing to his computer. "Try *JMMTrax*."

He did, but when he got no hits, he changed it to *JMTrax* and sure enough, a slew of results popped up, also linking the term to the failed invasion of Cuba that had been engineered by the CIA and scuttled by President Kennedy.

Puzzled, Mia said, "It's been over sixty years. What connection could the Bay of Pigs have to what's happening?"

JOHN WAS AS puzzled as Mia. "It can't be someone who was involved in the invasion. They'd be like what? Eighty years old?"

"*Mi abuelo*—my grandfather—is 87. I'm not sure how many survivors are still alive, but if they are, they'd all probably be in their late 70s, 80s and even 90s. Our attacker was young," Mia said.

"He was. If this is a real connection we've discovered, it's likely that our attacker is a 'grand,'" he said, using air quotes and continued. "Grandchild, grandnephew. Our generation."

Mia held her hands up as if in pleading, trying to understand. "But why? It happened sixty years ago."

"I don't know enough about it to say, Mia. But I think it's time to get everyone involved. Maybe even call your grandfather," John said.

Mia grabbed her phone, dialed Trey and explained what they had discovered.

John heard the murmur of his voice in agreement and when she hung up, she said, "Trey is going to set up a video call."

When a familiar tone announced the incoming call, he answered and cast the image to the television screen to get a clearer view of the Gonzalez family members.

Mia scooted closer to him so that she'd appear in the video as well.

"We think we've figured out the meaning of *JMMAD-DTRAX*," John said and quickly explained what they had unearthed.

The reaction of the other Gonzalez family members matched Mia's earlier reaction.

"That can't be," Trey said.

"But that's so long ago," Sophie said.

Robbie added, "Almost ancient history."

Mia shook her head, chastising her cousin. "That's because you two mostly grew up in the DC area. In Miami, it's still important, still a wound to a lot of Cuban exiles."

"Mia's right. When the sixtieth anniversary of the invasion happened in 2021, the veterans of the brigade were honored by the governor and others. That history is almost as alive today as it was sixty years ago," Trey warned his cousins.

Sophie lifted a hand to her chest in a gesture of apology. "So sorry. But if this is related to Grandfather Ramon, do we have to worry about him being attacked?"

"John can run that through his program to get the probability, but since *abuelo*'s staying put on Palm Island, *abuela* and he should be safe," Trey said.

"I will run it," John said, but as he went to the dashboard, he realized he already had a hit on an earlier operation he'd been running. Muttering a curse, he said, "I've got to finalize this dashboard."

"What is it, John?" Sophie asked, dark eyebrows furrowed with worry.

John waved off her concern. "I have the analysis of the cell-tower sites related to all those calls. It looks like there are about half a dozen locations where the calls were made. I'll send you the information so you can review it."

Sophie and Robbie nodded. "We will. We're still working on that cloud account and the tracker. It's still active and sending signals. Maybe to one of those cell towers on your list," Sophie said.

Mia said, "If there is a connection to *abuelo* and this stalker is mad at the family—"

"We can ask Ricky to chime in on that and maybe give us a profile," Trey said.

Mia spoke up again. "The gang member is related to

someone connected to the invasion somehow. Speaking of gang members, where's Roni?"

"At the precinct chatting up her colleagues about any connections to Cruz," Trey explained.

"If this is family-related, doesn't it make sense that it's not just a gang member? That it could be someone in Cruz's family?" Mia asked.

"It does make sense and we can start doing a search for relatives who might fit the other requirements," Sophie said.

Trey slapped the top of his desk. "Sounds like we each have something to do. I'll reach out to Ricky and Roni, Sophie and Robbie will keep working on the tracker and get started on any family ties—"

"We'll work on those also and any connections to our list of suspects. We'll also keep hammering at those cell sites," John said and peered at Mia from the corner of his eye.

She nodded to confirm it and so did her brother and cousins, who signed off one by one, leaving him staring at the image of him and Mia on the big screen. He signed off as well, faced Mia and said, "I guess we have our work cut out for us."

"We do. I'll go make some coffee."

HE HAD THOUGHT an attack would be difficult, but the more that he researched it, the more he realized it was nearly impossible.

Only one way off and on the island.

The house was on the southern-most tip, and while he had a clear shot at the front of Wilson's house from the golf course, the main living areas of the home were in the back as far as he could tell from the real-estate photos he'd tracked down on the internet.

Stillwater Drive was across the way, but the angle was all wrong.

The other way to approach the property was via Biscayne Bay, but the water would have to be like glass for him to use his 50 cal for a shot or any other rifle for that matter. Not to mention that the area was popular with boaters, creating all kinds of wakes to disrupt his aim.

He could steal a Sea-Doo, as he'd done in the past, but if there was a guard near the dock, he'd have to neutralize him as well. He already had one body to answer for, but that had been easy. Jorge Hernandez hadn't expected his hired hand to turn on him.

A paid security guard, especially one from the SBS group, would be harder to take down but he liked a challenge.

Pulling up a street view, he continued planning.

Chapter Nineteen

It didn't surprise Mia that quite a number of the areas identified via the cell-tower sites were in Little Havana. If the killer had a connection to the Bay of Pigs veterans, they were more than likely Cuban, and Miles had said the caller had an accent. While many Cubans had moved into other neighborhoods, there were still quite a number of Cubans in Little Havana and the nearby areas.

"Could you zoom in on the part of the map in Little Havana?" she said, and he did, revealing four different circles, which identified the general area from where the calls had originated. Despite John eliminating calls that he and his brother had made to the restaurant, a circle still covered the area for the location on *Calle Ocho*.

Running her finger from the restaurant to the other locations, she said, "You could walk these easily."

John nodded. "For sure. Go and get a morning *cafecito*. Run by at lunch hour to get a Cubano."

"A regular. Someone no one looks at twice. Just a neighborhood guy walking up to *La Ventanita* to get his coffee or a sandwich. Even Miles, if he went to pick up something and made a call from there," Mia said and leaned back in the chair, considering that possibility. She circled her finger around the area and said, "What else is around there? A bank or something else with a CCTV?"

With a shrug, John pulled up a street view for the area and swiveled around to examine the street. "Nothing here, but maybe farther up," he said and did the virtual walk away from the Versailles restaurant. Across the street was another eatery, *La Carreta*, with its kitschy wagon wheel on the side of the building. But directly across the street was a bank with an ATM machine that faced *Calle Ocho*.

"That's a good thing, isn't it?" Mia said, leaning close to confirm what she was seeing. A second later, a darker green circle appeared on the screen in that area.

John gestured to it. "You gave me the info for the cell-site location for the number we think is from the killer. This is where the computer says the call was likely made."

"We have the time it was made. Roni should be able to get the ATM footage from that location," Mia said and was about to call her best friend when John stopped her.

"Let's map the locations of the other two calls," he said and a second later, he zoomed out on the map to show where the two dark green circles were visible.

One of the locations was less than a dozen blocks away, on Flagler. "He could walk there," Mia said, pointing to the location.

As he had done before, John displayed the street view, but other than a few small stores and a used-car lot, there was nothing that would give them any information. But something niggled at Mia's consciousness about the location.

"Can you pull up the last one again? By the bank?" she asked and as he did so, she noticed it immediately. "There's a bus stop in front. I think I saw one at the other location as well."

He flipped back to the other location and sure enough, there was another bus stop in front of the used-car lot.

"That's too much coincidence," he said and immediately

checked the last location, which was in the downtown area, close to their old offices and the SBS building.

"That call from downtown is not far from our offices," Mia said, but then shook her head. "If this guy doesn't have a car and keeps stealing them, that just ups the likelihood that he gets caught while driving one. I'm not sure he's that stupid."

"I agree. From what I remember of your other recent cases, he has to have wheels of some kind."

"The bus route—I think it's the 208, by the way. Just coincidence?" Mia offered, eyes narrowed as she processed the information.

John likewise considered it but couldn't say. "I'm going to run this through the program. Let's take a look at something else, though."

He typed in the address for the downtown location and displayed the street view. Swiveling around to inspect the area, he stopped and tapped the screen. "Another bank right across from where the call was made."

"We need to have Roni get the ATM footage from those two areas at the time the calls were made," Mia said and texted her friend.

Need ur help. Emailing deets.

Got it, Roni texted back.

Mia almost collapsed into the chair, feeling like a weight had been lifted from her now that there was finally some progress on the case.

"We did good work," John said as he relaxed against the dining-room table. He gestured to his laptop and said, "It will take a few minutes for the probability and the family search may take hours. I don't know about you, but I'd like to stretch and maybe get some fresh air."

Mia eyed the back patio with both longing and trepidation. They'd be exposed out there, but it wasn't as bright as it had been yesterday, with the full moon, and the landscaping provided some privacy from the guard positioned near the waterfront. Not to mention that there was nothing but Biscayne Bay behind them for some distance. The closest land was the narrow spit of land for the homes by Stillwater Park and that was way off to the left.

Hopping to her feet, she held her hand out to John. "I'd like that. Just a short walk. Some fresh air."

JOHN SET ASIDE his laptop, slipped his hand into hers and stood. Together they walked toward the patio doors, and he slid one open. For parties and in nicer weather, the immense glass doors folded away to create a seamless open space between the living-room area and the outdoor-patio area.

Thick ground cover and the leaves of colorful caladiums around the garden spilled onto the edges of the travertine patio tiles, while lush elephant ears, with their immense leaves, provided privacy at the edges of the gardens. Here and there, taller papyrus swayed with the night breeze, and oleander and bougainvillea flowers provided pops of color against the deep greens and wood of his home. Jasmine scented the night air, and he breathed the smell in deeply.

They strolled along the patio and, seeing the guard down at the dock, pushed a little farther toward the edge of the pool, lost in their thoughts. Eventually they turned back toward the house and the patio.

"You have a beautiful home," she said as he guided her to a large chaise longue, where they lay down, hidden from sight by the lush greenery around the space.

It *was* beautiful. Feeling like it was time to share more with her, especially when she snuggled into his side as if it was just the normal thing to do, he said, "It's the first place I can really call home."

She hesitated for a moment, but then said, "I know it wasn't easy for you what with your dad and everything."

He nodded. "It wasn't. I try not to remember only…you don't want to throw out the good with the bad and there was good there. My mom was the best. Miles, too."

She stiffened beside him. "I get it, Mia. He betrayed me. Brought the devil right into our home, but…he's the only family I have left."

"I understand, only…you may forgive him, but the authorities might not," she said and stroked her hand across his chest.

The authorities wouldn't be too happy with his insider trading, especially since he had manipulated the stock's price with his leak. But he didn't want to talk about Miles.

"What do you see yourself doing in five years?" he said and hated that it sounded so businesslike and impersonal.

"Why? Are you hiring?" she teased back with a laugh.

"I'm not really good at people skills. I'm better with machines," he replied with a chuckle.

She shifted to lie closer and nuzzled the edge of his jaw with her nose. "I think you're really good with people, John. Especially me," she whispered before kissing him.

He answered her kiss, opening his mouth to her, urging her body over his to lie against his length. The kisses were soothing at first, but slowly deepened, demanding more with each breath they took.

HE WAS HARD against the softness of her midsection and dampness flooded her center at the memory of making love to him the night before.

She wanted to make love with him all night long. Maybe even for the next five years, or ten, or more, she thought but couldn't say.

Instead, she slipped from the lounge, stood beside him

and grabbed hold of his hand. "Come inside. I don't want the guard to see us get *nekkid*," she replied with a laugh.

He grinned, his smile bright even in the dim light. Jumping to his feet, he grabbed hold of her hand and tugged her into the house, stopping only to close and lock the patio doors.

Once the doors were secured, and his alarm system was set, they almost ran into the bedroom, then fell on the bed, laughing and kissing. They tossed aside clothing playfully until he was leaning over her, suddenly serious.

"I can't believe you're mine," he said, revealing his pain again. Not only that of his family's past, but also of what he was. A genius. A loner, but not by choice, she suspected, recalling how well he had meshed with her family in such a short time.

"You are a part of me, John. Part of me and my family. Never doubt that," she said and rose up to kiss away the hurt.

John took her kiss into him, let her love wash over him. As much as this house was now his home, he couldn't imagine Mia not being a part of it either.

But he tempered what he wanted to say because of all that was happening and might be clouding their emotions. Instead, he showed her with his kisses and body what he felt for her. How he cared for her, revered her.

She was everything he'd never imagined possible for himself. A bright and caring woman. A ready-made family because he had no doubt that the Gonzalez family was a package deal and surprisingly, he wanted to embrace it. Embrace the kind of family he'd never really had.

As passion rose, he opened his heart and body to her, holding nothing back. He wanted her to know just how precious she was to him.

Together they tumbled over and lay there in the after-math of their loving, content. Quiet.

But soon the *ding-ding-ding* of their phones interrupted the peaceful lull, reminding them that they had work to do.

With a final kiss and a promise for later, they gathered their clothes to answer the calls demanding their attention.

SOPHIE AND ROBBIE had gone on one of the genealogy sites to try and collect the names of Jaime Cruz's family members. His grandparents were both gone, but they had confirmed that Cruz's maternal grandfather had taken part in the Bay of Pigs. Cruz's parents and three siblings were still alive. Add to that four aunts and uncles, as well as over a dozen first cousins.

John's list, which he had pulled from not just those sites, but a variety of public databases, also included a number of second cousins.

"That's a lot of people," Mia said with a heavy sigh.

"But the connection is on his maternal side," John said, immediately zeroing on that connection.

Ricky, who had been pulled in for this discussion to offer a profile said, "I agree with John. If there is anger at our family, probably for some imagined wrong, it's likely that whoever is behind it is on that side of the family, since that was the grandfather involved in the Bay of Pigs."

With a few keystrokes, John eliminated any family solely on Cruz's paternal side. "That cuts it back substantially. The grandfather's name was Carrera. Do you think your grandfather might remember him?"

Trey nodded. "*Abuelo* may be 87, but he's still sharp. It's late though, so it may have to wait until morning."

"What about *Papi*? Would he know?" Ricky asked.

"Maybe. I'll reach out to him, but maybe we can do some digging on the internet," Trey said.

Beside him, Mia reached for some of the papers from

their earlier searches. Flipping through the pages, she said, "We have two Cruzes on the list of gang members but no Carreras."

John gestured to the numbers besides their names. "Those two are low probability. Nothing that says they have the skills to build bombs or be expert shots or work in the downtown area buildings."

Roni jumped in to offer her opinion. "My guys say these are just two low-level gofers in the gang and not anyone they see as a threat for violence."

"Two steps forward and one step back," Mia muttered from beside him.

"It's what we have to work on," Trey said, clearly resigned to following those leads.

"We'll get to work on it," John said, and everyone chimed in with their agreement, but not enthusiastically.

He understood. They'd expended so much energy and still only had a few pieces of the puzzle. But there were more and more pieces and he had to stay optimistic that soon they'd have the complete picture.

"John?" Mia asked at his prolonged silence.

"We have more than we think we do. We're just not seeing the forest for the trees," he said and offered her a reassuring smile.

"I'd like to take an axe to those trees," she joked.

He had just the axe to use. "I'm going to run all these names and all this data through the program."

Chapter Twenty

While John was using his program to pull data for all the various family members and figure out the probabilities for who might be behind the attacks, Mia decided to tackle it in another way: by finding out as much as she could about the failed invasion.

Her *abuelo* had sometimes shared stories, but not often. It had obviously been a very painful episode in his life between the actual battle, the imprisonment that had followed and the sense of betrayal that still lingered for so many Cubans even to this day.

Jumping on the internet while John worked beside her in bed, she pored over various accounts of the invasion and the aftermath, keeping in mind what her brother Ricky had said about someone harboring a grudge for some imagined wrong.

A wrong that had happened on the battlefield? she wondered, but from what she could see, the bulk of the stories were about the bravery of the men and how they had fought to the very last bullet before being taken captive.

Something in prison? Over a thousand men had spent twenty months in a Cuban prison until the United States had brokered a deal, providing fifty-three million dollars in food and medicine in exchange for their release in December of 1962.

Her *abuelo* had never mentioned anything at all about the prison and what might have happened there. Asking him might awaken emotional memories.

She hated the thought of doing that. She loved her *abuelo*. Looked up to him as a hero who had fought so hard for freedom and to give them all a better life.

John passed a finger across her brow, soothing the furrows there. "You're upset."

"It is upsetting. I'm so removed from this part of my family's past… Now I have to face it, embrace it, but it could be hurtful. Especially for *mi abuelo*."

"Hopefully we can avoid that," he said.

She nodded and murmured, "Hopefully. Do you have anything yet?"

"I have the list and one suspect who's slightly higher than the others on the list, but nothing earth-shattering. What about you?"

"Nothing about the Carrera grandfather. He's on the list of prisoners, but that's about it."

"Maybe it's time to make a call to one of the daughters?" John asked.

She nodded, but it was late. Too late to call someone, but suddenly her own phone chirped to warn of an incoming call.

Trey. She swiped to answer, worried that he was calling so late.

"What's up?"

"Can you get John? I'd like for him to hear this as well," he said.

Heat swept up her cheeks and she held up a finger to ask John to remain silent. "Sure," she said, then counted to ten to make it seem like they weren't lying together in bed and tapped on the speaker.

"He's here," she said.

"Great. I spoke to *Papi* to see if he knew anything about

the Carrera family. He said that he'd met the grandfather at some of the reunions of the Bay of Pig survivors. He also met the two daughters as well," Trey said.

"And?" Mia pressed, impatient to get to the important bits.

"It turns out that Carrera wasn't one of the men released in 1962. No one knows why, but Fidel kept him in prison for another fifteen years. Carrera was eventually released as part of some kind of exchange for a man the US had identified as a Cuban spy."

"I've spent most of the night reading up on it and didn't see anything about something like that," Mia said, imagining how the family must have felt having a loved one imprisoned for so long.

"Apparently it was all kept low-key because it involved national security. *Papi* wouldn't even have found out about it if one of his daughters hadn't accidentally spilled the beans at one of the reunions," Trey advised.

"Fifteen years in a Cuban prison. That couldn't have been easy," John said.

It was impossible to miss the harsh sigh that Trey let out before he said, "And it apparently wasn't easy for the family here either. With Carrera imprisoned, it was hard to get established the way *abuelo* did. Ricky said this might be for an imagined wrong and I totally see how a family member could think that.

"Their grandfather—because we know the person who's doing this is younger—rots in jail while the family flounders here. The grandfather gets released and there's no hero's welcome for a number of reasons," Mia offered.

"First, there's the national security aspect, but also, it's fifteen years later. People are thinking about other things. Some had even forgotten about the invasion, others were trying to move on with their lives," John mused.

"Cubans don't forget much about Fidel, but you're right

that for some who are younger, it's not as emotional as it is for their parents and grandparents," Trey said.

A long silence filled the room as they all thought about what Trey had just revealed.

John finally broke the silence. "Seems like the two Cruzes have to top the list, no matter how low probability they might be."

"I agree, but right now, we have no proof of anything. Roni is going to ask her guys to keep an eye on them," Trey said.

"Maybe those ATMs we identified will give us some video that might help," Mia reminded him.

"Maybe. We'll touch base in the morning. Try to get some rest," her brother said and hung up.

Mia laid her phone on the nightstand and tucked her laptop on its shelf. "I can't imagine holding a grudge for so long."

John likewise laid his laptop on the nightstand next to him and tucked her into his side. "I wish I could say that I didn't but…"

He didn't have to finish for her to know what was bothering him. She faced him, reached up and cupped his cheek. "Miles. He's had a gripe with you for a while." ·

With a grimace, he said, "Years, apparently, and I didn't see it."

She eyeballed him and he shrugged sheepishly. "Okay, I had some reservations after the leak, but who wants to believe that your only family is screwing you?"

"No one, but he's not your only family now. You have me and the rest of the crew," she said, then leaned forward and kissed him.

As they slipped down into bed, she held him close, wanting to heal his hurts. As he held her, peace settled over her, but she knew it wouldn't be a lasting peace until they stopped whoever was trying to kill her and her family.

She was impatient for it to be over, but if she'd learned one thing from Trey it was that impatience could be deadly. They would have to bide their time until tomorrow and whatever new information that day would bring.

JOHN WOKE UP with a headache after a night filled with memories of his father, Miles and cars for some reason.

He sat up on the edge of the bed, raked his fingers through his hair and glanced at the empty spot on the bed where Mia had been sleeping beside him. From the kitchen came the sounds of her puttering around and the blessed smell of coffee.

I'll need buckets of it to get through the day, he thought and massaged his temples to drive away the pounding in his head.

"You okay?" Mia asked as she walked over and handed him a cup of coffee.

"I didn't sleep well. It happens sometimes when I'm trying to work through a coding problem…and you snore," he teased. He accepted the mug from her and took a bracing sip.

She chuckled and sat beside him. "I could sleep in the guest room."

"Being next to you was the best part of the night," he said and leaned over to kiss her.

She tasted of her minty toothpaste and coffee, and as she dug her hand into his hair to hold him close, they kissed for long minutes until they reluctantly broke apart.

"I could get used to this every morning," he said.

"I could, too," she admitted and dropped another kiss on his lips before popping to her feet. "I made breakfast. Come and eat. I feel like this is going to be a long day."

Feeling the same way, he grabbed his T-shirt from the floor, slipped it on and followed her to the breakfast bar in the kitchen, where she had laid out place settings on the granite counter.

Mia worked at the stove, gave a last stir to the eggs and came over a minute later to serve them. She followed up by bringing over buttered toast and crispy slices of bacon.

"Looks good," he said and dug in, hungry despite the headache, but it lingered.

Mia must have sensed it. "Can I get you aspirin or something?"

He shook his head. He didn't think aspirin would drive away the thoughts unsettling him. "Just some weird things in my brain."

"Like what?" she asked.

Appreciating that she was trying to help him, he said, "Thoughts about my family and cars for some reason."

She grinned mischievously. "Missing the Lamborghini?"

He barked out a laugh. "I don't even know how I'm going to explain that to the insurance company," he said and forked up some of the eggs.

"Maybe that's why you're thinking about cars, only… We were talking about buses and cars yesterday. Didn't we also see a used-car lot in one of the street views?"

He scrunched his eyes tight, trying to recall the image. "I'm not sure but let's do the search again."

Suddenly eager to get back to their investigations, they scarfed down their breakfast.

John grabbed his mug and worked while Mia loaded the dishwasher.

He opened his laptop and immediately noted that his program had finished the analysis of the various family members, but there hadn't been much of a change from the probabilities they'd had days ago. The two Cruzes who were gang members had the highest scores, but as everyone had noted, they both seemed to lack the requisite skills to carry out the attacks. None of the other family members had set off whistles.

With the words on the screen jumbling together as his head continued to pound, he printed the report so he could take a closer look later. Whenever he had an issue, he found it easier to locate it when he printed it out, which made sense. He'd read studies that said people recalled things better when they were on paper.

Mia must have heard the whir of the printer. She pointed to his office and said, "Do you want me to get that?"

He nodded. "Please."

Pulling up the results from the cell phones, he once again wondered at the overlap between the places where his brother had made calls and the calls the killer had made.

Had the killer been following his brother, or was it just happenstance that their paths had crossed?

Mia returned and sat next to him, the report in hand. Seeing that he'd paused on the results rather than recreating their street view, she said, "What's worrying you?"

He gestured to the intersecting areas of red and green circles. "I can understand that last connection. It's right before we were attacked at the office so I'm assuming he and Miles talked or texted. But these other two?"

"Maybe one is where Miles dropped off the money?" Mia said offhandedly while skimming through the report he'd printed.

"Maybe," he said and pulled up the street view for the second location they'd examined the day before. As he swiveled the view around and around, he saw it. A used-car lot just behind the bus stop.

"Is that it?" Mia asked, but even while she did so, she was perusing the list of family members. Suddenly she stopped and jabbed a finger on one of the entries.

"One of the Cruz cousins owns a used-car lot in Little Havana. Could it possibly be that one?" she said and pointed to the screen.

"Let's get the exact location," he said, then switched to a map view to get the address and read it off.

"That's it. Cruz owns that used-car lot," Mia said, excitement ringing in her voice.

Maybe that's why the thought of cars had settled into his brain much the same way a troublesome piece of code would sometimes do. The pain in his head popped like a balloon that had been overinflated, bringing welcome relief. And with that came another thought.

"Looks like we're going to buy a car."

In the hope of not being recognized, Mia had pulled her hair into a ponytail, slipped on a baseball cap from John's prodigious collection and added sunglasses.

"You look…like Mia," John said with a chuckle as they pulled out of his driveway for the trip to the used-car lot in Little Havana.

"And not one of 'the Twins,'" she said with a shake of her head.

"Not one of 'the Twins.' This you…" he said and eyed her up and down. "I like this you, but I like the other you, too. Actually, I like all the different yous."

She grinned, appreciating his honesty. He'd never treated her as a trophy, but as a real person. She realized then that she had treated him much the same way, more interested in John the man instead of the reclusive multimillionaire.

"I like the different yous, too," she teased back, but even as she did, she pulled down the visor to keep an eye on the road behind them and kept her head on a swivel to make sure they weren't being followed.

John was vigilant as well, constantly checking the road, mindful of the danger of being tracked by whoever wanted them dead.

They traveled along the A1A until they slipped onto the highway and finally pulled off onto the side streets to head to the location they had identified from the street view. When they pulled into the parking area for the business and stepped out of the car, a thirtysomething man stepped out of a building on the lot.

Victor Cruz was dressed like many Miami Cubans in a pale blue *guayabera* shirt and dark dress pants. Smiling as he saw them, he greeted them when he approached.

"Good morning. How can I help you today?" Victor said.

"My wife and I are looking for a second car," John said.

Mia added, "Nothing fancy. Just something to run errands."

"Sedan? SUV? Truck?" Victor asked.

"Truck," John said at the same time that Mia said, "Sedan."

Victor laughed and nodded. "Sedan it is. Come this way," he said and guided them in the direction of the building.

As they neared, Mia realized that the building housed not only an office area in the front, but also what looked like a repair area in the back.

"Do you fix cars also?" she asked and gestured toward the open garage doors. When they got closer, she could see there were two bays, and a car was up on a lift while a mechanic worked beside the car.

"We do. We offer a limited warranty and if anything happens during that time, we'll take care of it for you," he said and waved his hand in the direction of a long row of late-model sedans.

She and John strolled up and down the row, chatting while Victor extolled the virtues of some of the cars. She felt guilty wasting his time because they had no interest in buying a car.

Hemming and hawing, giving one excuse after another, they delayed, trying to get a feel not just for Victor, but whoever else might be at the location. As they did, she noticed that the trucks were a few rows back and much closer to the garage area, where the mechanic was still at work and where a second man had joined him.

"I know you wanted a truck, *amorcito*. Let's take a look at those," she said, then slipped her arm through John's and dragged him in the direction of the larger vehicles.

"Of course, *mi amor*. Anything for you," he said.

"Lucky man," Victor said and when she glanced over her shoulder, she caught the salesman leering at her backside.

Anger rose up, but she tamped it down and approached the row of trucks. She intentionally moved them toward the trucks closest to the garage and as they got there, the mechanic she'd noticed earlier stepped into view.

She was sure he was one of the Cruz gang-member cousins and as the man saw them, his eyes widened and to her surprise, he raced off down the side of the lot.

"He's in a hurry," she said, drawing Victor's attention to Cruz's retreating back.

Victor waved her off. "Ignore him. He's a little *loco*, but a good guy."

Not *loco* but someone who clearly knew who they were and didn't want to stick around.

When she met John's gaze, he'd realized the same thing.

They hurried off, saying they had to think about it, hopped in the car and circled around to go in the direction they'd seen Cruz take off. While they did that, Mia called Trey, who immediately conferenced in Roni.

"That was a risky thing to do," she said while the sounds of station-house activity filtered across the line.

"We had a hunch. The lot belongs to Victor Cruz, one of the cousins," Mia explained.

"Stay put. Roni will meet you there with backup," Trey said.

"He's already on the run. We're trying to track him

down," Mia said, craning her head every which way to see where Cruz may have gone, but it was no use. Behind the car lot were a number of stores, and he could have easily slipped into one or found a hiding place in any of the alleys.

"Go back to the location and wait for me. In the meantime, I just sent Sophie and Robbie the ATM footage from both of those banks. Hopefully they can find something," Roni said and hung up.

Mia looked at him, but he had heard the conversation. "The risk was worth it," he said and steered back toward Cruz's car lot, but parked on the street to wait for Roni.

"It was. If he ran it's because he recognized us and knew why we were there," she said in agreement while they waited.

It didn't take more than about twenty minutes for Roni to pull up in a nondescript sedan with her partner.

Mia and John left their car to meet them, and Roni introduced her partner. "Detective Heath Williams. Meet John Wilson. I think you already know Mia."

"I do," he said with a smile and held out his hand to John. Williams was a good-looking man who seemed better-suited to a modeling gig than being a cop. Just over six foot, he had a lean muscular build, ice-blue eyes, boyish dimples and hair the color of chestnuts. She'd dated him once, and once had been more than enough, but he was a good cop.

"Hang back while Heath and I speak to Cruz," she said.

Roni was in cop mode and Mia always marveled at all the different roles her best friend seemed to handle with such ease. Today she was dressed in her black suit and was all business, but she'd seen Roni dressed to the nines for undercover work and totally casual when she hung out with the family.

As they strolled toward the building, Roni and Williams looked around, taking in the location.

Cruz must have seen them coming since he hurried out of the office area to greet them.

He looked from Roni and Williams to them, brow furrowed with puzzlement. "Officers. Mr. and Mrs... I never did get your names."

"John Wilson and Mia Gonzalez," John said, gesturing between the two of them.

Victor clapped his hands and laughed, seemingly unperturbed by the presence of the police. "I knew I recognized you even with the disguise."

"Mr. Cruz. We need to ask you some questions," Roni said.

He seemed startled by her tone, as if finally realizing that this was serious. "Sure. Come into the office," he said, inviting them in with a sweep of his hand.

Roni jerked her head in Williams's direction, instructing him to hang back by the door while they entered.

Inside, Victor went to a desk and sat, but the three of them stood there while Roni began her interrogation.

"I understand that your cousin Alejandro Cruz works for you," Roni said.

Victor flipped a hand in the direction of her and John. "Like I told them, there's no need to worry about him."

"I ran his record on the way over. Breaking and entering. Assault and battery. Seems like a reasonable person might be worried about having someone like that around," Roni pressed.

Victor raised his hands for understanding. "He's family. I couldn't say no even if he has problems."

"Has problems? Want to explain?" Roni said.

Victor circled an index finger around his temple. "He thinks he and his friends are going to invade Cuba someday and set it free. Be just like our *abuelo*, who took part in the Bay of Pigs."

Roni looked over her shoulder at them, eyes wide in disbelief, before she schooled her features and returned her attention to Cruz.

"How do they plan to do that?" she asked, a too calm chill in her voice.

For the first time since they'd gotten there, Victor started to fidget. He picked up a pen from his desk and flipped it from end to end. "It's nothing serious. Just a couple of guys on the weekends. Camping and stuff."

"Stuff. What kinds of stuff?" Roni pressed.

"It's a free country, *sabes*. They're not doing anything illegal," he said, but the flipping of the pen got faster and faster.

Roni reached out and stopped him. "Why don't you let me be the judge of that?"

Victor eyeballed Roni and then them. With a shake of his head, he said, "I'm not the guy to tell you." He grabbed a piece of paper and wrote something down. Handed the paper to Roni. "Sam Hidalgo is the head of the group. They call themselves the Cuban Democratic Army. He'll be able to tell you more."

"Thanks," Roni said and began to turn away. But then she faced Cruz again and said, "If your cousin comes back, play it cool and call us." She took a business card from her pocket and handed it to him.

With a tip of her head, Roni instructed them to exit the office.

Mia went first, with Roni following and finally John. They met Williams, who jerked his chin up in question. "Get anything?"

Roni waved the piece of paper with the name and number. As she did so, a trio of chirps sounded from their phones.

Almost in unison they whipped out their phones to review the message they'd just received.

The message was from Trey and as Mia pulled up the short video, she gasped.

Chapter Twenty-One

"That's him," Mia said on a shocked breath.

John paused the video and zoomed in as a man bumped into Miles, seemingly accidentally, only they all knew there had been nothing accidental about it.

"That's Alejandro Cruz," John said and shook his head. "That's when he must have put the tracker on Miles."

"That cinches it. We have reasonable cause for a BOLO," Roni said, and Williams nodded in agreement.

"What about the group? What do you do about that?" John asked.

Roni smiled harshly. "If it's one of the 500 or more militias scattered across the US, we should probably check with the Feds before we do anything."

Williams nodded. "We don't want to step on one of their investigations."

"500 or more?" Mia almost croaked.

"That's actually down from the over 600 in 2018," Roni said with a shake of her head.

"What do we do now?" John asked, worried that with Cruz on the run he might be even more deadly.

"Go home and stay home. A cornered animal can be dangerous," Roni said.

While John didn't like the idea of hiding, he also didn't

want to risk Mia's life and she and the rest of the family were Cruz's primary targets.

"We'll be there. Call us if you have any developments," John said and escorted Mia back to their car.

Once they were buckled in, he took off for home, but nervous tension filled the vehicle.

"I almost can't believe we have him," Mia said.

He couldn't believe it either. Wouldn't believe it until their attacker was behind bars. "We still need to be careful."

Come to think of it, so did Miles. "Can you do me a favor and send that video to Miles and warn him about Cruz?"

"I will," she said.

From the corner of his eye, he watched her texting away, but then he returned his attention to the road, vigilant for signs that anyone was following them. His eye caught Mia beside him, also attentive to what was happening all around. Thankfully, they arrived at his home without incident.

As soon as they walked through the door, Mia wrapped her arms around herself and said, "I can't just sit here and do nothing."

"Neither can I," he said and immediately raced to the wall safe in his bedroom, where he had locked up his laptop. He hadn't wanted to haul it with him and had secured it until their return.

When he went to the dining room, Mia was already sitting there on her laptop. "These guys—the Cuban Democratic Army—they're dangerous. Over ten years ago they were responsible for an attack in New York City that killed five FBI agents and wounded three others."

The articles that he pulled up were older, mostly around the time of the New York City attack. "Not much new information," he said, wondering if it was because most of the members had been jailed or gone into hiding.

"Nothing really, and Cruz would have been young during that big attack. Only fifteen," Mia said.

"But his older cousin was twenty and already involved with the gang. Alejandro Cruz goes from being groomed there to somehow connecting with the militia and it makes sense. He's got a beef with your family about whatever happened to his grandfather. A man he idolizes to the point he wants to be just like him and liberate Cuba."

"And the militia clearly had the capability of making bombs and training him to shoot," Mia repeated.

"The program was useless because there wasn't enough data about the militia and how Cruz was connected to it," John said with a shake of his head.

"Garbage in, garbage out," Mia said sympathetically and slipped her hand over his.

With a laugh, he said, "I'm almost relieved about that. I was so worried about this becoming something all-knowing and so dangerous."

"Enough data and it could be, but I trust you not to let it get that way," she said.

"You have a lot of faith in me," he said and twined his fingers with hers.

She smiled, her blue eyes dark, but happy despite everything that was happening. "I do because... I love you, John. It's crazy and it doesn't make any sense—"

He cut her off with a kiss because he didn't want to hear all the buts. Lord knows he'd been thinking about them from the day he'd first met her and now...

"I love you, too, Mia. You are such an amazing woman," he said. He cradled her cheek and stroked his thumb across her smooth cheek.

He was leaning in to kiss her again when his phone chirped. He wanted to ignore it especially when he saw it was Miles, but swiped it open.

Cold filled his core at the photo of Miles tied to a chair.

A bruise marred his cheek. His shirt was torn open and stained with blood.

"John? What's wrong?" Mia asked.

John held up his phone and Mia's face turned a sickly green.

"No. That's not possible. We just texted him."

But when he checked the time, he realized it had been over an hour since Cruz had run away from the lot.

Another text arrived. Call the cops and I kill him.

"We have to call Roni," Mia said.

John shook his head. "We can't. He'll kill him."

Mia laid her hand on John's. "He's going to do it either way. You know that."

Another ding. His hands shook as he read it.

I want Mia and a million dollars. Small bills.

Ten million. No Mia.

A long pause followed, but then Cruz responded. K. Tomorrow. Noon.

Where?

I'll let you know.

JOHN AND MIA sat with the family at his dining-room table, while Roni, her partner and someone who Roni had identified as FBI Agent Garcia zoomed into the call.

"Agent Garcia is familiar with the CDA. He was one of the agents wounded during the New York City attack," Roni explained.

"Thank you for being with us, Agent Garcia. My family appreciates any help you can provide," Trey said and dipped his head in greeting.

"Thank you, Mr. Gonzalez. We've been watching the CDA for years," the agent said.

Garcia was a recklessly handsome man in his late thirties with just a hint of gray at his temples. Light green eyes were striking even via the camera.

"Why are they still in business?" Mia asked, frustrated that the dangerous group was still in existence.

The agent's lips firmed, and his gaze hardened. "The situation was complicated. We charged those we could but didn't cut the head off the snake."

"And they reorganized and survived," John said.

Roni and her partner shared a look. "Agent Garcia is not sure the CDA is behind this abduction."

"Why does that matter? Isn't kidnapping a federal crime?" Mia challenged.

"This kidnapping normally wouldn't fit the criteria for us to have jurisdiction, but since it does include a CDA member, we're willing to provide assistance," Garcia said.

Mia was about to lose her temper, but Trey gently squeezed her hand. "We will get the help we need, *hermanita*."

"We're determining the location of the call and we have an inside man who might be able to provide more info," Garcia advised.

"What do we do next?" John asked, worry etching deep lines onto his face.

"He'll be watching, so we'll need to be careful," Garcia advised.

"I'm ready. Whatever you need," John said with no hesitation.

Mia wished she could be as sure. Fear twisted her guts into knots and it didn't unravel as the video call ended and her family rallied around them.

"It's going to be okay," Sophie reassured her, but Mia wasn't an idiot. It was impossible to miss the worry on the faces of her family as they sat around the table.

"The FBI will provide everything they have on the militia. We'll process it and devise our own plan, just in case," Trey said.

"We will," Robbie chimed in.

Mia forced a smile and glanced at John from the corner of her eye. His face reflected what she was feeling, but she put a brave face on for him.

"It'll be okay. We're family and we take care of family," she said.

MIA PACED BACK and forth and waved her arms wildly. "Why do you have to do this?"

"It's what he instructed," John said as Trey adjusted the straps on the bulletproof vest. "Should it be so tight?" he asked.

Trey tugged on the bottom. "We have to make sure it covers all the vital spots."

"Vital spots! Is it going to stop a head shot?" Mia nearly screamed.

John met Trey's gaze and the other man left the bedroom. John walked over to Mia and slipped his arms around her.

"It's going to be all right. The FBI has a team ready—"

"But they can't plan for every contingency," she said as tears glistened in her gaze.

"Is this my kick-ass warrior? The woman who can handle anything—"

"Except watching you have your head blown off," Mia challenged, but she was calmer than before.

"Which won't happen," he said, and they walked out of the bedroom to where Trey stood with FBI Agent Garcia.

Garcia handed him an earpiece. "We need to do a sound check."

John slipped it in and nodded. "I'm ready."

"Everyone check in," Garcia said, and, in his ear, John heard the various agents in and around the Bay of Pigs Monument confirm they were in position.

He nodded to acknowledge that he'd heard, and Garcia said, "Good. You remember what to do?"

The texts from Cruz with the directions had been straightforward. "Bag with the money goes in front of the monument."

Garcia handed him the reusable grocery bag from a local store. Cruz had insisted on that and the FBI had filled the bag with bundles of counterfeit hundreds.

"Leave it and walk away. As soon as you do, we'll move in as well as raid the CDA location where we believe Miles is being held," he said.

"Are you sure about that?" Trey asked. He'd been standing off to the side, arms tucked across his chest, Mia beside him.

"We're pretty sure. Our inside man identified it as a shack the CDA has on the outskirts of the Everglades," Garcia said and peered at his watch. "Time to go."

John nodded but took a quick second to hug Mia. He whispered in her ear, "Don't worry."

He glanced at Trey, silently begging him to take care of her and his friend nodded.

His friend, he thought. If this was going to be it, he could at least say that he had friends, even family, who cared about him.

Grabbing the bag, he stepped out of the home the FBI was using for the operation. It was a short distance to the corner, and he turned onto *Calle Ocho* in the direction of the memorial honoring the heroes of the invasion.

Head on a swivel, he looked around for Cruz. Nothing.

Just typical lunch-hour traffic at the fast-food chicken place and strip mall across the way. He crossed over to a small local supermarket—the one that gave out reusable bags just like the one holding the ransom money.

On the other side of *Calle Ocho* was a black hexagonal column honoring the Bay of Pigs martyrs. The column sat on two hexagonal tiers of black and was surrounded by chains. He crossed the street and placed the bag in front of the monument, as he'd been instructed.

But he hadn't taken more than a step or two when a commotion across the street made him stop. Suddenly, nearly a dozen women, all carrying the same reusable shopping bags as he'd laid at the monument, streamed out of the supermarket and headed in the direction of the square.

"Keep your eyes on that drop. Keep moving, Wilson," Garcia instructed over the earpiece.

He wanted to hang back, wanted to see if Cruz was somehow in that gaggle of women, but he did as he was told and walked up *Calle Ocho*. He wondered if at the far end, which ran deep in the Everglades, the agents had been able to rescue Miles.

"I think I see him," Garcia said over the earpiece.

He headed back toward the supermarket and the home where Trey and Mia were waiting with Garcia for word that Cruz had been apprehended.

"Tracker says he's on the path toward the next memorial," one agent said.

He faced SW 13th Street, where some of the women were also strolling down the island in the middle of the street. But suddenly a quartet of agents streamed in, and the women scattered like pigeons in a park chased away by a determined dog.

It happened so fast it almost didn't seem real. One second there was what appeared to be an older woman standing there, but then she was suddenly on the ground. When two of the agents hauled her to her feet, the wig flew off.

Cruz.

It's over, he thought, relief washing over him.

As the agents walked Cruz toward the street, an unmarked FBI sedan pulled up.

John stood there watching. Barely a few minutes later, Mia was wrapping her arms around him.

"See, head still intact," he teased, but her body jumped beside his as something punched into his side.

Two agents rushed off in the direction of a nearby strip mall and opened fire on a car that was parked there. Glancing across the street, Cruz smiled at him before the FBI agents hurriedly stuffed him into the sedan.

As Mia's knees folded, he gently lowered her to the ground, in disbelief at the sight of the blood seeping from her side. Garcia's frantic calls in his ear, screaming for an ambulance.

"Mia," he said as he cradled her, but she'd passed out.

Trey kneeled at his side, shock on his face, then he went into action, ripping off his shirt and tearing it in half. He wadded the fabric and said, "Apply pressure."

Apply pressure, he thought, thinking this couldn't be real. But the warmth of her blood against his hand was only too real.

He placed one wad at her back while Trey took the other and applied it to the exit wound. She moaned, bringing joy because that meant she was still alive.

The wail of the ambulance filled his ears as it screeched to a stop.

EMTs jumped from the vehicle and took over, moving Mia onto a gurney and loading her into the ambulance. He stood there, her blood drying on his hands, as the ambulance raced away.

Garcia approached, his face somber. "We should have seen that coming."

"We should have," Trey chimed in, shoulders slumped. His voice was filled with guilt and...defeat.

"She'll be fine," he said to convince Trey and himself.

Barely a breath left him before Garcia's phone chirped. The agent answered and his mood stayed stoic.

John's heart pounded in his ears, so loudly he didn't hear what Garcia had said. It was Trey who repeated it and he finally understood.

"They have Miles and he's okay."

Okay. Miles was okay, but as he peered at his hands, the blood there warned that nothing was okay and might not ever be again.

JOHN SAT BESIDE Mia's bed, holding her hand. Tubes and wires ran from her to assorted monitors that beeped and blinked with signs of life while Mia lay uncomfortably still.

Complications during surgery. Coma.

The words kept on repeating in his brain throughout the night and into the morning, but nothing changed except for the ebb and flow of the Gonzalez family members coming and going from the room.

He left her side only to relieve himself and grab a candy bar, stale and tasteless, from one of the hospital vending machines.

"You need to go get some rest," Trey said and laid a hand on his shoulder.

Looking up at his friend, John wondered if he looked as bad. Smudges dark as bruises sat below his aqua-colored eyes. He obviously hadn't been getting any rest when he wasn't at the hospital.

"We'll stay with her," Roni said. She was tucked into her fiancée's side, offering support.

"I'm not leaving."

Realizing that he wouldn't budge, Roni said, "I'm going to get you something to eat."

With a kiss on Trey's cheek, she hurried from the room and Trey almost toppled into a chair that protested his weight with a worrisome creak. "She's going to pull through this," he said, but his voice lacked the usual confidence he had come to expect from Trey.

He wanted to believe it even as frustration at being helpless made him clench his fists. "I wish there was more we could do."

Trey bowed at the waist and leaned his forearms on his thighs. "They say people in comas can hear what you say."

With a shrug and a shake of his head, he wondered what he could possibly say besides that he loved her. He was grateful he'd already told her before…

"You were always trying to pry it out of me, so here goes."

At Trey's puzzled look, he explained. "She wanted to know more about me. About where I came from. Things like that."

"As good a thing as any to tell her," Trey said with a tired smile. He sat back in his chair, prepared to listen as well.

Normally John wouldn't share such personal things with strangers. But Trey wasn't a stranger. He was a friend, but more importantly, he was family now.

"I was born in Lancaster County. My dad's family settled there in the early 1800s, but my dad lost the farm when I was six and we moved to Philly," he began. He talked until Roni came back with a sandwich and soda for him.

Trey took over, sharing a story about when he'd tried to cut a wad of gum out of her hair and nearly scalped her, and another time when Ricky and he had embarrassed her when they'd found her necking with a boyfriend at the movie theater.

Roni chimed in, regaling them with a tale about their antics at a college frat party.

He finished his sandwich and resumed his position at Mia's bedside, sharing bits and pieces from his past, tag-teaming with other family members until night came again.

This time it was her father who urged him to go.

"Samantha and I can do the night shift," Ramon said and jerked his head in the direction of Mia's mom as she entered.

"I'm not leaving," he said, but gave her parents space so Mia would know they were there.

They left around midnight, and he resumed his vigil, softly sharing his life with her until his voice was hoarse, his throat sore, but the pain didn't silence him. Sleep claimed him in the early morning hours.

Her voice drifted into his dreams. "Philly?" she said.

Philly? he thought and jerked awake when he heard it again.

Mia's eyes fluttered open, and she grimaced. "Hurts."

"I'll call the nurse," he said, but she grabbed hold of his hand.

"No. Okay. Philly? Really?" she said, her words clipped as if each one brought pain.

"You heard me?" he asked, thinking back to when he'd been sharing with her. He didn't recall any moment when she'd seemed lucid.

She nodded. "I heard. I love a guy from Philly," she said, slightly stronger and with a shadow of a smile.

"And I love you, Mia. I don't want to spend another moment without you," he said and gently leaned over to press a tender kiss on her temple.

"I'm not going anywhere without you," she said, and her smile strengthened.

"No, you're not."

Epilogue

Why have only one wedding when it was just as easy to have two? Mia thought. Especially since she and Roni were best friends and would have the same bridal parties and guests.

Mia watched Roni walk down the aisle to meet Trey at the altar of the cathedral. The organist paused and started the wedding march again.

"Are you ready, *mi'ja*?" her father asked and slipped his arm through hers.

She nodded. "Never more ready, *Papi*."

Together they marched down the aisle to where John waited for her along with the rest of the bridal party. So-phie, Carolina and Mariela wore gowns in a pale shade of coral. Opposite them, Ricky, Robbie and Miles stood hand-somely in white dinner jackets, black pants and coral bow ties and pocket squares.

She had been surprised when John had asked about having Miles in the bridal party, but since the kidnapping, the brothers seemed to have reconciled to some extent.

John, she thought with a loving sigh and met his gaze down what seemed the too long length of the aisle.

He stood beside Trey—both of them were breathtak-ingly handsome in their dinner jackets. Roni was already at Trey's side, waiting for her best friend.

Mia quickened her pace, earning a hushed *"Cálmate."*

Sucking in a breath, she calmed herself and her pace until she reached him.

He seemed just as anxious, since he stepped down from the altar to take her hand even before her father could hand her to him.

It prompted laughter from everyone around them, but she didn't care.

He was nothing like what some might call the perfect man, but he was the perfect man for her.

"I love you," he whispered and guided her to her spot on the altar.

JOHN HELD HER hand tightly, almost not believing that they were here. That they were getting married.

It had been weeks since she'd been shot, but he'd been with her every step of the way, sharing his Indian Creek home with her as she'd slowly healed. Sharing the bits and pieces of his past as they built their future together. Even the painful past about his father and his mother's death and the fresh pain of his brother's betrayal.

He shot a quick look over at his brother. They'd had a reckoning, the two of them, about what Miles's role might be in John's new life. Miles had understood.

They'd always be brothers, but nothing else. John wasn't sure he could ever truly trust him again.

Unlike the woman beside him. Brave, intelligent, caring. Strong, so strong.

She was the kind of woman any man would be lucky to have in their life. A life that included her amazing family as well.

Mia squeezed his hand tight, yanking him from his thoughts. She tilted her head in the direction of the priest, who repeated, "Do you, John Xavier Wilson—"

"I do," he interrupted, eliciting waves of laughter again from everyone in the church.

The priest shook his head, chuckled and glanced at Mia. "Do you—"

"I do," she answered, and he knew everything was going to be more than okay.

It was going to be perfect.

* * * * *

COMING SOON!

We really hope you enjoyed reading this book.
If you're looking for more romance, be sure to
head to the shops when new books are
available on

Thursday 2nd February

To see which titles are coming soon, please visit
millsandboon.co.uk/nextmonth

MILLS & BOON

THE HEART OF ROMANCE

A ROMANCE FOR EVERY READER

MODERN

Prepare to be swept off your feet by sophisticated, sexy and seductive heroes, in some of the world's most glamourous and romantic locations, where power and passion collide.

HISTORICAL

Escape with historical heroes from time gone by. Whether your passion is for wicked Regency Rakes, muscled Vikings or rugged Highlanders, awak the romance of the past.

MEDICAL

Set your pulse racing with dedicated, delectable doctors in the high-pressure world of medicine, where emotions run high and passion, comfort a love are the best medicine.

True Love

Celebrate true love with tender stories of heartfelt romance, from the rush of falling in love to the joy a new baby can bring, and a focus on the emotional heart of a relationship.

Desire

Indulge in secrets and scandal, intense drama and plenty of sizzling hot action with powerful and passionate heroes who have it all: wealth, status, good looks…everything but the right woman.

HEROES

Experience all the excitement of a gripping thriller, with an intense romance at its heart. Resourceful, true-to-life women and strong, fearless me face danger and desire - a killer combination!

To see which titles are coming soon, please visit

millsandboon.co.uk/nextmonth

LET'S TALK
Romance

For exclusive extracts, competitions
and special offers, find us online:

f facebook.com/millsandboon

🐦 @MillsandBoon

📷 @MillsandBoonUK

Get in touch on 01413 063232

For all the latest titles coming soon, visit
millsandboon.co.uk/nextmonth

JOIN US ON SOCIAL MEDIA!

Stay up to date with our latest releases, author news and gossip, special offers and discounts, and all the behind-the-scenes action from Mills & Boon...

 @millsandboon

 @millsandboonuk

 facebook.com/millsandboon

 @millsandboonuk

It might just be true love...

GET YOUR ROMANCE FIX!

Get the latest romance news, exclusive author interviews, story extracts and much more!

blog.millsandboon.co.uk